SIX

By

Liz Moran

To Chris,
    "Permanence, perseverance, & persistence
in spite of all obstacles, discouragement, &
impossibilities: It is this, that in all things
distinguishes the strong soul from the
weak." (Thomas Carlyle).

    Thanks for perseveing!

        Kind regards

        Liz Moran

First published in Great Britain

By

Moranweb Press

www.moranweb.co.uk
publishing@moranweb.co.uk

First Published - December 2005
Reprinted with corrections – April 2006

ISBN- 10: 0-9551643-0-3

ISBN- 13: 978-0-9551643-0-9

Cover Design and Print layout by JMJ Technologies Ltd
www.jmjtech.co.uk • info@jmjtech.co.uk

Printed in Great Britain by YPS Ltd
www.yps-publishing.co.uk

SIX

The Synopsis

This book is based on the true story of six Yorkshire men in WW1. Five of the six are actually brothers. They are the Jackson boys. The sixth lad to join them is a best friend of one of them. His name is Albert Seal. In a ritualistic display of merging his blood with the blood of the youngest brother, John, he becomes one of them. The link is then forged and they become six brothers at war.

Their futures are set. Their country needs them. There's nothing special about them. They are just ordinary lads. Any one of them could be your brother, or mine. On the brink of embarkation, John falls hopelessly in love with a young girl called Alice. She becomes the one to keep his body and soul together against all odds.

The story of the six is told by John, and begins in 1919. His narrative takes Alice on a journey to see what he saw, experience what he felt. All of the six flirt with death. All of them lose sight of God, denying His existence. The six have little choice but to kill or be killed. Not all survive.

It's a story of love, hate, war, life and death, with devastating consequences too cruel to believe. A story that ends with the haunting echo of six brave young lads etched on your mind, where nothing is ever the same again.

They are simply: SIX. And Alice needs to know what went on…

SIX

THE SIX

Albert Seal

Robert Jackson

Matthew Jackson

George Jackson

Fred Jackson

John Jackson

Acknowledgement & Thanks

To Grandad who was the 'spark'.

Special thanks to my family, who were fantastic.

To the writing group who gave invaluable advice.

To York Archives and Library, for their research services.

To David Allen, whom I will always be indebted to, for it was he who photocopied numerous War Diary entries and enabled me to walk in the footsteps of brave men.

To Trish Wilson, Kay Edgar, and Jennifer Snowden.

Lastly, to various others who have given me their support and encouragement. You know who you are.

Thank you all.

Liz Moran

SIX

Foreword

This book is dedicated to

John Edgar Jackson, my grandad.

"Dear Grandad…
For a little while, I have tried to walk in your shoes,
To feel what you felt,
To see what you saw,
and have attempted to do justice to the many stories you told."

This book has been written as a testimony to the thousands of young men who bravely fought in WW1, and the strength they possessed to just wake up each morning, and to carry on through such adversity during those terrifying years.

The price they paid for freedom was twofold. They sacrificed their youth and dreams and became men much too soon. Some gave the ultimate… their life.

Liz Moran

June 2005

SIX

Chapter ONE

John's Story
Countdown to War

Alice and I sat on the grass with our backs propped up against the trunk of the old oak tree, watching dappled sunlight display kaleidoscopic colours all around us. The sounds of summer and the smell of freshly mown grass assaulted our senses. Alice was content. War was finally over and the summer of 1919 was a glorious one. I took in a deep breath and, for the first time in years, realised what it felt like to be alive.

The scene of tranquillity and peace all around me momentarily faded the last four years into a distant nightmare. People were wandering about, enjoying their morning stroll in the park, oblivious to the mental torment which continually haunted me. My eyes eagerly absorbed the view, attempting to keep madness at bay.

I turned to Alice.

"I wish things could have been different. I wish I could go back and change it all," I said, in an effort to make normal conversation.

I swept my hand in front of me as if trying to wave a magic wand to do just that.

"We were bloody fools, Alice. That's what we were. Bloody fools and now it's too late…"

Alice picked up my now motionless hand, looking at the neatly trimmed nails that had once been ingrained with dirt and blood, and entwined her fingers in mine. She gave them a gentle squeeze of comfort.

"It's always the 'if onlys,' John…What's done is done and sadly can't be undone. It wasn't your fault. It was circumstance," she said, matter of factly, trying to snap me out of my morose mood.

"Nothing can change that now," she added softly, brushing her warm sun-kissed face over my cheek to rest it on my shoulder as she snuggled up to me.

Her hair smelt of apples, reminding me of childhood days, and her soft body moulded itself to mine, like a sticking plaster trying to make things better.

I tried desperately to hold on to the moment, to put everything behind me, not even daring to close my eyes for fear of losing it, but within minutes that tranquility was gone and the images of death and horror transported me back in time. With it came the stomach-wrenching fear which tore away at my insides, as my thoughts drifted back to that fateful day in August 1914 when it all began, when youth was foolish, and the age of innocence was about to be lost forever. War in Europe had begun.

I remembered it clearly. I had been with Albert Seal, my best friend. We had both been just sixteen and in the back yard of 15 Brunswick Street, a small mid-terraced house in York which had then been my home. We had been whispering together, making plans as to how we could fool the authorities into letting us join up. Little had we realised that our plans and actions that day would regrettably change our lives for ever. Neither of us had known then what we had really been doing. We had been bloody fools, that's what we had been... and Alice had to be told the truth.

-o-o-o-o-

1914

"Well, what did George say?" I asked quietly, as I repeatedly scuffed the back yard wall with the toe of my shoe and put my hands in my pockets to keep them warm.

I started to shiver and jig about. The afternoon had become cloudy and there was a distinct chill in the waning August day.

"All he said was to be there on Saturday," said Albert.

I thought for a moment, as Albert's pensive gaze caught my eye.

"Do they suspect anything?" he added, referring to my parents as he inclined his head towards the house.

"No," I replied with confidence.

"Nor my Dad," he reiterated.

"None of them need know anything just yet, and what they don't know won't hurt them. In any case, they'll be too busy nattering over our Charlie and Wilf to notice what I'm doing, and by that time, it'll be too late," I reassured him.

"They'll kill you," he muttered, as he lit up a cigarette, looking around to make sure no one else could see him from the kitchen window.

"Well, at least bloody Jerry won't have to do it," I said, laughing out loud.

"What do you think your Dad will say?" I now added.

"I dunno. He's always saying it's about time I grew up, so I expect he'll be proud that I'm doing something. He'll never guess what it is though, until it's too late. Then he'll have a duck-fit, but like you say, by that time, it'll be too late to stop us." Albert replied confidently, as he offered me one of his cigarettes before putting them away.

"No thanks," I said, shaking my head.

Suddenly, footsteps approached the back yard gate. I touched Albert's sleeve and motioned with my finger on my lips for him to be quiet, just in case he hadn't heard. We listened intently, and waited to see who it was. Albert quickly stubbed out his cigarette as the six foot creaky gate swung open to reveal my Mam slowly emerging from behind it.

"Now then you two, what are you up to?" she enquired, as she struggled to close the gate behind her.

She had sausages from the butcher in one hand and her hat and handbag in the other and looked distinctly hot and flustered.

"You look as thick as thieves with your heads together like that. I can see you're up to no good. What've you been doing?"

"Nothing," we both replied, hastily turning away to hide the guilty looks, now menacingly written on our faces.

My Mam had a knack of detecting something was up by just looking at you, and once alerted wouldn't let it go until she was satisfied she knew all there was to know. She could tell a lie a mile off. Albert, looking uneasy, surreptitiously checked the end of his cigarette behind his back and gave it another squeeze between his thumb and forefinger before gingerly placing it in his pocket.

"Well if you aren't doing anything, isn't it time you went home, Albert?" she said suspiciously. "It'll soon be time for tea and your Dad'll be waiting."

"I'm just going Mrs Jackson. Bye John. See you tomorrow."

Mam continued making her way towards the back door, seemingly agitated, as we both heaved a sigh of relief. Albert, now genuinely pleased that he didn't have to explain himself further, headed across the yard towards the gate. With my arm on his shoulder, I reassured him.

"Don't worry. She'll think it was catching you smoking that accounted for our guilty looks. She'll have smelt it in the air. Anyway, see you tomorrow."

As he quickly went down the narrow back alley, I headed towards the outhouse in the corner of the yard to scrub up for tea. I smiled to myself when I thought of Albert still in awe of my Mam. She'd been a kind of stand-in mother to him and his sisters, after their mother had died in June 1898, not long after he'd been born. His father, Stephen, had then had the difficult task of raising six motherless children as best he could with her help and advice. It hadn't been easy for him but living just a short way down the street from us, and a long time friend of both Mam and Dad, he'd coped.

Stephen Seal was now sixty-three and beginning to look his age. With only Albert at home to care for, he had more time to spend reminiscing about the old days with Dad. Mam had a soft spot for him and always admired him for doing his best after Hannah, his wife, had died. As each of his daughters had flown the nest, he'd regarded himself fairly well off and with Albert working and bringing home some money, he'd often spoken with Dad about retiring fully. He and my Dad dreamed of such indulgences… they were the pipe dreams of the future… that was, until the likelihood of War began to threaten such things.

By the time I'd had my wash and brush up, tea was ready and everyone was sitting around the kitchen table waiting for Mam to serve it up. My Dad was known to everyone as Thomas, but had actually been christened John Thomas Jackson. He was sitting in his usual place at the head of the table with my Mam next to him on his right. His greying hair, his wrinkled weather-beaten face and gnarled fingers, told their own story and left no-one in any doubt that he was a hard-working man, a man I was proud of and pleased to call Dad.

Fred, my older brother by three years, always sat on Dad's left. At nineteen he thought he was the 'bee's-knees' especially as he'd just recently mastered the cut-throat razor on his virtually hairless baby-skin face. I often caught him admiring himself in the small outhouse mirror, as if proving to himself he was a man like Dad now. The chair next to him was mine. I could see that everyone was becoming impatient, so I sat down quickly.

As I looked up, my brother Charlie, who was three years younger than me, was grinning like a Cheshire cat from where he sat opposite, hoping I'd be in trouble for keeping everyone waiting. Much to his annoyance, I wasn't and when everyone's attention was diverted to Dad, I pulled a face, sticking my tongue out at him, as if to say, 'see, you were wrong.'

He was fat in comparison to the rest of us and always acted the clown so that his presence was seen as well as heard. At the end of the table facing Dad was Wilf, the youngest brother at eleven. He always sat there so Dad could keep an eye on him. Being the 'baby' of the family, he could get away with murder. Mam was always saying that "butter wouldn't melt in his mouth," and she was right.

Satisfied we were all ready to eat, Dad clasped his hands together and lowered his head.

"For what we are about to receive, may the Lord make us truly thankful, Amen."

"Amen," we mumbled, now waiting for Dad to load up his first forkful, before all of us did likewise.

It was always the same: Dad would start, and then almost as if nothing else mattered in the world, the rest of us would then tuck-in. Now, with a large mouthful of mashed potatoes in my mouth, I looked around at the familiar happy faces that made up my world, and felt safe and content.

I should have known then that it couldn't last, and heeded the sudden warning which coursed through my body as if someone had just walked over my grave, setting the hairs on the back of my arm on end. I took a deep breath to lessen the sensation which passed just as quickly as it came. No-one else seemed to notice, but it left me with the overwhelming emotion that nothing in the world would ever be the same again.

I tried to discard the sad, intense feeling I felt, as Mam interrupted my thoughts.

"Slow down now boys, there's no need to stuff food into your mouths like that. Anyone would think you were animals!"

SIX

Despite raising all of us to be mindful of good table manners, and being used to us eating as if our legs were hollow, she still felt it necessary to harp on about such things and woe-betide you if you didn't heed such warnings. Provoking her wrath by ignoring her was not a pleasant experience as it was often accompanied by a clip around the ear-hole, unless of course you managed to duck in time.

Briefly complying with her scolding, my attention was gradually drawn to Charlie. He was slowly scooping food into his mouth with exaggerated movements, obviously adhering to her warning to the 'letter'. He chewed each mouthful purposefully, savouring every minute of its taste, before repeating the action again and again. After watching him doing this for several minutes, I burst out laughing, just as Mam gave her usual smack over the ear-hole for his cheek. Turning away, she hid her own smile, as the rest of us carried on eating and normality settled over the Jackson household once again.

At one time, there would have been nine of us around this small kitchen table, but Thomas had died two years ago at the age of nineteen from peritonitis. It had been a devastating blow to all of us. Now, every time any one of us gets a stomach-ache, Mam quickly drags us along to see old Dr Jones down the road. She often goes shopping for him and in return he keeps an eye on us. The fact that he's been retired for years and she pays a penny a week to another local doctor, doesn't seem to matter to her. Then there was William, who had been the youngest, but he had died last year from whooping cough at the age of four. Mam had had him much later in life. There had been seven years between him and our Wilf, who was now regarded as the 'baby' of the family.

Fred, Charlie, Wilf and me, are the only ones still at home. I'm their sixth son and by far the most dashing and modest with it too! George and Robert, two older brothers, are married. George lives not far away in Emily Street, with Harriet, his wife and their three children. Robert moved a few years ago to Colchester when he married Gladys, so we see very little of him. Matthew, another older brother, is footloose and fancy free and living in Australia. He emigrated there to become a sheep farmer in 1911. We haven't seen him since he went, but he writes often.

Mam's always thanking God that she still has seven healthy sons, and reckons in this day-an'-age, it's a blessing. She's always telling us that there's many a family not so lucky, though that doesn't stop her from crying every now and again when it would have been Tom's or Will's birthday and she thinks no-one is looking.

SIX

"Where's the newspaper?" Dad queried, unable to see it on the floor by the hearth. Fred got up to retrieve it for him.

"Oh don't let's spoil our tea with reading the newspaper at the table, Thomas. It's bad enough you have to read it at all with all what's going on, let alone when we're eating. It's bad for the digestion," Mam cautioned.

Dad continued to open the newspaper as if he hadn't heard her. He was the only one I knew who could ignore her and get away with it, and he immediately started to eat and read at the same time as we looked on and envied him his defiance.

"I heard talk at work today that Germany's at war with France," he dryly uttered.

"There's also talk that Italy is being dragged into it, despite trying to stay well out of it, and Belgium says it's not going to allow any German troops through her country," said Fred, proudly demonstrating his knowledge of such things as he tried reading the headlines over Dad's shoulder.

"That's probably why it says here then that Germany's now declared war on Belgium," Dad replied, tapping the newspaper with his fork to show him, before putting another large piece of sausage into his mouth.

"'Ere, listen to this," he said spluttering with his mouth full.

Fred leant over to have a look, under the disapproving glare of mother as she sighed, letting her annoyance known. Swallowing quickly, he read out a headline he'd just noticed...

> *"At 4pm today, the British Cabinet ordered mobilisation of the British Army…"*

"Ee bah gum, that sounds ominous."

"Mm… I reckon it'll only be a matter of time before we get involved. That'll sort the buggers out," exclaimed Fred.

"Language!" Mam exclaimed, no longer able to contain herself as she looked around to see if Charlie and Wilf had been listening. Exasperated, she turned to Dad.

"Can't we have tea in peace? Thomas, you're frightening Wilfred."

Dad sighed, and after a further cursory glance at the daily headlines, threw the newspaper onto the chair in the corner. He was just about to open his mouth to say something else, when he thought better of it, and chewed another mouthful of sausage instead. Mam's irritable manner had at last annoyed him. Tea continued in silence, as each of us became immersed in our own thoughts. I was thinking of Saturday, whilst Dad and Fred appeared to be still thinking about the news, as after tea, they both resumed their conversation about the way the hostilities seemed to be escalating overseas.

The following morning, Dad was out early collecting the York Herald newspaper for old Mrs Lofthouse who lived next door. He was eager to see if there was any further news. For his trouble, she let him read it before her if he had the time, and if not, she'd save it so he could read it in the evening. Mam was still upstairs. The stove was lit and the kettle was on by the time he got back and sat down to read it for a few minutes before going to work.

"'Ere John, listen to this…

> 'Last night at 11pm Britain declared war against Germany, the only allied country to do so.'

What did I tell you?" he said, clearing his throat before he read on.

> "'The British Government will be taking over control of the country's railways under an act of Parliament passed in 1871.'

Looks like you'll be affected at the Railway then son." He continued…

> "'Admiral Sir John Jellicoe has been appointed Commander-in-Chief of the Grand Fleet and the Kaiser has issued an Order of the Day to his first army to "exterminate the treacherous English, and walk over General French's contemptible little Army." At his office in St. James's, Sir Edward Grey commented with sadness that, the lamps are going out all over Europe; we shall not see them lit again in our lifetime.'

Contemptible little army indeed! Who does he think he is?"

He put the newspaper aside in disgust and looked up at me.

"Well, that's it then son. We're at war," he said, outwardly disturbed by the news, as he frantically puffed on his pipe to get it going again.

He shook his head in disbelief, even though he had suspected it would come to this.

"Mary," he shouted, using Mam's proper name, instead of Polly, her nickname.

"It's blooming happened. We're at War with Germany."

SIX

His words hung ominously in the air, trapped in the cloud of smoke rising above his head. As he wearily stood up to get ready for work, the lines etched on his face showed he was worried. On hearing the news, Charlie and Wilf pointed imaginary guns at each other, shooting one another from behind the door, and I quickly put on my coat with equal excitement and anticipation, ignoring Dad's consternation.

"Where are you going son?"

"I'm just off to tell Albert about the news. He's probably not heard yet."

"What about breakfast?"

"I've had some. I got some bread and dripping while you were out. Tell Mam I'll be back in time for dinner. Albert and I are just going down town to do a few things and then we'll be back," I said excitedly, and before Dad could ask any more questions, I slammed the back door behind me and was gone.

"Just wait till Albert hears," I muttered under my breath, as I headed down the street towards his house.

On turning the corner of the alleyway, I bumped into Mr Hepplethwaite taking his daily walk.

"Morning Mr Hepplethwaite. Have you heard the news?"

"Aye lad, I heard it this morning. Blooming wars. Talk is that it'll be all over by Christmas, though I doubt that," he remarked.

"Really? Well whatever, we'll show em, we're going to knock em dead," I said, thumping the air, confident that this would be the case.

"Aye lad, I've heard it all before," and not wanting to dwell on such things, he changed the conversation to pleasanter matters.

"Was it you I saw out with George Johnson's girl last Sunday? What's her name, Alice isn't it?" he continued.

"Yes, smashing isn't she? I'm seeing her later today. Anyway, got to go. I'm meeting Albert and we've got things to do."

"You lads are all the same, always in a rush."

As he continued his journey slowly down the street, his shoulders hunched over like those of a man twice his age, he sighed, shaking his head as he acknowledged the impetuousness of youth. It started to rain just as I reached Albert's house and turned down the little snicket to his back door. Only visitors ever went the front way and got shown into

SIX

the best room. Those in the know though, always entered via the tradesman's entrance. I knocked, and as I looked through the kitchen window, Mr Seal waved me in.

"Eee lad, what are you doing here so early when you don't have to be at work today?" he exclaimed, as he continued cooking porridge on the stove.

"We're at war with Germany. Have you heard? Does Albert know? Is he up yet?"

I looked down the hall passageway, hoping he would materialise so that I could tell him. Mr Seal continued to potter around the kitchen muttering about bloody wars, whilst I, unable to contain my excitement any longer, headed to the hall doorway.

"Albert, are you up?" I shouted.

Within minutes, Albert staggered into the kitchen looking half asleep with his hair all dishevelled and his clothes I guessed, hastily put on, as they were twisted around his body as if he'd been wrestling with a crocodile.

"What's up?" he muttered, as the cold from the stone floor sucked the heat out of his feet.

"We're at war with Germany," I eagerly told him, tugging at his sleeve to wake him up and make him take note.

"War?" he said, repeating the word as if he hadn't understood. We huddled together and lowered our voices.

"You mean it's really happened? Britain's at war?" he said, now whispering incredulously at the thought of it.

On seeing Albert was up, Mr Seal started to serve up the porridge, muttering about this and that and about what the world was coming to, but we weren't listening. By now, our undertaking to enlist on Saturday had become firm and the lies we were about to tell, were forming in our minds. The most important thing we had to do now, though, was to carry on as if nothing had happened.

"Hurry up and get washed Albert. We've got things to do…" I said impatiently.

Chapter TWO

The world has no room for cowards.
We must all be ready somehow to toil, to suffer, to die.
(Robert Louis Stevenson 1850-1894)

The next few days passed quickly, and following the news that we were at war, the Government decided to extend the bank holiday to Friday, the 7th August. Everyone we met was talking about what was happening in Britain and in Europe. The street newspaper stall was busier than ever. Albert and I listened with excitement and exchanged knowing glances, as the secret of our coming action increased inside us. We were dying to tell someone but knew it would be our undoing if we did.

On Thursday, Lord Kitchener was appointed Secretary of State for the War Office and the following day, he called for 500,000 volunteers, 100,000 to be raised forthwith. That settled it then. As far as Albert and I were concerned, it was official, he'd called us up, and at first light on Saturday morning we were both at the beginning of the queue outside the Army recruiting station on Tower Street.

As we entered the imposing building, which doubled up as the Territorial Force drill hall, we were ushered down some stairs into a large room with a huge ceiling. On opening the door and entering, we were hit by the smell of fusty stale air. About fifty of us piled in behind the admitting officer. He pointed to a dozen or so chairs.

"Take a seat, lads. We'll be with you in a minute."

The first of us instantly did as we were told, excited and eager to please. The rest stood in a long line, which stretched through the doorway and back up the stairs out of sight. An expectant pent up silence descended within the room as various army officials entered.

Opposite us were six large trestle tables arranged next to one another making one long table, which now had army officers sitting about three feet apart down one side. We assumed they were the enlisting officers who would take our details. Their backs were butted up against the high windowed brick wall. In front of the tables, empty chairs were now strategically placed. At the nod of the head from one of these men, the admitting officer, who'd initially told us to take a seat, tapped Albert and me on the shoulder and pointed to the first table.

"Sit down. Name?"

SIX

"John Edgar Jackson, Sir."

"Address?"

"15 Brunswick Street, York."

"Age?"

Now this was the tricky bit. I looked across at Albert who was also going through the same process.

"Eighteen," I replied, just the same as him.

"Come on son, when were you born?"

We'd already done the calculation so I replied more confidently now.

"28th February 1896."

"Stand up lad," the army officer ordered, talking a look at me for the first time.

"How tall are you?" he enquired.

"Five foot six, Sir," I lied, though I was only five foot four, and he knew it.

With that, he tore up the sheet of paper in front of him, thrusting it into my hands.

"Go home son. Put some newspaper in your shoes to make yourself taller and come back next week when you'll not only be taller but older as well."

"Next," he bellowed to the officer organising the queue, sighing as he did so. It was going to be a long day.

I turned, horrified, to see Albert who was even shorter than me getting the same short shrift. Having felt we'd got away with lying about our ages, neither of us had anticipated we'd be too short. Collecting together our deflated egos we both hurried up the stairs, crestfallen, and rushed out of the door, fighting our way through the excited crowd of lads queuing to join up.

"What are we going to do now?" I said to Albert, when we got out into the fresh air, feeling totally dejected and let down.

"I'll tell you what we're going to do. We're going to do exactly what the bloody man says, but instead of coming back next week we're going to come back this afternoon and hope to God there's been a change of faces. That's what we're going to do!" exclaimed Albert, determined not to be brushed off so easily.

SIX

"And this time, we're going to do it proper!" he added.

With newspaper wedges in our shoes and spit on our hair we queued again in the afternoon, just as Albert had insisted we should. The queue had ebbed somewhat and the admitting officers in the afternoon were indeed different from those in the morning. One of them in particular didn't appear to be too choosy about who he accepted. In fact, he went through the whole process as if bored, hardly glancing up. Albert and I manoeuvred ourselves to make sure that he would be the one to take our details. When we told him we didn't have our birth certificates with us, he matter of factly waved the regulations saying "no matter," and in return, gave us a slip of paper telling us to report on Monday 17th August to York barracks.

"Make sure you say goodbye to your families. You're in the Army now," he snapped, and he stamped an endorsement on the papers in front of him. We left triumphant.

Christ... we were so euphoric, it was unbelievable. We'd fooled the authorities and were in the Army...

Once outside, the smiles on our faces expressed the excitement we couldn't contain any longer. The rest was going to be easy. We were going to tell our parents that the Railway required us to undergo some 'home front' training with the Territorial Army. They wouldn't realise we'd actually joined up properly, especially knowing we were underage. In any case, they'd think it was logical for boys of sixteen to eighteen, and those too old for the army, to undertake such training to protect the homeland, should it be needed of course.

What better than those unable to enlist to do just that! We'd, of course, have to tell them that we would have to wear a uniform so that people would recognise us as 'home front soldiers,' and we'd no doubt have to go away to do this training. The plan was perfect. It'll be 'just what the doctor ordered,' as Mam would say.

We were certain that no questions would be asked and neither my parents nor Albert's dad would realise our deception and lies, until it was too late. By then we would be fighting abroad for our King and country. Of course, as far as the army was concerned, we were eighteen and we weren't going to tell them otherwise. In the event that the 'cat did get out of the bag,' we were sure everyone would get used to the idea, and might even be proud of us. We patted each other on the back, pleased that things were going according to plan. The whole thing was fool-proof.

SIX

Turning the corner of Castle Street, we bumped into Arnold Doherty and Peter Walder who appeared equally excited.

"Hi Arnie, Pete, any luck?"

"You bet! And you two?"

"Yes. We've to report on the 17th," said Albert.

"What about you two?"

"Same here," chirped Arnie, and we all shook hands enthusiastically congratulating each other on our good fortune.

"Have you heard about the other lads?" I asked, referring to Jimmy, Alf and Phil.

"Yes, they've all got through, and Joseph Smallwood too, that little chap who works at Rowntrees. God knows how he managed to get accepted, but he did," said Pete smiling.

"He probably got the same enlisting officer as us! I doubt if he even saw him!"

We all laughed at the vision of little Joe balancing on his tiptoes in an attempt to make himself taller, and the enlisting officer not even noticing. As if under the influence of liquor, we walked arm in arm down the road together in an exuberant state. All of us would tell our parents the same story about 'home front training' with the Territorial Army, just in case they bumped into one another and started to ask questions. That way, we reassured ourselves, no one would give the game away and the truth would be kept hidden for as long as possible.

Before parting, we all decided to give our notices in at work on Monday morning. Albert and I worked as clerks in the Railway office at York Station, whilst our friends worked in and around the city not far away. As we approached the entrance to the park, I reluctantly said goodbye to the lads, telling Albert that I'd meet him first thing on Monday when we could hand in our letters together, and he agreed.

When I eventually caught up with Alice by the large oak tree I could sense she was furious.

"You're late," she pouted.

"Yes, sorry," I said breathlessly, gently kissing her cheek and then briefly her lips, before looking around guiltily to see if anyone was watching us.

SIX

We were really only at the holding hands and kissing cheek stage, but occasionally I would catch her off her guard like today, and gently kiss her lips. They were soft and yielding, almost beckoning for more.

I restrained myself, not trusting myself to do it again, as uncontrollable urges awakened within me. For a moment, I imagined making non-stop love to her. I often dreamed of what it would be like. I was sure she sensed that too, and so gave me little encouragement. I liked to think she couldn't trust herself, but I knew I was only fooling myself. She was like Sleeping Beauty waiting for her Prince Charming to awaken her, and I was going to be him! I knew I couldn't rush such things or all would be lost, and so I just held her hand.

The day was glorious… just perfect. Alice tried to distance herself, still angry with me.

"Where have you been?" she enquired, her face flushed with agitation.

"I've enlisted with the home front section of the Territorial Army to protect the Railways," I declared matter of factly.

"What does that mean?"

"Well, it means I'll have to go away for a few months to learn how to protect the railway, in the unlikely event of an invasion here at home. Will you miss me?"

She didn't answer, but instead asked, "Do you think it will really come to that?"

"Nah," I said reassuringly.

We walked together towards the river, still hand in hand and I promised I'd write if I went away, all the while good-humouredly reassuring her that, as her very own Sir Galahad on my white horse with my banner flying, I would be there to protect her.

"Will you miss me?" I asked again, on a more serious note, now unsure of myself. She hesitated once more as I waited for a reply.

"Yes, of course," she finally answered, all the while looking down at her feet as if uncomfortable at being asked such an intimate question.

"I'm going to miss you too," I said gently and lifted her face up to look at her.

For a brief moment our eyes met and I raised her chin up towards me to kiss her lips. She didn't resist. Instead the kiss was more lingering, mixed with a teasing desire and a promise of things to come. Her light-

SIX

hearted flirting masked the innocence of her body and at once I knew she cared for me. My heart raced uncontrollably as my aching body cried out for hers.

"Oh Alice, you are so lovely."

Chapter THREE

How can you hesitate? Risk! Risk anything!
Care no more for the opinion of others...
(Katherine Mansfield 1888-1923)

Alice lived on the other side of the town and the park was halfway between our two houses. Her dad knew my Dad. I first met her one Saturday a few years ago. She was smiling at me whilst her father discussed with my Dad a problem he had with one of his dray horses. Her brother Ted was also with them. He was three years younger than her, and when he'd changed schools, I started bumping into him on a morning as I went to work. He never failed to stop to have a quick chat with me, and I would ask after Alice. I don't know what it was about her that fascinated me, but there was just something that attracted me.

Several months after that initial meeting, Alice started working at Rowntrees, and to my delight our paths also crossed every morning. Knowing that I liked her, Ted told me that she usually had her lunch in the park by the old oak tree, and so I 'accidentally' started bumping into her at lunchtime as well. Albert said I was mad, saying that something as beautiful as the likes of her couldn't possibly fancy me. How wrong he was, and I told him so when he saw her waiting for me one day in the park looking lovelier than ever before. When I realised that she liked me too, I was over the moon, and now to my delight she was even going to miss me!

When it came to telling my parents about what Albert and I had done, that too was easier than I had first anticipated. In fact, though somewhat worried about the war in Europe, they seemed quite pleased with our actions, and felt it would be good for us to be occupied. Of course they also believed that the war would be over before it would affect any of us, especially as it had been reported in the newspaper that H.M.S. Birmingham had sunk a German submarine the previous Sunday. I almost felt guilty at lying to them, but justified the lies by saying to myself, there'd be one less mouth to feed and that must be a blessing. We weren't well off and Dad's weekly wage didn't often stretch the whole week without him doing the odd favour or two for someone else as well.

Albert had a similar response from his dad. It was a mixture of satisfaction and pride that his son was trying to help in some small way, and he too believed that the war would be long over for it to matter. And so it was that, under the guise of a lie, Albert and I went to war.

We gave in our notices at the main railway office, which was about a hundred yards away from the little office on York Station where we worked.

"Now then Jackson and Seal, what's all this about?"

"We've joined up in the 'Home front unit' Sir," said Albert.

"It's just whilst the war's on Sir," I added.

"Good show lads, that's the spirit. That's what I like to see. When you've finished your training, I'll make sure your usual job is waiting for you. Just make sure you ask to see me."

"Thank you Sir," we both replied, pleased this too was going to plan.

When we went to say 'cheerio' to those in our little office, we were told we had to be back in time to buy a Christmas drink. Mr Prince wasn't too sure about it all and in no uncertain terms told everyone. Albert and I laughed at him for being such a pessimist. In his defence, he told us that Great Britain and France had declared war on Austria and Hungary and he could see the war beginning to escalate out of control. As it happened, he was right, but we were too young and naïve to realise it then.

Good old Rodney Green jiffled in his chair breaking the silence which followed, and asked if he could look after my ebony ruler and borrow my chair which was comfier than his.

"Sure mate," I said, "but only until I get back," I warned.

"Great!" he said, as he stood up and instantly swapped our chairs over and lifted my ruler off the top of my desk, placing it on his own.

"Bloody hell, Rodney, I hope you don't jump into my grave as quick!" I quipped, as I cuffed him one for his cheek.

I now looked around realising I was going to miss the old place; the smell of smoke from the trains which billowed through the top stained glass windows into the office; the guard's two-toned whistle which saw the trains out of the station; the many faces that came and went. Yes, I was going to miss it all, especially all the hustle and bustle, but as I turned to leave the office for the last time, it was then that I suddenly realised it was Alice I was going to miss the most.

I said goodbye to Alice on the Sunday afternoon in the park. She clung to me with tears in her eyes, not caring who saw us, and I was thankful now that I hadn't told her the truth. She would have blown our cover for certain. The lies once more slipped easily off my tongue as I tried to reassure her.

"I'm not going away for long. It'll fly by and I'll write to you as often as I can," I said, all the while kissing her eyes and stroking her hair away from her face to tuck it behind her ears.

The salted tears lingered on my lips and stirred inside a protectiveness that overwhelmed me.

"I'll be back soon," I promised as I hugged her.

I didn't really know how to handle her emotion and as we stood clinging to each other I began to feel miserable at having to leave her. Leaves were fluttering to the ground all around us heralding the end of summer and a cool breeze caused goose pimples on our bare arms. As a leaf fluttered off the tree in front of me, I moved Alice aside to catch it. I kissed it, and gave it to her, though what possessed me to do such a thing I had no idea.

Surprised by my action, she tenderly tucked it into her pocket and in return pulled out a beautifully laundered, small soft-laced handkerchief, delicately scented with the 4711 cologne she always smelt of.

"Come back soon," she whispered, her large brown doe eyes pleading with me. I sniffed the handkerchief and placed it in my breast pocket.

"Of course I will," I promised, both of us now a little shy at the declaration of our feelings.

We walked along the riverbank and I made her promise not to come to see me off in the morning. I told her that I wanted my last memory of her to be by the river with the sun shining on her face and the wind gently blowing through her long hair. I hadn't realised it was going to be so difficult to say goodbye, but she complied with my request and in the end, that was how I left her.

"Now have you got everything son?" enquired Mam, fussing.

"You will write and let us know how you are getting on won't you?" she continued, not really waiting for my reply.

"Shall we take you into town?" she hurriedly nattered on, busying herself with the fastenings on my small brown suitcase.

"No, it'll be fine. Albert and I will manage. I doubt whether Albert's dad will be going either so don't worry about us, we'll manage and I'll drop you a line to let you know we've arrived safely."

"Now son, just watch yourself and keep out of trouble," Dad said, with his pipe in his mouth and his arm around my shoulder.

He wasn't much for demonstrative overtures, but the squeeze of his hand on my shoulder told me he cared. Mam was just Mam. She hugged me so tight and kept fussing with my tie and made sure I had handkerchiefs in my pockets to blow my nose. She checked my shoes had been polished, and then as she continued to fuss, Dad eventually managed to prize her from me.

"Come on now, ole' lass, let the lad get off."

That morning, the newspaper reported the government had sent four infantry divisions, an infantry brigade and a cavalry division from Britain to France. Things were beginning to happen and my excitement was mixed with exhilaration and an urgency to be a part of it all.

My goodbyes to my brothers was met with utterances of "good riddance," and much banter about me protecting England and a fat lot of good I would be in protecting the homeland. I left the family on the doorstep, and then at last, with all goodbyes said, I gave a final wave. By the time I'd reached Albert's house, there was just Mam and Dad in the doorway, my brothers obviously having better things to do. Mam was waving her white handkerchief as well as mopping her tears. I touched Alice's handkerchief in my pocket, reassuring myself it was still there and with one last look at them, I was gone.

For the first time, I felt a pang of uncertainty as I headed down the back way to Albert's house, and an unknown future. It was the first time I'd ever been away from home and I felt excited and panicky at the same time. It was peculiar really, and I laughed at myself for being so daft. I couldn't wait to see if Albert felt the same.

Chapter FOUR

But risks must be taken
because the greatest risk in life is to risk nothing…
(Author unknown)

Monday 17th August 1914 was destiny day for Albert and me. This was the day that we were to relinquish the courtesy title of Mr, to become known as Privates Jackson and Seal, Numbers 1857 and 1858 respectively. We were now a part of the Prince of Wales Own, 1/5th West Yorkshire Regiment.

We arrived at York barracks on Fulford Road at nine o'clock, where we, and several of our friends, were allocated to a barrack room and ordered to report at half past nine to draw uniform kit. There were ten pristine red-brick barrack buildings in all, each two stories high, and split up into four dormitories. Every dormitory housed twenty-six men. Albert and I were fortunate enough to be billeted with a lot of the lads from York we already knew, so it was a bit like being with my brothers at home. All of us were eager and excited, full of bravado and desperate to become soldiers. We were still wet behind the ears, but we looked the part, and that was all that mattered.

"Which bunk do you fancy Albert?"

"I'll take the top one as I don't fancy your fat arse falling down on me," he said, as he quickly heaved his suitcase onto it.

"What do you mean, my fat arse? You cheeky bugger!" I replied, throwing myself onto the bottom bunk, amid much amusement from the lads around us.

"In any case, I'm fitter than you and can clamber up here without getting out of breath," he said, as he scaled the frame of the bunk, and launched himself onto it, just as I simultaneously rolled off mine onto the floor in fear of him coming through and landing on top of me.

The laughter from everyone grew louder and eventually caught the attention of the Sergeant who banged his stick on the door frame to regain order. All of us sobered up immediately.

"Right now gentlemen," he boomed. "If you've found yourself a place to put your cases, let's be having you outside, lined up on the pavement, ready and waiting to collect your kit. Come on, come on. Jump to it."

In an instant, we rushed to his bidding, and lined up outside waiting for further instruction.

"Now then you lot, stand up straight, shoulders back, stomachs in, arms by your sides, and follow me, up two, three, four, ... left..., left..., left...," he said, swinging his arms as he briskly marched us across the yard.

"Come on, come on, let's be sharp about it, you're in the Army now, not at home with your mothers, still having your ears washed," he shouted.

We headed across the parade ground at break-neck speed where several other soldiers could be seen undergoing marching drills.

"Eyes right," shouted our Sergeant. "Now that's how it should be done, so let's have you lot doing the same. Left, right, left, right, up to it, come on, up to it. What do you think this is, a Sunday school outing?" he continued.

There were a few mutterings along the line which were silenced by the Sergeant's glare, very much like one of Mam's, as we continued at a fair pace in a higgledy-piggledy fashion. We passed the sports field and the married quarters, which housed three-hundred-and-ten men, mainly of officer status, and made our way to the end building where the barrack stores were located. Most of us were out of breath by the time we got there. It was obvious we were an unfit bunch of lads.

Once inside the stores, there were rows and rows of different piles of uniform to be collected. These were accessed in an orderly fashion when we started at the end nearest to the door and worked our way round.

"Okay, son, what chest size are you?"

"Er, I don't know," I replied, aware that the vast majority of my clothes were hand-me-downs from my brothers.

A jacket was held up against me, and then thrust into my hands along with another. It appeared that you got two of everything, one for best and one for field gear.

By the time I'd gone along the various rows, the pile had become virtually unmanageable and I, like the rest, teetered outside with my bundle. These included two of everything: service jackets, shirts, trousers, web belts, puttees (which looked like large bandages), hobnailed boots, shorts and sandshoes for athletics, helmets with nets, general service caps, cap badges, shoulder title patches, divisional wool patches, braces and gaiters. And finally, one large overcoat, a British rain cape (which would double up as a ground sheet) and several regulation vests and underpants.

"I didn't think we'd need a raincoat overseas. Isn't it supposed to be sunny all the time over there?" enquired Phil.

"Nah, I think that's just wishful thinking mate; it rains every bloody where," replied Jimmy, and we all agreed.

It took us forever to stagger back towards our barracks, as most of us kept dropping various items, which the Sergeant deftly picked up with his stick and unceremoniously draped over us. Jimmy ended up with his regulation underpants perched on his helmet, which was on his head.

There was little he could do about how he looked, so he brazened out our laughter with a huge grin and acted the fool. Fortunately, I was carrying my helmet.

"Cor, this lot's bloody heavy. How are we supposed to wear all this and carry the rest of our kit as well?" asked Jimmy of the Sergeant.

"Don't worry lad, when you do pack drill and a route march of twenty five miles, day in and day out for several weeks, it'll be like carrying a feather," came the reply.

We all laughed. However, Albert and I looked at one another unsure whether he meant it or not. Certain that he didn't, we continued laughing, now definitely believing it to be a joke.

As I took off my civvy clothes and packed them neatly into my little brown suitcase, I felt as if I was removing all traces of who I was. I caught my reflection in the windowpane and saw the outline of a stranger staring back. I was Private 1857 of the 1/5th West Yorkshire Territorial Regiment. That's who I kept telling myself I was and it felt very strange. With the transformation almost complete, I realised that the stores Sergeant had guessed my measurements very well. Only the trousers didn't fit. They were about six inches too long but when folded over at the bottom and covered by the putties, they weren't really a problem. In any case, it didn't matter, I'd grow into them.

Others weren't so lucky and it was only after there had been various swapping of jackets and trousers that they found the right size and the desired results they were looking for. With the donning of the uniform came a feeling of importance, and for several days all of us could be caught glancing at our reflections in various window panes we passed. For me, it was like looking at someone whom I couldn't take my eyes off. I felt I'd already grown two inches in height with the importance of being called Private Jackson.

"'Ere mate, I reckon we look a bit of alright in this gear, don't we?" commented a lad, also called John, as he tightened up his belt.

"Yes, great," I boasted feeling just as eminent, not caring that the uniform itched like blazes.

"We'll have the girls all lining up to go out with us," said Albert, excited at the thought. "All the girls like a man in a uniform," he continued.

I wasn't worried about any other girls, just Alice and wondered if it would make a difference to our relationship. I couldn't wait to show her.

We attended our first parade that evening, where we were told that in two weeks time, we would be sent for war training at Strensall Camp, six miles outside of York. If we proved ourselves to be worthy, we'd be allowed some free time to go home on the Saturday before. I'd show Alice then, I thought to myself. Until then, we were told we had plenty to learn, and had to knuckle-down.

The following afternoon we had the regulation short back and sides haircut. Each of us lined up to await our turn. As we looked on, Albert reckoned that his father's pudding basin cut was better than the army's cut. After the haircuts came the cursory medical, which we all passed, and then the last collection of kit. This consisted of a toggle rope, a whistle (which we all blew to check it worked), webbing to hold ammunition, a bayonet with scabbard and frog, entrenching tool, a pair of basic universal pouches, a big pack with shoulder straps, a small pack with belt straps, a water bottle and holder, a web rifle sling, a torch, shaving roll, soap, flannel, towel, a pocket jack knife with a marlin spike, and a first aid kit complete with a field dressing in it.

In addition, there was a housewife sewing kit known as a hussiff, a brass plate button cleaning protector, for use when brassing our buttons, a knife, fork, spoon, tin square with folding handle to eat out of, and if necessary to cook with. Also an enamel mug, two grey blankets rolled up, a shoe cleaning kit, a Prayer Book and a soldier's book with a Will in the back of it, which had to be filled out. Lastly, the best bit of all was a Number Four Mark One Enfield rifle. The kit was endless, but we were soldiers now, at least in looks.

SIX

Having collected our kit, we were shown how it all fitted into the various packs. The big pack housed clothing and the blankets. The small pack contained our eating equipment and washing stuff. Various pockets on our service jacket and trousers held other bits of kit. The belt had shoulder straps, which also held the bayonet and other pouches.

We were given a powder called blanco, which was to be used on various bits of webbing and our belts, for when we were on parade or needed to blend into the environment. We were told that it usually came as a powder, though sometimes it would be issued in a cake form, which would help renovate our webbing, or change it to a more acceptable colour. Khaki webbing, we were told, stood out amongst the terrain of Northwest Europe and so it was a job that we had to be familiar with, in the event we should end up there. There were excited murmurings at the prospect of such a thought.

Our webbing, when worn in the field, would hold 150 rounds of ammunition, though for now it was empty, which was just as well given the fact that half of us couldn't walk in a straight line, let alone fire a bullet straight. Having intimately explored our kit and fiddled with the jack knife and marlin spike, we spent the rest of the evening sewing on the various patches and Regimental badges to both uniforms.

"This bloody needle; the hole's too small; I can't thread the dam thing, ouch! Bloody 'ell, I've pricked myself, I'm bleeding," echoed throughout the barracks.

It was obvious men's fingers were not ideally suited to the finer art of sewing and would take some practising. My Mam would have been proud of me though as I deftly knotted the end of the cotton between two fingers, just as I'd seen her do many times before.

At ten o'clock, the lights went out, and, blinking in the darkness, I lay awake on the straw filled mattress listening to the loud snores from several of my bedfellows who'd fallen asleep as soon as their heads had hit the sack. Under the blanket next to me was my rifle. I secretly touched it, excited that it belonged to me. Little did I realise that it would be the first of many nights that I would sleep with it in my hand, but under very different circumstances. For now though, I was reminded of Alice. I would write to her, tomorrow.

Chapter FIVE

*Life is short and we have not too much time for gladdening the hearts of those who
are travelling the dark way with us.
(Henri Frederic Amiel 1821-1881)*

"Wakey, wakey, rise and shine, hands off Percy, the morning's fine, so move it," said a cheeky young Sergeant, who we'd not seen before.

At first, I thought he meant my rifle, and wondered how he knew I had it under the blanket, but then Albert enlightened me as to who Percy was and the penny dropped!

"You know, John, when it comes to some things, you're remarkably stupid," he said, as if knowledgeable in such matters.

The Sergeant paraded up and down, hitting the bottom of our bunks with his baton to make sure we'd heard him, as I gently slipped my rifle onto the floor. We soon discovered he'd been assigned to our barracks. His name was Pickles, but it wasn't too long, before we christened him, 'Old Picky'.

The day started with reveille at seven-thirty and a visit to the latrines at the end of the room, quickly followed by a wash in tepid water. It took us a while to get dressed in the hard itchy uniforms and put on the awkward cloth puttees from the top of our boots to our knees. They were supposed to keep dirt and other foreign matter out, however, there was a knack to winding them and several of us had the problem of them unwinding at embarrassing moments, much to the glee of those who'd mastered the art. It was almost worth sewing them in place each time, but as usual, time did not allow. Coupled with that, our stiff black leather hobnailed boots chafed and seemed as if they would take forever to soften to the shape of our feet. This resulted in us hobbling everywhere to the sounds of "ouch, 'ow, sss," and such likes, as each part of the rubbed foot touched the ground.

"Right now, fall in, on the double, Atten...tion," shouted Sergeant Pickles.

It was his job to teach us how to salute and march in time, or so he said. We all stood to attention. At least that's what we thought we were doing until he came along the rows prodding and poking us in various parts of our bodies to tuck bits in and straighten up. Once happy with the results, he made us stand like that for a good ten minutes whilst he wandered over to talk to another group going through the same drill. His eyes never left us though, and on return he pointed his stick at several of us.

"You, you and you, stay behind. The rest of you, fall out and report back here after breakfast at o'nine hundred hours."

Poor buggers. We watched them continue standing to attention for a further fifteen minutes before he let them join the rest of us.

After breakfast, it was the same thing, only this time, we were taught how to march in step.

"Left, right, left, right, left, right," reverberated in my head.

The problem most of us had was in the coordination of our arms with our legs. The marching action consisted of the left arm and right leg working together, and the right arm and the left leg working together, and if you had difficulty in telling your left from your right, or your brain was wired up wrong, as in Smithy's case, it was a bloody nightmare. A nightmare that for some would be visited time and time again, until it was automatic and the action branded in our brains.

The Sergeant tried making it easy for us by saying that one doesn't work without the other, so if your left arm moved, then your right leg did as well and so on, but poor old Smithy had a devil of a job getting it right. Whenever he moved his left arm, his left leg moved. The problem was though, that until he got it right, Sarge wouldn't let any of us stop. Only after several hours, with someone walking behind Smithy to kick his right leg, did we manage to get Sarge to call it a day. We were none too pleased with Smithy, I can tell you.

In the end, the sore feet turned into blistered feet and on top of that, I had a headache from the constant wearing of the tight-rimmed cap, which had for some reason, become too small. Albert reckoned my brains had grown from all the information it had to take in! Fortunately, Phil's cap was too big for him, so we did a swap, which solved the problem for both of us.

"Oh, I'm dead beat," I said, aching from top to toe.

All I wanted to do was to throw myself onto the bunk and rest my weary bones and go to sleep.

"It shows you're unfit," Albert chuntered, also hobbling around the bunk, though pretending that he was as fit as a fiddle.

"That's a laugh. What's up with you then?"

"Oh mine's not to do with fitness. I've just pulled a muscle," he lied smiling.

"Great food though," he continued, as he lobbed himself up onto his bunk.

At last, our first few days as a soldier were almost over, and Albert had been right. The best thing about them had indeed been the meals. We had three square meals a day and plenty, in comparison with the smaller portions most of us got at home. With the food and the training, Albert reckoned it wouldn't be too long before we'd all "put some muscle on our bones," as Mam would say, and these uniforms would really fit us all perfectly.

Just before lights out, most of us were already top-side on our beds. A few were boot cleaning, some were practising puttee wrapping and though I wasn't one for writing letters, I scribbled a hasty note to Alice:

> *"Dear Alice,*
>
> *Meet me in the usual place on Saturday, 29th at 2pm. I've got a few hours leave before they send me to Strensall Camp. I can't wait to see you.*
>
> *Yours truly,*
> *John."*

I'd never written to Alice before, so I wasn't sure how to start or end my letter. I wanted to say, "Dear Sweetheart" and end it, by saying, "Yours forever," but being chicken-livered, I did neither and kept it short and somewhat formal.

I also wrote to Mam and Dad telling them I was settling down nicely and that the Army officers were looking after me. I told them I'd see them on that same Saturday for a few hours and would tell them all about it then. I smiled at the thought of them seeing me in my uniform, and me having to reassure them that we had to look 'the part' even though we weren't proper soldiers. I just couldn't wait.

The following morning, every muscle in my body ached. I'd stiffened up completely. I groaned. Today there would be more marching drills on the parade ground but this time with our rifles, learning how to present arms.

SIX

"I'm going to shoot Smithy if he gets it wrong today," I said, to a few of the lads as we prepared for morning drill.

"Yeah, you won't be the only one," replied Albert, and the rest agreed.

"Smithy," shouted Phil, hoping that he'd hear, "I hope you've got that piece of string tied from your right boot to your left hand, or you'll be dead."

"No problem lads. I've got it cracked," he said, appearing from nowhere, having heard the banter.

"Look…" and with that, he gave us all a quick demonstration as to how it was done.

"I've been practicing it in my dreams," he reassured us.

"Let's hope his bloody rifle doesn't mess it all up," said Phil, laughing.

"Nah, not a chance. I tell you, I've got it sorted. Just don't distract me."

Smithy was true to his word. His every thought was on getting it right. His lips silently mouthed, "Left, right, left, right," in keeping with his arms and legs, exposing the workings of his brain as he concentrated hard. No, it wasn't Smithy who let the side down and kept us practising until we got it right, it was me! I had two left arms. I just couldn't get used to the rifle being held on the left side with the right arm swinging in time with our marching. Being left handed, it just didn't feel right and it put me completely off my stride until I eventually got it drilled into my head. And, I was made to pay for my mistake. It cost me a packet of twenty 'Wills' and two tins of snuff, before I was forgiven. Still, as I was collecting the "British Empire" cigarette cards, I was only really out of pocket with the snuff.

Later on in the week, we were promised a route march in full kit. Sarge told us they would go easy on us to begin with and would only make us march five miles for the first time. After that, we would build up to twenty-five miles in the one day. It was now apparent that the Sergeant we'd first seen hadn't been joking. We were told we'd be walking at about four miles per hour, which was about average.

"No wonder they call it a route march!" said Albert.

By Wednesday of the second week, marching in full kit and a five-mile distance had been mastered, and we were feeling pretty good about it.

"There's nawt to it," said Albert, and we all agreed.

It was now only a few days away from the big twenty-five miles march. On that day, an army truck was to take us up into the Yorkshire Moors, and drop us just outside the town of Pickering for the big hike home. From there we had to march in full kit and be back at the barracks no later than four o'clock, giving us a leeway of about one hour. We had maps just in case we got lost. However, sad to say, we failed miserably. We didn't make it back until six-fifteen. The heavens had opened almost as soon as the trucks had left us. The weight of the rain had added to the weight of our packs and despite the maps, we got lost and spent valuable minutes arguing as to which way we should go. The torrential rain was relentless. God was in his heaven, but all was not well. It felt as if we'd walked fifty miles.

It stopped raining just as we staggered down Fulford Road, almost on our knees, and when we turned to go through the Barrack gates, Sergeant Pickles greeted us. He must have had a lookout to tip him off that we were coming. He was tapping his stick on his hand, like a headmaster about to use the cane.

"Fall in, at the double. What time do you call this?" he boomed across the courtyard.

Silence ensued, partly because none of us had the energy to respond.

"Well, you despicable lot, you are going to do this exercise again tomorrow, and the next day, and the next, until you get it right and complete the task in the time allotted, and all leave will be cancelled until you do. Is that clear? Well, is it?"

"Yes Sir," we responded.

"Right then, fall out, and get cleaned up."

Somewhat despondent, our feet and backs killing us, we all knew that we couldn't take much more of this gruelling task. And to cap it all, it only gave us two days to get it right or we'd miss out on Saturday's leave. No one wanted to forgo the plans we'd all made. Besides, none of us could face repeating the exercise day in, day out, until such time as we did get it right, so we decided to get our heads down, and give it our best shot again tomorrow, aiming to start at sunrise when we'd all be fresh.

Spurred on by the thought of failure and having to do it all again, we started out once more and made excellent time. We completed the exercise at record speed, in just less than six hours, at the average of four miles per hour as instructed. The weather was fine and we even managed to catch 'Old Nit Picky' off his guard.

SIX

Pleased with our efforts, he let us off with only light duties for the rest of the day. What he didn't know was we'd flagged a couple of large butcher's carts down on their way to Malton market to pick up cattle, and so only had to walk twelve miles. Well, what 'Old Picky' wasn't privy to wouldn't hurt him we thought. After all, we couldn't miss out on Saturday's leave as it approached, now could we? How we all laughed knowing we had fooled him.

Chapter SIX

Endurance is one of the most difficult disciplines,
but it is to the one who endures that the final victory comes.
(Buddha (Gautama Buddha) 563 BC - 483 BC)

At last, the big day home arrived. Having had the lecture from Sarge about how to behave when in uniform, I headed for home with Albert. We walked proudly through the town, appreciating the attention girls gave us as they passed by. When we got to Albert's house, I told him I'd catch him later and journeyed on to my place.

As usual, the back door was off the latch, so I walked straight in.

"Halt, who goes there?" I said, as Dad entered the kitchen to find me standing by the table.

"Well, well, well, son. Just look at you. Polly, it's our John," he shouted.

"Oh, son, you do look different," said Mam, as she came rushing in, crushing me in a bear hug and showering me with kisses.

Full of pride, her eyes filled up and tears threatened to cascade down her soft cheeks, just as she sniffed them away.

"Aw Mam, lay off will you. I've not been away two minutes and you're already getting soppy."

She took out her handkerchief and blew her nose, still overcome with emotion at seeing me. On hearing the commotion, Fred, Wilf and Charlie piled into the kitchen to see what all the fuss was about.

"Cor, look at our John! He looks a right old dandy in that uniform," said Charlie.

"Have you killed any Boche yet," said Wilf, half expecting me to say "yes."

"Aw, give over. I haven't been anywhere to see any."

"I heard last Sunday that Japan has now declared war on Germany. They're also saying there's been five and a half thousand Belgians killed already," said Dad, looking worried.

I reckon that's just German propaganda, don't you John?" said Fred.

"Yes, bound to be. Anyway, enough of that… how's everyone?" I enquired.

It turned out that everything had gone on much the same without me, just as I had predicted it would. Old Mrs Lofthouse next door wasn't too well, and they'd heard that the girl two doors away, Ruby, had been mysteriously sent away to family at Romford. It wasn't common knowledge but apparently everyone was whispering about it.

I could now hear Mam's voice clearly.

"It wouldn't surprise me if she's got herself into trouble, always surrounded by boys like a dog on heat. It's disgusting. She can't be more than twelve or thirteen. Well, fingers get burnt if you play with fire. It'll be that Alice Johnson's turn next, you mark my words."

"Nah Mam, give it a rest. Alice isn't like that," I said, and nearly added that I should know, but thought better of it.

"In any case, you don't know if that's the reason why Ruby's gone to Romford. It might be her chest that's giving her problems."

"Mmm, we'll see... you mark my words," Mam retorted.

"There's no smoke without a fire," she continued, as she gave another appreciative look at me in my uniform.

"Have you heard from our Matt and the likes?" I hastily asked, distracting Mam's thoughts away from the Johnson's.

"Yes. We had a letter from him the other day. It appears he's got himself a sweetheart. She's called Mary same as me. He says that she's a lot younger than him, but he's quite keen on her. Says she's the sheep farmer's daughter. I do hope he knows what he's doing," she nattered.

"Oh, and our George is going to be a dad again, and guess what," she said, looking at me half expectantly, as if I might already know, "so is our Robert, so there's plenty going on. I expect they'll want me to help."

"George is going to have his work cut out to feed four of them then, isn't he?

"Mmm."

"I bet our Robert's pleased. It's about time he got his finger out."

"Oh aye, he's like the cat who stole the cream," replied Mam, beaming.

"And how are you getting on, lad?" asked Dad.

"Oh great Dad, just great. We're going to Strensall next week for proper training. They reckon we'll be there until the end of October and then we'll be back in time for Christmas, though I doubt whether we'll get much time off."

"How's Albert doing?"

"Oh, just fine, just fine."

Mam had done us proud and cooked a slap up dinner to celebrate my visit.

"It's one of Mr Haigh's rabbits," she said, and it was one of the best stews Mam had made.

The meat just fell off the bone. Well, only the best was good enough for one of her boys she remarked as she cleared away the dishes. Dad settled in the fireside chair and out came his pipe as he watched us play cards on the cleared table. Nothing had changed, or so I thought.

Just before leaving, Fred called me aside as he went into the back yard for a smoke.

"I haven't told Mam and Dad yet, but I'm going to join the Durham Light Infantry next week," he said, lighting up a Capstan. He preferred those to Wills.

"Aw Fred, don't. Wait until they call you up, or at least leave it a few more weeks until they get used to me being away."

"No, I've made my mind up. I've always wanted to go in the Army and now I've got my chance. It's not as though there's a girl holding me back, and it's not like you, it's the Army proper," he continued.

"When are you going to tell them?"

"I'll tell Dad tomorrow and no doubt he'll break the news to Mam later. I've been talking about it for a while now, long before the war broke out, so they won't be surprised. Our Matt's also been talking about joining the Australian Imperial Force as well, especially if this sheep farming lark doesn't get going."

"Bloody hell! It just needs our George and Robert to join up and except for the young-uns, we'll all be gone."

"Nah, George and Robert are family men. They're not going to want to join up unless they're forced. Anyway, keep your mouth shut. Charlie and Wilf know nothing about it and I want to keep it that way for as long as possible before the cat's out of the bag."

In a serious mood, Fred shook my hand and both of us uttered our goodbyes, promising to write. He promised to let me know if any new developments occurred. I was going to be late if I didn't get a move on, so for now, I left it at that. The last thing I wanted to do was to be late seeing Alice. Once outside, I waved frantically at the family, and ran like a bat out of hell towards the park. As soon as I entered the main gate I saw her, wearing her red dress… my favourite. Within a flash, she was running to greet me, almost falling into my arms. I just couldn't contain myself and in full view of everyone, I kissed her frantically without saying a word. Her lips parted slightly under the pressure of mine and the tip of my tongue accidentally touched hers. It was electrifying. I thought I was going to die in ecstasy. She instantly backed off as if something had stung her.

"Oh Alice, I've missed you," I uttered, in-between a further onslaught of kisses.

For once, I wished we were somewhere other than in the park, in the full gaze of everyone. She tried putting a halt to my ardour and pushed me away slightly to catch her breath.

"For goodness sake, John, stop," she said, now continuing to push more firmly.

I backed away and reluctantly let go of her.

"We mustn't," she said.

"I know, I know. I'm sorry Alice, but you're so lovely. I just couldn't help myself. Don't you feel the same way?"

"Of course I do. At least, I think I do, but you're getting carried away and I'm just not ready for anything like that yet," she said, all of a sudden shy.

I knew at once I'd gone too far, but it was impossible not to touch her, so in desperation I put my hands in my pockets, aware of my passion.

We talked about Rowntrees where she worked. We talked about Strensall camp and about home front training. She didn't mention anything about how I looked, or that she was pleased to see me.

"What do you think of the uniform then?" I asked, unable to contain myself any longer.

"I like it, though you look so different. You seem to have grown taller. I expect it's because I've not seen you for nearly two weeks."

"You'll not know me after two months then, when I next see you."

"Will it be that long?"

"Yes, from what they say."

We walked towards the town in silence, each of us deep in thought. It left me feeling unsure as to whether I'd gone a bit too far in my passionate onslaught of her.

"Can I still write to you?"

"Sure."

"Does this mean you forgive me?"

In reply, she turned to kiss me briefly, but before I got a chance to catch hold of her properly, she wriggled free and teasingly sprinted away. I chased after her, only managing to catch up with her as we reached the main road of the park and the bustle of people doing their last minute shopping. The moment was gone and I could see that Alice felt safe again in the crowd of people milling around, leaving me frustrated at having to share her again with so many.

We walked through the town and to the top end of Fulford Road before saying goodbye. I leant against the wall and she innocently pressed her body against mine, as we stood together. I pulled her closer to feel her properly, as my lips hungrily searched for hers. I wanted to rip my jacket open to feel her breasts through the thin red dress as she pressed up against me, but by the time the thought had occurred, she was disentangling herself from my arms. Before I could catch hold of her again, she turned and was gone from my reach.

"Goodbye," she said, reluctantly.

"Don't forget to write."

I stood for a moment watching her in the distance, as my body continued to ache for hers. I tried to put all thoughts of her from my mind as my ardour cooled, and I headed back to the barracks.

"John, John," shouted Albert, who was running hard to catch up with me.

"Had a good day?" he said breathlessly.

"Sure, though that Alice is driving me mad with desire. I'm sure she's doing it on purpose. One minute she's all over me like a rash and the next minute she's as cold as ice."

"I shouldn't worry mate. That's girls for you," said Albert, reassuringly as we headed back to base.

Chapter SEVEN

I was taught that the way of progress is neither swift nor easy.
(Marie Curie 1867-1934)

By the time we'd got back to the barracks and slipped into army routine again, all thoughts of Alice had gone. Over the next few days, we prepared to journey to Strensall for proper war training. Our excitement was difficult to contain and there was plenty of teasing about which one of us would be able to shoot straight and be the better soldier. Alf reckoned we ought to take bets.

When we eventually arrived at Strensall, it was completely different from what I'd imagined. For a start it was mainly tents with very few brick built buildings, and it was vast.

"Crickey Moses Albert, we're going to have to live in tents," I said excitedly, catching the look of amazement on his face.

There were rows and rows of conical shaped white canvas tents, which brightened up the landscape. The camp was split into various areas, one part being divided into the tented area, others into rifle ranges, arm-to-arm combat areas, rope scaling tower platforms, woods and trench sections, nets to climb over and under, and streams to ford. The area extended further than the eye could see.

"It's going to be brilliant," said Smithy, and I had to agree.

"How big is this place, Sarge?"

"It's about 1,800 acres in total and home to some ten thousand men from other regiments, all who will be involved in tactical exercises with us," said Sarge.

"Their skills will be pitted against ours, so you'd better learn fast. I'm counting on you all to be the best."

He allowed us a few minutes to take in the scene before us. We were developing a bit of a soft spot for old Pickles. He was strict in some things, but always extremely fair, and a thoroughly decent chap. I think he had a soft spot for us too as he now called us "my boys," and all of us were keen he should be proud of us.

"Don't let me down now lads," he said, as he tried to curb our enthusiasm.

"There's going to be plenty of opportunity to get stuck in, so for now, just familiarize yourselves with the tented area that's to be our home for the next two months. Let me assure you, by the time you're leaving here you'll be glad to see the back of it."

We unpacked our gear into a storage tent and went to inspect the night-time arrangements. The tents were huge, made up of twenty-six panels, a panel to each man, with enough room for other men to sleep down the middle if necessary. Albert and I decided to put our blankets on two of the camp beds in the bell end, away from the possible draughts that might emerge from the middle entrance area. Alf, Smithy and Phil followed suit. We were then ordered to fall in line and given a conducted tour of the rest of the camp.

The weather was quite fine and the going under foot was easy. Along one side of the tented area were makeshift latrines. There was also a wash area which had tables made up from three long planks of wood supported by trestle ends. The tops were strong enough to support several tin washbowls for the morning wash. A two-inch plank was suspended above the planked top supported by smaller crossed pieces of wood every four feet. This acted as a shelf. On the floor, were batons of wood joined together to make a raft, to stop you from slipping and sinking into the ground, which I suspected would be a quagmire in the wet weather. All could be easily moved and reassembled elsewhere should the area become too muddy, and by the looks of it, this had only recently been done. Dad referred to these rafts as duckboards and after the Boar war, had made one for Mam to stand on by the big kitchen sink.

In the distance was the garrison church, attendance at which was compulsory on Sundays. I knew that Mam would be pleased about that. There was a large area called Queen's Parade where Sarge told us three to four thousand men could be drilled and manoeuvred at any one time. The whole place was immense. There were also several mess huts, kitchens, and canteens, which served the various regiments. A large area had also been designated for several skittle alleys, three cricket and lawn tennis grounds and a commodious theatre, all of which were provided for our recreation and amusement. Yes, it was going to be great here.

"Only one problem with the place," said Albert.

"What?" I replied, wondering what on earth could be missing.

"There are no girls," he moaned.

"Bloody hell, Albert. Who wants a girl here when we've got all this?" said Phil, who had yet to discover the delights of the opposite sex.

"I do," said Albert, disappointedly.

Albert did have a point. However, we couldn't have everything and I told him as much, as we walked on to investigate the Telegraph Office and the Savings Bank that had just opened on the site. I was hoping to buy a postcard to send a message home.

On our way, we passed what was supposed to be a semi-permanent Medical Centre. It was constructed of a brick base, with a light steel frame, filled in externally with rough cast panels, and internally with plaster. The roof was made of asbestos cement tiles which were the forerunner of the light barrack construction, now up and coming.

"I think we should send Phil in there to check whether he's got any balls," Albert said, worried about his lack of interest in girls.

We all laughed, but Phil refused to comment.

"'Ere, Phil. You have got some balls haven't you?"

"Bugger off you lot and the same to you, but with brass knobs on," he replied.

"I tell you what, Phil. This 'ere place is big enough to provide us with a knocking-shop. I'll ask Sarge where it is and we'll point you in the right direction. The girls there will sort you out," said Albert, not letting up on him, as he pretended to look around for Sarge.

"My Dad always calls those places a kip-shop. Do you reckon there is one here?" I said.

"Don't talk wet! Why do you think they put bromide in our tea?"

"Really?"

"Well I'll get Sarge to put two spoonfuls in your tea then, Albert," said Phil, hoping to get back at him.

"Better ask him for me as well then, 'cos Alice is just about driving me mad," I quipped, as we walked on.

I didn't just buy one postcard, but half a dozen from the Telegraph Office before we headed back towards the tented area to report for final drill practice of the day. Tomorrow we would be practising rope climbing and rifle shooting. I couldn't wait to see what kind of a shot I was going to be and Albert couldn't wait to have a go on the ropes. It was going to be a great day, and all of us were excitedly looking forward to it.

It was hot and clammy in the tent that first night and I tossed and turned most of the time amid the smell of sweating bodies and snoring. By morning I was just dozing off into a deep sleep when the bugle sounded to get up. Albert had to kick me twice before I could drag myself out of bed and gather my wash things together and head towards the washing area. I joined a sea of men, wearing only their trousers, vests and braces, all heading in a state of semi-consciousness to the area where the tin washbowls awaited us with cold water sloshed in them.

"Bloody hell, that water's cold enough to freeze the balls off me," I said, immediately wide-awake as I gasped for air from the dowsing of water on my face.

"You'd better get used to it, Jackson. It's as good as it gets," remarked Sarge, as he passed on his way to the canteen.

I certainly didn't linger over the activity and hurriedly completed my toilet in super-quick time. The September mornings had more of a chill in the air so I wasn't going to hang around any longer than I had to.

After roll call, we changed into our gym kit and proceeded to the rope climbing area where we were introduced to the physical training instructor, Sergeant Baker. He was a tall athletically built man bouncing with energy like a tightly coiled spring about to unwind. He had us running on the spot, jumping in the air flapping our arms up and down like birds, followed by fifty press-ups before we could say "Jack Robinson." It was his way of getting us warmed up to start the planned activity.

To tell you the truth, we were all knackered after that, and that was before we joined him at the rope-climbing tower! I had cramp from the blood running out of my arms during the wing flapping, and still breathless, we stood and watched him scale up this rope to the top of the tower as if he had ants in his pants.

"Do you think he has a rocket up his arse?" whispered Albert, and I laughed out loud at the thought of it.

"You there, what's your name?" Sergeant Baker bellowed from the top of the platform.

I looked around, not sure who he was referring to, and when I caught his eye again, he said, "Yes, you."

"Who, me, Sergeant?"

"Who else do you think I'm pointing at?"

"It's Jackson, Sergeant," I replied, my heart catching in my throat.

"Well then, Jackson. You seem to have found something funny to laugh about, so I'd like you to climb up here and tell me all about it."

I gingerly pushed to the front of the group, making my way towards the bottom of the rope, amid mutterings and smiles from my fellow comrades. I took hold of the two-inch thick rope and looked up. Christ, it must have been at least twenty feet to the top. I raised my hands as far up the rope as I could, and gripped tightly as I heaved. I tried desperately to wrap it around my legs to get a better grip as I heaved again. The progress was slow. About half way up, I glanced down, now unsure of what to do. I was too far up to let go and drop to the ground, and yet I was too exhausted to carry on.

"Pull with your arms and get a grip with your knees, lad," boomed the command from above.

"Pretend you're a caterpillar," shouted someone from below.

"That won't work," said Albert. Then he shouted, "Pretend it's Alice trying to get away!"

A peal of laughter erupted as Sergeant Baker's voice bellowed out to silence them.

"Put some muscle into it, Jackson."

"Someone needs to put a bomb behind him, Sergeant."

I continued to inch my way up, resting every now and then, whenever I managed to get a good grip with my legs. As I looked up, I'd only got about another six feet to go. My hands were white and I couldn't feel my arms anymore. The blood had completely drained out of them. It was then that I made one final fatal mistake. I relaxed my grip and lowered my arms to shoulder level. As the blood came flooding back into them in, a wave of pins and needles, followed by severe pain erupted. I couldn't hold on any longer and letting go with my arms, my legs took the full weight of my body. The rope started to slip between my legs, burning the skin on the inside of my thighs, as I slithered down a few inches.

SIX

On seeing what was happening, Sergeant Baker quickly scaled down the rope adjoining mine and reached out with his legs, wrapping them tightly around my body. He gripped me to him to prevent me from falling down any further. There were gasps from below as several of my mates rushed to the bottom of the rope to break my fall, should it be necessary.

"Now then, Jackson," he whispered in my ear so no one else could hear, his breath rasping on my face.

"We are going to finish climbing up this bloody rope as if a Jerry is on your tail, and we are going to do it before I count to ten, or you are going to be on sanitary fatigue duty for the duration of your stay here. Is that clear, Jackson?"

"Yes Sergeant."

"Right then, get a grip," he said, as he gingerly released me, "one… two… three… four…"

I grabbed the rope, and holding my breath, pulled myself up the remaining section of it, gripping alternately with my hands and knees, scaling it as if I was a rat going up a drainpipe. I clung onto the top of the tower, all energy expelled, as Sergeant Baker hauled me up onto the platform by the scruff of my neck. I sat exhausted, weak-kneed and retching. Vomit came into my mouth and I quickly swallowed it again, desperately hoping it would stay down.

"Right then, you lot down there. Who's next?" Sergeant Baker shouted, as he slid down, leaving me with my head between my knees to keep the vomit from coming up again.

He used the rope so effortlessly, that all I could think of was that he must have been brought up in the jungle. After no one volunteered, he proceeded to show everyone the necessary technique. By wrapping the rope around the left foot and trapping it with the right foot, and at the same time gripping with the knees, you could anchor yourself firmly, he told us. It was then just a case of releasing the foothold as you pulled up with the hands. If you timed the coordination just right, the whole procedure was easy.

He then threw a length of thinner rope up to me on the top of the tower, and after he'd tied the other end around the waist of Albert, he told me to take up the slack. After my ordeal, he obviously wasn't going to take the chance of anyone falling and breaking their neck, before they left for France. As it happened, Albert didn't need any help. He was up to the top in no time.

"The secret is, mate, you've got to do it in the quickest possible time or you run out of steam. Your problem was you took your bloody time," he said to me.

He undid the rope from around his middle and threw it down for the next man up. This time he took up the slack, and at the same time, I descended the other rope. Now that I was fully recovered, going down was much easier. The main problems were counteracting the weight of my body with the pull of gravity, and the rope slipping through my hands causing friction burns. However, I made it without too much trouble. Gradually, as each man underwent the same ordeal, Sergeant Baker had us running on the spot whilst we waited to go again. The idea was, we should go up and down the rope automatically and be back forming a queue to do it all over again. The activity should be on a continuous, rotational basis, until he told us to stop.

By the end of the morning, we were all shinning up and down the rope pretty well. I and a few others were still a bit on the slow side but we were getting there. Albert insisted I was unfit and therein lay the problem.

"Put a sock in it. You're talking rubbish. In any case, there's more to fitness than just climbing ropes," I retorted, knowing that he was a poor swimmer.

"You wait till you need piggybacking across a river. There'll be no question of whether I'm fit or not then. Maybe I'll accidentally let you slip into the water and see whether you sink or swim. I bet you won't be telling me then I'm unfit, will you?"

"Course not. What do you think I am, bloody daft?" he replied grinning. His laughter danced on the wind as he gave me a hug, as if to say he was only joking.

Chapter EIGHT

Learning is not attained by chance,
it must be sought for with ardour and attended to with diligence.
(Abigail Adams 1744 - 1818)

I fared much better than Albert doing rifle training in the afternoon. The camp had five rifle ranges dotted amidst wooded areas and we couldn't wait to get out there. The only slight stumbling block to our enthusiasm was that we had to know every inch of our S.M.L.E. rifle before any bullets were fired and the only way to do that was to clean it said the ammunitions Sergeant. S.M.L.E stood for Short Magazine Lee Enfield rifle or Smellies as they were nicknamed.

We learnt how it came apart and how it all fitted back together again, which was just as well, as my only experience of taking things apart resulted in not being able to put them together again. We learnt how the bayonet should be attached and how the grenade launcher was connected on. The Smellie had wood all the way to the muzzle, with a flush metal cap over the end, and a round stud at the bottom for the bayonet attachment. When clean, the whole forty-four and a half inches of it, was like pure silk to touch.

The magazine held ten rounds of ammunition at any one time, which was a great improvement on its predecessor, known as the Long Tom, which Dad had used in the Boar War. By the time we'd learnt all about the rifle, and the trajectory of bullets, we were ready to see which one of us would be the best shot. The targets were placed at different distances and it wasn't long before most of us had got the hang of it. Those who had, progressed to firing from different positions, from laying down on our bellies and crawling on the ground using our elbows and knees to move ourselves forward, to shooting from standing and other stances. The noise was deafening.

"Try not to hit anything other than the target," exclaimed Sergeant Terry, the ammunitions instructor.

To my delight, Albert was having problems and I smirked when I realised that at last, I had found my forte. I was a pretty good shot and Sergeant Terry thought that with a bit of training, I'd make a good marksman. At the end of the session, he singled a few of us out to talk about what this would mean. Albert struggled on all afternoon getting more and more frustrated.

"The trouble is, my rifle's not straight," he whined, using it as an excuse for not hitting the target once.

"Maybe I'm blind in one eye and don't know it," he continued.

"Oh yeah, pull the other one. Why don't you try pulling the trigger with your right finger instead? It looks awkward the way you're holding it."

In desperation Albert changed it around and sure enough, he began hitting the target with ease.

"You'll almost be as good as me if you practise," I quipped.

"Watch it, John-boy! I might be better!" he replied laughing.

As time went on, all of us became adept at firing from different positions. We were told this was to take into account any eventuality and it was great fun. We extended our rifle training into bayonet practice, and with great gusto, we ran, yelled, and stabbed the bayonets into hung up bags of sand and straw.

"Louder," shouted Sergeant Terry.

"You're meant to be frightening the enemy, not pussy-footing around," he added.

This only had the effect of making us laugh even more at the thought of any of us frightening anyone, let alone the enemy. Still, we all obliged him with louder "aaahs" as we mercilessly pulverised our hung-up Jerry into empty shreds of sacking.

We learned about various other weapons, such as machine guns, trench and mortar guns, big berthas and howitzers, and guns that delivered shells with apparently devastating results, which we still had to witness. We played with dummy hand grenades, learning how to alter the timing of them by using a fingernail in the slot located on the bottom of them. Turning it in a clockwise direction enabled the timing to be changed from a few seconds detonation to several seconds, depending on the situation.

We were told that if we were walking past a window and wanted to just slip one in, then the detonation time needed to be short, as we didn't want to give any time for it to be thrown out again. However, if we were going to lob it some distance by using the clip attachment on our rifles, then the timing of the explosion would need to be much longer.

"You'll soon get the hang of it," Sarge informed us.

SIX

Our brief introduction to grenade training was just a taster, said Sarge, as our proper instruction would be after Christmas on the East Coast beaches. Smithy was relieved to hear this as he relentlessly bit his nails to the core. He now had a few weeks to grow a thumbnail sufficiently long enough to do the job, and we were all co-opted into helping him.

Whenever we caught him biting any of his nails, he got a clip around the ear-hole, just as Mam would have dealt.

"At this rate I'm going to be dead from all the blows I get," he exclaimed, following one hit that caught him unawares and knocked him sideways onto the floor.

"It's for your own good," chirped Phil, who had struck the blow. "You'll be thanking me when you need that nail to pick bogies out of your nose," and we all laughed.

"Don't be so disgusting," Smithy added.

We continued to do pack drills and route marches in full kit and also learnt about arm-to-arm combat, how to kill quietly and how to knock our opponents off balance, but to all of us, it was just play and we found it hard to take it all seriously. We even enjoyed cold showers and the thought of 'jankers.' However, none of us had committed any real misdemeanours to warrant such drastic action. The closest we ever got to any punishment was when all of us were confined to barracks for three days, followed by three days digging a new latrine trench, and all for failing to own up to a prank which none of us had done.

The prank had been committed against our Commanding Officer. Every day during morning roll call he would salute the Union Jack, which flew high on the parade ground. One particular day, someone had swapped the flag for a pair of his smalls. He was so angry, that he confined everyone to barrack duties until the culprit owned up. Unfortunately, the culprit never did and so after confinement and the three days latrine duties, he gave us a monetary penalty as well, thereby saving face. Rumour had it that it was one of the Durham Lights who'd committed the crime, but we never did find out.

After a few weeks, we were pretty much set in the camp routine. The weather had been kind to us, very much like an Indian summer. As I headed for the canteen, I heard Smithy calling after me.

"Hey-up, John-boy. There's a letter for you."

I quickly looked at the envelope but didn't recognize the postmark. I expected it to be from Alice or Mam but it was neither. On opening it, I discovered it was from our Fred:

"Dear John,

Just a quick line to tell you that I've been and gone and done it! Yep, I've joined up with the Durham Light Infantry and I shall be based with the 2nd Battalion. There's talk of our lot briefly coming to Strensall, possibly at the end of October. How come you are there and for how long? Maybe we can meet up. Mam and Dad took the news fairly well. They just said they wished I hadn't, but realized they couldn't stop me. The talk on the street is that they need soldiers for the defence of Antwerp so I don't think it will be long before I go overseas. I expect by then John, you'll be defending York if it comes to it. Anyway, take care of yourself old lad. Maybe I'll get a few days leave at Christmas before I go abroad and I'll see you then. By the way, Alice is pining for you! Don't worry, I haven't said anything to Mam and Dad. It's about time you wrote to them though, just to let them know you are all right.

Your ever-loving bro,
Fred."

I tucked the letter into my top jacket pocket and hoped to God he didn't arrive at Strensall before we left, or the cat might be let out of the bag for real. He would then cotton-on there was more to the 'home front' involvement in this war than just staying at home. He's going to be surprised when he hears they plan to send the West Yorkshire's overseas and sees us fighting alongside the 'real' army, as he keeps referring to it. Hopefully, he won't be any the wiser until its too late, and in any case this was such a big place it would surely be virtually impossible to locate me.

That night I wrote home telling Mam and Dad I'd heard from Fred and reassured them that he'd have a great time if he came to Strensall. I also wrote to Alice:

"Dearest Alice,

I'm in A1 condition, and apart from missing you, it's not bad here. How are you? I'm sorry that I haven't written for a while but when we do manage to get a few minutes to ourselves, I've been so tired that I try to get some sleep. It's not helped by the fact I'm trying to sleep with twenty-five other men all snoring and talking in their sleep. I'm a light sleeper at the best of times. Maybe if I had you to tuck me in at night I might sleep better?

How's everyone else at home? I had a letter from our Fred today. He's joined up with the Durham Lights. Anyway, the last post has just been sounded so I'll end now and get this letter off to you tomorrow. Take care of yourself. I really do think a lot about you and like you lots. Some might even say that I love you. It won't be long now before I see you again and then I can tell you what I really feel about you.

Yours Forever,
John.
p.s. Have you been to see the oak tree recently?"

I'd secretly carved a heart on the trunk of the old oak with "JJ loves AJ" inscribed neatly within it and hoped that Alice would be pleased with my efforts. The tree didn't seem to mind, and now, I only hoped she didn't either. I was beginning to wonder if I'd done the right thing. After all, I still wasn't a hundred per cent sure of her feelings for me.

As I began to think about the war, the camp lights went out. I searched my jacket pocket for Alice's handkerchief and held it close to my nose. The smell of her cologne made me ache with desire. Only about one more month to go and then I could hold her in my arms again.

Chapter NINE

*You gain strength, courage and confidence by every experience
in which you really stop to look fear in the face…
(Eleanor Roosevelt 1884-1962)*

Back at home, Alice was in the kitchen of 4 Bexley Square, re-living some of her nightmares. As winter approached, it was something which often happened.

It was always the 6th December 1911, which came flashing back. Alice had been ten then, and had been kept off school to look after Molly and her younger brother Alfred, who was four months old. Her sister Molly had been one month short of her fifth birthday. Molly's proper name was Hilda, but to family she was simply, Molly. Their mother had left Alice in charge, while she went around the corner to help her aunt paint her front room, but to Alice it had been a million miles away, when she had needed her.

Alice could still hear the screams, could still see Molly in flames as she'd ran crazily around Alfred's bedroom, setting fire to everything before becoming quickly engulfed herself. It was the day that haunted Alice, and she remembered every detail… her own hands burnt as she'd tried to lift the Holland pinafore dress over Molly's head, her desperate efforts to make her stand still as she clawed away at the rubber buttons on her clothes to get them off her. Her futile attempt to get the fire away from her. Yes, she remembered everything.

When Alice realised the ineffectiveness of her actions, she remembered the seemingly endless run for help, and the horror at having to leave Molly still ablaze, with her screams echoing after her. Eventually, minutes later when she'd returned with her mother, the house was silent, and both of them ran upstairs to find Molly curled up in a flaming heap on the ground, with the bedroom on fire. Yes, she remembered it well, just as if it was only yesterday.

Mercifully, the other young ones had been at school. George, her older stepbrother from her father's first marriage, was married and lived away, leaving Alice as the next eldest, to help her mother. Connie was just two years younger than Alice, but always suffered with her chest so was rarely well enough to help. Then there was Ted, Molly, and Alfred. Edna, and Ethel, had been born a few years after that fateful day though Ethel had died the following February aged six months, leaving Edna as the baby of what had once been a family of eight.

Alice recalled the minutes before the fire. Alfred had been asleep upstairs in his cot. Molly was upstairs bent on waking him and wouldn't come down. Angrily, Alice had pulled her out of his bedroom and had dragged her to the top of the stairs, where she'd left her sulking. She always proved difficult when Alice was left in charge, and as there were still the chores her mother had left her to do, she left Molly sitting there. It was shortly after that when Alice had heard Molly's screams.

Earlier that day, her mother had put the morning's wet bedding to dry in front of the open fire in Alfred's bedroom before she'd gone out. Molly, not doing as she was told, had gone back into the room and had walked between the wet bedding and the fire, where her dress caught alight. There was little Alice could do. By the time their mother had arrived and had scooped Molly up off the bedroom floor still ablaze, it was too late. Eventually, it was Mr Hepplethwaite who had the foresight to smother both Molly and her mother in a rug as they came down the stairs with flames still licking everywhere, and it was he who managed to put the human inferno out.

Alice could still remember seeing Molly, as she lay unrecognisable in her mother's arms like a black, charred, limp rag doll, mewing pitifully. She was barely breathing. A passing hansom cab took them both to the hospital, and that was the last Alice had seen of her. Molly had died three hours later. At the inquest the following day, the surgeon who'd attended Molly said the only bit of her that hadn't been burnt was a small area on her ankles and the soles of her feet. She hadn't stood a chance of surviving.

The coroner had praised Alice for her efforts, but she blamed herself, and now, as she stoked the kitchen fire, she could hear the echoes of Molly's screams again and again in the empty house, and wished that she was dead too. She was sure it was her fault. It was always the same, if only… if only she had made Molly come downstairs… if only she'd known to smother the flames with a rug… if only she hadn't been too busy and had played with Molly, then she wouldn't have been bored and gone near the fire. It was always 'if only'.

From that day, the house had changed. Her mother and father, after months of arguing and accusations, became strangers, hardly talking to one other. Nothing had been said, but Alice felt her mother in particular, had blamed her for not taking better care of Molly. This was reinforced when, despite Alfred initially surviving the fire with just smoke inhalation, he too died four months later from bronchitis, as a result of a weak chest. Her father had continued to go out to work as a carter and her mother continued to take in other people's washing to make ends meet, but the house had lost its sparkle. They were all like lost souls going about their daily tasks, with no heart left in it. Molly had taken that away with her.

The whole family had been the talk of the neighbourhood for months, especially when the inquest was reported in the newspaper. Her dad couldn't read, but her mother could and had been mortified by the accusations directed at her. Maybe that's why her mother blamed Alice, or so Alice thought. She never openly said anything, other than to admit that Alice was nothing but a child herself and was not responsible, but Alice felt it. It had taken many months to face all her friends again and she became somewhat withdrawn.

The Coroner, in his summing up, had said that it was just another case which showed the folly of people leaving children in the house with open fires not protected by fireguards. The case had occurred early in winter, and he hoped that it would be a warning to others not to leave their children alone with unprotected fires. He'd again said he thought Alice, who had given evidence, was a very capable child, and had done everything she could for her sister, but that was little comfort to her. She couldn't look at a fire without hating it for taking Molly away. Molly, who had been so full of energy.

Her last memory of the Coroner's Inquest had been when one of the jurymen asked her mother if they possessed a fireguard, her mother's reply being that they hadn't one, as they couldn't afford one.

"Damn being poor!" Alice had wailed out loud.

Again, it was the same old thing, if only... if only... It was then that she made a vow to herself that she would never be poor. She would marry a rich man, a man who could buy her everything she could ever dream of, especially a damned fireguard. Oh yes, they did get one. The Coroner had ordered the court to provide them with one, but the papers referred to it as...

> *"Shutting the door after the horse had bolted."*

How cruel those words had been.

SIX

Her parents continued to blame each other: Her mother blamed her father for not having a job that paid more, and he blamed her for leaving Alice with the little ones, and so it had gone on. As if that hadn't been bad enough, after Molly and Alfred's deaths, the gossips were saying that her mother had a fancy man, William Lofthouse. Alice had been too frightened to believe it, and had worried for months about what would become of them all if it was true, especially when her mother became with child again.

Everyone knew that William Lofthouse and her mother had been childhood sweethearts, but then after an argument, had both married different people. But that was in the past, and now at last the family was slowly beginning to heal.

As the door banged startling her, her father ambled in. He had one leg shorter than the other and walked with a limp as a result of polio as a child. Alice wondered if her father had ever suspected her mother of having an affair. She desperately wanted to talk to him about it, but was frightened she might say something to upset the apple cart. Such things were never spoken of in the house, and after Edna and Ethel had been born, a general calm had descended, so she didn't want to open up any old wounds, nor create any new ones. Better to let sleeping dogs lie she thought. If he did suspect anything, he didn't show it, and despite everything, he appeared to love Edna as if she was his own, so maybe she was and the gossips were wrong. She put the guard in front of the fire and started to prepare some tea for when her mother came in.

Alice had no idea that back at the camp, I was still thinking about her. I was wondering about when she would next write to me. The following day was a workday, so she would probably write to me before going up to bed. As I continued to think about her, I recollected how snobbish my Mam had become where she was concerned.

Mam liked to think we were from better stock than Alice's family and though both our families were poor, mine was certainly better off than most, due mainly to our prudent existence, Mam would say. We were a Church-going family and Mam had a strong sense of right and wrong and duty. Of course, as a matter of main concern we had fireguards for all our fires. Mam was very strict about such things, but then I suppose she had to be when trying to raise high-spirited boys. She kept her softness hidden behind her harsh exterior and that's how she kept control.

Dad, on the other hand, was quiet and had fewer complexities than her, but the two of them somehow went together like bread and jam. He was a gentle man who hardly ever got ruffled. He liked nothing better than to smoke his pipe and sleep on any problems. He was never given to quick decisions. It was Mam who 'wore the trousers' as the saying goes, and my Dad let her, until such time as she went too far and then his word would become the final one. The best quality he possessed, though, was his ability not to interfere and for that, all of us loved him.

With only Charlie and Wilf now at home, Mam and Dad rattled around in the house. Mam couldn't quite get used to it and said it was too quiet. However, Dad enjoyed the peace it brought. He felt old and tired at the age of forty-nine and was quite happy to have a bit more time to himself on his one day off a week. He liked to doze in the chair in front of the fire, given half the chance. He had worked hard as a farm labourer for many years but had fallen on his feet when he became the head groom on Sir Francis Dunnell's estate. He'd worked there for the last ten years now. Sir Francis had been the solicitor and secretary for the North Eastern Railway Company, until he had been appointed solicitor to the sixth Earl of Harewood and his wife Mary, the Princess Royal, daughter of King George V.

Dad had often accompanied Sir Francis on the many hunts he'd been invited to at Harewood House and so was privy to the kitchen gossip, where the many rumours about the Earl of Harewood and Mary, suggested it was not a happy marriage. Most people thought Princess Mary led what the locals called, "a dog's life," but despite Dad being aware of such goings on, his counsel was always the same:

"What God has put together let no man put asunder."

He always minded his own affairs, leaving others to mind theirs, and that's what I especially liked about him.

Mam was older than Dad, having just had her fifty-second birthday. Not that they celebrated such things in any great way.

"It's just like any other day and there's too much to do without stopping for birthdays," she would say.

Back at home, there was a knock at the door and Mam went to answer it.

"Oh, it's you Mr Rourke. What have you there?"

"Looks like you've got a letter from your Matthew," he said, as he handed over the post to her.

He couldn't recognise the handwriting of the other letter, but she instantly realised it was from me.

"How's your lad doing, Mr Rourke?"

"Oh, he's doing nicely, Mrs Jackson, thank you for asking. He joined up last week and he's with the first-tenth Manchester Regiment. He reckons he'll be going overseas next week."

"Gosh really, and so soon? Our Fred joined up a few weeks ago with the Durham Light Infantry. I wonder how long it's going to be before he goes overseas then?"

"I don't reckon it'll be too long. They say things are getting worse over there. Anyway, if I hear anything, I'll let you know."

"Thank you Mr Rourke," Mam said, being slightly bothered as she closed the door, and looked at both letters in her hand.

She opened the one from me first. Being the younger of the two, she worried that I might have a problem.

"Who was that?" Dad shouted down the hallway.

"Only Mr Rourke with two letters. It looks like our Matthew and our John have written us."

The letter from me was brief, telling them that I was having a great time and that they weren't to worry. I had jokingly added that I'd be the one to protect them as they slept soundly in their beds.

"That sounds just like our John," said Dad, when Mam read the letter to him.

"It's all just a game to him," he continued, as he shook his head wondering if I'd ever mature.

"Never mind, love. Why worry? There's plenty of time for him to grow up, let him have his childhood and his fun," said Mam, in no particular hurry for me to change.

"Aye, I reckon you're right. In another two years he'll have no choice but to be a man. What's our Matt got to say?"

"Oh, things seem to be going well for him. He's moved to a place called Geurie in New South Wales with Mary's family. They've bought another sheep farm, and they want our Matt to manage it for them when they get it all established. I must make a note of his new address," she said, looking for a pen and piece of paper.

"Does he say what's happening to the old place?"

"Yes, they've got another manager in to manage that for them. I wonder why they didn't ask our Matt?"

"Well, they hardly know him, love. Maybe they want to see if he's capable of it first," said Dad, ever practical about such things.

Later that day, as Mam put the milk bottles out on the step, she saw Mr Seal coming down the street.

"Hello, Stephen. How's your Albert doing?"

"Oh, he's doing grand, just grand, thanks Mary. I had a letter from him the other day and he sounds just fine. How's your John?"

"Having the time of his life, by the sounds of it. We had a letter from him this morning. I'll be glad to get him home though. I expect you're the same aren't you?"

"Oh definitely. It's so quiet about the house now. I'm really lost without him," he said, now looking much older than his years.

"Has Albert said anything to you about when he'll be coming home?" she continued.

"No, but I don't think it'll be too long. They've been there almost eight weeks now and he did say they'd be back by the end of October, so it should be any day now. I expect they'll let us know soon enough," he replied, as he made a move to continue on his way, now eager to get on.

Mam closed the door, thinking of Hannah, Stephen's wife. She could only have been about forty-six when she died. Dad was always surprised they'd only had six children in the twenty-eight years they'd been married, and once jokingly said to Mam that they couldn't have been doing it right. After all, he'd only to look at her and she'd be in the family way again! Dad was always full of bright ideas and had jokingly offered to give me and my brothers a few tips as to how it was done, but Mam had put a stop to that, threatening him with her hand to keep his mouth shut, or else! Such things were not spoken of, even within closed doors.

"What on earth would God think?" she'd told him.

Dad didn't think God really had very much to do with it, but didn't say so, for fear of upsetting Mam's puritanical beliefs. Mam was a devout

SIX

Christian, and he knew better than to challenge her, but at the time she'd grinned at him mischievously. He'd caught hold of her and had given her a quick kiss.

"What's that for?" she said.

"Oh nothing, love. I just wanted to."

Mam and Dad had been married for thirty years, and in that time, she'd been with child twelve times, but three had died not long after being formed, too weak to survive. Much to her relief her curse had stopped after William's birth.

A bit later, Mam decided to give the bedrooms a good clean in readiness for me coming home too. She eagerly made a start, as she knew the weekend would be upon her soon and, apart from going to Church on the Sabbath, no other work would be done. Most families adhered to the Sabbath being a day of rest and prayer, and ours was no different. Charlie and Wilf hated it. It meant having to get dressed up in their Sunday best and staying clean.

"Out of respect for our Lord and Father, you will visit his house," Mam said, in response to their moaning, and visit it they did... twice, once in a morning and once at night.

It was a family thing. All self-respecting families did that sort of thing, all except for the Johnsons she'd said, unaware of my love for Alice.

Chapter TEN

Christmas comes but once a year…
(Proverb)

Albert's father had been right. On October 28th, we were packing up our kit and being route-marched back to York Barracks.

"'Ere, Sarge, you were wrong," I said.

"Wrong about what, Jackson?" old Picky replied.

"About us being glad to see the back of this place."

"Ah well, you've been fortunate with the weather. You should feel very sorry for the poor buggers who will be coming to Strensall after we've gone, when winter's set in, then it's a hell hole."

"Still, I'm going to miss the place," I continued.

I looked much healthier than when I'd first arrived. I'd grown at least another two inches and my exposed skin had turned a golden brown. I also had to shave every day. The bum fluff on my face had definitely turned into whiskers and required the regulation shaving on a daily basis. Only Smithy escaped this ritual. His skin was still as smooth as a bairn's bottom. Albert, of course, had been shaving for a while despite him being younger than me, but regardless of that, I now felt as though I was a man. The boy I had been was quickly fading into a distant past.

It started to rain as we arrived back at York. The rain looked set to last for the rest of the day, but it was good to be back. We were allocated to new barracks, as our old one had been commandeered for the raw recruits still enlisting in their droves. The camp was fit to burst with keen lads all wanting to fight for their country and it was obvious that we had now become the envied. We were almost fully trained soldiers, fit for anything and our eagerness for war had not waned.

We heard that the British Army had made one last attempt to turn Germany's northern flank back and that the battle of La Bassee and Messines was now well and truly under way, as was the battle of Armentieres, Sarge told us. The last lot of recruits sent over there had been deployed to support those involved in the battle of Ypres, which was escalating, as the Germans raced to the sea.

At a briefing given by our commanding officer, he reported that both sides now held an entrenched line which stretched for twenty miles, and as both armies were growing in size, this was extending all the time. A few days later, we heard the fighting was now from the sea at Nieuport, to the La Bassee Canal, almost forty-five miles in a direct line. Old Picky showed us this on a map. Our allies had been forced to retreat, which we found difficult to understand, looking at the position we held. The main objective was to hold the Germans on the Marne, and to reverse the flow. Unfortunately, this wasn't achieved until our lot had dug in on the heights, north of the Aisne. Sarge referred to this as trench warfare. We'd heard so much about it, but we still had a lot more training to do in this.

All the foreign place names we heard during our tactical training heightened our eagerness to be there, and the mundane tasks of pack drills, roll calls, cleaning equipment, and barracks, added to our frustration and raised questions as to when it would be our turn.

"Aw, just send us over there, Sarge. We'll show 'em," said Albert and some of the others.

"You'll be there soon enough, Seal, so keep your hair on. As I've said before, there's still a bit more training to do yet. The plan is, you'll have two weeks leave at Christmas, then back here to await orders. At some stage we'll go to the Lincolnshire coast for trench, grenade, and sea defence training, and then on to a camp at Gainsborough. After that, it will be France and Flanders. As I keep saying, Seal, it'll come soon enough."

"Not soon enough, Sarge," said Smithy, just as anxious to be there, and we all agreed.

Time continued to drag, and most of our conversations were about the news we heard regarding overseas activities. I had a letter from Fred, who was now at Strensall, where it had rained ever since he got there and with the volume of men, had indeed become the waterlogged miserable existence we'd been warned of. No one had heard from Matthew since his letter to Mam some time ago, and I hadn't heard from Alice since I'd written to let her know we were back in York. I was getting a bit worried that my declaration of love had frightened her off, so I decided to write to her again to say I would explain my feelings properly when I saw her. I was also feeling pretty rich and wanted to buy her something special, if she'd let me.

The battles abroad continued. The main German objective to capture the town of Ypres had been thwarted. Sarge told us the fighting had been fierce, as the Germans had centred their attack on both sides of the Menin Road, a main road leading into Ypres or Wipers, as Sarge called it. The British had successfully withstood the continuous attacks south of the road, but the Germans had broken through on the north. It appeared there was nothing to stop them from taking Ypres, apart from a single line of British guns.

Fortunately, Sarge told us, the Germans had hesitated at that crucial moment and a counter attack by an improvised force of cooks, assistants, batmen and every Tom, Dick and Harry who had all fought magnificently to save Ypres, had succeeded. This, we were told, was the symbol of allied resistance and what the Germans had to contend with. It was held up to us all as an example of true British grit, and a huge cheer for our lads was let rip.

"He who hesitates is lost, eh Sarge?" said Phil.

"Absolutely, so bear that in mind all of you," he added, not wanting to waste an opportunity to get a message across.

Though we were told nothing about the loss of men on both sides, we'd heard on the grapevine that French and German casualties had been much higher than our own, so our spirits remained high, and our eagerness to be there, in the thick of it all, became overriding.

Meanwhile, the war at sea had been taking shape and we heard that on December 8th Admiral von Spee attacked Port Stanley in the Falkland Islands. He was apparently misled into thinking the British communications centre and coaling stations were undefended and so he had decided to attack. What he hadn't bargained for was the presence of our Grand Fleet with two battle cruisers, the Invincible and the Inflexible, on hand to greet him when he arrived to reconnoitre the place. We all cheered when we heard this, and imagined his utter horror at seeing the British ships waiting for him. As soon as Spee had realised his mistake, he'd tried back peddling at full speed with the British fleet in pursuit.

"I wish we could have seen his face," said Albert gloating.

"I bet he almost shit himself," added Phil, whose brother was with the grand fleet, and the source of our information.

The battle cruisers dealt with the enemy's main ships, sinking the Scharnhorst and Gneisenau, and our Glasgow and Cornwall boats sank Leipzig. Kent sank the Nunberg, but the Dresden got away. It was the only one to escape.

"It was a great victory," said Phil's brother, and we excitedly told old Picky about it, demonstrating our knowledge about such things.

"The Germans lost almost two thousand men that day," remarked Phil.

"They must have fought with great guts and nerve," said Smithy.

"Oh they did, but they didn't do much to us. We hardly had any casualties," continued Phil.

"Was anyone else there we knew, other than your brother?" asked Albert.

"No. Not that I'm aware of," replied Phil, now pleased he was able to tell us about how the battles were going.

Oh yes, we were definitely winning the war.

On the day we were going on leave for two weeks, the camp was buzzing with the news of a German FF29 seaplane, which had attempted to conduct an air raid over Britain and had dropped bombs in the sea near Dover. It was the first air raid of its kind and Sarge told us to be ready in case we had to be recalled before our leave was up. We all chatted excitedly about this prospect and couldn't wait, secretly hoping it would be the case. As we packed our stuff for home, our spirits were high.

"Not long now lads," said Albert.

"Gosh, Mam's going to have a duck fit if she hears about this," I said to Albert and the others, as I hurriedly forced the last bit of clothing into my kit bag.

"Yeh, I reckon all of them are going to be panicking. I don't think they ever thought it would come to this and they'll be thinking we really do have to start defending Britain at home," said Alf laughing.

"Yes, except that we'll not be defending them at home, we'll be defending them over there," I said, tilting my head in the direction of Belgium.

"Just think, lads, all of us in a foreign land. Do you think they'll speak English?" said Smithy.

"Nah, they're not that clever," said Albert.

It was good to get out into the fresh air and head for home and familiarity once more. Mam and Dad were glad to see me and insisted that I had a professional photograph taken in my uniform to mark the occasion. It hadn't occurred to me they would now think my home front training was finished, and so I had to tell them I was only home on leave and that I'd still got a bit more training to do. To soften the blow, I agreed to have the photograph taken as a Christmas present to them. I knew that deep down they would be pleased with it and would take extreme pride in showing it off to family and friends.

During that week I did my Christmas shopping, which I thought had gone quite well. I bought Fred a packet of Capstan's, Charlie a catapult and Wilf some rope for the cart Dad had come across and had renovated as a surprise for him. I spent the majority of my pay though on Alice. I bought her a nine carat gold locket in the shape of a heart. I got it quite cheap from the jeweller in town in exchange for posting a few advertisement leaflets through some letterboxes on my way home. Virtually all my money had gone by that time, but I knew my other older brothers, George, Robert and Matthew, wouldn't expect anything from me, so I was well pleased with myself and the presents which I'd bought.

Christmas day fell on a Friday, and I arranged a special meeting with Alice after Church. She'd been unable to get away from work to meet me before then and we'd been forced to cancel our pre-Christmas get-together. She wasn't even too sure whether she could meet me then either, as she'd been told she'd have to help her mother. However, she did promise to try and so we had arranged to meet at half past ten under the oak tree.

My Christmas present to Mam and Dad was well received. They opened it on Christmas Eve, along with their other presents but as usual, we weren't old enough to stay up and open ours. We had to wait until the morning, when Dad would shout up the stairs to say that Father Christmas had been! It was a ritual that, despite our ages, was always done and we played along with it for the sake of Wilf. This year we were hoping he'd get a bag of soot to scare him.

Mam and Dad gave me a pair of woollen socks which she'd knitted and was particularly adept at making. Fred bought me a leather collar stud box, which he'd sent to Dad to give to me. He had hoped to get home, but in the end, couldn't make it. Charlie offered to brass my uniform buttons, and Wilf promised to polish my shoes for when I went back, as well as offering me a go on his cart, which he was over the moon with. Sadly, the bag of soot didn't materialise!

We'd been given a Christmas goose by Sir Francis Dunnell and sufficient vegetables from the estate to feed an army. It was the only benefit Dad got, but it was worth its weight in gold. Mam spent

Christmas Eve getting everything ready and promised us a meal fit for a King. She always plated up a meal for old Mrs Lofthouse as well, even though she went to her son's for the day. Mam knew she would reheat it later and have it for her tea.

On Christmas morning, the service seemed to go on forever. Wilf and Charlie fidgeted in their seats and pulled faces at the Naylor girls sitting two rows behind until Mam stopped them with a smack from the back of her hand just as the Minister was telling us all to, "love one another." He seemed to look directly at Mam as he said this, and she blushed, as the rest of us giggled.

It was the best bit of his otherwise dull sermon. As my mind started to wander again, I thought of dinner, and in response, my mouth began watering. The Minister droned on and on above the rumbling of my stomach. Fortunately, there wasn't another service on Christmas night, so it meant we could all look forward to spending the evening at home playing family games.

When the service was over, I knew there would be the inevitable small talk afterwards, as to it being a wonderful sermon, and yes, wasn't the weather kind, and no, they hadn't heard about when Fred would be home… which would go on and on, unless I could make my excuses to get away. Mam and Dad knew I was seeing Alice, so when the minister shook Mam's hand, I seized the opportunity.

"I'm off now Mam. I won't be long," I said, hurriedly squeezing past her, to make my escape.

"Don't you be late for dinner my lad, or else! It'll be on the table at twelve o'clock sharp, and woe betides you if you're not there!" came a warning from Mam, as she continued to thank the minister.

"I won't, I promise," I remarked, rubbing my empty stomach at the thought of missing it.

"Even Alice doesn't come before food," I joked, indicating that Alice meant nothing more.

By the time I got to the park it was just turning ten thirty and there was no sign of her. I waited and waited, listening to the Minster bells chime eleven, but still there was no sign of her. At quarter past eleven, I decided to call it a day and reluctantly headed home. Just as I reached the entrance to the park, I turned to take one last look to see if I could see her. In the distance I caught a glimpse of someone running and waving their arms and I heard frantic shouting. It was Alice.

SIX

By the time we reached one another, we were both out of breath, but it didn't stop me from scooping her off her feet and swirling her around and around as I hugged her tightly. Dizzy, we both fell over and landed in a heap on the cold, damp grass. My hand landed on her bare thigh and before I could stop myself, I pulled her roughly towards me to explore further, the bulge in my trousers becoming more and more evident as I touched her. For a brief moment, Alice gave way to the intensity of her feelings and rubbed her breasts against me, as she gasped at the stroke of my hand, trying to make a half-hearted attempt to stop me.

"Oh God Alice, you're so lovely," I uttered, as I rolled away from her in an attempt to regain some control.

All I could think about was the ache in my groin and the need to satisfy it. Alice's lips were so full and inviting. Her hair was all tousled, her legs spread-eagled exposing more of her than I'd ever seen before. She lay there ready for the taking. The park was deserted, but as quickly as the emotions had surfaced, they were lost in frantic moments of embarrassment, with both of us hurrying to our feet to straighten our clothing.

"I'm sorry Alice. I don't know what came over me." Alice laughed and brushed her skirt.

"No matter," she uttered, almost as if she'd surprised herself, and now didn't know what to say.

I heard the bells ring the half hour, and I quickly took her present out of my pocket and gave it to her. As she carefully opened it, her face lit up.

"Oh John, it's the best present anyone has ever given me. It's lovely."

Her eyes filled with tears as she retrieved her present to me, which was in a brown paper bag on the floor, looking like a piece of rubbish.

"My present isn't half as grand as yours, but it's made with lots of love."

And with that, she handed me the bag. It contained a pair of grey woollen knitted gloves.

"I made them, and constantly thought of you as I did. I made them to fit Ted's hands, knowing that if they fitted him, they'd probably fit you. I hope you like them?"

"Oh, they're just what I wanted," I said, kissing her briefly to thank her.

SIX

I was careful to keep my body away from hers, as I was still reeling from my earlier encounter, and on hearing the Minster bells chime again, I reluctantly stuffed the gloves in my pocket, and prepared to make my way home.

"I'm sorry Alice, but I've got to go, or I'll be late for dinner and Mam will be really cross if I am. Meet me here again tomorrow at one o'clock and we'll go somewhere else."

"OK. I'll try not to be late this time. Bye then, and oh! John…"

"What?"

"Merry Christmas," she said shyly.

"Merry Christmas, Alice."

Chapter ELEVEN

I go, I go, look how I go,
Swifter than arrow from the Tartar's bow.
(William Shakespeare 1564 - 1616)

The following day, I heard Mr Johnson in the kitchen talking to Dad, and when I saw him standing by the back door looking serious, I nearly died. Guilty thoughts immediately struck me dumb. I could only imagine it must be something to do with what had happened in the park the day before between Alice and me. Maybe someone had seen us. Maybe he had found out about the expensive Christmas present I'd bought her and was wondering what my intentions were.

Overcoming my anxiousness, I managed to say as politely as possible, "Hello Mr Johnson."

"Now then, lad, I hear you've been seeing my Alice," he remarked.

I groaned inwardly and guiltily looked towards Dad before answering. I was uncertain now as to what had already been said between them.

"Yes, Sir," I answered gingerly.

"Well, she'll not be seeing yer today, lad, as she's come down wi' a belly sickness. 'Ere... she's gee-en me this to gee yer," and he handed me a small grubby-looking sealed envelope.

With that, he turned back to talk to Dad, as I, thanking him, nonchalantly took Alice's note, relieved it hadn't been anything else. Her letter was brief and to the point, saying:

"Can't see you today. I'm not well. What about next Saturday?"

My heart sank. That was the last day of my leave and we had to be back at the barracks first thing. The chance of seeing her again before then would be remote, unless I tried to meet her outside Rowntrees after work to walk her home. I couldn't see Mr Johnson being too happy about that, not with the dark nights prevailing as they now did. In any case, she always walked home with one of her aunts who also worked at the factory, so it would be virtually impossible to do that.

Deep in my own thoughts, I barely heard Mr Johnson leave. I quickly stuffed Alice's letter in my pocket as Dad looked up questioningly at me.

SIX

"Well? What's this about you and Alice?"

"Oh, nawt really Dad… I like her, but it's nothing serious," I lied.

"I see her every now and again, that's all. Albert likes her as well," I continued, hoping to make it sound as if it was no great thing, as I tried to hide the disappointment on my face at not being able to see her.

I was pleased that Mam was out and not privy to Dad's questioning. She'd see through me straight away and would want to know more. Then I would no doubt get a lecture as to the in-appropriateness of girl friend. Ever since I'd won the scholarship to attend the well-known Archbishop Holgate School in Lord Mayor's Walk at the age of eleven, Mam had been conscious that I should mix with the right class of people and not people below me, as she thought the Johnson's to be. Not that she had anything against their kind, she would often remark, but I knew that she fervently hoped I would marry 'well' one day.

She was always keen for me to accompany Dad to Harewood House with Sir Francis, when he was invited to the many hunts they held there. Oh yes, I knew what she was up to every time she encouraged me to go with him. As head groom, Dad held quite a high position and was frequently introduced to the important guests that the Earl of Harewood and the Princess Royal often had staying with them. Mam dreamed that one day I would marry a lady of the Royal household. That was a laugh. Little did she know that my heart was already firmly Alice's.

As the night closed in, so did my mood. I was fed up with everything. I couldn't see a way to see Alice by herself before returning to camp and it would be months before I would get another opportunity, which depressed me even more. Maybe Alice had cold feet, and it was just an excuse not to see me again. My mind started to run away with itself and despite Alice sounding cheerful enough in her note, I began to worry that maybe she had appendicitis, and would die like Thomas.

When I talked to Charlie about it later, he reckoned it would have been her curse.

"Do you think so?"

"Yeh, they always use that as an excuse," he replied, as if knowledgeable about such things.

In the end, the torment was too much and I kicked the table and went to bed, in the hope that I could shake the dark thoughts off. The darkness of the night would be good company to the way I was feeling.

Maybe tomorrow would lift my spirit. I tossed and turned most of the night, so much so that I disturbed Charlie and Wilf, much to their annoyance. They told Mam that I'd kept them awake, but fortunately, before she could say anything, there was a knock at the door. It was Mr Rourke.

I could hear Mam chatting about something but couldn't hear the detail. As she came back through into the kitchen, she handed me a telegram.

"It looks official. What have you been doing son?"

"I dunno, nothing that I know of," I said sheepishly, and proceeded to open it under the glare of the whole family, who were now taking an interest in what was going on.

"Well, come on lad, what does it say?" Mam persisted.

"It's from Sergeant Pickles. He says I've to report back to the barracks immediately as everyone's on alert. I'd better get ready."

As I stood up, the chair on the tiled floor scraped noisily. Mam quickly lifted it off the floor to prevent it marking the tiles and moved it out of the way, as I hurriedly left the room to pack. Everyone began to scurry around collecting various things for me. Wilf picked up my boots and started to clean them, as he'd promised, and Charlie ran around to the barking of Mam's orders to get clean hankies and underwear out of the cupboard by the range.

"She'd make a good Sergeant Major, she would," said Dad, laughing at the flurry of activity.

I ran up the stairs, taking two steps at a time, and hurriedly searched for some paper to write a quick note to Alice. Typically, I couldn't find any and so taking her note out of the envelope and putting it safely in my pocket, I wrote on the back of the cover. I quickly jotted down about being ordered back to barracks and told her I would write to her properly when I got the chance.

"Charlie," I shouted, now folding the envelope over to hide my message.

"Here, do us a favour. Get this to Alice, and tell her what's happened," I said, as I hastily thrust it into his sweaty hand.

"Don't let on what you're doing, there's a good fellow."

"It'll cost you."

SIX

"What?"

"A penny for some sweets."

I dipped my hand into my pocket and gave him a penny, to shut him up.

"Thanks John-boy… it's as good as delivered," he said, beaming.

Collecting my bag and other bits of kit, I said my goodbyes to everyone and was running down the street to Albert's house, before anyone could say "Jack Robinson," leaving everyone somewhat bemused as to why I'd been called back to camp so early.

Albert was just coming out of his front door as I arrived. I raised my hand to wave to his Dad, who was standing motionless by the living room window, watching us both walk swiftly down the road. There was no time for deliberation, no time to figure out what lay ahead of us, as we headed back to the barracks like ants to a nest under attack. I suppose it was fortunate that things had happened the way they had. It prevented answering all those awkward questions Mam seemed to ask, especially as it was becoming more and more difficult to evade telling her the truth, without her suspecting.

One thing for sure, Mr Hepplethwaite had been wrong when he had said the war would be over by Christmas. It was becoming increasingly obvious that wasn't going to be the case. We flew back to the barracks, meeting most of our friends on the way. It was quite laughable really. Albert likened it to bees flying back to a honey pot, old Picky being the pot and none too sweet either. We were one of the first to arrive. The rest came in dribs and drabs depending on Mr Rourke's route around York. As soon as all of us had reported in, we were called together for a briefing.

It appeared that the French Commander in Chief, Joffre, had launched a major offensive, which extended along the front line from Nieuport to Verdun, throughout the Artois and Champagne regions. The battle of Champagne, as the 'big-wigs' called it, had started on 20th December, before we'd actually gone on leave. It had been the first significant attack against the Germans since the construction of the trench system.

Despite heavy fighting at Givenchy, Perthes and Noyon, there had been minimal allied gains, and now, the British battalions were required to shore up the attacks. It was therefore imperative that our training was completed in readiness for us to be shipped out. Some units had already left York, and the plan was to get the Territorial Force into shape in case more were needed. It was official; we were now under orders proper.

The next few weeks hurried by. We spent those following commands without question, doing keep-fit workouts, marching drills and learning a little bit about lines of attack so that we would appreciate orders given out on the battle fields. We were told that no credit would be given for thinking, and all of us began to realise there'd be no point in challenging anything anyway. It was a case of doing exactly as we were told, even if we did think to the contrary.

"Understand this, none of you will be aware of the greater picture, so it's imperative you follow orders to the letter, no matter what," said Sarge.

"If I say jump, you jump, understand?"

We understood OK. Albert said it was just like being back at school.

At last we had a purpose. I wrote home reassuring everyone I was champion. However, the news of the war raging in Europe and on the Caucasian front was grave, and everyone was worried, including Alice. She wrote to say she regretted not being able to say goodbye properly and had enclosed a photograph of herself in her red dress, which she'd been going to give me. I too was disappointed at not having had a chance to say goodbye properly, especially when I felt Alice was now becoming relaxed enough to let me near her.

I looked longingly at her photograph, and remembered the silkiness of her skin when my hand had accidentally touched her thigh, the heaving of her breasts against my chest as I'd kissed her, and her gasp of delight as my hand tried to explore further unfamiliar parts before we'd come to our senses. Oh God, why was this existence so cruel? I now doubted that I'd ever get another chance to get so close to her. The moment had gone, and I feared that when I next saw her, it would most probably be the old Alice... the Alice who didn't do such things.

Chapter TWELVE

There is a pleasure, sure,
In being mad, which none but madmen know!
(John Dryden 1631 - 1700)

A few weeks later, I got a letter from Mam, telling me Matthew had joined the Australian Imperial Force. He'd already been shipped out from Geurie to Gallipoli on active service. Mary had written to them, saying there hadn't been much time, and that Matt had asked her to let them know he would be in touch when he could. No one had heard from either of them since, and it was now almost the end of February, and my seventeenth birthday.

Mam and Dad sent me a birthday present, and with it, a brief letter from Robert to say that he'd joined up with the Durham Lights. He had hoped to be in the sixth battalion with Fred, but Fred's battalion was already on trench training on the Northeast coast, almost ready to be shipped overseas, so sadly he'd ended up in the second battalion instead. Mam and Dad were upset, as it meant Robert would miss the arrival of his first bairn.

"He wants his head examining," Mam added.

It didn't take brains to realise they were worried. She wrote to say they hoped I'd be home soon, and wished me a happy birthday. When I opened the present she'd sent, it was another pair of knitted socks. I could tell it was her way of making sure all her boys were warm.

"You can catch your death from cold feet," she said.

"I've now got enough pairs to supply most of the bloody army if I wanted to," I joked, as I held them up for Albert to see, genuinely proud that she cared.

"Not another bloody pair," he said jealously. He had to rely on his older sisters for such things, and there wasn't much chance of that, as none of them could knit.

"'Ere, I could get Mam to knit you a pair if you want?"

"No thanks mate, just give me some of yours when it's my birthday," he teased.

"In any case, your Mam's got a soft spot for me. She'll no doubt be daft enough to knit me some anyway. She'll not forget my birthday," he laughed.

"What date in June is it?"

"The 28th."

"I'll tie a knot in my hanky."

"Don't worry, I'll remind you," he replied.

I suspected Mam somehow thought she was protecting us in lots of ways by knitting such things for us. With a bit of luck, I hoped it would be a fair-isle pullover next time. Albert reckoned that if she could give us the moon, she would, and he was right. For a moment, I realised I missed her, and as I lifted the socks up to my face, they smelt of home and apple pies.

Further down her letter, was the news that George had also enlisted, and I found this added bit of information very disturbing. He was a family man with three kids to support and another on the way. What on earth was he thinking of? Mam said that some woman in the street had hurled abuse at him for not being in uniform, and had given him a white feather, telling him he should be ashamed of himself. He'd been quite shocked when she ended up calling him a coward. Mam told him not to take any notice, and in no uncertain terms reminded him that his place was at home with his family. She told him she'd got enough to worry about without worrying about him as well, and had prayed to God that he'd listen to reason. Unfortunately he didn't, and a few days later, he went to enlist.

Not long after, I heard from Dad, telling me to take care. With it was a cutting from the Herald's front page. It reported a major loss of life in the ongoing battle of Champagne. France's Commander in Chief, Joffre, had now called off the offensive in order to regroup. The report said that allied casualties numbered some ninety thousand, but all of us suspected it was just propaganda. No one for one minute believed it was true. We tried cornering old Picky about what was happening, but he couldn't enlighten us, as he hadn't had any official reports about the numbers involved. There were lots of rumours though.

His evasiveness left us unsure of what to make of it, especially when Smithy's older brother sent a letter, telling him about the unusual Christmas day he'd had in the front line trenches. It appeared they'd struck up some kind of a truce with the Jerries and ended up standing with them in no-mans-land, shaking hands and exchanging food, buttons, badges and cigarettes. They'd even had a game of football with an empty bully-beef can, and a sing-song. It had initially started with a few of them striking up a conversation across the lines, telling stories about Christmas and home, and then a couple of them had raised their heads above the trench to throw Christmas cake across no-man's land and when they hadn't been shot, they got braver and eventually secured a truce, and the Jerries joined in as well.

He didn't say who'd won the friendly football match but continued to say our adversaries had sung "Stille Nacht, Heilige Nacht," and Smithy's brother's battalion had responded with a similar British Christmas carol. This bizarre kind of friendliness and openness had apparently gone on for a few days, and for a short time, all fighting had been forgotten. Some even forged friendships, and swapped addresses, promising to get in touch after the war was over, if they survived of course. It was only when orders from above put a stop to it all, that they resumed their positions again, and the fighting carried on.

"Bloody hell, that must have been bloody strange," said Phil, when he heard this.

I must admit, it did seem amazing to think of the enemy as being as sentimental and as daft as us.

"I had thought it was only us who celebrated Christmas. Are the Jerries Christians as well then?" I asked innocently.

"I doubt it. They're foreign aren't they," said Phil, as if that made a difference.

Smithy continued to read from his brother's letter and remarked about the enemy being young lads, just like us. It became hard to believe these lads had mothers who loved them just the same as ours. After all, they were the enemy weren't they?

"I wonder if they feel the same as us then?" Phil continued.

Smithy doubted that, and in any case he didn't think we'd ever get the opportunity to find out, especially after one of the lads in our barracks called Jim, had heard his brother Joe had been killed. It was then that all thoughts of Jerry being the same as us disappeared, and we became intent on avenging Joe's death.

"Don't worry Jimmy, we'll make 'em pay."

Chapter THIRTEEN

I love to travel,
but hate to arrive.
(Albert Einstein 1879 - 1955)

On 31st March 1915, the West Yorkshire battalions became part of the 1st West Riding (Territorial) Division and at last, had been selected to proceed to France as a complete unit. Embarkations were due to take place sometime in April, and so we now found ourselves within a matter of days being transferred to Gainsborough for the final part of our training, just as old Picky had predicted. All of us from York came under the banner of the first-fifth, a small cog in a big wheel, but we still felt important. As far as we were concerned, we were soldiers now, and strutted around as if we knew everything, basking in the awesome looks from new recruits who continued to follow in our footsteps.

We arrived at Gainsborough and before we knew it, found ourselves on the final leg of our journey to the East coast for our trench, grenade and mortar combat training on the beaches. All of us were excited. At last, we were getting nearer to being dispatched overseas. As we boarded the train for the coast and approached the coastline we could smell the sea air and hear the gulls screeching out our arrival. We'd heard so much about the sea, from stories such as Moby Dick and the escapades of Sir Walter Raleigh, though few of us had ever seen it. Now we eagerly waited our first glimpse of it.

"Maybe we could buy some rock and post it home," joked Albert excitedly, knowing visitors did that when at the seaside.

"Don't be bloody daft. You'll let the cat out of the bag," I responded, before realising it was a joke.

"'Ere, quick, look, there's the sea!" exclaimed Phil, and we all piled to his side of the train to take our first look at this mythical beast.

"Cor, look at it!" exclaimed Smithy.

"Looks bloody cold, if you ask me," I added.

"'Ere, who can swim?" asked Phil.

In our immediate billet there were twenty-six men. Only nine of us could swim and from the sound of it, some not that well. I'd learnt to swim whilst fooling around in the village beck at Ebberston and had perfected my own unique technique in the Ouse. My best asset though was the ability to be a natural floater. Albert on the other hand was just the opposite and despite several attempts to learn, he still ended up flailing about, sinking like lead to the bottom. A worried look came across his face.

"Don't worry, mate," I whispered. "We won't be swimming. We have boats to do that for us," I told him reassuringly.

"In any case, stick with me and you'll be fine. With what little brains you have, it shouldn't take too much to keep your head floating above water," I joked and stepped back, as he took a swing at me and missed.

In less than an hour we'd disembarked from the train, and in full kit found ourselves heading towards the promenade for action. Albert was enthralled and showed no sign of his earlier fear of the water as he stared at it, mesmerized. We noted that there were other units on the beach in various stages of digging trenches, filling sandbags, and blowing up various flag poles stuck in the sand, which we presumed acted as targets for the grenade throwers. Amidst the loud dull thuds of grenade explosions and billowing sand, which rose several feet in the air, we made our way to the far side of the beach. We set up camp and waited for old Picky to give us a briefing as to what we would be doing next.

He duly gave the orders. The cooks and ancillary staff were to set up the camp kitchen in the dunes, which were a little way back from the front, whilst the rest of us were split up into small units. The sand baggers were to start making sandbags with wet sand near to the receding tide. These would be used to shore up the sides of our trench when it was dug, and would be stacked between pit props which would be strategically hammered in along each side. They'd also be placed along the top edge of the trench to give it some stability and hopefully prevent it from caving in.

Some of us would actually start digging the trench and clear away the heavy sand making a channel several feet wide and deep. Picky told us that it had to be fifty feet long, not a foot less or a foot more. Once it was dug and shored up safely, we were to put duckboards on the floor to make movement within it easier. After that, we could then begin making small staging platforms every ten feet along the side of the trench to act as a step-up from which our grenades could be thrown. Ladders were to be strategically placed so that we could propel ourselves up and over the top as if following through with an attack. All of us would have a spell doing each activity, Sarge informed us, so with shovels and pit props in hand, we got to work.

It wasn't easy going and before long, we were puffing and panting like old men. Old Picky told us to put our backs into it, as he wanted the job finished before mid-day, when we would be stopping to eat. The afternoon was scheduled for grenade training and would include all members of the battalion, including the cooks and any other ancillary staff lurking about.

"That'll be a laugh. I wonder what old Frederico will make of it," said Smithy, referring to our cook, who was great at concocting a variety of meals out of nothing, but who we'd yet to see in action.

Rumour had it he was a dab hand with a rifle, and in his spare time, could be found on the rifle ranges practicing his shot. When not in his cooks' garb, his jacket proudly displayed a crossbow badge, which he'd got for being a marksman. He wasn't one for boasting and never showed off, and that's what all of us liked about him. He was an East Yorkshire lad from Hull. His real name was Frederick. However we only knew him as Frederico. He'd inherited the nickname due to his dark Italian looks and the artistic gesticulations of his hands as he spoke, probably due to the fact he had a speech impediment from being a child, and stuttered constantly.

"His stutter is going to make him even worse. I reckon he'll be speechless by the time Old Picky's finished with him," said Phil, and we all fell about laughing, as we placed bets as to how well he would fare throwing a grenade from our makeshift front line.

"A packet of Wills for everyone if he comes within ten feet of the flag," I offered and before long, all bets were on.

We told Frederico what was in store for him as he served up the usual bully-beef stew with not a care in the world.

"I can't fff...fff...flipping well hit the fff...fff...fire at home with a ppp..ppp...piece of fff...frigging ppp...ppp...paper, let alone hit a bbb...bbb..bloody fff..fff...flag, so you'll be lu..lu...lucky," he casually replied.

Confident that he wouldn't let me down and get anywhere near the target, the others now tried to wriggle out of the deal.

"All bets stand," I quickly re-inforced, as we eagerly waited to see who would be the victor.

As it stood, if Frederico's past performance had anything to do with it, I would secure five packets of cigarettes, and I couldn't wait to be proved right.

Despite it being a cold day, he emerged in his white short-sleeved tee-shirt and regulation trousers covered by a large, not so white apron, along with the rest of the canteen staff. He was puffing and panting a bit as sweat poured off him, which we assumed was due to the hot steamy environment of the cookhouse, though several of the group thought it likely to be nerves at having to handle a lively bit of equipment, instead of the usual innocuous stuff he dealt with.

At the top end of the trench, Sarge demonstrated how to arm the grenade and lob it at the flag, which was some thirty yards away. For safety's sake, only one soldier at a time was allowed in the trench. Sergeant Pickles remained topside to see the outcome and make comments.

With grenade in hand, Frederico headed for the first platform. We all watched with bated breath as he climbed into position in an ungainly fashion. He took a huge intake of breath, shook himself down as he got ready to throw and then in one swift movement, closed his eyes, ducked his head, swung the grenade and lobbed it as far as he could. We watched in wonder as his hand caught on the back wall of the trench, and the catapulted grenade flew through the air, landing just topside of the sandbags, barely two feet from where he stood.

Not aware of his blunder, and with a big smile on his face, he now raised his head above the parapet to see where it had gone, his nose just inches away from it. As he peered over the edge, old Picky took a flying leap at him, knocking him off his feet and into the bottom of the trench to protect him from the blast. Instantaneously, the side of the trench wall went up in a grand majestic aerial show of sand, sackcloth and pit props, all dancing in front of us, before landing down on top of them, burying them alive.

There was no doubt about it, Sarge had certainly saved him. Poor Frederico, dazed and unsure of what had happened, tried to crawl from underneath Sarge, who was equally attempting to release both of them from amidst the debris. The rest of us quickly went to their aid.

As they dusted themselves down, Picky had one final comment to make.

"Get yourself flipping well out of my sight and back to the bloody canteen where you bloody well belong, and take the rest of those brainless bleeding imbeciles with you!" he said, referring to the rest of the kitchen staff.

SIX

As he collected himself, and the cooks sheepishly made their way back, I held my hand out to collect my dues, with the biggest grin on my face you could ever wish to see.

"I bet he did it on purpose," said Albert, as he grudgingly handed over my spoils.

Chapter FOURTEEN

Practice makes perfect...
(Proverb)

We spent several days at the coast perfecting our throwing, digging and bagging skills, despite the atrocious wet weather which set in, attempting to put a damper on things. Frederico and his fellow workers got on with the job of feeding us, which lifted our spirits. Meanwhile, I heard from my brother Matt, who was having his own fun and games on the Gallipoli Peninsula. He'd been sent to the Eastern front line. It was hard to imagine him being out there, scorched by such heat, when over here it was so bloody cold.

Still, it didn't sound as if it was a bed of roses out there either. He told me they'd spent several days just getting a foothold at a small cove, on the peninsula, which they named ANZAC after themselves. The cliffs and rocky terrain enabled the Turks to have an advantage over them, and hundreds of lives had been lost in securing the small area. However, they had dug in, and were ready for battle. Matthew's lot had set up camp, as instructed, near some bushes in the inhospitable landscape. As many tents as possible were placed near them, which they hoped would give some protection from the sun and keep them sheltered at night, when the temperature dropped markedly. The heat during the day had been unbearable, and mosquitoes and other biting insects plagued them mercilessly. They'd been issued with some liquid insect repellent, which they constantly doused themselves in. However, he wrote to say that nothing had changed and he was still extremely tasty to the critters, especially at night, when he and the rest of them were relentlessly bitten.

After a few days, Matt had decided to wage his own war on this virtually invisible enemy, and in an attempt to combat the problem, he'd obtained an old flit-pump from supplies and managed to con his mates into donating their supply of insecticide. The pump was a piston-driven, hand powered spray gun with an attached refillable can. As mosquitoes came near, the saying soon became, "Quick, Matt, the flit!"

One particular night, determined to beat the little buggers at their own game, he had poured the liquid into the pump and sprayed four tents, inside and out, and his mates and himself in the stuff as well. They'd then turned in and hoped for a better night. I smiled to myself as I imagined him zapping the air shouting, "Take that, and that and that," convincing everyone he'd solved the problem, as they crawled into this bug-free environment created especially for them.

His glory had been short lived though. As the following morning dawned, each of them had awoken to arrows of intense sunlight streaming through large holes in the tent fabric, as if shards of glass had been run through them. After they had tried to make sense of such an effect in the dazed period between asleep and full consciousness, it had become obvious that the once strong canvas fabric had disintegrated during the night, and the tent poles were now left supporting flimsy bits of material that gently rippled in the Turkish wind.

Not letting on to his Sergeant what had happened, Matt had managed to convince him that some sort of caterpillar must have been in the bushes and attacked them in the night. It wasn't until six other soldiers emerged from their tattered tents with uniforms in shreds as well, and no evidence of any insects, that it had started to be a little harder to explain.

"These 'ere critters are mighty ferocious, Sarge. Maybe it was a plague of locusts," he'd offered, as a way of explanation.

The Sergeant, completely baffled as to the cause of such destruction, had ordered them back down the line to collect new equipment. As they'd headed towards the support area, Matt turned to the rest of his mates.

"Bloody 'ell, what does this stuff do to us, if it does this to our gear?"

He reckoned they should take bets as to what would kill them first, the insect repellent, or the enemy they were fighting. He suggested in his letter to me that the British Army ought to get some flit, to use as a chemical weapon.

As I read his description of events, I smiled to myself, remembering our Matt as always being the resourceful one in the family, always looking for an easier way to do things, only this time it had back-fired. He reckoned his mates had praised him for his ingenuity, before they'd all returned to the intensity of fighting which lay ahead of them.

I put away his letter in my large pack. For now, we had our own war to contend with, and by 9th April, we were back in Gainsborough awaiting final orders. Eventually they came through saying we were shipping out on the 14th and would be in France by the 15th. It was now time to write our letters home, fill out our wills, and be jabbed against typhoid.

SIX

I thought long and hard about my letter home and started it several times, trying to make it sound as if it was no great thing going to France. Deep down I was excited at the prospect of killing Germans, and in my head I saw a glorious picture of myself holding my rifle and spraying bullets "der... der... der... der... der," as I killed the enemy in one grand swing of my gun. The dream of valour and praise bestowed on me as a result of my action made me swell with self-importance at the knowledge of how proud my parents would be. However, such thoughts gradually faded and I tried to concentrate again on writing the letter. There was going to be no easy way to tell them, so I decided to say it straight:

"Dear Mam and Dad,

I hope this won't come as a big surprise to you and I don't want you to worry, but by the time you get this letter, Albert and I will be in France with the Territorials. It happened so quickly. We were asked if we wanted to fight overseas and so we said yes. I didn't tell you sooner as I didn't want you to worry. I'm sorry I kept you in the dark about it. It was with the best of intentions. Anyway please don't worry; I'll be fine and so will Albert. We'll both look after each other and I'll write to you as often as I can. It's too good an opportunity to miss and both of us are excited. Take care of yourselves. I'll be in touch again soon.

Your loving son,
John."

I wrote a similar letter to Alice, though I added that I'd miss her and would remember the sweet smell of her, the softness of her skin, the loveliness of her hair, and the tenderness of her kisses. I hoped she would understand, and told her that I still had the picture of her, as well as her scented handkerchief, hidden away next to my heart, along with a picture of Mam and Dad that I'd pinched the last time I was home. I didn't tell any of them I'd no idea when I would see them again, but reassured them it was a chance to prove myself, and an opportunity which I couldn't possibly miss.

There were so many things I really wanted to say. Anxieties kept creeping into my mind, such as, would they be alright when they heard where I was, what if I got injured in some way, causing them to worry. Or worse still, what if I was to get killed and never see any of them again? I shook myself, putting all negative thoughts behind me, and reasoned they would be fine with it.

Fortunately the concerns I had about their reactions, were fleeting. I paid no further attention to them as I sealed both letters. It was only afterwards I wished I'd written a word or two about how much I loved them all. Again I rationalised my reason for not doing so, by telling myself I didn't want to worry them. Saying something I rarely verbalised would give them the impression I was unsure of things and would only add to their fears.

The deed now done, I waited for Albert to finish his. We both agreed to post them on the day we were being shipped out so that it would be too late for anyone to do anything about it. We commissioned Frederico with the task, as, sadly, he was being left behind.

Two days earlier, he'd met with an unfortunate accident, after an argument between a boiler full of porridge and his foot. The boiler stood about three feet high, supported off the ground by sleepers and had a large inner tub with a hinged lid on the top of it. At breakfast time, it held our porridge. To cook the contents of the boiler, a coal fire was set underneath it and an integral chimney at the back of it channelled the smoke away. All the lot was transportable into the field and was an essential part of kitchen field equipment.

On this occasion, some clown had not stood the boiler properly on its supports and out of the corner of his eye, Frederico had seen it going over. As he'd rushed to catch it, a large dollop of porridge lifted the lid and hurled itself onto the vest he was wearing. In an attempt to prevent burns to his chest, and yet still support the boiler, he'd quickly pulled his vest away from his skin with one hand, using the other to support the boiler. Regrettably, the jerkiness of his action created another large dollop of porridge to cascade out over the top and straight into his partly laced up boot.

As he'd hopped around in agony, frantically trying to get his boot off, and secure the boiler back on its supports, he was unable to prevent his foot from getting burnt. As a result of this, he was now laid up having his foot painted every few hours with gentian violet by the prettiest nurse you could ever have wished for. And, to cap it all, he was put on orders for not having his shoe laces tied up, not that he was bothered! A few weeks with a pretty nurse would be worth it, he told us grinning.

Unfortunately for us, it now meant he would be staying put in England. All of us were really sad at losing the best cook we'd ever had and hoped he would be able to rejoin our unit later. Meanwhile he promised to see that our letters were posted, and after we'd exchanged good luck wishes, and a wink and a nod in the nurse's direction, we left him, fervently hoping he'd catch up with us soon. With a large grin spreading from ear to ear, he waved us off.

With months of training now complete, we left Gainsborough early on 14th April and journeyed to Folkestone, and an unknown land. At last, our once in a lifetime adventure had started for real.

"It's going to be bloody great," I excitedly remarked, to the sea of happy faces now surrounding me.

SIX

Chapter FIFTEEN

Time and tide waits for no man…
(English Proverb)

With thoughts of our past lives behind us, we stopped just outside the town of Folkestone, waiting for our turn to march into the busy port directly in front of us. From our holding position, we could see several large steam ships in the harbour and what looked like hundreds of brown ants scurrying in and out of them. Each battalion numbered about nine-hundred-and-forty men, and Lieutenant Colonel Wood, who commanded our particular one, reckoned that the four West Yorkshire battalions were up to War strength and ready for action.

There was a pent up feeling of anticipation as we made ready to move out. With our faces glued to the scene in front, we joined the throng of shoulder-to-shoulder men heading towards the dockside. As we got closer, the brown ants became connected with reality. Sarge assured us that within the chaos there was order and purpose, though how anyone worked this out was beyond my understanding. A low rumbling sound was emitted by the revving vehicles with huge red crosses on them, and as we made ready, the racket increased, engulfing us as we headed towards the ships.

There were people shouting, horns blaring, and orders being bellowed out as men shuffled towards the dock, just as another equally chaotic stream of men and trucks headed away to unknown destinations. An order came for us to keep to the right. We were so packed together that I could almost lift my feet off the ground and still be carried along in the mass of heaving bodies around me as we moved ever closer to our intended destination.

Every now and then we came to a halt, whilst an assortment of wounded men disembarked from incoming ships. The starkness of the red-soaked bandages stood out against the grey backdrop of the fading day, punctuated only by the off-white butterfly caps of the young nurses silently fluttering amongst the broken bodies. As we got nearer, the sounds of moaning and strident unearthly screams of pain could be heard.

"'Ere mate, watch what you're doing," interjected the voice of a stranger, as he wrestled his way past us.

"Sorry," I replied, realising I'd accidentally caused him to drop his cigarette amongst the trampling feet.

"'Ere, have one of mine," said Albert, saving the moment from turning nasty, as he got one out for himself as well.

"Are you coming or going?" Albert continued, tilting his head back and forth to indicate what he meant.

As he struck a match and cupped the flame up towards the man's face, the glow revealed the weather beaten features of an old man.

His sombre eyes met ours, and his cheerless mask relaxed just enough to expose the deep brown eyes of a much younger lad, which shocked us. He was probably not much older than us.

"I'm coming," was his calm emotionless reply, savouring the lungful of smoke as if it was his first one for a long while.

"What about you lot?" he now said, blowing the smoke purposefully skywards and relaxing even more so as he did.

His action seemed almost as if he was blowing demons away.

"Oh, we're just going," I eagerly exclaimed.

"Well, good luck. You're going to need it," he responded, with a distinct edge to his voice, as his face once again regained its former guise.

I was about to ask him what he meant when he was unexpectedly swept along with the moving crowd and was now several feet away. He looked back at us in sudden panic as if trying to tell us something important, maybe warn us, or capture our faces in his mind's-eye, almost as if he was desperately trying to hold onto us somehow. Just then, we too started to move in the opposite direction, swallowed up in the confusion of bodies all around us.

Albert and I looked at each other, unable in our high spirits to understand his meaning, and the moment was quickly forgotten. As we stood a short while on the dockside, the S.S. Victoria emerged resplendent in the misty fading light. She was awesome and, as we now eagerly neared the gangway getting ever closer to being on board, Albert held onto my kit bag in fear of being separated from me. The thought of being on the sea still disturbed him and like a child, he held on tight. I was his lifesaver should anything happen and he wasn't going to let go of me without a fight.

SIX

Eventually, movement on the gangplank started to go in our direction and at last the embarkation process started for real. Sarge told us to find a place to rest and make the most of what sleep we could get. It was going to be a long night. We found a sheltered spot on deck and huddled together. Our eyes remained stubbornly open for fear of missing anything, and the strange noises in the gloom sharpened our senses as we tried to make out the sounds in the descending darkness. Albert was still concerned about being on water and any slight movement of the boat produced a look of anxiety and a tightening grip on my arm. To reassure him, I put my arm around him like I would one of my younger brothers, and as we huddled closer together to keep warm, wrapped in one of our army blankets, we slipped soundlessly out of port into an unknown world.

Only the moon, now shining dimly on the surface of the sea, guided our path. It was then that I thought about a poem Longfellow had written, and knowing that Albert would remember it from our school days, I whispered it to him and he closed his eyes, savouring its familiar words:

> "Ships that pass in the night, and speak each other in passing;
> Only a signal shown and a distant voice in the darkness;
> So on the ocean of life we pass and speak one another,
> Only a look and a voice; then darkness again and a silence."
> (Longfellow)

Somehow, it became a comforting thought as we left England and all that was familiar to us behind. With the calm sea and the reassuring gentle rocking motion of Victoria, we both eventually fell asleep. Whilst we slept, I was blissfully unaware that my brother Fred was also crossing the channel that night with the Durham Lights, and he too was equally unaware Albert and I were now snuggled up together on a similar journey. Robert and George had already beaten us to it, and were advancing through Belgium to the front line. And Matthew was firmly established on the Eastern front. None of us had any idea we were now all, 'SIX' at war.

In the warmth of bodies, I dreamt of home and Alice. In my dreams I could hear her saying, "Be sure to come home to me," and I replied with passionate promises that nothing would stop me, not even a war would keep us apart for long. She was so real, so perfect, and lovely. In my dream we were as one, sharing the same heart and soul, and body. The warm glow of the dream washed over me. It was then I knew for certain I loved her. Did she dream such dreams too, I wondered?

SIX

As Albert stirred, I continued to hold him. Under the weight of his slumbering body, my arm lost all feeling, the stiffness of its position now waking me fully. The ship's engines stopped and unaccustomed to the pitch of the night, my eyes had difficulty seeing anything. A low whisper was heard, ordering us to maintain silence as we neared the port of Boulogne. It would still be some time before we would enter and disembark, but as my eyes became familiarized to the darkness, I was content to watch the dawn loom slowly in a foreign land, exposing the French coastline for the first time.

As we came into port, the scene was very much like the one we had left in Folkestone harbour, though the noises were muffled and more sombre, and it was obvious that, just as we were desperate to arrive, hundreds of others were desperate to leave for home. It seemed as if thousands of solitary men, their inner spirits extinguished, were everywhere. Some didn't appear to move and for a moment I thought they were probably dead, though Sarge just referred to them as the sick and wounded. The sight was pitiful, and inwardly, a fear of horror and confusion assailed my thoughts.

We were quick to dismiss the scene, refusing to gaze at this sea of humanity, fooling ourselves that it would never be our fate to writhe in agony on a cold dockside, waiting to go home. We pitied their foolishness, as if it were somehow some fault of their own. Suddenly, there was a commotion on the dock side. It seemed a mistake had been made and our boat had docked in the wrong place. There was frantic waving and an urgency to get us out of the way. Orders to move out were hurriedly shouted, as we were ushered quickly off board.

Amidst the chaos, one of the men on a stretcher at the bottom of the gangway feebly reached out his hand to grab hold of Albert.

"'Ere mate, got a smoke."

Stopping to look down at him, Albert was taken aback to see the man only had one arm and was heavily bandaged about the torso and head. The bandages unsuccessfully attempted to conceal the mass of destruction to his body. Alarmed and too frightened to touch the man whose eyes betrayed a kind of madness, Albert threw the last few cigarettes he had in his packet onto his chest and quickly moved away.

"Thanks mate," the man gasped, all energy now expelled.

Albert continued to move quickly on, not stopping to light up for him, fearful he was the bogey man out to get him.

SIX

The words "Poor buggers," were heard in the midst of unrest. Albert agreed silently to himself, as he briefly took another glance at the man now behind him, fearful he might have got up to follow him, not realising that the words hanging in the air were actually meant for us. I had not mistaken the meaning and as I stole a look at the grotesque bodies all around me, a premonition of something horrible swept over me. It was a feeling of danger. Albert did not feel the shudder go through my body as he pushed me on, away from it all, putting further distance between us and them. As we left the scene behind, my confidence slowly returned, as did Albert's now his feet were back on terra-firma.

Within a short while, Albert was so full of expectation and excitement that he no longer seemed to hear the fading cries of pain in the warm gentle early morning breeze, as we continued to march with purpose, but I did.

"We're here!" he exclaimed, laughing.

None of us in our wildest dreams could ever have imagined we could be abroad as we now were. The prospect of being able to tell everyone at home registered itself. To Albert, it was just as if he'd fulfilled a dream and as we marched swiftly to the nearby holding camp, he threw his arms in the air and jumped for joy, just as if his heart would burst with pride at being British, and at war at last.

With his manic outburst over, normality reigned triumphant once again, almost as if the whole event had been imagined.

"Is he alright?" Phil asked me.

"Yeh, I reckon it's just the relief of being back on dry land, or maybe a reaction to that man grabbing hold of him. He was quite taken aback by what he saw."

"Weren't we all," Phil agreed, as the rest of us marched on in sombre thought.

Chapter SIXTEEN

All men are fools, but all fools are not men…
(Proverb)

It was strange to think of life at home continuing, with us miles away.

"Morning Mrs Jackson," said Mr Rourke, as he handed her a letter, and tipped his cap by way of a greeting.

"Nice morning. Looks like a letter from one of your lads," he said, as he handed it over to her.

"Aye, by the looks it's from our John. No doubt he'll want something," she laughed, as she put my letter in her front pinafore pocket, and turned to go indoors.

The kettle was boiling. Dad had long since gone to work, the boys were at school, and this was her time. She sat down, deciding to have a cuppa before starting the day's chores, smiling that the day was now her own. Content, she sipped her hot cup of tea and pulled out my letter to read.

"Oh my God," she cried, as her hand clutched at her throat, and her eyes re-read the words over and over again, as if unable to believe what she was reading.

"The bloody fool," she uttered, in her desperation, still unable to believe the words written so plainly in front of her.

"What on earth does he think he's playing at?" she voiced out loud, to herself.

Her tea completely forgotten, her mind working overtime, she quickly and desperately tried to think of what to do. She must get word to Thomas, right away, and of course she must go to see Stephen Seal immediately. Jumping up, she reached for her hat and coat, and clutching the letter in her hand, rushed out into the street, with all plans for the day ahead now gone.

With her feet barely touching the ground in her impatience to get to Albert's house, she continued talking out aloud like someone possessed, not aware of the strange looks she was starting to get from passer-bys.

"I hope this won't come as a big surprise to you…"

"What does he think it'll come as?" she shouted out, telling 'all-an-sundry'.

"It happened so quickly..."

"Too bloody right it did!"

"We were asked if we wanted to fight overseas and so we said yes..."

"What on earth were they thinking of?"

"Your loving son, John..."

"I'll give him "loving son John" and the back of my hand when I get hold of him," she continued, heading for the Seal's back door.

Stephen Seal had already heard and was sitting rubbing his hands on his head. Albert's letter was open on the table in front of him. His eyes were saddened, and he was unable to respond to Mam's sudden entrance, almost as if he was paralysed with fright. He was a quiet sort of a man, whom Mam often thought lacked a bit of a backbone when it came to a crisis.

"You've heard then," said Mam.

"Come on, get your coat on. We've got to go and see what we can do about it," she declared, and without further ado, and with her leading the way, they set off to Tower Street enlistment station, like bulls in a china shop, calling both of us all the names under the sun.

On reaching the building, they fought their way through the crowd of lads all eager to follow in our footsteps, and Mam in no uncertain terms pushed her way through, telling them all to go home to their mothers.

"Now look here, you just can't come barging in like this. We have a set of procedures to go through. You're interfering with army business. Have you got an appointment?" said the flustered enlisting officer, confronted by my irate Mam.

By now she was at the front of the queue demanding attention, with Stephen Seal hot on her heels.

"Forget an appointment. What are you going to do about getting our sons back from France? You've shipped out two underage lads who shouldn't be there," shouted Mam, as she grabbed Albert's letter out of Stephen's hands to wave both letters under his nose, as if to prove the dastardly action they'd done.

"I'm sorry, Madam, but there's nothing I can do about it. It's not my job to sort this out."

"Then get someone whose job it is then!" shouted Stephen, before Mam could respond.

Mam turned, surprised, and gave him an appreciative smile, realising there was nothing like a parent's protectiveness to bring out the mettle. Both stood firm, refusing to budge until someone addressed the issue.

With a sigh, the enlisting officer held both the letters up, summoning an orderly.

"Take these two 'ere persons to Captain Pickard's room," he commanded, now eager to be rid of them.

It was obvious he had no time for irate parents, probably because he didn't know how to handle them and probably because he was, as he said, powerless to help anyway.

They were ushered along a narrow winding corridor to a door right at the end. The orderly told them to wait whilst he informed the Captain of the circumstances. Within minutes both were propelled into a drab, but spacious room, and ordered to take a seat. The stern, sallow looking man behind a large desk stood up and gestured to the chairs in front of him and waited until they were settled before seating himself back down again.

"Now then, I'm Captain Pickard. What can I do for you good people?" he said, as he twiddled the ends of his long moustache into points, coiling the tails to emphasize his charming smile, which he obviously reserved for such occasions.

Mam explained the situation, her anger now vanishing under the subtle tones of reassurances that 'all stops would be pulled out.'

"Of course you do realise, Mrs Jackson and Mr Seal, that these things do take time," he explained.

"I will of course need evidence of their ages."

They agreed to produce this as soon as possible.

"… and you do understand how difficult it is going to be to locate two young boys out of so many that are overseas?"

Mam nodded.

"Especially with the various units on the move all the time," he continued.

"I will of course do my best to get word to their commanding officer to say that both boys must be returned forthwith. Will that be alright?"

"Yes, thank you," uttered Mr Seal, and Mam nodded again.

His charm oozed out, pouring over them in a 'there, there' manner, soothing their anxieties and reassuring them that everything possible would be done. He stood up and offered his hand to both of them, as he led them to his door and called for the orderly to escort them out. As they went one way, he entered the door opposite to where another orderly was typing.

"Alfred, see what you can do about finding the whereabouts of Privates Jackson and Seal, will you? Don't spend too much time on it. Just do enough to show that we've tried to do something about getting them home again. Silly buggers were under age." And with that, he turned and resumed his work.

Meanwhile, Mam and Stephen set off for home, convinced they had done something positive to bring Albert and me back to England. Little did they realise they'd only been on a fool's errand. Mam took comfort in having Mr Seal with her as they hurried down the street, content we would be back home soon.

Alice's reaction was somewhat different. On receiving my letter, she wasn't sure what it really meant and wrote back asking if it was just for a few weeks or for a few months, or what? She was proud to be able to tell her close friends that I was in France fighting for her and yet on the other hand, suddenly thought that she might never see me again. It wasn't so much about the fact I could die, but that I would meet some French woman and fall in love.

She'd heard all about these French girls, the way they dressed, the way they painted their lips red and wore silk stockings. Oh yes, she knew all about foreign women, and forgetting there would be little opportunity for such shenanigans, she'd become consumed with jealousy.

"It's typical of the way a woman's mind works," said Albert knowingly.

Before I had time to reply, Albert and I were on the move again. We arrived at 7.30pm by truck at a small village called Merville. Then in the darkness we marched to Le Sart, a few miles away, where our billet was to be for the next few days. Tired, we dropped our kit, left it where it landed and scrambled into bunks, aware of nothing but the need to sleep. It had been a long day.

As dawn broke, we were refreshed and ready for action. Whilst checking our stores and kit, we chatted excitedly about our platoon officers and N.C.O's attending a briefing. Phil ran up to us, and breathlessly reported he'd overheard one of them talking about going to Fauquissart to see the 21st brigade in action in the trenches. A short while later, we watched them go, knowing this would determine where we would possibly end up. We waited with excited anticipation and kept a watch out for their return. The waiting seemed endless.

Eventually, orders came to say we were going to Estaires instead, but we didn't care, we were going to kill Jerry, and that was all that mattered. Albert and I, and the rest of our battalion, travelled with the Grenadier Guards and headed up into the front line trenches for instructions. Despite the weather being fine, we sank into at least six inches of mud and squelched our way along the communications trench towards the sounds of battle.

"Keep your flipping heads down. There's live ammunition out there and bloody crazy Jerries wanting to blow your bleeding brains out," came a stern rebuke.

A gruff-looking officer watched us heed the warning, before turning to his mate in despair.

"This lot aren't going to last five bloody minutes out here, and it'll be us who have to pick up the bleeding pieces," he uttered, his mate nodding in agreement.

"Too damn right," his mate replied.

We continued to keep our heads ducked in response and made our way sheepishly down the line. As we got nearer to the main frontline trench, the whistling of bullets and the odd shell exploding, didn't take us long to realise our survival did indeed depend on keeping our heads low. As we got closer, an automatic ducking action took over, as mud and dirt continually rained on us. This was trench warfare, and we were about to learn how men survived it.

It quickly became engraved on our minds. As the noises reverberated in my head and my heart permanently resided in my throat, I was horrified to discover that the reality we'd all been eager to experience, was not as I'd imagined. At one stage, I thought I was going to die of fright. As I turned around to look at Albert, he was mouthing the Lord's Prayer and marking himself with a cross, whispering to himself, "in the name of the Father, the Son and Holy Ghost, Amen."

Turning, I clung on to him, terrified. We were both shaking.

"We're going to be fine Albert," I said to him, more to reassure myself than him.

"Just fine…" I repeated, scared stiff.

On our return to Le Sart, twenty-four hours later, we overheard one of the platoon officers reporting we'd all had a 'quiet' day in the trenches, with nothing much happening.

"What's a noisy day then?" remarked Albert, as we despairingly took to our beds and thanked God we'd survived.

By 29th April, the battalion had been in the trenches twenty-four hours, and to our amazement, we had suffered no casualties. A few men had been sick, a couple had been given commissions and had returned to England, a pack horse had died from pneumonia, but Major Wilkinson reported he was pleased with our adjustment, and informed us we would be moving out soon, where the real action would begin.

We were all still pretty scared at the thought of 'real action,' now that our taster period was over, and on May 1st, our moving out day, I woke and muttered "white rabbits," softly to myself, hoping it would bring me luck. Orders came to "stand to arms" at 6.30am, and before we knew it, we were travelling in trucks back to Estaires again. The guns greeted us, as we marched to Bac-St-Maur and were allocated billets on scattered farms. Sanitary conditions were pretty poor, compounding our fears.

Smithy, Phil, Archie, Arnie, Pete, Jim, Albert and I, and a young kid called Joe, managed to be billeted together in an old farm building belonging to Roĝer and Monique Lizeul. They had a young son called Pierre. Madame Lizeul brought us bread and cheese and fresh water, and made us very welcome, whilst we lounged around, looking lost, waiting for orders.

Runners kept us up to date with information, and within a few days we were led towards the front line trenches under heavy gun fire by a stupid guide who managed to get us lost. We were some time before we found out where we should be, and because of this, ended up relieving the lads going into reserve much later than anticipated. By the time the relief was finally complete at 9pm, we were ordered to dig in for the night and keep watch. As the night became quiet, I began to relax thinking this wasn't so bad after all. My eyes became heavy and kept closing as I tried desperately to stay alert, but I just couldn't keep them open. Every bone in my body was telling me to sleep. It wasn't until I heard a branch cracking and some German voices that I became instantly awake, wide eyed, and ready for action.

My heart drummed in my ears so loudly, that I felt Jerry must be able to hear it. We all waited and watched with bated breath. There was a sudden burst of fire down the line and a distant cry, as the bullets hit their mark and then all was silent again. Straining to hear more, with sleep completely banished, I gingerly raised my head above the parapet to strain my eyes for any movement. None was seen and I carefully lowered it again, relieved there wasn't any.

"Keep your bloody head down, Jackson, unless you want it bloody shooting off. Use the periscope if you want to see what's going on," hissed Sarge, as he threw the box at me.

"Sorry Sarge," I mumbled.

The following day, several of us went to shore up the communication trench, making it ready to withstand further action, though it turned out to be a quiet day, followed by another relatively quiet night, and gradually my nerves began to settle again. One soldier was wounded by a chance shot, reinforcing the warning to keep our heads down as the days and nights dragged on. One evening, a mortar attack demolished our number one parapet with a direct hit, but fortunately, two other shots did no damage, and two enemy planes came over and fired a few rounds at us but soon went. Sarge reckoned it was to cover Jerry's change over of men in their front lines.

The planned attack by our lot, due on the 8th, was postponed for twenty-four hours and rescheduled to begin at 5am, before sunrise, on the 9th. No-one told us why, and so we waited, cold and miserable.

"The wire cutters will go in first, then the artillery bombardment of enemy trenches will start from the big guns behind us, then it's us," said Sarge, informing us of the attack plan.

When the battle started, Jerry retaliated with a number of shells killing one man and wounding three others, burying them in debris. The stretcher bearers hurriedly carted them away, though not before we saw the mess. Albert turned away, as he vomited. I felt sick and feared I was going to faint. Gulping gallons of air, I grabbed hold of Albert and moved down the line away from it all.

By 4pm, only our own artillery was firing. Jerry had gone quiet. We were covered in a layer of dirt, almost at one with the ground. My skin was becoming perpetually brown, ingrained with stuff no decent person could ever imagine. I felt dirty, no matter how much I washed it and came to the conclusion that no amount of rubbing would get rid of the filth of war.

We continued to fire at Trivelet, a stronghold of the Boche, and though our first shot wasn't bad, we wasted the remaining eight shots, mainly due to tiredness But despite that, we must have had an effect as our ration parties were able to deliver food and hot coffee without being fired upon. It was the same the following day, when twenty-four shells hit the enemy's barricades. Our guns made short work of their trenches, which was just as well, as by that time we were dead on our feet. We desperately awaited relief, which came in the end on the 15th. It was then that we crawled back to our billets, punch drunk by the constant noise of guns, having spent eleven days in the trench. In that time, three men had been killed and fifteen had been wounded, though mercifully, Albert and I had escaped, albeit scared witless, with nothing more than a few scratches.

Chapter SEVENTEEN

It is only the dead who do not return...
(Bertrand Barere 1755 - 1841)

"Get cleaned up all of you," said Sarge, the next day.

We were all given a bowl of luke-warm water to scrub up in and each of us took pleasure in washing for the first time in days. I didn't realise a wash could feel so good and scrubbed every inch of my skin till it glowed, not that it made much difference to the brown staining.

Smithy had the trots and was fair buggered with it. It left him with little energy to wash. All he kept saying was, "Later chaps, I'll do it later," and so we left him to sleep. We knew he needed every ounce of energy to be ready for trench relief tomorrow night, so told him it didn't matter if he wasn't clean, the rats weren't choosy and there was another chance to wash his exposed bits tomorrow, if he felt up to it.

The next day came all too quickly, and as we went to relieve our comrades, just before midnight, it was tipping it down with rain. The low cloud hid any moonlight there might have been, and the silence of the night made everything eerie. I hated it at night. This spookiness prevailed for five whole days, and the silence became just as un-nerving as the deafening noise of shelling. We methodically made repairs in the various trench systems as best we could, especially in the communications trench, and began a different battle, the never-ending one against water.

One man was wounded by a sapper during a small advance mission, but generally, despite our nerves being on edge, these few days passed uneventfully in terms of action. Shortly after, we were relieved by the 1/7th West Yorkshires and went back into reserve again. Ironically, after we'd left, officers had been to inspect our work and had been met with a series of heavy shelling which had undone all our repairs, so it had all been for nothing. It was as if the bloody Jerries knew we'd just finished them!

Archie was sent to the Rue Petillon number one section of trenches, where little had been done to improve them. His platoon had been ordered to do what they could, but the stink of dead bodies turned his stomach and he kept retching as they cleared away the debris. His face was pale when he returned to our billet, and the sight of food was too much for him, so much so, that we ended up sharing his rations as he settled for a cig instead. We were tired and miserable. Bit by bit our resolve was slipping and the tension we felt was almost tangible. Home seemed so far away now, and close to an eternity had lapsed since we'd arrived, or so it appeared. We had no word from family, neither had we had a chance to write either, and tomorrow was going to be the first of June, another 'white rabbit' day. God, I was tired!

Within a matter of days, we had plenty to thank Archie for. His clearing out of the Rue Petillon trenches, meant we were only knee deep in slime, though Archie reckoned the stench of dead bodies remained. All of us gave him and his mates a few fags for their effort, and the glory went to Archie's head. When we bombarded the German lines with our big guns called Archibald, he boasted they'd named these guns after him and bragged about how big he was where it mattered. We all ribbed him about it, trying to take our minds off the visions which still haunted us, as rats swam in the quagmire beneath us and clambered over our feet and legs.

When we later fired fifteen shells overhead, all were good, landing directly in our enemy's trenches successfully silencing retaliatory mortar for over half an hour. Everything was going well until Jerry started his sporadic shelling again, sending shrapnel in all directions. As I ducked down below the parapet, my trench took a direct hit and it blew up before me. The moment of reckoning had finally arrived and everything went black. As the darkness encased me, I was not aware of slipping into this unknown world.

I knew nothing of the scrabble to dig me out, nor anything of the blood that oozed out of my body, or the many hands that tried to stop its flow, as shells continued to land all around.

"Is he dead, is he dead? For God's sake tell me, is he?" said Albert frantically.

Friends dragged my body down the line, packing the hole in my shoulder, shouting for stretcher bearers as they bundled me along. Albert sat with his head in his hands in six inches of cold water, all energy now spent in getting me help, still not knowing if I was dead. Out of the corner of his eye he saw a rat about to bite him and in an instant, picked it up by its tail and banged its brains out. It was six days before relief came and he got his answer.

When I finally came to, the eyes of a young girl were smiling down at me.

SIX

"Bonjour Monsieur, Je suis Elise. You are awake, yes?"

A thin shaft of light shone brightly behind her and for a moment I was confused.

"Where am I? Is this heaven?" I asked, now uncertain where I was.

"Qui," she said laughing, and then, reassuringly, "No, no, no, Monsieur, you are in casualty clearing. You 'ave 'urt your 'ead, and shoulder, but are fine."

Dazed, my head registered pain and I put my hand up to touch where it hurt. She patted my chest with the palm of her hand and smiled again before moving on with a tray of shiny instruments. Her lovely face now gone, I thought of Alice as I slipped back into a deep sleep. By the time the lads came to see me, I was well on the road to recovery. The blast had temporarily knocked me out, leaving me with one cracking headache and, embedded in my shoulder, a large piece of shrapnel which had been successfully removed. All in all, I had been lucky. My wound was healing well, and apart from aching all over, I was almost back to normal. All recollection of the event had been erased. The last thing I remembered was being in reserve on the farm.

Albert, now excited to see me, grinned from ear to ear.

"'Ere mate, some people have all the luck!" he joked, as he flung his arms around me and then, embarrassed, quickly offered me a cig. The others grasped my hand and ruffled my hair in turn, as they pulled up chairs around the narrow metal bed, obscuring me from any nurse whilst I smoked it.

"That's the best smoke ever," I added appreciatively as I handed the stub end back to Albert for him to put out for me.

"When are they going to let you out?" asked Phil.

"I dunno. Soon I hope," I replied. I wasn't sure, but thought it could be any day.

"The doc says they'll let me back on light duties for a day or two until I'm fit for full duty. They'll even send me for a spell of convalescence. Maybe I should try it?" I laughed.

"Just you dare," uttered Albert, aghast at the thought.

"Don't worry mate, I won't. In any case, there's no guarantee I would be sent back to you lot."

"Well tell them we're in reserve for two weeks, so if they sent you back now, the timing couldn't be better," said Albert, desperate for my return.

The lads chatted excitedly as they gave graphic details of my rescue, embellishing it somewhat, telling me I 'owed them' and that they would collect their just rewards when we were next having a beer. They assured me it would cost me 'an arm and a leg' to repay them. Archie said he would collect his dues now, and would settle for a date with Elise.

"Fat chance mate, she's already spoken for. There's a ring on her finger," I said, and he sighed wistfully, muttering to himself.

"Why is it all the pretty ones are always taken?"

I was sad to see the lads go, and so started to nag the medics to let me return to my unit. Apart from wanting to be back with them, the comings and goings at the casualty clearing unit had become too depressing and I had begun to realise the fragility of life. It was a case of, one minute you're here, and the next minute you're gone. I took comfort knowing that in the blackness of the unknown, I had not been aware. I imagined death to be like that.

I started to think about 'heaven' and what it would be like and wondered how you got to it from the darkness. Did one rise from the dead on the third day like Christ? For a while, I couldn't get this out of my mind, and thought maybe I was going a little crazy. I tried talking to the chaplain about it, but all he could offer me was reassurance that God would take care of me. I somehow began to doubt this. Where was God in the hospital? Where was God when lads were screaming out for release from pain? I found no evidence of God in the carnage around me, and in my betrayal of Him, I could hear my Mam's voice clearly saying, "Go wash your mouth out with soap!" and so, trying not to think of such things again, I returned to my unit.

Chapter EIGHTEEN

Courage is the thing; all goes if courage goes...
(Sir James Matthew Barrie 1860 – 1937)

When letters from home caught up with us, I had three, all from Mam. Looking at the postmarks, I decided to open them in order. The first one was nothing but a tirade about how stupid Albert and I were, and telling us we had to get ourselves straight back home immediately. How could we do that, I asked myself. Mam didn't realise that if we were to come home, half the bloody battalion would have to be sent home too and then the Army would be buggered! How could we leave other lads our age in this hell-hole and hold our heads up on the streets of York, and live with the guilt? We'd be labelled scrimshankers. No, Mam had no concept of the difficulties we would have in coming home again.

The old saying, "You've made your bed and now you lie in it," came to mind and I realised it would be something we'd have to live with.

The next letter followed the same thread, only this time she referred to a letter she'd written to Major Wilkinson, thinking that if I got letters, then he would too! It wasn't long before Albert and I were summoned to headquarters, both of us knowing what it was about. The Major had two letters in front of him. Albert's father had also written, no doubt prompted by my Mam. It was obvious they were desperate to get us home by any means.

The Major was a tall, unassuming man who appeared on the surface to be concerned about our welfare.

"Now then lads. I'm in a bit of a predicament here. Your parents want you home as you're underage. Now if I send you home, I'd have to send others home too, probably half the blooming army. I'd also have to acknowledge that mistakes have been made," he said, pondering what to do.

He continued to tell us how proud he was that British lads such as us had enlisted. It demonstrated to him how remarkably brave we were. He made us feel that every man in his unit mattered to him, which made it all the more difficult when he passed on to us the decision regarding whether we should return home or not.

"Well, lads, it's up to you, but it would be a shame to lose you," he added, making our decision overwhelmingly difficult.

For a brief moment, the urge to go home was intense. But how could we really choose to do so? He would think us both cowards. We knew in our hearts we couldn't desert our friends. We knew what we had to do. I looked at Albert.

"I won't think any the less of you if you want to go home," I uttered miserably to him.

"I won't, honest… I'll understand," I continued.

"We're in this together," he said, just as downcast.

In acknowledgement of our answer, Major Wilkinson didn't ask us how old we were. Maybe he knew, but he didn't say. As far as he was concerned, we were men, despite Albert's seventeenth birthday being only yesterday. And so it was, on 29th June 1915, our fates were sealed.

Mam's third letter was even more frantic than the other two. This letter revealed a desperate yearning for any news from either of us. She hadn't heard from me in quite a while, so an acknowledgement of our continued existence was now essential. Unable to prolong the suffering I knew I was causing, I immediately wrote home, indicating no knowledge of her previous requests for us to return. I sent a reassuring letter, to say we were both keeping well and that the army was looking after us in this fair and agreeable land. Not much different from being at home, I told her.

I didn't tell her of my injuries, or what it was like in the trenches and the misery life could be there. I didn't tell her I had renounced God in this unspeakable place, as I knew she wouldn't understand. I wrote instead begging for news of my brothers and of Mrs Lofthouse, and of the everyday lives of people nearby. I needed the tangible reminder of why we were fighting. I needed to know that what we had done had been right and for a reason. I begged her and Dad for forgiveness and their approval, all the while reassuring them that Albert and I were fine, a statement that belied the truth even as I wrote it. Nothing could ever be 'fine' out here.

As the weeks passed, we slowly moved north into Belgium, and gradually settled into a different way of life. We marched to a place called Turco Farm, two miles north of Ypres, amid heavy shelling half a mile away to our left. We were entering new territory and another miserable existence. As we dug in, aerial torpedoes rained down on us causing everything, including the earth, to take on a different look. We were back to surviving in the trenches, but instead of holding our position, we fought to gain precious ground. In doing so we beat the Germans back in a 'blood-bath' of a battle.

Then an alarm was raised as gas shells landed around us. It was our first experience of this iridescent, mystical, drifting mist, and though the effect was small due to the southerly wind, by the time my trembling fingers had got my mask on, my eyes were smarting and my nose was running. I started to cough inside my mask and the urge to rip it off my face to take a deep breath was overpowering, even though I knew it would be the wrong thing to do. There'd been only a second to get the mask in place and yet in that time, I'd been affected and now desperately wanted to take it off. I started to sweat with panic as the cloth hood clung suffocatingly close to my face.

"Keep calm Jackson. You're alright. Breathe slowly. Try not to panic. That's it. You're doing fine. You're alright," Sarge kept telling me, over and over again, as I heard the noise of others coughing all around me.

When I turned towards the noise, I couldn't actually see the two men near me clutching their throats in the last throes of death, their bodies twitching as life left them. I could only hear the guttural choking sounds they made as they gasped for air. Was this the 'death rattle' my Mam often used to refer to when someone was in the final stages of dying? I didn't know, but it was dreadful, and I clutched at my own pulsating throat wondering if I would die, as I coughed and choked.

"Don't worry about them Jackson. Just keep looking at me. You're doing OK," Sarge said, as he turned me away from their writhing bodies.

When the all clear came and I removed my mask, I saw the black-purple faces of these two men, their gaping mouths with tongues outstretched and their eyes wide open, revealing the horror they had endured. No, there was no God in this place. He had forsaken us all. Others saw it too. Smithy made the sign of the cross on his chest, as if not wanting to believe God had truly left us.

As the gas dispersed, heavy trench mortar bombardment started. Sixty pounds and more were dropped, causing six yards of parapet to be blown in, in two places. Four more men were killed instantly, eleven were wounded. Then two more were killed and fifteen more wounded. The numbers of dead and wounded rose with every passing minute. In retaliation, our bombers put eleven hale bombs into the German line causing loss, and howitzers breached the German parapet at Estaminet. We fought our enemy with a fanaticism to kill and maim in return, despite the reality that none of us had ever seen this faceless foe, only the massacred bodies of their destruction.

The skirmish was at last over, and the dead and wounded lay ready for collection. Now the sounds of war were replaced with sounds of cries for help. There had been damage to our communication trenches near Turco farm and massive destruction around Algerian Cottage. Until the communication trenches were repaired, the dead and wounded would have to wait in no-man's land for the cover of darkness and retrieval. Some we knew would die in agony in the waiting.

That night, all who could be saved were, which was just as well, as numerous gas shells burst on the canal bank and bridge the following day, killing even the rats. The 1/6th West Yorkshires, took over and we returned to billets close by. As we moved away from the front line, a bird fluttered to the ground just in front of me, its wings outstretched, its beak open, beautiful in death as it had been in life. I stood looking at the pitiful thing. It was then that I cried. I cried for this innocent being and all that it stood for in my mind. I picked up its still warm body gently and held it in my hand willing God to let it live. What had it done to deserve this end? I cried fearing I would never stop as the tears flowed freely, and the pent up emotion of living with death all around me was released. No-one said anything, and Albert took the bird from me quickly burying it by the side of the road, using the heel of his boot to make a hole, before then filling it in again.

"Come on mate. Let's get back," he said, with his arm around my shoulder.

Everyone understood. Something inside of me had broken and I couldn't make sense of anything anymore as I arrived back at our billets, detached and in a daze. Albert lifted my heavy kit off and laid me on the straw in the corner of the barn. Long after that, when there were no more tears left, I drifted into an uneasy sleep and dreamt of Alice and home.

The old oak tree was in full splendour, with its branches swaying gently in the breeze and sparrows squabbling furiously all around as they darted in and out of it. Alice was sitting naked beneath its bows, smiling, happy, and smelling of nectar. She was exquisite and in the lingering breathtaking moment when our bodies touched, we became oblivious of the world around us. I savoured every touch, every feeling, as my lips brushed hers and my whole being became one with hers as our bodies merged together. She was stunning, wonderful, full of

SIX

excitement and vitality, and I drowned in her beauty. As her essence flowed, I became alive again, filled with her life-force as she willed me to live. Just as I lay back, content, the old oak tree took a direct hit and blew us both up, taking her away from me. I woke up in a sweat, screaming out loud, clinging onto the barn wall as if I'd been splattered against it. For a moment, I had no idea where I was.

"It's ok, mate. Go back to sleep. You've been dreaming," said Albert, as he wrapped his arms around me, holding onto me to ward off my demons.

I settled back down again and dozed once more, only to wander the misty void of no-mans-land, calling out for Alice, but there was no-one there.

"Oh God, Albert, it was awful," I said to him, as I recounted the dream in the cold light of day, remembering the hell that had nearly sent me mad.

Gradually, as the fear in the pit of my stomach settled, I prepared myself to face another day.

Chapter NINETEEN

God grant me the serenity to accept the things I cannot change,
Courage to change the things I can, And wisdom to know the difference.
(Reinhold Niebuhr 1892-1971)

It was five days later when fate decided to take a hand in things, and it changed everything. We were back fighting near Turco farm. The fighting was fearsome and for a while, a kind of madness ensued. Amidst it all was a beautiful blue sky with cotton wool clouds floating peacefully by, oblivious to what was happening. I stopped to watch the sun playing hide and seek, before the madness started again. In between the shelling was this surreal quietness, punctuated occasionally by the song of a skylark piercing the warm balmy July breeze. It too was confused. In a sense it was like living in two worlds: Heaven above, with all its beauty; and Hell below, with all its hideousness. It reminded me of the sermons back home when the vicar talked about 'Hell on Earth'.

Disillusioned, I realised this once peaceful landscape was now in Hell, stained red with the blood of our men.

"Spilled for what?" the crows seemed to screech, as they flew overhead amid grenade and mortar onslaught.

Behind me, on the distant horizon way behind the front line, I could see cows grazing as if nothing untoward was happening. They grazed on ground now landscaped by war, oblivious to the noise and mayhem now happening where I was.

I looked affectionately across at Albert. I'd known Albert for as long as I could remember. We had grown up together, had been at school together, and had lived almost next door to one another. We had laughed together, shared our boyhood dreams, liked the same girls and had even become blood brothers when one day in the park we'd cut our wrists and mixed our blood together, like the Native American Indians did. I looked down at the faint scar and ran my finger over it. It had been so natural to enlist together and come to war, to fight as we now did, side by side, brothers at war. We had believed ourselves to be invincible, but even that conviction was beginning to waver amidst all this carnage.

Now, with our naïve illusion of heroism gone, this war had robbed us of our dreams. Fighting for freedom? Proving ourselves to be men? What bloody fools we had been. I could hear the guns, smell the stench of death, and realise the misery of those left dying in the dirt in some unknown spot and imagine what they must feel. I hated the thought of being blown to pieces, pierced by shrapnel, or just left to rot in this war torn earth. The more I thought of it, the more I could taste real fear, and feel the wretchedness of our folly in wanting to grow up too soon. This was not the first time this had happened. It had happened before, but I had never dared to acknowledge it.

Our recent experiences preoccupied me. There we both were, killing other young boys in order to simply stay alive. A case of kill or be killed, either by our enemy or by our own men in front of a firing squad. A no-win situation whichever way you looked at it. It was madness. Madness which we had entered into without question. At the entrance to the trench system, I could see the battle policemen with guns to hand to prevent desertion and wondered how they felt as they watched us die.

Just then, I heard the feared whiz-bang sound of a bullet, and felt it graze the side of my head. As it parted my hair, eliciting an automatic ducking response, I followed its path with my hand.

"Bloody 'ell!" I uttered, my heart pounding, my breath held until I registered I wasn't hurt.

Scared witless, I put my tommy hat on, which should have been on in the first place, and breathed a sigh of relief, unable to believe my luck.

"Did you see that?" I said, as I turned to Albert. "Too bleeding close for…"

My heart missed a beat as a giddy feeling of terror washed over me and I clutched my mouth in horror. Albert slowly fell to the ground, instantly halted in life, shock frozen on his face, stilled by the bullet which had passed by me on its journey straight through Albert's head, taking with it all the fears and images of death he'd had, as the possibility of his final demise became reality.

Disbelieving the vision before me, I instantly caught him, softening his fall, preventing him from slipping into the watery depths of hell, crying and begging him not to leave me, telling him to hold on, telling him everything would be alright, washing him with my tears in utter desperation as I shouted for someone to help me, holding him tight, impotent to do anything else. As I looked down at him, cradling him like a baby, his beautiful face was serene and calm. His eyes were wide open, staring vacantly into mine. His innocence, his boyhood dreams were now gone, taken from him by a bullet which had been meant for me. I was certain it had had my name on it, not his, and yet here he was, lifeless in my arms.

He was unresponsive as his colour gradually drained away. There was just a small hole in his forehead where the bullet had entered, but as my hand cradled the back of his head, I knew from the size of the exit hole that his brains had been blown away. My hand caught his blood as he ebbed away. I cupped it and smeared it all over me, trying to prevent it from reaching the ground in the desperate hope I could give it back. Once it entered the ground, I knew there would be no getting it back. The ground took a man's existence away in an instant. I followed the stretcher bearers with his lifeless body sprawled between them. Phil intercepted my step.

"Leave it, John, leave it. He's gone, it's no use."

He was finally taken to Hospital Farm, a casualty clearing station in support of the front line, but I knew it was futile. I knew in the depths of my soul he was dead. By this time, there was nothing but utter numbness and the echo of Rossetti's words:

> *"Remember me when I am gone away, gone far away into the silent land,"*

…only it was the silent voice of Albert who spoke them as he was taken from me. It was then that I prayed to God not to take him, and in my panic, I was horribly struck by the thought of how to tell my best friend's father about the death of his only son. Should I tell him he died a hero's death? Tell him it should have been me? Tell him he was just one of the thousands who slipped into the earth and was greedily swallowed up, and I hadn't been there? Or pretend it was all a bad dream and none of this had really happened?

A gust of wind whipped around my legs as I pushed Phil aside and ran after Albert, not caring I was leaving my post. I wasn't going to let him go without me, no matter what.

"Oh God, don't take him… He's my best friend. He's my brother," I said, desperately trying to turn the clock back.

"Please bring him back," I yelled, running after him.

SIX

On the 23rd July 1915, just ninety-nine days after we had landed in France, Albert's body was lowered into the ground in the makeshift cemetery behind Hospital Farm. He was seventeen years, twenty-five days old. He should never have seen the horrors he'd seen, none of us should have. We had just been boys wanting to be men, "playing with fire," as Dad would have said, until Albert had paid the ultimate price. What utter fools we had been. Oh Christ, what had we all been doing?

I looked around and felt the veil of peace now surrounding Albert and the makeshift graves of all our boys who were sleeping. I could see the freshly tilled earth where poppies grew creating a resplendent Garden of Eden for them to admire. Albert's war was now over.

With the Chaplin's echoing words of "ashes to ashes, dust to dust," floating on the wind, I left him. The image of his face was firmly imprinted on my mind. I made a silent vow to avenge his death and promised him that one day I would return. I took one last look at the improvised wooden cross hammered into the ground to mark his grave, and went back to my unit. It was then I realised the true anguish his dad would go through, and realised for the first time the fear all parents must experience when they watch for the telegraph man walking down the street with the inevitable telegram from the War Office. Soon, Stephen Seal would experience that horror for himself, when the telegraph man would stop at his door. I imagined his distress, as well as my own parents' torment, and how they must feel believing it was only a matter of time when he would come knocking at their door.

Albert was just one of many to die that day. Major Wilkinson wrote the typical "How sorry I am to have to inform you" letter, and Albert's meagre non-perishable belongings were parcelled up and sent home, no doubt bringing little comfort to his dad. The rest of his stuff, his chocolate, his cigarettes, were given to me to share amongst the others. I put them in my pocket and fingered the cigarettes in the packet. I visualized him smoking them, his soft lips encircling the butt ends, lips that had never really kissed a girl's... lips that had once spoken of future dreams. It was impossible to imagine he'd left me and wouldn't be coming back.

I then wrote the hardest letter ever. I wrote home telling Mam and Dad about Albert's self-sacrificing death, his constant companionship, and how I was going to miss him deeply. I told them it was bureaucratic red-tape which had caused his death, and blamed the Army for his loss, not wanting to admit to any part in it. I tried to reassure them I was fine and would, I hoped, return home soon when I would visit Mr Seal.

SIX

What I didn't tell them was of my intention to fight on to the bitter end, and my resolution to 'get even' for my best friend's death.

As the days came and went, anger festered within me, growing all the time and I gradually started to take risks which I would not otherwise have done. I lost all regard for my own safety and in this new found bravado, earned myself the position of Lance-Corporal, heading small platoons of men into no-man's land, fighting the enemy on his own ground. It was then that I came face to face with my foe for the first time. I saw them as the scum of the earth to be got rid of. Each bullet I fired was for Albert, and then more and more, for the sake of all mankind.

Gradually, I began to distance myself from the rest of my pals. In my quest to avenge, I didn't realise until much later that Pete and Jim had been killed, and Phil and Smithy had been severely wounded. I didn't know where Joe or the others had got to. Maybe they were dead too. I only knew I had to go on. I spent all my time killing the enemy, with this anger welling up inside me, spurring me on to kill more and more, filling me with hate.

My letters home became brief and hardly worth the effort. I didn't even bother to tell them I'd been made up to a Lance Corporal. I wrote without thinking to Alice, telling her I loved her, almost as if I needed to write the words to prove to myself I was still capable of loving, knowing deep down reality said otherwise. The hate burned within me. Secretly, I was terrified my resolve would crumble and I would inevitably fail Albert and all those who had died.

And so, as I automatically wrote the words of love to Alice, without any emotion attached to them, I prayed she never detected how I really felt.

Chapter TWENTY

When brothers agree, no fortress is as strong as their common life.
(Antistheses 444 BC - c. 371 BC)

As time went on, my day to day existence took on a life of its own with me being taken along for the ride. I was no longer in control. I just existed, either in the endless hours of trench warfare, or resting in temporary billets with the smokescreen of pleasure in the local estaminets, singing, laughing, toasting my missing friends, and drowning my thoughts in the up-surging hatred for my enemy. And, just as the days went on, so did the weeks and the months in this place where all dreams were lost. With the hate, came fear. Fear that tore at my insides. Fear that yesterday's sunset would be my last.

Mam continued to write, each time wanting to know when I would be home. Home. God how I wished I was at home and this mindless war was over. She wrote to tell me Matthew was in a second field ambulance hospital somewhere in Gallipoli, with severe trench fever and badly damaged feet, "whatever that is?" she said. She'd immediately posted him some of her knitted socks, blaming herself for mistakenly thinking it was hot out there. I smiled to myself at the lack of comprehension Mam had about such things. None of the family had any idea what lay behind the words they so readily read.

They hadn't heard from Robert, Fred or George. They were all fighting, "somewhere overseas," God knows where. With the worrying snippets of news Mam and Dad heard on the street and read in the newspapers, they desperately prayed for all of us to return home safely again.

She also wrote of Mr Seal, saying he'd lost a lot of weight and that they hardly saw him. As the weeks had gone by, it had become too painful and embarrassing to talk about all of us, who were mercifully still alive, when his precious Albert was dead.

"How can you possibly understand?" he had said to Mam one morning, and Mam had agreed as she had looked at his gaunt face, into his sunken eyes, with their sparkle now gone.

The news of lost loved ones, sons, fathers, husbands and brothers, was now common-place. Almost every household either knew of someone close to them who'd been killed, or had lost a loved one themselves. Even the postman, Mr Rourke, had lost his Granville somewhere near

Ypres, and gradually, it became more and more obvious they all had one thing in common, the impotency of being able to do anything about it.

By November 1915, winter had set in, and my battalion was in reserve at Coppernolle. Major Wilkinson left for London to take command of another battalion and Lieutenant Ousebourne started his duties as Acting Adjutant, waiting for Major Oddie to arrive on the seventh. All of us were involved in laying tramways and erecting huts for our winter quarters.

I heard by chance that my brother George was nearby. He was with the Royal Engineers 118th Railway Construction Company. I managed to get a message to him to tell him about Albert and he sent one back saying Robert, who was with the Durham Lights, had been wounded and shipped back down the line to only about a mile away from where we both were. I hadn't even realised he was in the area.

"'Ere, Sarge, I've heard my brother's copped a blighty, can I go see him? He's just about a mile away. It's quiet here, so I won't be long. What do you reckon eh?"

"Make it snappy then. Tell the battle police I've sent you for some supplies, and you can pick me up some cigs whilst you're at it," he said, feeling particularly generous.

By the time I managed to find Robert, it was too late. He was dead. Company Sergeant Major Robert Henry Jackson, my beloved brother, was dead. Another one to add to the list. He was twenty-seven years old, and had never seen his son. George was with him. When he saw me, we both sobbed, unable to take it in.

"Bloody 'ell! Dead!" I said, intensely overwhelmed by the news.

"Our big brother, dead!" I repeated, hardly believing it. George nodded, also shocked.

"He'd been fighting at Essex Farm, which had taken heavy shelling. Some shrapnel hit him," said George, who'd been told by another lad brought in at the same time.

I kept telling myself I should be grateful he wasn't one of the many to lie in no-man's land suffering a painful lingering death alone, left to rot for days or even weeks, eaten by rats and maggots waiting for his body to be retrieved. At least this way he would be buried with dignity. Little comfort, I knew, but I was thankful all the same.

SIX

We went to collect his belongings and it was then George told me about the French medics not even managing to assess Robert. He'd been tagged in the field, and had been waiting for their help.

"It was only when I grabbed one of the medics to take a look at him, they realised the urgency," uttered George distraught.

"By that time, he was too far gone. He died before anyone could do anything," he continued.

"Did he say anything to you?"

"No. He just squeezed my hand. He knew I was there though. When he looked at me, his eyes said it all. He knew he was going to die and he held on to me for as long as he could before his grip loosened and he finally slipped away," said George, distressed with emotion.

Overwhelming hatred for the French for letting him down engulfed me.

"And that's the thanks he gets for helping them in the war is it? Bloody Jerries! Bloody Frogs!" I said, loathing them all.

George clung on to me, still unable to take it in, and for a while, it was good to be hanging on to each other before each of us had to get back. Time was running out and both of us had to go. I waved to him until he was out of sight, before heading in the opposite direction. It was bitterly cold and I felt sick inside. I told Bill, a chap I'd teamed up with, that if I'd have known sooner I could have been there. Bill had just joined my lot, and his quiet manner reminded me so much of Dad. We had taken to each other the moment we met.

"You couldn't help that," he replied kindly. "He didn't die alone. He was with family," he added, to soften the blow.

I mechanically wrote the date, 10th November, in my pocket diary and drew a small cross on the white paper next to his name, fearful I would lose my mind and forget him.

Two days later, my lot were sent to Essex Farm. I fought like an avenging angel and stood up firing my rifle aimlessly across no man's land, until someone knocked me off my feet into the mud and grime. It was Sarge.

"It should have been me," I sobbed, until all my energy was gone.

"Get a hold of yourself, Jackson," said Sarge, shaking me until I was under some modicum of control.

"Go and get cleaned up, and come back when you're respectable."

I didn't write home to tell them of Robert's death. They would hear that for themselves soon enough. No doubt Gladys would write a simple letter to them with the sad news. Again, I made another promise to myself that, if by some miracle I survived this hell, I'd make damn sure Robert junior would one day know of his father and his bravery.

Eventually, my continuing sporadic manic outbursts caught the attention of a doctor. He'd heard about the death of my brother and came over to me.

"He's with God, now, my son," he reassured me.

I listened politely feeling sorry for this man who still managed to hold onto his faith in the carnage that went on around us. His words held little comfort, and he suspected I was close to breaking point. After a few words with my commanding officer, he immediately ordered me to take two days' sick leave and to come back after I had rested. Before I realised it, I was being escorted by his orderly to a house in Poperinge, called Talbot House. There, I was told, I would get a bath, a complete change of uniform, a hot meal and the chance to sleep in a proper bed. The place was fast becoming known as Toc H, after the signaller's code, a 'home from home,' lads were saying. I'd heard of it, but had never been there.

It had been open only a few weeks, by an Army Chaplain known as "Tubby" Clayton. With his friend, Neville Talbot, they'd converted it from a hop merchant's home into a kind of rest centre, in memory of Neville's brother, Gilbert. Gilbert had been killed a few months ago in a particularly sad situation and this house was in honour of him. It was just a few miles behind the front lines and had been designed to offer a place of respite to all soldiers.

As we drew up outside 43 Rue de l'Hopital, the three storey building looked grand. There was a sign saying 'working man's club' swinging high above the wrought iron doors. The orderly lifted the heavy door knocker and rapped it hard several times. The door was opened by a young girl, which surprised me. She invited me in to the dark interior as if I was expected.

"Com' zist way," she said, in broken English, indicating I should follow her.

The orderly tipped his cap at both of us, and left.

I followed her through the large hallway towards the back of the house, passing a room on the left where a small group of soldiers were having a sing-song around an old piano. She headed towards the back door as if to go out into the garden.

"Don't look surprised, lad," said one of the men reassuringly, as she opened the door and I followed her outside.

She carefully closed the door behind me and hurried down the garden path to a small brick building on the right, which was apparently the bath house. There was an ante-room leading from it, which originally must have been a store room but had been converted into a sort of wash room. In the corner of this room was a charcoal fire, heating buckets of water. By the side wall, an old tin bath had pride of place, underneath a tiny frosted glass window, barely twelve inches wide.

The young, strikingly pretty girl was called Lisette, and she instantly began filling the tin bath with bucketfuls of hot water, indicating that I should bathe, no doubt as part of an essential admittance rule. When the desired water level had been achieved, she gave a soft smile and closed the door, leaving me to enjoy it. I peeled myself out of my uniform and piled it in a heap in the corner on the cold red brick tiled floor. I dipped my toe into the hot water creating ripples on the surface, checking the temperature before gingerly submerging myself fully. The heat slowly warmed through me. I had forgotten what it was like to be engulfed in water up to my neck, and its soporific effect not only washed away the lice which fed constantly from me, but months of pent up anger as well. I remained in the water until it was lukewarm and then hastily dried myself before putting on some clean stuff Lisette had left for me.

It appeared Lisette was a local girl, who occasionally helped out at the house. Normally, someone on the staff would have greeted me, but as they were particularly busy, Lisette had been told to look after me. Now, feeling more relaxed, I heard a small tap on the door. The door slowly opened and a young lad looked in.

"Hello mate," he said quite jovially.

"Left you on your own, eh? Been quite bad has it?"

I nodded.

"Well you're the lucky one tonight. You've got the bed! It's just what the doctor ordered, eh?" he continued, smiling.

"Get the rest of your clean stuff, mate, and I'll take you up."

I picked up my belt and slipped on my boots again and followed him back through the house and upstairs, to where an iron bed regally stood, in what he called the General's room. I thanked him profusely.

"Right then, I'll leave you to it," he said, closing the door behind him.

I stripped off completely and climbed in between the deliciously crisp white linen sheets of this amazing yielding bed, and instantly fell asleep. I didn't register the soft knock on the door later that night, or the face of Tubby which peered around the door frame to see if I was alright, as I slept solidly for twelve hours.

By mid-morning the following day, the sun was streaming in through the window, bathing me in a shaft of sunlight. There was a brisk tap on the door.

"Come in," I shouted, suddenly wide awake.

It was Lisette. She was carrying a large tray with a mug of tea, some freshly baked bread, butter and a small amount of jam. She carefully put it down on the little bed-side table. By now I was quite hungry and quickly started to devour the delights she had brought. I'd never had breakfast in bed before, and it felt decidedly wicked.

"Merci, Lisette," I added, showing off my pigeon French.

"You are welcome," she said in perfect English.

As she left to fetch me a bowl of water to freshen up in, I hastily got up and wrapped a towel around my lower half, conscious that I was naked under the sheet. I had only had just enough time to wrap it around me, when she returned. When she left, I began washing my face and underarms, feeling decidedly wholesome again. It was bliss. Unexpectedly, Lisette returned with my uniform, which had been laundered. She must have retrieved my dirty clothes from where I'd left them in the bath house. She smiled at me as she put them on the side, and just as she was about to leave again, offered to wash my back. Before I could answer, she took the washcloth out of the water, and motioned with her hand for me to turn around.

For the first time in my life, I was shy. Not even Mam had seen me bare-chested since I'd grown up and though the towel still covered my essential parts, I was nevertheless slightly embarrassed. She seemed not to notice my discomfort and matter-of-factly washed my back until it glowed. I closed my eyes savouring the sensation.

The window to the room was slightly ajar and instead of the noise of constant shelling, there was music and laughter, and the sound of people milling around outside enjoying themselves. I couldn't remember the last time I'd heard anyone truly laughing and as a shaft of sunlight glistened on the bowl of water, I forgot there was a war on, and pretended I was at home again by the fire in the kitchen. I could hear Mam singing and my brothers laughing, and smell the pungent smoke from Dad's pipe.

Lost in thought, Lisette began rinsing my back with her bare hands; she massaged my firm muscles, briefly touching the scar on my shoulder where I'd been injured.

"Qu'est-ce que?" she enquired in French.

I told her about the trench blowing up, and about the shrapnel, and about Albert and Robert. She politely listened, only understanding bits of what I was saying, but it didn't matter, she just let me pour it all out until I was suddenly sobbing. As she put her arms around me to comfort me, I clung to her, desperate to feel alive again, and before I knew what I was doing, I was kissing her lips and her neck and pushing her towards the bed. I sensed her reluctance but didn't care. It was only when my towel fell to the floor, that I realised what I was doing.

"Pardon, mademoiselle. Je suis désolé."

I was utterly appalled at my actions, and I turned away to hide my shame and embarrassment. She put her hand on my shoulder.

"No matter, cela ne fait rien... I don't mind, I understand," she gently answered as she left, closing the door behind her.

Ashamed, I quickly finished dressing and made my way downstairs, eager to hide in the midst of other men.

"Hello there, lad. The name's Pettifer. What's yours?"

"Jackson, Sir."

"Have you met Tubby yet?"

"No, Sir."

"'Eee lad, there's no formality here. It's just Pettifer. Come on, follow me and I'll introduce you to Tubby."

The rooms were heaving. Some men were playing cards, others were drinking tea, reading, or writing letters home. The whole place was buzzing with people relaxing and enjoying themselves. We made our way back up the stairs to the first landing again to find Tubby coming out of his room.

"Now then, son, good to see you," he said, as we approached him. He held out his hand to welcome me and shook it vigorously.

"I looked in on you last night, but you were fast asleep. How are you feeling now?"

"Much better, thank you, Sir."

"Oh for goodness sake, call me Tubby, everyone here does," he said, ushering me towards his room.

Above his door was a plaque which proclaimed,

"All rank abandon, ye who enter here."

He followed my eyes as I read it, and carried on to tell me it was a deliberate misprint from the sign above Hell in Dante's "Inferno".

"Not all who see the sign would grasp the reference," he proceeded to say, "but its meaning is clear," he continued, as he proudly told me that all idea of rank, class and background was actually left at the front door.

As we entered his room he went on to explain that the philosophy of the house was to cater for the mind, body and spirit of those who entered.

I briefly thought of Lisette, and instantly realised he didn't mean those bodily needs, and I became conscious that this kind man mustn't be taken too literally as he offered me a drink. We continued to talk about my brothers and home as he brewed up. He told me about the Chapel in the loft of the house where once hops had been dried, and suggested that I might find some comfort there. I nodded in agreement.

"Let's leave this to brew then shall we, whilst I take you up there," he said, now eager to act on my affirmation.

"I'll catch you later, Jackson," said Pettifer, as he left us.

"Yes, thanks," I responded to the retreating figure, as Tubby casually shepherded me through the crowd of soldiers up onto the next floor.

On the landing, we stopped to talk to some Scottish lads who were playing billiards. They were cheerful and chatty.

"Mind the steps lad," said one of them, as Tubby guided me to the left, where a door opened straight onto the narrow staircase, leading up to the Chapel.

The steep steps were difficult to climb in my hobnail boots and I automatically leant forward to crawl up them, using my hands for balance, just like a baby learning to walk. Tubby laughed as he watched me struggle up them.

"It's even worse coming back down. I suggest you come down backwards," he said, warning me.

Slightly puffed, I emerged at the top of the stairs to see that the whole of the hop store area was now one large Chapel.

"It's almost the size of St. Margaret's Church in York," I told him amazed at its size.

"Yes, it's bigger than you think," he said, proudly.

"The makeshift altar, over there, was made from a carpenter's bench which we found in the garden shed. The candlesticks were fashioned out of bedposts," he continued, as he pointed out various aspects of the room.

"And there's the 'groan box,'" he said, merrily using his affectionate name for the portable organ regally placed to the right of the room.

"We acquired the wooden benches from various churches, which were damaged in the area," he continued.

"And the altar cloth was donated."

Tubby beamed, obviously proud of his achievement.

Who would have thought this oak-beamed space at the top of the house could create such a beautiful, simple place to worship in, and become a humbling sanctuary for those in need of respite? He followed me around, telling me about other acquired artefacts in the room, before finally making his way to the top of the stairs again.

"When you're ready, lad, I'll make another brew," he said, now leaving me.

"Stay as long as you want," he shouted, as he clattered down the steps, closing the door at the bottom.

The room suddenly became deathly silent.

SIX

At a loss as to what I should do, I sat down on one of the benches, and closed my eyes, absorbing the tranquillity within this makeshift Chapel, and automatically started to pray to God. With my head in my hands, I could see nothing but death and destruction, dying and decaying bodies, and felt utter despair and sadness at the pointlessness of it all.

"Oh God help me," I cried out, the words now echoing in the void.

God's reply entered my consciousness.

"I am with you always, even unto the ends of the Earth"...

The scene in my head recalled nothing but the 'ends of the Earth'.

"What happens after the ends of the Earth? Where will you be then? Will you still be with me after all the men I've killed and the sins I have committed?" I asked, forlornly.

In the abyss, I waited for God's reply, but there was none. I sat quietly feeling dead inside, as all hope faded. It was then that my eyes caught sight of a small Bible on the bench in front of me. I hadn't noticed it before. Instinctively, I picked it up and blindly opened it, and there was God's answer.

"The Lord shall preserve thee from all evil; he shall preserve thy soul..."

It was then I prayed in earnest. I prayed for Albert and Robert, and all those who had died in this senseless war, and when I was all washed out of emotion, I prayed the rest of us would get home safely.

It was several hours later before I eventually crawled backwards down the stairs, as instructed, into the body of the house again. The house was still teeming with men, and this time, I entered into the spirit of things. The rest of the day passed quickly and after another good night's sleep in the wonderful iron bed, I was reluctant to leave. I'd become almost human again. Somehow, this old house had restored my sanity.

I found Lisette in the kitchen, and said "Goodbye", thanking her for everything she'd done.

"Come back any time," she said shyly, shaking my hand, holding onto it a touch longer than required.

"I will."

We smiled at each other.

"Tubby is upstairs," she said, now embarrassed.

"Thanks."

I rushed up the stairs striding two at a time and headed towards his door, which was open.

"I'm off now, Tubby," I said, stretching out my hand to shake his.

"Good show, ol' lad. You're welcome anytime," he added.

"Thanks for everything."

"Anytime… anytime," he said sincerely, as he headed down the stairs with me to see me off.

Sensing a kind of peace within myself, I went back to my unit, a much calmer person. The last two days had enabled me to gain some composure of myself. When I reported back to my commanding officer, Bill caught sight of me.

"Good to see you back again, mate. You OK?" he said, shaking my hand.

"Yes, I'm fine. It's good to see you too. 'Owt happened whilst I've been away?"

"Nah, just the usual. Here, I've got these for you," he said, handing me a letter from Mam and one from Alice from out of his jacket pocket.

"I've been looking after them for you. Anyway, I'll catch you later," he said, leaving me to read them.

I walked on, looking for a peaceful spot to sit down. I opened Mam's letter first. It was brief, as she'd wanted to get it in the post to me! She told me Matthew had returned to his unit and was now in Egypt at a place called Alexandria. She'd also heard the devastating news of Robert and from what she didn't say, I knew it had hit her hard. Throughout her missive, she continually begged me to come home and hoped it would be before Christmas.

Alice's letter was not as demanding. She wrote of her love for me and the normality of home. I suddenly thought about Lisette and felt guilty that I'd almost betrayed Alice. What a good job I hadn't. Sarge strolled up to me, pushing all thoughts of betrayal from my mind.

"Not long now," he interjected.

"Not long to what Sarge?"

"Not long to the La Belle alliance battle. We'll be moving out in a couple of days' time. No rest for the wicked," he exclaimed, as he sauntered on by.

Only a few weeks had lapsed since Robert's death and yet it had seemed like a lifetime. Work in the trenches had gone on in readiness for our forthcoming attack. The days had been tranquil, which was most unusual for this area and the quiet nights which followed became the lull before the storm, which came all too soon. In no time, we were in position, ready for battle, with the 1/6th West Yorkshires on our left and the 1st Shropshires on our right. Sentries heard the beginning of Jerry's attack. There was a shout, followed by the firing of several coloured rockets, indicating a gas assault had started, and the usual kerfuffle of getting our masks on ensued.

The hiss of escaping gas was distinctly heard as dense white vapour blew across our trenches, driven by the prevailing north easterly wind. A further alarm was raised and an urgent warning sent to headquarters by wire. It was the only wire message to get through, as Jerry subsequently cut our line in the bombardment which followed.

Undeterred, officers sent runners to get further messages through, and despite our company on Canal bank being cut off, Jerry didn't seem to realise this, as they sent only three small parties to continue their attack. We caught them between the lines of our machine gunners and rifle fire. After that, no further advance was made by them, even though they kept up a heavy bombardment all day.

That night, we heard eighty casualties had copped it, largely as a result of the gassing. The stretcher bearers had been brilliant in bringing them in, but because of the large numbers involved, we were all directed to help out. We took most of the casualties to the dressing station on the Canal bank. The ground had been heavily shelled and retrieving all the bodies proved difficult.

For some of us, the after-effects of the gassing continued well into the next day and a further forty men were taken to hospital, suffering from the effects. A few men even showed effects the day after that. I was once again one of the lucky ones. This time only my eyes were affected. This gassing lark was beginning to be a regular thing, and a few days later, new tube helmets were handed out. The big-wigs assured us they would protect us from phosgene gas as well as chlorine. I felt they served only to remind us of the futility of those who'd already died and couldn't help but think about the old adage Mam used to say about 'closing the door after the horse had bolted'.

Early the following morning, another of our lads, a machine gunner, was killed. I'd forgotten it was Christmas Eve, not that it mattered. Men died most mornings whether it was Christmas or not. I didn't know his name, in fact, that's how I preferred it to be. I'd long since reasoned that if you didn't get to know a person, then you couldn't be hurt when they inevitably died. He lasted well really. I heard he'd survived the trenches for several months, which was a rarity. The average life span in the trench was three weeks, so he'd outlived his time. I, and a few others interred him at Essex Farm after dark, and the Chaplin said a few brief words. No one hung around when doing this job, and I tried not to give it another thought, not daring to wonder how his parents would take the news. The Chaplin talked once again of God's everlasting love and I turned away, recalling God's words,

"I am with you always, even unto the ends of the earth."

Had God been with this man I wondered, trying to reconcile such horror with God's so called, everlasting love.

Death was commonplace now. I'd seen more dead bodies and bits of bodies than I could recount. As I watched the early morning sun rise low in the sky, I couldn't help but wonder when it would be my turn. I lit up a cig, crouching down in the trench as I tried to keep warm and noticed under the duckboard two rats mating, which was unusual for this time of year. Maybe they sensed their numbers were dying out as well. It was over in a flash, just like life really. Nothing had changed. War was still war and I remained within its grasp.

Chapter TWENTY-ONE

From the body of one guilty deed,
a thousand ghostly fears and haunting thoughts proceed.
(William Wordsworth 1770 - 1850)

Christmas day was calm. The only present we got from Jerry was one shell, dropped into the dug out company line, which injured a few men. The rest of the day was quiet, probably because they'd suddenly remembered what day it was. By 9pm we were relieved and spent the following day clearing up after the 1/7th West Yorkshires who looked as if they'd had a party, whilst we'd shivered and kept watch.

We heard we were moving out at first light and would be heading to Elverdinghe, from where we would march to Houtkerque, a further six miles on. As we packed up and readied ourselves to move on, we watched another load of fresh lads arriving, eager to fill our shoes. I couldn't help but wonder how many of the poor sods would be alive tomorrow. Instantly, I recalled the face of the stranger on the dock-side whose expression I now comprehended, and just like him, my pity reached out to them.

The journey to Houtkerque was arduous. It rained, just as if someone had turned a tap on. When we arrived, we stayed for twenty-four hours in reasonable billets, before marching on again for Wormhoudt, another six miles on. In the morning it just drizzled but by afternoon, it was raining heavily again. It didn't really matter as marching was preferable to being left standing in several inches of mud, freezing to death, with shells exploding everywhere or worse still, six feet under like Albert and my brother Robert.

As we systematically walked in step, the rain merged with unexpected tears, as thoughts of my brothers kept entering my consciousness. The light was fading as we watched distant shells exploding. Some poor souls were in for it. As the thoughts continued to intrude, I tried to think of pleasanter memories. Robert had been ten years older than me. There'd always been an unwritten rule in our family that older brothers should look after us younger ones. All of my older brothers had looked after me, and when Robert left to get married, I thought the rule wouldn't apply, but I could still hear him saying with sincerity, that no matter what, he'd always be close by. Well, where was he now when I needed him the most?

In my loneliness and misery, I thought of the time when I was eight and all of us were around the old kitchen table eating dinner. Robert had convinced me that Mam's sago pudding needed salt on it. He proceeded to shake the salt-cellar over his pudding and then passed it on to me for me to do the same. I dutifully did, and repeated the action again when he told me it needed more. I eventually discovered that when he'd salted his, he'd had his finger over the end of the salt-cellar, covering the hole and I hadn't noticed. When I came to eat mine, it was vile. How they all laughed! Mam gave him the usual 'ear-hole clip' and told me to get on with it. I struggled to swallow it down amidst muffled sniggers from the rest of my siblings. I later discovered I was not the only one in the family to fall for this prank of his. He laughed about it for years and said I was gullible.

George had had to tell me what that meant. Now, as the wind whipped the rain into a frenzy lashing my face, I could hear Robert still laughing at me and feel the weight of his arm on my shoulder comforting me. I knew my mind was playing tricks with me. I knew he was dead, and yet I could now distinctly feel him with me as I marched on, weighed down by my wet kit. Albert's smiling face was there too, and the three of us trundled along the road together as if on a boy's outing to the local football match, laughing and joking as we used to do. Their voices kept jabbering on and on. I was happy to be with them.

"You alright there, Jackson?" asked Sarge, in response to a manic outburst of laughter from me.

"Yes, sure Sarge, why shouldn't I be?" I replied, shaken from my celestial existence.

We arrived at Wormhoudt, and were billeted there for two weeks before being route marched to Calais. We set out on a bitterly cold January day and travelled seven miles before resting. Our breath gave off billowing clouds of steam as it came in contact with the freezing wind. The landscape was flat and stark, and flakes of snow fluttered and swirled all around confusing the way in front. The cold air froze our noses and numbed our ears. My brain was empty of thoughts and my body moved automatically, desperately trying to generate and retain heat.

The next day, we marched seventeen miles, which brought back fond memories of York. The memories didn't compare to this though, nor to the following day when we walked a further nineteen miles to Calais with not one single man falling out. An achievement to be proud of in winter months, I can tell you.

SIX

I don't really remember much about the next few months. They just seemed to come and go, and before I realised it, 1916 had well and truly dawned and I'd missed it.

On 1st February, we went by train to Amiens and then marched to Ailly sur Somme. By the twelfth, we'd moved on to Martinsart, just north of the town of Albert and there on the twentieth, we went back into front line trenches where we resumed the usual pattern. I slept only in brief moments, dead to the world. I ate, killed others, moved on, spent endless hours living in dug outs and wet trenches. I was rained on with mud and bits of human flesh, which added to the crust covering my skin where lice now lived again. Always waiting, waiting... waiting for fate to take a hand.

I don't remember having my official eighteenth birthday at the end of February, probably because we were under attack at the time. One of those Jerry "rum jar" shells fell at the head of the communications trench, just as one of our platoons was taking over. They all died where only minutes before my platoon had passed. How funny fate was. It seemed to be playing games with me.

The intensely cold weather and heavy snowfall bit at my hands and feet, making movement difficult. We were told to keep moving or we would freeze. The penetrating cold made me tired and I longed to sleep, for in the depths of sleep there was nothingness. One night I even prayed for death, but God didn't hear, and I began to think I'd been right all along. He'd deserted us. It didn't matter now that no one knew the day or the hour, or what we were fighting for. Nothing made sense anymore and in any case, who really cared? Even the bigwigs disregarded our lives as they sent us into these senseless battles.

I vaguely remember Mam sending me another pair of her grey knitted socks, and some chocolate. I think it had been for my birthday. I tried desperately to remember whether Albert had got any for his. In one manic episode I gave him a pair, carefully burying them in the ground, certain he'd find them. As I tried to make sense of it all, I convinced myself I was not mad.

Eventually, we were withdrawn from the line more dead than alive, and spent some time getting refitted and regrouping. Something else was definitely afoot, but none of us knew what. We spent the next four months undergoing more training in preparation for this unknown event. Whatever it was, it was going to be big.

With the misery of the recent battles in Ypres Salient still fresh in my mind, we finally moved on, all of us hoping this unknown destination would be better than the one we were leaving behind. The days were warmer now and as we became more active, so did the lice. I became obsessed with finding them and cracking their plump red bodies between my nails. It was a pastime that whiled away the hours as we waited, waited for the 'big noise' at the top to tell us what to do.

By June 1916, all four territorial battalions were in place for a big offensive that was in the planning. Our unit had been issued with Lewis guns and a proper machine gun company of men. Mam wrote to say Matthew was in Marseilles and that she'd also heard from George and Fred. They too were in France. She proudly wrote to tell me Fred had been awarded a Military Medal and a Certificate of Distinguished Service after he'd apparently held a shell-hole single handedly for two days until his unit could reach him. Not knowing how big the country was, she thought the four of us could meet up with one another and celebrate, especially as he was now a Company Sergeant Major and should be able to pull some strings. I laughed out loud at the thought of him doing this.

"'Ere Sarge, listen to this," and I repeated what Mam had written.

"I bet you can't do what our Fred can," I said, ribbing him.

"Yeh too right I can't. All my strings have been pulled," he joked. "Is your Mam still trying to get you home?"

"Nah, she's given up now I'm of age. She's taken up praying instead," I replied. Sarge laughed.

"Fat lot of good that will do her," said Jock, a big fat lad from Scotland who'd been listening in on our conversation.

"They should have given our Fred the bloody Victoria Cross," I said, as I re-read her letter, feeling a sense of pride wash over me. "Mam's no idea what's entailed in holding a shell-hole single handedly. If she had, she'd be insisting King George himself did the honours to fix the medal on him," I added.

"And so she should. Write and tell her," said Sarge, now winding me up.

A few days later, I had a letter from Alice. In it she wrote about how the display of daffodils on the banks of the City walls had now gone. She wrote of green fields and birds singing, of the knocker-upper signalling the start of the day, and the factory hooter jarringly telling everyone it was time to go home. She asked constantly if I still loved her and thought about her. Her letter seemed to depict a different universe, miles away from here. In my world, I lived from day to day, not knowing if it was my last. God, how I missed her and home!

As the seasons changed, she told me about the old oak tree and how it changed too. At present it was in all its glory, and she was sitting under it writing her letter and dreaming of me. Little did she realise that in solitary moments like these, I too thought of her and the tree, and smelt her perfume on her handkerchief. I took out the now crumpled grubby photograph of her, remembering how she had looked in her red dress, and I desperately wished she was in my arms.

The summer of 1916 was in full bloom, and all of June was a flurry of activity in preparation for this big battle, soon to take place. New roads, camps, tented areas and light railway networks were constructed. By the 20th we were ready, and all four territorial battalions were camped very near to Aveluy Wood, waiting for the battle of Albert to start.

Sarge told us there would be a series of battles along the front line from Belgium to the Swiss border and these would take place simultaneously. The date still had to be determined, but it would be very soon. He collectively referred to it as 'The Battle of the Somme'. Everything would depend on timing, so it was important to be prepared.

Late morning, on 26th June, the Brigade Commander inspected our battalion, and informed us that the forthcoming offensive was now scheduled to take place on 1st July. It was a stirring address and yet it filled me with scepticism and fear.

By the 30th, orders to move forward into trenches in Aveluy Wood were received. The big push was on schedule, and we had to be ready. I felt sick with worry, and a feeling of foreboding descended as we headed into the dark eeriness of the wood. By mid evening, we were in place, and now waited in silence for dawn to break.

It had been some time since our last battle and the sickening remembrance of such things came flooding back. I passed the time away, biting my nails down to the quick. When the stroke of midnight came and went, I remembered I hadn't said "White Rabbits." I knew it was only supposed to be said in months which contained an 'r' in the spelling, but fearing bad luck would come, I said it anyway, just in case. I watched Bill make the sign of the cross, obviously making his peace with God.

SIX

"All the best, lad."

"You too, Bill."

As we waited, the tension mounted. It was going to be a long night.

As the sun rose, peeping over the hilltop bright and fresh, the eerie morning mist to the west lifted like a ghostly blanket being peeled back. It unfolded like a scene from one of Shakespeare's plays. The dawn chorus was now in full throttle, and the tension in the air was tangible. As we waited for the signal, the first warning of things to come interrupted the morning sequence.

It was 7.20am. There was a terrific blast followed by the earth shaking.

"What the bloody hell was that?" Jock whispered.

"Sounds like Hawthorne mine has been blown," said Bill.

"Jesus Christ, that's over five miles away!"

I checked my watch.

"It's gone off ten minutes earlier than it should have, hasn't it? I thought it wasn't due to be blown until two minutes before the whistle?"

Fear now struck each of us. Shivers down my spine set hairs on edge, and I had the sudden desire to empty my bowels. We continued to wait for our attack to begin, quiet as field mice, knowing now Jerry machine gunners would be alerted to our presence.

"The cat's out of the bloody bag for sure, and our cover's bound to have been blown," I whispered to Sarge.

He too looked at his watch.

"What bloody imbecile set the mine off too soon? I don't understand it," he said, also confused.

It seemed like an eternity. All birdsong had stopped. Even the birds sensed the forthcoming danger. Not a sound filled the empty void as we waited. I held onto my guts, squeezing my bottom cheeks together and watched the cornfields gently rippling in the distance as the wind blew through them. The first wave of our men would have to cross those fields and the Jerries would now know they were coming. And then it would be our turn. Oh God, it would be us! "Oh God, help us," I silently prayed.

SIX

At 7.28am, another loud explosion was heard, this time followed by shock waves reverberating through the wood. For a moment, the top layer of woodland lifted away from the ground and then fell back into place again. The mine at Lochnagar had been blown as planned. The blast still echoed in my head and though it was some way away, I automatically ducked down, as the sound continued to echo in my ears.

A message came to hold our position and we continued to wait in support of the first wave due to go over the top any minute. The two minute bombardment started, as we waited for the whistle. The effect of the mines going up was terrifying, and smoke drifted towards the wood filling our nostrils with the smell of cordite. At last, 7.30am heralded the signal we'd all been waiting for, and several blowings of the whistle now pierced the empty void. The piper played the battle tune, and the battle started. We could see our lads scrambling out of the front line trenches into no man's land, and watched in horror as they were shot to pieces before our very eyes.

They simply walked into a hail of bullets as Jerry machine gunners opened fire on them. Then an onslaught of shells rained down on them, fired from way behind the enemy front line. Jerry had been waiting for them, alerted by a full ten minutes, giving them enough time to spur into action, and thwart our element of surprise. As I watched the slaughter, I swore to kill the man who'd given the game away. Amid the bedlam of conflict, we heard the distant wailing of dying men above the piper still playing our battle tune, the sounds carrying on the wind. Lieutenant Colonel Wood gave orders for us and the 1/6th battalion, to move off along the railway embankment. We were to cross the River Ancre by the southern causeway known as the Passerelle de Magenta. From there, we were to take up position in the assembly trenches in Thiepval Wood.

As my platoon moved off, we came under heavy fire from Thiepval. We headed just east of the star cross roads towards the edge of the wood to secure our position on the right, and by 11.30am we were in position ready to follow the others who'd gone over the top before us. I briefly detected the heat of the bodies that had vacated these trenches minutes before, and felt I'd jumped into dead men's shoes. From this position, the view was obscured but the ongoing roar and din of the battle assaulted our ears. We were aware now, that our comrades would not have seen death coming until it was too late.

"This is it," I said, resigning myself to the inevitable.

Fear tore at my insides and my rifle acquired a fine tremor. I wanted to scream out that I was not ready to die and I suppressed the urge by rubbing my face in panic on my rough sleeve, trying to hide my fear from the others. I was desperately frightened of losing my nerve altogether, and I begged God to save me. I entered into a bargain with him, telling him I'd do anything, anything, even become a 'preacher' and preach his word forever, if that's what he wanted, as long as he'd save me.

Despite the sun now blazing down on us, I continued to shiver as we waited for the signal, all the while on tenter-hooks. By 2.30pm we were still there and I kept looking around, confused. Something was amiss.

"What's going on?" I whispered to Sarge, as he crawled along the line.

"God knows. I've got no bloody idea. Just wait for it Jackson, that's what we do, wait. Wait until we get the signal, OK?" he replied tersely.

The strain was beginning to tell on old Pickles too, as he shuffled along the line trying to calm others, telling them to wait for the signal. And so we continued to wait, and wait... Eventually, we received a message, ordering each of the battalions to send out an officer's patrol to do a recce, with a view of attacking Thiepval village itself. Selfishly, I again prayed to God it wouldn't be my platoon to do the job, and mercifully, it wasn't.

New battle plans were sent to Sarge, with orders to attack the village from the west at exactly 4pm, after a preliminary bombardment had taken place. The time was already 3.30pm, so there wasn't much time to consult with any other company commanders or N.C.O's, as we prepared ourselves once again to go over the top, just as we had done since dawn.

The reconnoitring patrols still hadn't returned, and all of us now knew the first wave of attack had failed. It was obvious Thiepval village had not fallen as envisaged, and so would have to be captured. Sarge quickly gave orders for us to attack from the right, the 1/6th battalion from the left, 1/8th in support and 1/7th in reserve. The frontal attack would be across six hundred yards, split between us and the 1/6th battalion.

The guns prepared our way, toppling a few buildings on the edge of the village. Several howitzer shells fell into enemy trenches but unbeknown to us, the Jerries had dug themselves in deep and had only suffered a few casualties. For some reason, the signal to my battalion to go over the top was unavoidably delayed, and so at 4pm when the guns stopped, the 1/6th battalion went without us. By the time our signal came and the whistle blew, my legs were like jelly and momentarily refused to move.

There was no turning back now, I thought, as we all started to scrabble out of the trench. Our own MP's pointed guns at our backs, waving them menacingly. None of us had any choice but to go forward as the 1/6th had done. This was it, and I wondered what the grim reaper would look like, as I prepared myself to do battle and meet him head on. Finally, with all the other poor sods, we reached the top of the parapet and onto the edge of no man's land. At long last, we'd gone over the top and were running…

In front of me was a drifting curtain of smoke from the remains of our bombardment. The 1/6th were way ahead of us having long since entered this eerie mist. It wasn't until I'd gone some way across no-man's land, dodging machine gun fire, and stepping over bodies, that I realised they were dead.

As the smoke lifted, the awareness of this spectacle began to filter through to those in charge. Suddenly, the whistle blew loudly, signalling a retreat. It was music to our ears. Not hesitating, those who could turned-tail, running frantically back to the safety of the trench, with the reaper running after us.

Bullets whistled all around me, as I ran in a zigzag pattern to avoid the Jerry machine gunners' aim. I flung myself back over the parapet, and nose-dived into the trench with others falling on top of me. My heart was thumping loudly, drumming in my ears as if it would explode with fright. Breathing heavily, I realised I'd out-run death. There was great confusion. We quickly collected ourselves together, and were told to immediately retreat up towards the Schwaben Redoubt to consolidate. Instantly, we started to head up there, with fear still pumping through our veins. When we arrived, three companies of the 1/7th battalion were also there. God knows what had happened to the battle plan, but it was chaos.

It later turned out that the 1/6th battalion had been the only battalion from the 146th Infantry brigade to fully carry out their orders. It was now clear the whole thing had been doomed from the start and almost all of the 1/6th battalion, some thousand men, had been wiped off the face of the earth. No-one knew how many others had been killed but the numbers missing were staggering.

SIX

As a cloak of darkness descended, we quickly moved up to Johnstone's post, amid a baying on the wind that became unbearable. Wherever we looked, there were hundreds of brown shapes, some writhing or moaning, some delirious and others just deathly still. As the battle waned, the Chaplin bravely crawled amongst the corpses, giving God's final blessing as he made the sign of the cross over their remains.

That night, rumours were rife as to what had gone on. It was thought over a hundred officers and about three thousand soldiers had been fatally wounded in this small area alone, lying somewhere amid the area now surrounding me. When dawn broke and stole across the sky, I saw for myself the rumours were true. My platoon, and several others, continued to hold the Redoubt with Lieutenant Colonel Wood and Major Thompson in the stronghold. The rest of the battalion centred on Johnstone's post.

We sustained further losses under heavy shell fire the following day. Four more officers were killed along with several other soldiers, and many more were wounded. The shells and the bullets tore at my clothing and splattered me in debris, but by some miracle, I remained alive. It didn't take me long to realise though, that being alive, came with another price. With the scene of death and destruction all around me, the cost of my pact with God included the burden of self-recrimination, loathing, guilt, and hatred of myself at killing others.

Every time I shut my eyes, I could see the charge of our men in the cornfields to the west of me, blinded by the sun's dazzle, simply walking straight into a line of German machine guns belting out their loads, cutting them down like scythes slicing wheat. Echoing in my mind was the horror that, "the Germans knew we were coming. They were ready and waiting for us." In my head, I could still hear the cries of the dying as they fell amid the noise of war. They didn't stand a chance. So many lives lost… so many still lying, waiting to be collected.

A haunting wind now gently blew amongst my platoon, as if the dead were acknowledging our presence. The guilt of being alive weighed heavy upon me. It was like a brick around my neck, a testament to my betrayal of them. It was then I prayed to God to let me die too, but he was no longer listening.

We had to leave the dead in the grotesque positions where they had fallen until it was safe to bring them in. They rotted amongst the cornfields, their blood fertilizing the ground. The Chaplin continued to creep amongst them, searching for the living amid the sea of bodies before us, but he found none. The stretcher bearers retrieved what men they could, under the continual assault from snipers. In contrast, the warm sun caressed my face, as we followed orders to walk back towards the assembly trenches in Aveluy Wood to regroup again and rest awhile. I was so tired.

As the sound of battle diminished, Summer resumed its relentless tune, punctuating the now silent breeze, as if nothing had happened. I felt the ghosts of our lads walk back with me, chiding me for my deceitfulness. Yes, God had answered my prayers and saved me, but I lowered my head in shame, as if I'd made a pact with the devil instead.

Chapter TWENTY-TWO

*It is better to decide a difference between enemies than friends, for one of our friends will certainly become an enemy, and one of our enemies, a friend
(Bias of Priene c. 566 BC)*

That night I got drunk and in my drunken stupor sang…

"I want to go home, I want to go home, I don't want to go in the trenches no more, where whiz-bangs and shrapnel they whistle and roar…"

And as I sang, the words became slurred and intermingled with,

"The bells of hell go ting-a-ling-ling, for you but not for me,"

followed by manic bouts of laughter, and heaving bouts of vomit, before drifting into unconsciousness, and being carted unceremoniously back to camp to sleep it off.

By 7th of July, my battalion moved forward to hold the front line of the Salient once more. I was told we had to hold it "at all costs." As we repaired the front line trenches and entered into spasmodic skirmishes with our enemy, we held our position with grand obstinacy. "The cost," was twelve more dead soldiers and at least fifty more wounded, but so what, we were just numbers to the bureaucrats who knew nothing of what they asked. After a while we stopped counting the dead and wounded, and started counting those still left.

In less than a month, we had only twenty officers and four hundred and thirty-eight men left in my battalion, out of the thousand we had had when we first arrived in France. And, over half of these were replacements from other units, being not part of the original number. Only God knew exactly how many of us were left from that initial voyage across the sea, when we had been full of spirit and excitement. The thought horrified me, and I wondered if anybody else was keeping count.

On 3rd August, after further engagements with the enemy, and little ground being taken, we went into reserve for a well earned rest. We were totally done in. I wrote several long letters home and tried to do normal things to take away all thoughts of war. As the days wore on, we swam in a shallow bomb crater and sun-bathed on its banks, just a few miles away from the horrors that still continued. I watched children playing nearby. They stood in awe of us. One brave soul, a little girl, came wandering up to me.

"Je suis Marie-Claire," she said, and held out her hand for me to shake it. In a grand show of manliness, I gently held her hand in mine and kissed it.

"Bonjour ma petite. Je suis John."

She couldn't have been more than seven or eight, and had the same haunting expression I'd first seen in Alice. Just as suddenly as she had appeared, she disappeared, hiding behind the shadows of a tree, giggling. Her friends congratulated her on her bravery and I smiled, remembering children at home.

The rest period turned into twenty-three days of near normality, with long summer days and cool summer nights. It was during this time that fraternising with the local girls became a regular thing. Several of my bedfellows could be seen swapping cigarettes for 'French letters' in their eagerness to indulge in such delights. I knew it wouldn't be long before the horrors of war would summon us, so who could blame them.

"Life's too short," said Jock, tapping me on the shoulder. "You should make the most of it," he advised.

"Yeh… sure… thanks for that," I laughed, agreeing.

I couldn't help but wonder about the consequences of their actions, and immediately thought of Alice. Bill reckoned the army had ran out of "number nine" (bromide), and now the local girls would cop the consequences of such folly. Being a married man, he wasn't interested in having sex with anyone other than his ol' lass. I wasn't interested in it either, though secretly I was concerned as to why not, after all, I wasn't married. I remembered a time when sex had always been on my mind, especially when I was with Alice. Maybe there was something wrong with me.

"Hey Bill, do you reckon it's normal not to be interested in the local girls?"

"Sure lad. It's not the be-all and end-all of everything. Don't worry about it. Being faithful to your Alice is probably blocking your interest," he said reassuringly.

"Yeh, you're probably right."

Both of us relaxed, enjoying the moment. He offered me a cigarette and we smoked together in silence, each of us deep in thought as we waited for the front line trenches to call us back once more.

It rained heavily as our orders came through to repair and hold the line before making another attack on the now, almost unrecognisable heap of rubble, called Thiepval. It had once been a pretty village, with a meandering main street through its centre, normally full of French families going about their business. With the advance of the German Army, everyone had upped and left in a panic to get away. It was now our turn, to oust the Germans out of their secure position, and give it back to the villagers, for what it was worth.

We took up positions on 3rd of September, at ten past five in the morning. My 'D' company crossed the Ancre without incident, but as the hours went on, the impetus of our attack slowed due to fighting for a small footing in the enemy's trenches, which completely shattered us. Unfortunately, the fullness of our attack failed like everything else, and we spent the rest of the month precariously clinging onto this small gain. It wasn't until the 26th, that Thiepval was eventually captured, but not by us, by the 54th infantry.

After that, we managed to turn our small gain into securing the whole of the front line boundary. The assault still took us nearly thirty hours, and fierce hand to hand fighting, to fully acquire it and transform it into the stronghold needed to protect the newly captured village, but we did it. In all that time we went without food or water. Then I got an unexpected 'blighty' which knocked me off my feet.

There was so much confusion. I was impaled through the leg by a Jerry who seemed to appear from nowhere. As he lunged forward, his bayonet plunged into my thigh. He twisted it upwards, slicing away at skin and muscle, trying to do the most damage, before he was stopped by a shell. His body took the full force of the blow, protecting me, as his right arm and part of his right leg were blown off. The force of the blast propelled me backwards and he landed on top of me, his bayonet end still embedded in my now open thigh. For a moment, we lay there together, stunned, until I managed to push him off me, whereupon he rolled over onto his back. Both of us were now looking directly up into a dreamlike smoky blue sky. Ironically, his attempt to kill me had actually saved me.

He yelled out in pain, momentarily closing his eyes. Through clenched teeth, he asked me in almost perfect English how badly he was hurt. I didn't have the heart to tell him that even if he was picked up in this instant, his label would still have "no" written on it.

As the fighting moved forwards, leaving us behind, only muffled noises now prevailed. I looked across at him, checking to see that he couldn't do any further harm, and then lit up a woodbine and placed it between his lips. He drew deeply on it, before realising his right arm had been blown away, and looking at me in horror, he screamed out, terrified at what he'd found. I tried calming him, telling him help was on its way, and together we talked about the futility of war, his fatherland, and home.

Time took on its own reality and the hours passed as if in no rush, and with it came the startling revelation that the enemy was human after all, with feelings and dreams, just like me. He was a country bumpkin and had come from a small village called Durnbach. His name was Schmidt.

"Ich bin Schmidt," he kept repeating proudly, followed by a whispered pitiful plea, "Ich sterbe, helfen Sie mir," as he lapsed in and out of consciousness.

"Come on, Schmidt, tell me more," I kept saying, tugging at his jacket to keep him awake and with me.

He was eighteen, the youngest of nine, and had hoped one day to work with horses. We talked of his sisters and older brothers and as we talked, I realised he had a family who cared. We lay together for several hours, impotent to do anything else, until he finally closed his eyes for good.

As dusk fell, I resigned myself to the same fate feeling no pain, no regrets, nothing. I watched the sun go down and absorbed the last remnants of its heat, as I closed my eyes. Sleep came easily and I drifted in and out of it amidst muffled calls for help. I thought the noise came from afar, but the cry came from me, as I waited for death to come.

"'Ere, Pete, there's one 'ere still breathing."

I looked up, and silhouetted against the moonlit sky were two dark shapes. At first I was unsure where I was, and as they started to move me, I screamed out. The bayonet end twisted in the wound, sending waves of pain down my leg. One of them placed a rifle under the top part of my legs and lifted, creating a kind of seat under me, so they could pick me up. They then sat me forward and placed their shoulders under my armpits and clasped their hands together behind my back, forming a kind of back rest. This makeshift stretcher chair enabled them to get me out of harm's way quickly. Unfortunately, the slightest movement caused me to yell out in pain again.

"Put a sock in it, mate, or we'll have the whole bloody Jerry army onto us."

With that, a flare was fired, lighting the whole battlefield area up. Instantly we fell to the ground.

"Don't move a muscle, sunshine, or we're done for," whispered one of my rescuers, as he jabbed me with some morphine.

I gritted my teeth and lapsed into unconsciousness. It was some time before I regained consciousness again. The doctor told me that the stretcher bearers had to wait until the flare had died away, before they could carry me back down the line into our own trenches.

From there, I was quickly moved further back, buffeted by the higgledy-piggledy movements of my stretcher bearer friends as they balanced me precariously between them. I eventually ended up in the confines of a makeshift bunker, which doubled up as a dressing station. I vaguely remember someone putting a tourniquet around my thigh and jabbing me again. Within what seemed to be minutes, I was being bundled onto a proper stretcher and taken further away from the front to the nearest casualty clearing station.

"Good luck mate," someone uttered, as I was whisked away.

Amidst a haze of smelly antiseptic and strong narcotics, the damage to my leg was surveyed. The main part of the thigh, its muscles and tendons, had been sliced away from the bone by the bayonet and I'd lost a lot of blood. The bone had been chipped and a slither of it had embedded itself in the surrounding soft tissue. Apart from that, I'd live, or so they said, after they'd sewed everything back together again. I was in no hurry to prove them right and after being transferred to another hospital near the coast, I wallowed pathetically for many weeks, waiting for the muscles and tendons to knit back together again.

It was a slow process, but the leg gradually healed, and I started to hobble around using a stick. It was going to be some time before I would be fit again for duty, but they assured me they'd get me back to my unit as good as new. The longer it was, the more I began to fear the thought of returning, and I started praying again. It's funny how my relationship with God was a part-time one and once again, I heard Mam's voice telling me I should be ashamed of myself.

It was several more weeks before I mustered up some energy to write home, telling them I'd been wounded, but was safe. When Alice's reply got through to me, she wondered if they would send me home for good. I wrote to say I doubted it very much, but would ask them if I could have a few weeks convalescing instead.

By some miracle, my request for leave was granted and arrangements were made to transfer me to Edmonton Military Hospital in England. From there, I could go home on two weeks' leave. I didn't argue with their decision and quickly started pestering them to parcel me up and ship me out as soon as possible. Sure enough, a few days' later, in the last week of November, I was loaded onto the SS Denis, and was at last on my way home.

After an initial assessment at Edmonton they released me, advising me to report back in two weeks' time for a final medical check-up. If all was well, I'd be sent back to my unit. Feeling much better, I began to feel guilty. I tried justifying the ache in my leg, as ample good reason for two weeks off, but these feelings kept persisting, probably because I didn't want to go back.

When I reached Edmonton railway station, memories of my railway life came flooding back and with pent up excitement, I headed for my train, determined now to make the most of my leave. I savoured the smell and taste of the smoke billowing from waiting trains. The engine smoke trapped by the skylights above, swirled downwards and for a brief moment engulfed me. Forgetting that my lungs had been exposed to Jerry gas, I inhaled the familiar smell deeply, and ended up coughing my guts out, almost choking on it.

"All aboard. Come on now, Sir, we haven't got all day. There's a war on you know," said the guardsman.

I limped on board the 11.10am train to York. I was at last going home. I had with me a small kit bag of clothes and a walking stick which had become my trusted aid. The clickety-click of the train, and the lurching from side to side as we hurtled along, made me feel a boy again, and I started to play the old familiar childhood game of counting how many rabbits I could see on the journey. As we passed fields, covered in a crisp white heavy frost, and familiar named towns along the way, my eyes grew tired, and I drifted off into a dreamless sleep.

Before I knew it, the train was pulling slowly into York station. I heard the guardsman opening carriage doors, and shouting, even though the train was still moving.

SIX

"York Station… This is York Station everyone."

When the train finally stopped, I hurriedly made my way onto the platform and stood awhile, buffeted by others now desperately trying to get on.

"All aboard for Darlington. This train is going to Darlington. All aboard," the guardsman bellowed at the top of his voice.

I listened to the familiar sounds of carriage doors slamming behind everyone, and heard the guard's double whistle signalling the driver to pull away. For a moment, I became confused, and suddenly found myself at the front line, scrambling over the top into no-mans-land, running blindly into a hail of bullets that went straight through me.

"You alright lad?" asked a stranger, who caught hold of me as I crumpled like a frightened child to the ground.

When the whistle blew again, my disorientation receded.

"Ye..ye..ye…yes, yes I think so, thank you. Yes, I'm ok. My leg just gave way, that's all."

I was unsure of what had actually happened. I smoothed my uniform back into place, just to make sure I was in one piece, and still somewhat dazed, I felt for the holes where I thought bullets had passed through me only minutes before. Sweat poured from me.

The stranger helped me up and handed me my stick, which had fallen some way away. I was quite shaken by my vision and stood still to regain my composure, before slowly moving off towards the station exit. Still disturbed, I decided to walk home rather than wait for a tram, hoping the fresh air might clear my head. It took me well over an hour to hobble the short distance from the station and I had to keep stopping as my leg ached continuously, but at least it took my mind off things. By the time I'd turned into Brunswick Street and steadily limped past Albert's house, with my head turned away, I was buggered. I hoped Mr Seal hadn't seen me. I couldn't face him just yet. I needed more time to work up to that ordeal.

Fortunately, the street was deserted as I slipped into the back alley and opened the familiar creaking back gate. As usual, the kitchen door was off the latch and I crept in. I was home at last. I looked around noting the remains of dirty tea pots still on the table.

"Anyone home?" I shouted.

SIX

Mam came rushing through the door and gasped, as if seeing a ghost.

"Oh my Lord, you're here, you're home," she uttered disbelievingly, almost knocking me off my feet as she rushed up to me.

Hugging me tightly, she burst into tears. Now, enveloped in her ample body, my own resolve crumpled, and I became a child once more, sobbing in her arms, wanting her to make everything better. The noise and commotion brought in Dad, Charlie and Wilf. They stared at the spectacle before them. I turned away quickly, rubbing my face with the back of my hand, as Dad came towards me. He patted me on the shoulder pleased to see me, noting how gaunt I looked, as I continued to brush away further escaping tears. Getting a grip on myself, I then turned to face my brothers, smiling.

"Killed any Jerries yet?" said the ever-questioning Wilf.

Chapter TWENTY-THREE

Difficult as it is really to listen to someone in affliction,
it is just as difficult for him to know that compassion is listening to him.
(Simone Weil 1909 - 1943)

It was just short of two years since I'd last been home. Mam had put on a bit of weight, and Dad had lost a bit more hair on top, but otherwise, they were just the same. Charlie had lost his roundness and Wilf had grown several inches taller. Both now towered above me. I couldn't believe how grown up they'd become. I'd forgotten Charlie was fifteen and Wilf almost thirteen.

"Well… have you killed any?" pestered Wilf.

He hadn't changed. He was still the one wanting to know all the gory details of war, and only thought of the excitement, as I once had.

"Leave him alone now Wilf. He's just got in and doesn't need you to harass him. He's probably had enough of that, eh son?" remarked Dad, who looked on worried at my state of health.

I turned to Wilf and with a wry smile, punched his shoulder.

"Yeh, lots."

"Wow!" he replied in awe, and with that, he shot out of the kitchen pretending to shoot Germans as he disappeared.

"One thing's for sure, he hasn't changed," I remarked to the three faces now staring at me.

"You've lost some weight, son," said Mam concerned.

"Have you been eating ok? Do you want something now?"

"No, thanks Mam, I'm alright. I just need some rest, that's all. It's been a long day," I replied, rubbing my aching leg.

Dad got out his pipe and lit up as Mam put a cup of tea in front of me. I savoured each mouthful. I'd forgotten what a real cup of Yorkshire tea tasted like, and my taste-buds responded appreciatively.

"Is there another in the pot?" I asked, unable to resist.

As Mam fussed around me, the kitchen grew progressively quiet. It was as if no one dared to ask about the war. In the end, the silence itself spoke volumes. Only the loud ticking noise from the grandfather clock in the hall punctuated the atmosphere, comforting our thoughts. I was home, and I felt as though a great load had been lifted from me. Mam decided that whilst there was hot water on the boil, she'd put a hot pan in my bed to warm it through. She thought I'd feel better after a good night's rest.

Not long after, she chivvied me up to bed, treating me like a child again. As I made my way up the stairs, Wilf was busily moving his things to make room for me. He'd been sleeping in my bed and was now grudgingly doubling up with Charlie again, just as he'd done before I'd left.

"Now, no troubling our John, you boys… let him get a good night's sleep," she said, as she left us all to it.

It was just like old times, all of us squashed into the one room. There were a few groans from Charlie, as Wilf pushed him over, and I methodically stripped down to my vest and underpants, and slipped between the crisp cotton sheets. Without any thought of putting a nightshirt on, I instantly fell asleep.

In my dreams, I was running, running through no-man's land, running endlessly towards nothingness. Every direction I took, a shell blew up causing the ground to disappear. All the while, I kept running, changing my path, until there was nowhere else to run and I was standing on the edge of a precipice with fire and damnation below me. In the end, some faceless bureaucrat with a gun, ordered me to jump. Seeing no way out, I stepped off the ledge, as the ground behind me gave way. I screamed and desperately clung on to bits of bodies and floating limbs, in a futile attempt to save myself. The blankets, now completely encasing me at the bottom of my bed, wrapped around me. It took all of Charlie and Wilf's strength to release me from their grip, allowing me to breathe once again.

Sweat was pouring off me, as Dad rushed in to see what all the commotion was about.

"It's ok, Dad, he's just been dreaming," said Charlie, as he patted my shoulder and told me to go back to sleep.

I didn't say anything. I lay there for hours, panic stricken, not daring to shut my eyes for fear the earth would swallow me up again and the disembowelled bits of bodies would come to get me, just like the bogie man would if I wasn't good.

SIX

I could hear faint whispers from Charlie and Wilf, though I couldn't make out what they were saying, and as daylight dawned, I fell back into a deep sleep. Everyone was up, dressed, and gone, by the time I got out of bed. Dad had left early for work, and Wilf had gone to school. I heard the back door slam as Charlie hurried to his ticket collector job on the railways. I came down the stairs to find Mam clearing away the breakfast pots. The kitchen was lovely and warm, but from the ice on the window, I realised it was bitterly cold outside, and began to think of the poor sods shivering in no-man's-land.

"The water's hot. Shall I get the tin bath and put it in front of the fire?" she asked.

"No, not today, Mam. I'll just scrub up in the outhouse for now."

"Well, wrap yourself up, there's a nip in the air."

By the time I'd had a strip wash and put on my old working clothes, I felt like a fish out of water. I'd been so used to the army routine that I now didn't know what to do.

"Sit there awhile," Mam said, as if detecting my unease, as she handed me a large mug of tea.

"Do you fancy some bread and dripping?"

"Yes, sure, anything," I replied.

By the time Wilf got in from school later in the day, the whole street knew I was home. He'd been blabbing. I should have told him not to let on for a while, but it was too late. In his excitement at having me home again, he'd told all who knew me and also made it his business to get a message to Alice to tell her as well.

"She says she'll see you tomorrow dinner outside Rowntrees," he continued, proud of his interference.

Mam clipped him one and told him he'd no business saying or arranging anything. I reassured her it was fine and she scowled as she continued to busy herself.

"When will you go to see Mr Seal?" she nonchalantly asked.

At the very mention of his name, I felt sick. The thought of having to see him and tell him what had happened, turned a knot inside me, but I knew it was something that had to be done and the sooner the better.

"I don't know, possibly tomorrow... yes, I'll go tomorrow."

SIX

That night, the dreams and sweats returned.

"Get him off, get him off me," I screamed, as once again, Charlie shook me awake, and then seeing the fear in my eyes, got into bed and held on to me.

I clung onto him as his strong arms encircled me. Wilf stood wide eyed wondering what was going on.

"Go back to bed, Wilf," said Charlie, with a flick of his head towards the bed.

From the shadows on the landing, I heard Mam say she was going to talk to old Dr Jones tomorrow, and then heard the click of their bedroom door as they went back to bed and I drifted into a more settled sleep.

In the morning, Charlie carefully disentangled himself from me, and crept out of bed, as I feigned sleep, embarrassed. I waited until everyone had left the house before rising. I couldn't cope with any more questions, especially from Wilf. Dressing as quickly as I could, I made my way to the wash house whilst Mam was upstairs, making her bed. It didn't take me long and just as I came through the back door and picked up my jacket and scarf to go out, she entered the kitchen.

"You're not going out without having a drink nor any breakfast, are you son?" she hastily asked.

"I'm sorry, Mam, but I'm going to see Mr Seal. I'll be back shortly. In any case, I couldn't eat a thing. I feel a bit queasy this morning. I think I might be sickening for something... so I'd better go now before it gets any worse."

Mam let me go without saying another word, obviously still concerned about me as she filled the kettle.

I put the collar of my coat up and hunched my shoulders high to cover as much of my neck as I could. The cold morning air hit me once again. It was a real pea-souper of a morning. Fog seeped into my bones and froze me to the core. There'd been many mornings like this in the trenches. As I headed towards the Seals' house, I could hardly see three feet in front of me. The eerie mist reminded me of the swirling smoke on the battlefields and I looked down expecting to see dead bodies under foot. I walked slowly in case I tripped over them, but this time, I saw only the dirt track of the back alley as I approached Albert's back door. I could just make out Mr Seal in the kitchen. He had lost a lot of weight. I raised my hand to knock and then instantly got cold feet. I couldn't face him and started to retreat out of the yard, as the gate opened behind me.

"Hello, John. I heard you were home."

I nearly jumped out of my skin as I turned to see Albert's sister all muffled up in her fur hat and scarf. There was no turning back now. With her hand on my shoulder, she guided me towards the door.

"Look who's here, Dad," she said, as we entered.

I took my cap off and held it in my hand, as I stood rooted to the spot.

"Well I'll be…Come in, come in… Sit down, lad," uttered Mr Seal, as he held out his hand to shake mine and directed me towards the chair he'd just pulled out. He appeared to be glad to see me.

"Put kettle on lass and make us a cuppa," he ordered, sitting down next to me.

"We heard you were home. Is it for long?" Mr Seal asked politely.

"Just two weeks, that's all," I answered nervously.

"We heard about Robert. Tell yer Mam and Dad I was sorry to hear about him," he continued, as his eyes saddened.

"Yes, I will. I'm sure they'd love to see you anytime you're passing, but I'll pass the message on," I replied.

There was an awkward silence as Mr Seal waited for the kettle to boil and I felt distinctly uncomfortable.

"The newspapers keep saying war'll be over soon. What do you think?" he asked.

For a minute, my mind went blank. I had no idea what to say. He now looked at me more intently.

"Er, it's difficult to know. They've been saying it'll be over for long enough and yet it seems to be never ending," I stuttered.

He nodded, agreeing with me.

As the kettle boiled, it whistled loudly. Albert's sister took it off the heat, turning quickly to fill the teapot up, just as I lifted my arm across my head to protect myself from the shell exploding in my face. For a split second, I was back in no-mans-land amid whistles and shells and a ground that was blowing up all around me.

The look of terror on my face said it all, and she instantly stepped back, shocked, as Mr Seal reassuringly tapped me on my shoulder.

"Its ok, son, we understand. Bad out there, was it?" I nodded, now distressed as tears threatened to spill over. I quickly stood up to hide my embarrassment, knocking the chair backwards with an almighty clatter.

"Sorry, I shouldn't have come. I just wanted to tell you Albert didn't suffer. He died quickly, without any pain or suffering. He died in my arms. He didn't even know what had hit him. I'm really really sorry… we just joined up for a lark. We wanted to prove something to ourselves. We were stupid, and now he's dead…he's gone…and it's all my fault…"

The pent up feelings came tumbling out in a torrent of words, as unchecked tears streamed down my face. I kept hastily wiping them away on my sleeve, and quickly headed for the door. Mr Seal stood up, barring my way, stopping me in my tracks, and wrapping his arms about me, he sobbed too.

"It's ok, John. Albert knew what he was doing. He was just as responsible for his actions. Thanks for coming to tell us. It couldn't have been easy for you. We do appreciate you calling."

As I regained my composure, Mr Seal encouraged me to sit down again and we continued to talk about Albert and what had been happening at home. I drank my tea with shaking hands, unable to look him in the eyes. The after effects of the ordeal left me with the jitters. I couldn't understand why I was having these flashbacks. After all, I'd been away from the front line for some time now.

"Shock." That's what old Dr Jones told my Mam when she'd gone hot-foot to see him, after I'd left the house.

"Keep him warm and quiet. Give him plenty of hot drinks and he'll be fine," he'd reassured her.

As I got up to leave Albert's house, his sister gave me a brief kiss on the cheek and Mr Seal shook my hand again, thanking me once more for coming to see them. He said I would be welcome anytime. I thanked them both and headed for home, my limp more pronounced than usual and by the time I reached the back kitchen door, I was washed out with the strain of it all.

"How did it go?" Mam asked, concerned.

"It was bloody awful. I can't put it right. I don't know what else to do. It was strange not seeing Albert there, and inside of me there's this big hole where he's gone and left me," I uttered in despair.

She gave me a brief hug, and as I sat down, she kissed the top of my head and smoothed my hair into place with her hand, just as she always did when I was troubled.

"It's ok, son, I understand," she replied.

From the wistful tone in her voice, I remembered Robert and my other brothers. We hadn't spoken of Robert's death and in the sickening reality of Albert's death, I'd almost forgotten about him. It was Albert's death that haunted me the most. It was Albert's angelic eyes which had stared vacantly up at my face, as death had carried him away.

Mam left me sitting by the range, and as the warmth from it seeped through me, I dozed off. I stirred at ten minutes to twelve, and slowly got up to put my hat and coat on again in order to meet Alice. Mam sighed as she saw me getting ready. I rubbed my leg which was playing up a bit and decided to catch a tram at the end of the street to take me the short distant to Rowntrees. I didn't have to wait long. The fog had lifted slightly and as the tram made good progress, I was there in no time. As it rumbled to a stop a few yards away from the iron entrance gates to the old chocolate factory, I could see her anxiously waiting for me.

Her face lit up when she caught sight of me descending the deep steps of the tram, giving me one of the loveliest smiles ever, as our eyes met. Her thick long dark hair was neatly piled up on the top of her head, leaving a few wayward wisps to frame her face. The sleeves of her blouse were rolled up and she was still wearing the large bibbed-apron she wore at work, almost as if she'd just popped out to see if she could find me. Her long skirt looked cumbersome underneath the apron, as she ran towards me.

"It's good to see you John," she said, eagerly grasping my hands in hers, before flinging her arms around me.

"I've missed you."

"Oh Alice, I've missed you too," I said, as I lifted her face up to mine and shyly kissed her soft yielding lips.

I kissed them again, and again, each time more urgently as if needing to prove I wasn't dreaming. Reluctantly, she turned away.

"I shan't be long… I've got the afternoon off. I'll just go and change and I'll be back in two ticks. Don't move…" she said, as if wanting to capture the moment forever.

True to her word, she was back within minutes, flushed with rushing. Her apron was now gone, her sleeves neatly buttoned at her wrists and her long hair flowing in curls behind her. She dragged her hat and coat in her wake. I'd forgotten how beautiful she was and as I watched her, I realised she was no longer a young girl but a woman in full bloom, and she was lovely.

We spent the whole afternoon in Lendal's teashop with a cup of tea and a toasted teacake each, much to the despair of the waitress who after three hours, was keen to clear away the table for someone else to use. We chatted about family and friends, and who was doing what and where. It was just as though we'd never been apart. At one stage, I tried telling her about Albert and all the others, but noting the difficulty I was having, she gently put her hand on mine.

"Don't blame yourself, John. Albert knew what he was doing. We both loved him, and Robert too. Give it time."

For a while, I couldn't speak and aimlessly looked around at all the faces in the room, all of them oblivious to what was happening in France. It was like another world out there. Was this what it was all about? Was this what we were fighting for? For a minute I wondered if it was really worth it. Alice gently touched my arm, breaking my train of thought.

"Mother's invited you to tea. What about tomorrow night?" she said.

Totally surprised, I wasn't sure what to say, and then thought, oh what the hell.

"Yes, if you're sure. Do they know about us?"

"Oh yes, they know alright," she said, smiling mischievously.

"Are they ok with it?" I tentatively asked.

"Yes, why not. Dad has known for some time, and reckons that you're a fine lad. Mam will probably tease you a bit, but I know she likes you. She knows about all the letters you've written as she always picks up the post. They wouldn't have asked you if there was a problem. Well, will you come?" she persisted.

"Yes, I'd love to," I said, with more confidence than I actually felt.

The thought I would be seen as something other than a school friend of Ted, made me a little anxious, but I smiled reassuringly.

I walked Alice part of the way home and arranged to meet her the following evening at six. I briefly squeezed her hand.

"You are lovely, Alice."

I couldn't take my eyes off her. She smiled shyly, pleased I liked what I saw, and not wanting to appear forward, gave me a quick peck on my cheek, as she said goodbye. I caught her arm, and pulling her back, kissed her fervently, telling her I loved her more than ever. She now responded just as eagerly, as our lips pressed together. In the two years apart, both of us had changed, but despite feeling slightly awkward and shy together, it was good to know our feelings were still the same.

That night, I slept soundly. No dreams interrupted my sleep and I awoke refreshed and eager for the day. I told Mam I would be having tea at the Johnson's house. Fortunately, she didn't put two and two together and assumed I would be there at the invitation of Ted. Dad was a little more astute and made a brief reference to Alice, and in passing I acknowledged she would be there with the rest of her family. He smiled knowingly, and gave me a little wink, which caused me to grin back at him. My fleeting look spoke volumes. He didn't say anything else, and I glanced at Mam who'd missed our interchange.

As the day passed quickly, I started to spit and polish my shoes, and smarten myself up. I combed my short hair, neatly parting it at the side and smoothed it down with a little water and grease. I lathered up my face and with the cut throat razor gave myself a close shave, feeling every inch of my skin to make sure it was smooth. I then donned my best clothes, and turned to see the final results in the small octagonal shaped mirror above the fireplace in the living room. If Mam didn't suspect anything before, she certainly would now, I thought.

"Don't be late now, son. I'll expect you to be back before ten. Don't forget to shut the door properly when you get in," she said, forgetting that I was nearly nineteen.

"Lay off it Mam. I'll be back when I'm back, and I've no idea what time it will be."

Dad touched her arm silencing her.

"Stop fussing, he's a grown man now," he warned.

She sighed, reluctantly acknowledging he was right, but nevertheless, muttered under her breath what old Dr Jones had said.

Though Alice lived at 4 Bexley Square, not far from town, I caught the tram to her house, as I didn't want to risk irritating my leg and limping badly. As I knocked on the back door of the small terrace house, Ted answered it with an exclamation.

"Ye Gods, Mam, it's that Jackson lad all tarted up!"

Alice came quickly to the door, pushing him out of the way, as she came to my rescue.

"Don't stand on ceremony, lad. Come in, come in," shouted her dad from afar.

Alice led me through the kitchen and into the front room, where the whole family was sitting waiting for me. There was Mr & Mrs Johnson, Connie and her young man, Herbert, Ted with his friend Pat, and little Edna, who was ready for bed. All eyes were now fixed on me. Mrs Johnson waved me in, and Alice pushed me in front of her, and let go of my hand, as if abandoning me.

"So… you've come a courting our Alice, have you?" Mrs Johnson enquired, as I blushed.

"Well, turn around and let me have a good look at you," she said, before I could answer.

As I slowly turned around, I saw the sniggering faces of Alice's siblings and her scowling face silencing them. My eyes rested back on the bountiful body of Mrs Johnson. She looked me up and down. The atmosphere was tense as everyone waited for her verdict.

"Well… I suppose you'll do, but if you don't treat our Alice right, you'll have me to deal with," she warned.

When everyone saw the look on my face, they burst out laughing. With the ice now broken, I was patted on the back and my hand shaken vigorously by her father, and the others. Alice's face was a picture. She beamed from ear to ear, satisfied that I'd passed her mother's inspection and had been approved. Herbert put his arm on my shoulder.

"Welcome to the Johnson family," he said, helping me off with my coat, as Mr Johnson had ordered.

SIX

"Come on, lad. Take off your collar and cuffs and roll up your sleeves… there's no standing on ceremony here," he assured me.

I was indeed made very welcome by Alice's family and got on famously with Connie and Herbert. Herbert took me aside and told me everyone secretly referred to Mrs Johnson as "the old battleaxe," but he assured me her bark was worse than her bite. Still, I didn't want to put a foot wrong, so I continued to be as polite as possible amid the fun they all made of me when I called Mr Johnson, "Sir" and talked with what must have appeared to them a plum in my mouth!

I felt at ease with the family and made several promises to call again. After tea, Alice said she'd walk me to the end of the square. The air felt bitterly cold. Both of us pulled our coats tightly around us, as the crystal clear night, with hundreds of stars all twinkling brightly above, created a magical scene. I felt very relaxed and pleased with myself. Her dad was especially easy to talk to. I kissed Alice goodnight in the darkness of a doorway much further up the street. The full moon cast shadows making everything enchanting.

"Will you marry me, Alice?" I whispered.

Her eyes shone brightly as she teasingly hesitated.

"I don't know. You'll have to ask my Dad first."

As she sensed my horrified expression, she quickly kissed me, and then more slowly, her lips parting seductively under the pressure of mine, in a much longer embrace.

"Yes," she said, breathlessly.

"Oh Alice, I love you."

My hands slipped inside her coat and caressed her. She responded warmly, pressing her body against mine, feeling my erection.

"Oh God Alice, you're so lovely."

Her nipples responded to my touch and she gasped excitedly as our bodies rubbed together. Suddenly, there were footsteps in the alleyway, and instantly, she jumped away, pulling her coat around her. Still reeling from the moment, we heard the voice of Ted.

"Mam said it's time you said goodnight."

"Alright, alright, tell her I'm just coming," she said, annoyed.

SIX

"Bye John," she said softly, giving me a brief kiss, under the inquisitive eyes of Ted.

As she turned to walk away, she clipped Ted over the back of his head, scolding him for embarrassing her in front of me.

"It's not my fault," I heard him say, as the two of them disappeared.

My two weeks' leave seemed to be running out quickly and, after a man to man talk with Mr Johnson in the kitchen of his house a few days later, I asked permission to marry his daughter. He hummed and arred a bit.

"What do you think, Lizzie?" he called out to Alice's mother.

"Oh for goodness sake, put the lad out of his misery," she shouted back from the front room.

"Alright lad… Yes, that will be fine," he said, shaking my hand.

Now, with only one more obstacle to go, I told Mam and Dad of my intentions towards Alice. Dad patted me on the back in his usual way of showing pleasure and then shook my hand. Mam bristled slightly, making light of it.

"Well, you'd better ask her home for tea then," she said reluctantly.

She made no further comment, and when Alice did turn up later that week, it couldn't have been more different from the reception I'd received at her house. Dad made most of the conversation, and fortunately, my brothers made up the rest. Alice didn't seem to notice Mam's indifference and I didn't enlighten her as to the disappointment Mam felt. I knew it was because seemingly, in her opinion, I was about to marry beneath me. I wasn't too worried though, as I was sure in time she would come to terms with it.

The following day, I made my way towards Walmgate to buy Alice an engagement ring, and instantly fell in love with three large rubies held delicately in place by several tiny gold claws. The rubies were arranged in a straight line and sat regally upon a simple gold band. When we sat in the park near the old oak tree, just two days before I was set to leave for Edmonton again, I pulled the small box out of my pocket and gave it to her.

"Oh, it's lovely."

Now pleased with myself, I put it on her finger.

"There, its official," I pronounced.

I could tell by her face just how much she really liked it. The rubies caught the piercing rays of the low winter sun as she held up her small pale outstretched hand, marvelling at how well it fitted her. She turned to kiss me, telling me she loved me and that it was wonderful. I told her red suited her, and the redness of the stones would go with the red dress I loved so much.

The news of my official engagement was still met with a nonplussed expression from Mam, and continuing hearty congratulations from Dad. Alice's family, on the other hand, cobbled together a small party at her house, on the eve of my departure. It seemed as if they needed no excuse to hold a shindig, and the engagement proved to be adequate justification. They generously extended the invitation to my family, but Mam declined saying it was too short notice and they were sorry but they had another obligation. I didn't challenge them, and instead turned up at Alice's house with an apple pie she'd graciously baked, along with some scones.

We had a great night, singing and dancing, with lots of hand clapping and drinking. I was slightly tipsy by the time I left. Alice apologised for her family's exuberance, but I could tell she was excited as she showed off her ring and kept looking at anything that would reflect its splendour. As I said goodnight to her in the back alleyway, her mood changed and her eyes filled with tears.

"Do you have to go?" she sobbed.

"I'm afraid so," I said, with an equally heavy heart. "It shouldn't be for long," I tried to reassure her, though my words belied what I really felt, "when I get back, we'll get married," I added.

Her wet cheeks and soft kisses stirred me, and I gently pulled her body close to mine. As my hands explored further, and her body yielded, she did not stop me, but reluctantly whispered in my ear.

"Let's wait, John. It's not for long, and then we can do whatever we want."

I craved to touch her all over and as I controlled my ardour, it lessened somewhat. I knew she was right. Sobering up, I realised the folly and possible consequences of continuing. I felt sure she wouldn't resist me if I persisted, but then, what if I didn't come back? What then? Where would that leave Alice? I could hear my Mam's voice.

SIX

"She'll be up the creek without a paddle, that's where she'll be!" and I knew she was right.

We held each other close, savouring the nearness of each other, before reluctantly parting.

"I have to go," I said.

"Write to me won't you?" she pleaded, and I nodded.

"Sure I will. As often as I can."

Chapter TWENTY-FOUR

You cannot escape the responsibility of tomorrow by evading it today...
(Abraham Lincoln 1809 - 1865)

The following day I donned my uniform and gathered my bits and pieces together, all the while singing softly...

> *"John Brown's body lies a-mouldering in the grave, a-mouldering in the grave, a-mouldering in the grave... John Brown's body lies a-mouldering in the grave; his soul is marching on... Oh, Glory, glory halleluiah..."*

The jolliness of the tune gave adequate cover to the real feelings I had about going back. No-one suspected how the words really heightened my fear, as I continued packing my bag. I even contemplated deserting, but where would I go? And then there would be the shame of it all. I couldn't let that happen.

As I closed my kit bag, Mam's smuggled tin of fairy cakes next to the extra socks and bars of chocolate she'd put in there, stuck out at an angle. It was her way of making sure I wouldn't want for anything. She clung to the thought that Edmonton Hospital might declare me unfit, and would send me home again, and she begged me to limp badly when they gave me a medical. I was to tell them I was in extreme pain, which I wasn't, and how much trouble it still gave me, which it didn't. I couldn't possibly climb out of a trench, could I, she reasoned as if talking to the medics, and I was to be sure to tell them that.

"Yes Mam," I dutifully replied, and for a brief moment I even wondered whether those excuses would work.

I smiled at her fabrications and admonished her for saying such things.

"What would God think?" I told her.

"He'd agree with me," she uttered desperately.

In her heart though, she knew I wouldn't lie, and eventually made me promise to take care and to write as often as I could.

Dad shook my hand and told me to get in touch if I needed anything. My younger brothers were also quiet, as if this time they understood the real meaning of war and what could happen. I even got a hug off Wilf, which was something he hardly ever did and I smiled at his seriousness and tried to lighten his mood by telling him I'd kill a few more Jerries for him, but he wasn't amused. He told me it was more important to come home in one piece, than to kill stupid Jerries. I realised that my poor little brother was growing up, and giving him one last smile, I promised I'd take care.

"If you see your brothers, tell them we love them, and to take care too," shouted Mam, as I hurried down the road.

"I will," I bellowed back, letting the words carry on the wind.

As I passed the Seals' house, Mr Seal came rushing out to wish me all the best, and told me to wait a minute. He hurried back inside to get something. He'd obviously been keeping a look out for me, and when he returned, he thrust Albert's pocket watch into my hand, saying Albert would have wanted me to have it. With tears welling up in both our eyes, I thanked him, telling him I would treasure it and keep it safe. As I gave him a brief hug and shook his hand, I promised to keep in touch and told him I'd call in to see him again when I got back.

"Hopefully, this terrible war will soon be over," I added, as I said goodbye.

As the train pulled out of York station, it too seemed reluctant to take me back, as it slowly set off. The excitement I had once had so long ago, was now replaced with a feeling of doom, and flashes of the mid winter misery of trench existence, with very little to keep body and soul together, kept coming to mind. I kept telling myself I owed it to Albert and Robert and the other poor souls out there. I felt I had no choice but to do my duty and go back for them, but with such mixed emotions, I hastily wished the train would pick up speed before I could get off and change my mind. Eventually I settled, believing once again, my fate was sealed.

"Good to see you back, Jackson. I can see the break has done you good," said the medic, as he declared me fit, just as I knew he would.

"Now then, you're to report back to your unit on the 23rd December. Here are all the relevant papers. You'll sail from Southampton tomorrow. Any questions?"

I shook my head, confirming none.

"Well, good luck then."

He grasped my hand, and dismissed me. With a heavy feeling inside, I knew there was definitely no turning back now. The gun was loaded and pointing at my back, pushing me on.

The return journey was bleak. I'd no sooner left Southampton port than I was seasick, along with many others. The sea tossed us about like rag dolls in a dolly tub and subsequently, the whole ship was awash with vomit. Even hardened sailors couldn't remain upright, so it came as no surprise that I clung hard-fast onto a rail and heaved my guts out, desperate to get off. I felt so ill that at one point I thought of jumping overboard. I even wished for a U-boat to put me out of my misery.

When I walked down the gang-plank on to the dockside at Boulogne, the concrete floor continued to move, and I staggered around as if drunk. In an attempt to settle my stomach, I gulped in a lungful of fresh air, as waves of nausea washed over me. My unit was located in the Bouque Maison region, and when I eventually found the right train, it was laboriously slow, but it didn't matter. I knew it would be several more hours before I would finally report to my unit as directed, but I didn't care. As long as I got there in time for the run up to Christmas and New Year, I was certain no one would give a damn. In any case, I fervently hoped that 1917 would see an end to this horrible war.

It took me a while to get my bearings amongst the crowd of young soldiers now milling around me, typical of the chaos that seemed to arise from so many new bodies joining the unit. I eventually caught sight of Bill trying to have a quick fag behind a supplies lorry.

"Now then, what's going on?"

"Oh it's you, John-boy. It's about time you got yourself back here. The whole bloody place is swarming with sixteen new battalions joining the West Yorkshire's, all waiting to be despatched," he said, now exhaling smoke.

"Christ, that's going somewhat!" I replied astonished.

More men, I thought, and wondered how long it would be before most of them would be dead. I kept visualising the lack of awareness on the faces of people in York. They hadn't a clue what was happening out here, and within a few hours of being back, it was just as if I'd never been away.

"Well... well... well..., if it isn't Jackson. What's the news from home?" said old Picky, who seemed to come from nowhere.

SIX

"Hello Sarge, don't tell me you're still here then?"

"'Fraid so lad," he said, confirming he was no mirage.

"Home is buzzing. Rowntrees are now producing ammo for our big guns. Alice seems to be enjoying her effort to support us, though she's no idea what happens to all the stuff after it has left the factory. In fact, all our industries seem to be involved, one way or another. They've even been melting down iron railings, so you wouldn't know the old place now!"

"That's no problem. As long as my ole' lass doesn't change," he replied, letting us know that's all he worried about.

"It's going to be another bleak Christmas away from her," he added wistfully.

His etched face and greying hair made him look old and tired, and I suddenly felt sorry for him. It was obvious the only thing keeping him going was his old lass. I became lost for words and longingly thought of Alice, knowing exactly how he felt.

Ironically, Christmas came and went like any other day of the week and by 5th January, we moved out of the Bouque Maison area and headed for Baillemont, eight miles south west of Arras. The inclement weather mirrored our mood, and didn't change when the following day, we relieved the 19th Manchesters in the front line. We spent the next month in and out of the trenches as if we were performing some sort of dance routine, 'now into the middle and out again, swing your partners, and back again'. The only difference being, it was hell, and to cap it all, the weather began to deteriorate. The ground was frozen hard, and overnight there had been a heavy coating of snow. The cold bit at our fingers and toes.

The general work of framing up the trenches became especially difficult during this time. We tired easily, and despite the freezing conditions, I developed scabies and a bout of diarrhoea, resulting in a brief spell back in billets. Even the few remaining lice huddled together in the warm spots of our bodies, in a desperate bid to stay alive.

The short daylight hours, combined with the bitterly cold weather, meant a relatively peaceful time over the next few weeks. It was only when the weather warmed up slightly, that the enemy decided to come out of hibernation to shell Gastineau, and the top end of Lincoln Lane. Fortunately, no one was hurt and they gave up trying as the weather deteriorated again. At night, each of our companies spent time wiring everywhere. Most units were putting out an average of twenty coils of wire each, mainly in a vain attempt to keep warm.

We were all grateful for this quiet time with only the occasional shell from Jerry to make sure we hadn't fallen asleep. Both sides still had plenty to do behind the lines without spending time trying to kill each other. My unit busied itself with trench repairs, whilst Sarge supervised the building of a large elephant dug out. Our artillery put out the odd shell to let Jerry know we were still around but it was winter, and a time for everyone to take stock.

By 11th February my scabies had cleared up, killed off by the obnoxious substance the medic gave me to paint on every day. There were quite a few of us dowsed in this toxic stuff, which we reckoned would knock the Jerries out with one whiff. Still, it was better than the livestock.

"Get ready to move your platoon out, Jackson," said Sarge, pushing his way through the narrow space of the trench.

"Who's going to hold the line?" I asked.

"The 1/6th West Yorkshire Battalion. Look sharp, Jackson, we've got to get a move on."

"What's the rush, Sarge? Something happened?"

"The big-wigs need us to prepare for a large offensive they're planning and they want us to be ready for when it starts."

"Where are we going, any idea?"

"I've just been told we're heading to Humbercamps for training. They want us to go via Berles and Pommier, to avoid getting held up in any skirmishes," he replied, now moving down the line to tell the others.

It didn't take us long to get underway, and we made good headway. By early afternoon we arrived at Humbercamps, and were spread out in various billets, where we spent the rest of the day getting cleaned up. Our billets for a change were unusually good and I managed to secure a warm bath for the five of us billeted in the big farmhouse.

"Can I go first, John-boy?" asked Bill.

"'Ere, that's not fair," said a scrawny lad we didn't know.

"OK, OK, OK… stop moaning. We'll determine the bath order by picking straws. That's fair," I said, trying to pacify everyone.

As it happened, Bill was first in line and I ended up being second, with the rest following on, almost as if I'd planned it that way. As each of us took turns to wallow in the murky water, the ones waiting badgered us to hurry up.

As the last one emerged from the now cold water, a runner arrived with a message from Sarge to say we had to attend an evening lecture about a new attack formation. It was just 4pm, giving us enough time to enjoy the large chunk of bread and cheese, brought by Madame Benoit, the farmhouse owner.

"Merci, merci Anglais," she kept saying, thanking us profusely for ridding her country of Germans, who she cuttingly referred to as vermin.

She was a small, dumpy looking woman, very much like Mam, and she spoke her mind, just the same. I suppose that's what I liked about her, and all of us were grateful for the small pleasures she afforded us in the time we spent there.

Over the next few days, all companies were busy. Sixty men from 'B' company were involved in tree cutting at Gaudiemare, not that there were many trees left standing, whilst 'A' and my company, 'D', were ordered to take baths in the makeshift army bath-house. We didn't let on that the five of us had already had a bath, as we knew this next one would enable another layer of ingrained dirt to disappear, and we'd also be issued with clean clothes, which we desperately needed. By now, the sight of naked men bathing together was commonplace. No-one seemed to mind about displaying their private parts in public as we laughed and fooled around.

When 'B' and 'C' company had their baths, 'A' company went to Bailleuimont to witness a practice attack by the Brigade school, and the rest of us, went on a route march to Bavincourt, to attend a matinee performance by 'The Tykes' who were the 49th division Pierrot troupe. I'd never heard of them, but Bill reckoned many of the cast had been part of a popular end-of-the-pier entertainment troupe on the east coast. It appeared they sang, danced, and were a mixture of slapstick comedians, jugglers and specialist acts. He'd heard a lot about them, but it was the first time any of us had seen them. The troupe was part of the Northumberland Fusiliers and when I watched them, I couldn't help but wonder how they managed to remain so cheerful.

When The Tykes took a break, one of the nurses was cajoled into singing for us. Her name was Yvette. I'd seen her on quite a few occasions in one of the local estaminets. She was a dark, sultry looking girl, and her figure was certainly an improvement on the performers we'd just seen! She sang "La Madelon," a rather boisterous song in any language, and her rather sexy interpretation of it had us all lusting after her, as she teased us with her exaggerated body movements. She was a good sport and was given an enthusiastic standing ovation, followed by several loud wolf whistles, which echoed throughout the hall. In response, she sexily left the makeshift stage, blowing kisses and waving both arms in the air, causing her breasts to move temptingly from side to side. She was every bit a woman, the sort I knew Alice would hate, for fear I'd be enticed away.

In some farcical sort of a way, the whole afternoon had been a roaring success and for a few hours, all thoughts of war had gone. The Troupe was just great, and on the way back to our billets, we raved about the various acts we'd seen and joked about meeting Yvette in our dreams. This extraordinary experience, gave us something to cling on to and I couldn't help but wonder when the bubble would burst.

As predicted, it wasn't long. Fun and games were definitely over. It was almost as if the army had been giving us last rites, before subjecting us again to trench warfare. We spent several hours practising a new attack strategy and were told we'd soon be putting it into practice.

We took the same route back to the front, and on 15th February at 7.45am, we went to relieve the bedraggled and cold 1/6th West Yorkshires in Sector C1. By 11am the exchange was complete.

"It's too bloody quiet," said nearly everyone we met.

Again, the quietness was slightly disconcerting.

Eventually, the thaw we'd all been praying for happened and work became much easier. Many of our trenches were still showing signs of serious collapse, and orders were given to shore them up as best we could. As we made a start, the 147th and 148th brigades were busy raiding enemy lines. They put up a barrage on the enemy sap on the Alouette – Ransart Road, and though the enemy dropped several trench mortars on Lincoln Lane in response, they did no damage.

By chance, my platoon managed to capture eighteen Jerries and marched them down our lines amid cheers and jubilation, swaggering as we did so. We'd been clearing up a trench not far from Jerry, when we heard a group of them on a reconnoitre mission. As we ducked down, they simply walked into our trench, not realising we were there... silly buggers. All we had to do was point our rifles at them, and their arms went in the air as they surrendered! I don't know who was the most surprised, us or them!

Throughout this relatively calm period, we continued shoring up the trenches. As the thaw persisted, the wet ground seeped through our boots and a few men started to go down with trench foot. Sarge secured some gumboots to attempt to halt this process, but this just swapped one problem for another as our feet, now unable to breathe, sweated profusely and grew fungus. I couldn't help but wonder how our Matt's feet were doing, especially as he'd been prone to this problem.

By 20th February, we were relieved again, and many of us were wondering what had happened to this big offensive the big-wigs were planning. Sarge had no idea and as soon as we were back to the comfort of our billets and the ever pleasing Madame Benoit, Bill and I didn't give it another thought.

That night, Sarge gave us the go-ahead to attend the local tavern and after a particularly enjoyable night out drinking, singing and fraternising with the locals, I fell into a wonderful dreamless sleep. The following morning, when we prepared for parade, most of us were slightly worse for wear.

"Cor, my bloody head!" Bill remarked, holding his head in his hands.

"Mine too. It's like a sledge hammer thumping away."

"Come on, you lot, look sharp. Time to move out," Sarge bellowed above the moaning and groaning.

"Where are we going?" asked Bill.

"You're marching to Lesouich, five miles north of Doullens. We'll be going through Lacauchie, Coiturelle, Humbercourt and Lucheux."

"Any particular reason Sarge?" Bill queried.

"Orders."

"And orders are orders," we all chipped in.

It was a good day for marching, not too cold or too warm, but bright and dry, perfect in fact, and despite the roads being in a terrible condition, we all managed to complete the route by late afternoon. We were allocated really good billets again, and commented on our good fortune.

SIX

Next day there was a full kit inspection by our commanding officer. He inspected the battalion by companies, in full marching order.

"No doubt for propaganda purposes," said Bill.

All the big-shots were present, as we lined up. When the commanding officer said we looked in magnificent condition, our officers preened themselves, as if they'd personally scrubbed us up. With a "Carry on" instruction to our Company Sergeant Major, new orders were given.

"Right then, let's look snappy. At 2pm, we'll be marching on to Bonnieres, via Bouque Maison and Monleblond," said Sarge.

We didn't ask why, as we knew what his reply would be. The weather was again fine and though we expected trouble on the way, there wasn't any. The difficult four mile stretch was undertaken with no stragglers, which was some achievement, as some of us were still suffering with foot problems. Once again, our billets were good.

We hadn't seen or heard anything from Jerry for days and I began to think the war had definitely ended and our CO's were making us trudge around, so that we could show off in the face of our enemy's defeat. None of us knew really what was happening, but the quiet time persisted uncannily.

For the next three days we marched daily, moving to Gauchin, via Frevent, eight miles from St Pol, then on to Fiefs, another ten miles on. On the third day of marching we stopped just outside Sains Les Pernes for dinner, and again met no resistance. Our spirits were high as we proceeded to march through the village to our billets. Locals cheered us along the way as we marched down the main street, with pretty girls draped all over us.

That night 'A, B, and C' companies slept in the huge Chateau at Fiefs, while my company moved to ordinary billets on the Heuchin Road. There was a lot of grumbling as we moved on, but when we arrived at our billets, Sarge reckoned we were better off.

"Hey Sarge, how did you manage to arrange these billets?" I asked, noting how comfortable they were.

"I pulled a few strings," he said laughing.

"You should feel sorry for the poor buggers cooped up in the old drafty Chateau; they've got the worse deal," he continued.

"What about a night on the tiles as well then Sarge?" Jock asked.

"Why not… it's thirsty work, all this walking."

"Is that an order then Sarge?"

"Sure is," replied Sarge, grinning.

The local estaminet was just down the road, and 'as ordered' we sang with the locals who applauded our efforts. Girls showed those who wanted an especially good time. I joined in with the singing and the drinking, but that was enough for me. I was content to watch men with girls coming and going through the tavern doors, with not a care in the world.

By ten past eight the following morning, some of the men could hardly stand upright. As our unit regrouped to get ready to march on to St Venant, via Nedon and Lillers, the majority were regretting the night before. Sarge said it was their own fault and refused to give them any sympathy.

Days of unrelenting marching continued. None of us knew what it was about, and my leg started to ache, causing me to limp badly. Normally, my leg didn't give me much trouble, but it had become irritated by all the walking. As a result, I was beginning to be weary of the towns and places we passed through. When the pain in my leg became much worse, I started to fall back down the line. The cobbled road from Lillers to St Venant was particularly difficult, and Sarge, seeing my difficulty, slowed the pace down so I could still manage to keep up.

"Not much further now, Jackson. Then you can rest up," he said, recognising the problem.

By the time we arrived on the St Venant – Gauarbecque Road, with only an hour's stop for lunch, we'd marched another whole day. By then, all of us were feeling the strain. Sarge yet again, allocated me excellent billets. That was the best thing about old Picky, he never said anything, but you knew he cared.

As time went on, we were beginning to feel uneasy about our unknown destination. When orders to fall out for the night were given, Bill stopped to light up a woodbine for Sarge.

"Any idea what's going on, Sarge?" he asked casually.

Sarge shrugged his shoulders as if to say, your guess is as good as mine. As far as he was concerned, daily orders were given to him and apart from that, he knew little of the final destination.

"Orders are orders, so we just have to get on with it," he unenthusiastically remarked.

If he did know, he was keeping bloody quiet about it.

Twenty-four hours later, once more refreshed, we took to the road again, and blindly followed those daily orders. The day was bright and fresh. I took in a deep breath, and for the first time in a long while, was thankful to be alive. It was my nineteenth birthday.

I thought of past birthdays spent with my brothers at home and smiled to myself.

"What's up with you Jackson?" asked Sarge.

"Nothing much, Sarge. Just another birthday."

"Well, well, well, birthday boy. 'Ere you lot, Jackson's reached another birthday," he bellowed.

Those close to me wished me a happy birthday and gave me cigs and bits of leftover chocolate they had tucked away in their kit bags. A few patted me on the back and knocked their knuckles on my tin hat rattling my brains. Deep down, everyone knew what an achievement it was in the current climate, and decided it was something to celebrate.

"Here, Sarge, don't you think Jackson's birthday requires a toast?" said Jock.

"Why not? Good idea."

Sarge broke into the daily rum ration, giving us a bit more than usual. It was bad luck to toast to a long life, so instead he just raised his glass.

"Bottoms up," he said, to all of us.

"Bottoms up, Sarge," we replied.

Eyes locked onto mine, silently wishing me all the best. I felt the warmth of their thoughts, as the rum seeped down into the pit of my stomach and put a glow on my face.

We hadn't seen any mail for a few weeks now, probably because we were on the move, and it looked as if today was going to be no different. I knew Mam and Dad would be thinking about me and would have sent something, and I tried sending happy thoughts to them, in the hope they'd know I was thinking of them too.

We headed for Bout Delville, via Beaupre and Lestrem, and word was out our destination was in the new sector of Lys. Our time on the move was nearly over. It had taken us from 21st February until 1st March, a definite "white rabbit" day. None of us knew exactly how far we'd walked in all those days, but Bill reckoned it must be at least two to three hundred miles.

Within hours of arriving in this new sector, we went straight into trenches in a support position at Laventie and Rue Bacquerot, relieving the 1st Queen's Westminster Rifles. The reason for our time on the hoof was now obvious: we were again to be used as front line fodder, in the in-out existence of trench life. We groaned at the repetition of this performance, and Old Picky told us there was no rest for the wicked!

"Christ, all of us must be bloody bad then," I said to Bill, as he took up first watch position.

Eleven days later we were relieved, and mail finally caught up with us. We were beginning to think every one had forgotten we were here. I had several letters all at once, and I was a little concerned that Mam didn't refer to Alice in any of her letters, despite my constant mention of her in mine. I did hope in time, she'd get used to the idea, but so far it was looking bleak. Alice spoke about how lovely her ring was and how everyone admired it. She said she felt very lucky. I smiled at the thought of her. I missed touching her lovely smooth skin, and kissing her soft lips. I also missed the sensual way she looked at me now we were engaged to be married.

Connie had told her she couldn't wait for Herbert to ask her to marry him. Alice had laughed, telling her she'd better resign herself to waiting a few more years. Deep down though, she was pleased Connie wanted to copy her. She knew she was jealous, and for once it was obvious that Alice liked being the centre of attention.

With the post came two parcels and in one of them was a fruit cake from Mrs Johnson, which she'd taken the trouble to bake. Alice said her mother was the best cook for miles, and, after only a mouthful, I had to agree, but I wasn't going to admit that to anyone. My Mam was a pretty good cook too and the last thing I wanted was a war between prospective in-laws, as to who could bake the best cake!

As I ate Mrs Johnson's cake and read Mam's letters, she told me Matthew had been admitted to the 15th Australian Field Ambulance Hospital in France and had been transferred to the 3rd Canadian Field

Hospital at Boulogne, where he'd then been sent to Edmonton Military Hospital in England. Apparently his feet were in a dreadful state again. He had weeping ulcers that wouldn't heal and a worrying fever with it. I imagined he must be pretty bad if they'd shipped him back to England. Mam said they hoped to get down to see him, especially when the telegram said he was going to be there for a few weeks and it would be some time before he'd be able to walk again. She'd immediately written to the Australian war office, asking if they would transfer him up to York hospital, but it appeared too much red tape was involved to secure such a move. Secretly, I thanked God he was safe on English soil. He was better out of this war, even if he did have sore feet to contend with.

Mam asked if I'd seen anything of Fred or George, and again I smiled to myself. Obviously everything I'd told her about how big France was had been like water off a duck's back. Still, I wrote back, and promised to keep an eye out for their units, and would make attempts to see them if they were nearby. It kept her happy, however unrealistic her hope was.

As it turned out, they were to see Fred before me. On 6th April, as my unit was being relieved from another spell in the front line, Fred had been severely wounded in a skirmish many miles down the line from me, and had been quickly shipped home. They didn't know any more details, but Mam and Dad had been summoned to his bedside where he was described as critical. With Matthew at Edmonton and now Fred in another London hospital, it left only George and me on French soil, and only God knew where George was. Nobody had heard from him for several weeks. Uneasy about the news, I eagerly waited for more, knowing there was nothing I could do.

Chapter TWENTY-FIVE

Troops of heroes undistinguished die...
(Joseph Addison 1672 - 1719)

By mid April, we were ten miles north-east of Bethune relieving the 1/6th West Yorks battalion in the Fauquissart sector. All of us crept into position as rain poured down relentlessly, dripping off the tips of our noses into the sludge under foot. By late morning, the relief was complete with all of us looking like drowned rats, a truly miserable sight, and it depicted exactly how we felt. 'A' company was in support. 'B' company to the left, 'C' in the centre, and my lot to the right.

The rain continued for days, and became the sort where all of us wished we were sitting in front of a roaring fire, with a cup of English tea. We were wet, cold and badly in need of some nourishing food, instead of the slop now being served up in the front line. As I settled down to the long cold stretch of time facing us, a whiff of food assailed my nostrils, and I started to dream and salivate over the thought of Mam's rabbit stew and chunks of home made bread.

In anticipation of something edible, I looked down into the food bucket which had made its way to us. The greasy, watery substitute of soup now in front of me looked disgusting, and as the young lad lifted up a full ladle for me, I was disappointed.

"No thanks mate. I'll just settle for the bread."

The ladle fell back into the brown swill, as he diverted his attention to the loaf of bread tucked under his arm. He tore off a chunk with his grubby hands, and returned the loaf to his armpit to continue down the line, instantly turning my stomach as he did so. For a while, I just held the slightly stale bread in my hand, swallowing down excessive saliva, as I tried to pretend it didn't matter. Food was food and in any case, my stomach was shouting out to be satisfied, no matter what it was.

We ate silently, and the rain still continued. It poured down incessantly, rolling and splattering everywhere. There was only the occasional Jerry aerial activity, to break its monotony. With Jerry machine gunners and mortars quiet, it was apparent they had also resigned themselves to sitting it out, no doubt as miserable as us. With no let up, this grey blanket covered us all.

Eventually, thoroughly fed up and soaked through to the skin, the big-wigs decided it was time to do a couple of reconnoitre missions using men from 'B and C' Company to see what Jerry was up to. Sarge reckoned it was only to satisfy their curiosity before it got the better of them, and of course, it gave us something to do.

Whilst the rest of us waited, the rain mercifully stopped, and the night began to grow really cold. I pulled my sodden outer coat tight around me, as my body started to dry out. Our breath made cloud patterns as it hit the cold air. I prayed the moon would stay hidden so that the steam, now climbing upwards from our drying bodies and clothes, wouldn't be seen by Jerry. The last thing we wanted was to inadvertently give our whereabouts away. All of us kept a sharp eye out for our returning parties. When they did finally return, we discovered they'd been held up by vast pools of water near the German parapets.

They had seen neither hide nor hair of Jerry, and had thought they'd be able to get across these stretches of water by means of a small makeshift bridge into their front lines. However, with little cover of darkness remaining, Sarge decided to abandon any further efforts until the following night, when patrol parties could be sent out with adequate bridging equipment. He was in no rush and reckoned Jerry had probably gone home anyway!

The next day passed slowly. We kept our feet raised off the ground to wait for the cloak of darkness. There was no point in subjecting our extremities to more insult than was necessary, so we huddled together to keep warm whilst we waited. Little was said. No one felt like talking. All our energies were taken up keeping body and soul together until such time as action was required. I didn't even have the strength to worry about death anymore. As we waited, I checked to see that Albert's watch was safe in my pocket, conscious of time marching on. I looked at the twelve inches of water now covering the duckboards, and couldn't see an end to this insanity. I thought of Alice, wondering if she would understand if I chose to end it all.

Eventually, in the early hours of the morning, three patrols were sent out. Bill took the first party of twenty men, carrying a makeshift bridge to scale the vast areas of water. He managed to get through to the enemy's front line trench, and discovered about thirty Germans, totally unprepared for an attack. Shots were fired, and all hell let loose. Several of the Germans were killed. The skirmish went on for a considerable length of time until his party withdrew.

When everyone got back, Bill was missing. Immediately, two others and I went back to look for him. We saw him just yards away from the Boche wire. When we reached him, we were so close we could hear Jerry licking his wounds. Crawling on our bellies, we managed to slide him from under their noses and safely away from their parapet. Fortunately, Bill was repairable, and as we shunted him down the line, he gave us a cheery wave, glad to be out of it for a few days.

The second patrol managed to get within fifty yards of Jerry before machine gunners, spooked by our first patrol's attack, fired aimlessly into the night. The patrol couldn't locate the gun but managed to reach Jerry's parapet, only to find it empty. The trench was in a poor condition but they noted it was nice and dry, and immediately returned to report back.

The third patrol went down by the side of the drain to Jerry's lines there. They were deserted and full of water. They then went to the next line, but only got a further twenty yards before being stopped again by vast pools of water. They stayed there an hour-and-a-half before returning, to report no sign of Jerry.

As the information from the three recces was collected and analysed, we waited, doggedly holding our position whilst decisions were made. Listening patrols at night reported the enemy way back in his support line, but they didn't trouble us and our unit resigned itself to the continued monotony of waiting, whilst rain beat relentlessly down on us once again.

The 11th Company Commanding Officer, stationed at Merville, decided this relatively calm period was a good time to present medal ribbons, and so a few days later, on a much brighter afternoon, some of our men attended a special parade to receive the Military Cross. Captain Mackay, 2nd Lt Saxby and Captain Freeman, from our lot went. Pell, Rayner, Pattison, and Farnhill got the Military medal and bar, and numerous others received commendations and certificates. We were proud some had got recognition. I overheard Freeman telling Sarge he couldn't have done it without us, and I instantly thought of all the lads who'd given their lives for it.

On their return, our peace was shattered by Jerry shelling the junction of Picantin Road and the Rue Tilleley, damaging the reserve company's cook house and wounding a couple of lads. I thought about Frederico and couldn't help but wonder where he'd ended up. None of us had heard any more about him.

SIX

"Wherever he is, I hope someone is appreciating his bully beef stew," said Sarge.

"Oh shut up Sarge," we all chirped, realising how hungry we were.

It would be several hours before the food party would get through to us, and my stomach was already growling to greet it!

"There's one thing for sure, he's not one of our cooks," he exclaimed, and we all agreed.

Chapter TWENTY-SIX

Great is the glory, for the strife is hard!
(William Wordsworth 1770 - 1850)

By May 1917, Lt. Col Bousfield counted our lot and reported to headquarters, he had forty-one officers and eight-hundred and fifteen other ranks, me being one of them, and we were ready for anything. He received orders saying it was time for our battalion to regroup, and enter into a programme of training once again. Bill, now fully recovered, managed to be posted back in time to join us.

"Parades, parades, parades!" I uttered. "That's all we ever seem to do these days, when we're not stuck in a bloody trench."

"Now, don't exaggerate. There's a bit of bayonet fighting and musketry training as well," said Bill, as he swaggered up, pleased to see us.

"Now then, ol' lad, how are you? Good to see you mate," I said, shaking his hand fervently, pleased he was up and about again. "What took you so long? We thought you'd been sent home for a spell," I mocked.

He just shrugged his shoulders.

"There's no point in me doing that, John-boy," he said miserably.

"My ol' lass had grown tired of waiting for me and has upped and left."

His eyes glazed over as he talked of her, his spirit broken and all reason for fighting now gone. I put my arm on his shoulder and tried pathetically to console him.

"I'm sorry to hear that, Bill."

Trying to change the subject, I started to babble.

"It seems ludicrous that we've been here over two bloody years fighting the Boche, and the big-wigs still think we need more bayonet and musketry training! Still, it's a relief to sleep safe in our beds for a while, don't you think?"

Bill just nodded, not really interested, as I jabbered on.

"Never mind, it'll give us time to write home again and catch up with the latest news," I said, realising instantly I'd said the wrong thing.

"Sorry mate," I said, but he didn't seem to notice.

His thoughts were now far away. I lit up a fag for him, deciding silence was better than words.

As we sat for a moment, he took some chocolate out of his pocket and gave me a bit.

"Any news about the war?" he asked, thinking we might have heard some rumours about what was going on.

"Well, only that America has broken off its relationship with Germany, and decided to declare war on them."

"Bloody 'ell! What caused that?" he said, now interested.

"Sarge thought it was something to do with sinking the Lusitania with about twelve hundred people on board."

"That was ages ago."

"I know, but they haven't forgotten it."

"Well, if that's the case, Jerry can't possibly win! It'll be over before we know it. Why couldn't they have done that a bloody year ago?" he said angrily.

"I wouldn't bank on it being over, Billy-boy. I can't see Jerry giving up without a fight to the death," I said, trying to appease him.

"Did you hear masses of Froggies mutinied as well? They reckon Pétain is set to take over from Nivelle, but nothing's been confirmed yet, so Jerry might still win if we're not careful."

Bill just grunted.

"Bloody typical! If it had been us lot, we'd have been bleeding shot," he replied.

On parade the following morning, the voice of Lt. Col Bousfield boomed across the terrain. He fiddled with his thick moustache, and demanded utter silence, before delivering his orders.

"'A' company: bayonet fighting and musketry training, then at the disposal of company commander; 'B' company: full attack practice, then bayonet and musketry training; 'C' company: under specialist officers, then at the disposal of company commander; 'D' company: at disposal of company commander, and then under specialist officers. Is that clear?" he bellowed.

"Right-oh then, take them away Sergeant," he ordered, as he saluted and turned on his heel, leaving everyone to get on with it.

SIX

His orders reverberated in the air, for four days, in various sequences. None of us learnt anything new, but the break from trench monotony enabled us to take out any frustrations we had on the straw and sand Jerry replicas. The afternoons were slightly different. Our officers and N.C.O's attended lectures, which we weren't privy to, whilst we had parades and updates as to what was going on from Sarge. In the meantime, the front line lads remained on alert. Bill reckoned Jerry hadn't heard about the French upping and leaving, or they might have tried their luck at defeating us, before the Yanks got here.

Over the next few days, several letters from home caught up with us. There was a couple from Alice and Mam, one from Mr Seal and another from Matthew. Alice said that every time she looked at her ring she thought of me. She kissed it often and hoped I'd be home soon. How I longed to be the ring, and feel her soft lips on mine again. I thought about her, and prayed she would never leave me, as Bill's old missus had.

Mam wrote about food shortages and how worried she was about managing. She also worried about us, in particular Matt and Fred. She cried when she saw the state of Matthew's feet, and had to hold a handkerchief to her nose, as the smell of rotting flesh turned her stomach. It was going to be a long time before they'd heal completely, but she thanked God he was alive.

It was touch and go with Fred. She and Dad had been told he was in a critical condition, though stable for now. He'd been awarded the Military Medal, this time for skill and courage when he had rushed a machine gun post, capturing two guns and seven prisoners and killing two men. Not satisfied with that, he had then gone back to take two extra sections, and had proceeded to rush another machine gun, capturing it and one prisoner, before killing eight Jerries, and being wounded himself. Mam felt a mixture of pride and anger at the same time, calling him a silly bugger, and wondered what he was thinking of to do such a thing. She told me she couldn't wait for him to get better, so she could knock some sense into him! Dad said very little, understanding the situation was very grave.

Matthew's letter said nothing of his feet, just that he was doing alright and hoped to be back soon. I felt his letter needed to be answered first, if only to stop him from making a big mistake. I had to make him see sense, if that was possible. Maybe he'd listen to his little brother.

Mr Seal's letter was a polite, enquiring one, asking how I was doing and telling me how he often thought of me and of his beloved Albert. He asked whether Albert's watch was keeping good time and whether I would be home soon. I was touched by his thoughts and vowed to write to him as soon as I had the chance.

Eventually, the big-shots felt Jerry was too quiet, so orders came through for us to take a look at what they were doing. On 10th May, just after writing all my letters home, we went back into front line trenches again. Sarge sent a patrol from each company into no man's land to see how far we could get without getting our heads blown off. Yes, we were back to the life we were used to, living like rats in a sewer!

With the exception of one or two places along Jerry's line, most of us could get through to the next line. One patrol was stopped by a vast lake of water, fifteen feet to fifty feet wide, which they couldn't breech, though the land beyond appeared to be dry as this was higher. The bit of land between the drains was also dry, though where the drains hadn't been kept in good order, water had overflowed and merged into small lakes making it impossible to cross.

Opposite the centre and to the left where I was, the land seemed much drier. The enemy wire was strong in places and weak in others, namely where water had become the natural barrier. We sent out further patrols to get a better feel for the layout and spent half an hour in the Boche's line before returning. My lot by chance found a sentry post near the head of Bertha trench, not far from where we'd been fired upon the previous night. It appeared to be derelict. Whilst held up there, we saw a Jerry patrol of about fifteen to twenty men who came down Irma trench into no man's land, moving south. The patrol saw us and signalled with a flash light before disappearing. Three mortar guns immediately opened fire, but fortunately their loads fell short, giving us just enough time to move away. Our listening posts didn't come across anything else until much later, when they heard four Jerries laying down wire. After we opened fire, they too disappeared.

Sarge reckoned the discovery of the sentry post near Bertha's trench was too good an opportunity to miss, and on speaking with our C.O, it was decided to secure it properly. He felt it was just a matter of finding the best route to approach it. With that in mind, several reconnoitring parties were sent out to find out the lie of the land around it. One of the returning parties ended up making a run for it across no-mans-land in broad daylight, which had been pretty scary. All of us knew it was suicidal to raise even a whisker above the parapet to look out onto this

SIX

revered piece of land in daylight, let alone attempt to cross it without the cover of darkness unless we were forced to. Bill reckoned Jerry must have been too amazed at what he saw, or he was asleep.

Eventually, the plan was to approach the sentry post from the left flank. Using an aerial photograph to assist us, we marked out a dummy sentry post with tape behind our line. The few chosen to undertake the raid practised the assault with precision. The attack was to be silent but deadly. One that would leave the Jerries wondering what the dickens had happened.

As our assault team perfected their offensive, one of our lookouts could clearly see Jerries placing wire inside their parapet in front of the sentry post, almost as if they knew we were coming. Even the best laid plans are thwarted, and this was no exception. In response, our C.O. mounted another survey at dawn to see if there was another way round it. We found a route which led straight to the rear of the post avoiding the wire. Pleased all was not lost, our men rested in readiness to carry out the offensive before anything else could deter them.

In the early hours of 20th May, two officers and sixteen men from 'A' company crept silently into the night. Half of the party would carry out the assault. They would work their way round to the rear of the sentry post, whilst the others would take up position on the left of the old crater, and act as cover for them. Once in position, they waited for sunrise.

Like a cat pursuing its prey, they crawled slowly forward in a stalking movement, and took the sentry post by surprise. Nine German soldiers, one being an officer, were all caught napping. At first, they appeared to surrender without a fight, and then three of them changed their minds. One cried out for grenades and was killed at once with rifle and revolver. One made a run for it and then couldn't be extricated out of very deep water and so was shot, and a third tried to slip away. He too was shot. After that, the rest gave no resistance and readily trundled to our lines without a problem. Sarge said Jerry had been caught with his trousers down, and we all laughed.

The raid was carried out in complete silence and apart from four shots, nothing else was heard. My company was ordered to put up a protective machine gun barrage, after the usual signal, but in the end, it wasn't necessary. By the time the sentry post was secured, everyone was safe. Jerry put out a sharp burst of machine gun fire when they realised what was happening, followed by a few shells, fired into 'Rotten Row' trench, but by then, it was all over. They'd lost this particular battle, having left it too late to muster up any more action, and they knew it. We had certainly caught them unaware.

Eventually, the six prisoners were taken away and questioned. They were from the 263rd German Regiment. Our interpreter confirmed they had indeed been surprised at our cheek and were caught off guard.

A few days later, Lt Col Bousfield received a letter from Major General Perceval, the commanding Officer of the 49th Division. Clearing his throat, he proudly read out its contents.

> *"The preparations for the operation and the determined and skilful manor [sic], in which it was carried out, reflect great credit on all concerned, and the Battalion may be rightly proud of capturing a complete hostile post, with the employment of so few men, and bringing in six prisoners, the remainder having been killed. The absence of any casualties on our side shows that great care must have been taken in working out the plan."*

The letter had been forwarded with Major General Perceval's personal congratulations, who felt they'd been well earned by everyone. It was rare to get a commendation from a Major General, and Lt Col Bousfield basked in the honours bestowed on him, and us. By word of mouth, we also learned the 1/5th West Yorkshire's, not only received congratulations from the Major General, but received a great deal of respect from the regiments we fought alongside. When they recognised someone's worth, it was praise indeed, and it was their approval which made the difference. Now they knew we were just as good as them!

Chapter TWENTY-SEVEN

A fool sees not the same tree that a wise man sees...
(William Blake 1757 - 1827)

As spring moved into summer, Alice wrote saying she wished we were married, and had a house, and children, just like George and Harriet. She often looked after their brood to give Harriet a break, and now she wished we had children. She wanted a part of me, like Harriet had a part of George. She couldn't bear the thought I might end up with another girl, and was jealous of the French beauties she believed I was surrounded by.

I kept telling her she had my heart, and tried to reassure her that all the French girls had left when the Jerries moved in, so there was no chance of me ending up with anyone else. I also told her that with my heart, she had my soul for safe keeping, so she did have a part of me to hang on to and she'd better look after it! I assured her that if anything was wrong... she'd know... she'd sense it... and I gave her my word that I only had eyes for her.

Hoping my reassurances would be enough, I took her photograph out of my top pocket, and gazed at the now crumpled, grubby condition of it. Her face was difficult to see, and I panicked. She had to know I loved her more than anything.

I carefully flattened it out before reluctantly placing it back in my pocket, imagining her being with me, and me holding her in my arms. In response, an ache rippled through my body. I too wanted something to hang on to. I thought of our last night together when our bodies craved the touch of each other and now desperately wished we'd given rein to our feelings and not stopped. Then, I would have had the memory of her. For once we should have listened to our hearts and not our heads. Damn Mam's sanctimonious words of warning, I cursed.

I continued to worry about Alice. If she thought for a moment I would forget her, she might start looking for someone else. I mustn't lose her... I couldn't... I panicked. I tried wondering what it was like for her... the things she read in the newspapers, the intense u-boat actions with horrific losses, the hospital ship that went down with over a thousand soldiers on board, and the horror of all the battles. I wondered what she thought of England's dead youth, lying in their thousands, covered in wriggling loathsome maggots, eaten by rats, before being boiled up for German fat reserves, as propaganda would have us believe. What would any of them at home make of it all? They had to be here to believe it. I wiped a stray tear away as I looked around at the destruction of buildings and the obliteration of people's lives, trying to comprehend what we were doing here and I desperately wished to be with her, just as Bill had desperately wanted to be with his old lass, before she'd decided she couldn't stand the uncertainty anymore and had left him.

As the sun cast its shadows, I re-read her letter. I tried concentrating on the bits about daily problems, such as short food supplies, and everyone having to pull together to grow food. She asked whether I knew about Charlie and Wilf helping on the Dunnell Estate. Her graphic description made me smile at the sudden image of Wilf with a pitch-fork in his hand, doing his bit for England, no doubt using it as a pretend bayonet, killing and lifting his imaginary dead Jerries onto old Bessie's cart to be turned into flour. Gradually, my panic began to settle.

She asked if we'd seen anything of the Americans. She knew President Wilson had declared war on Germany, and wanted to know if we'd seen them. The rumours we'd heard about more than thirty-thousand French troops deserting in the North, she said were true. It had been front page headlines in the Herald. What she didn't realise was, it had only been after the Nivelle offensive had failed, leaving thousands dead.

Sarge sauntered towards me interrupting my thoughts. As I looked up, he threw me a woodbine.

"What do you reckon then Sarge? I asked.

"About what?" he replied, as he bent down to light up for me.

"About the Frogs deserting… where does that leave us lot?" I asked, concerned Germany might now win the war.

"Well, Pétain is now Commander in Chief, and he's said to have built up the force again and restored operational efficiency. They're certainly getting better treated than before, so Jerry's unlikely to take any chances," he concluded, sceptical at anything being under control in war.

I didn't set much store by the news, and with both of us deep in thought, I continued to peruse Alice's letter as Sarge smoked quietly beside me. She'd heard Fred was still in a dreadful state and wondered whether he would ever be fit enough to return. He still needed more surgery and even now, after all these weeks, he remained quite traumatised and was having nightmares. She'd also heard about Matthew. His feet were healing well and he was up and about. They reckoned he would be fit for duty again within a matter of weeks.

"God forbid," I uttered.

What with Robert and Albert dead, Fred and Matthew in hospital and George somewhere in France, I suddenly felt alone. It was strange to think of being lonely with so many people milling about. Faces kept changing so quickly, only Old Picky still sitting quietly puffing away beside me, and Bill, seemed constant in this madness called 'life'.

I closed my eyes to shut the world out. The feeling which had once washed over me all those years ago, when I sat around the kitchen table staring at the familiar happy faces which made up my world, became clear. It was just as if I'd been transported back in time, and with it came the realisation we'd all changed and I was right to think that none of us would ever be the same again. Deep in sombre thought, I tried once again to discard the feeling of being lost. Amidst my despair I heard Mam's voice.

"Take care son and come home safely…"

Old Picky tapped me on the shoulder making me jump.

"It's time to go John."

I hastily stuffed Alice's letter in my pocket and picked up my kit-bag, now heading with the rest of my lot towards Lestrem station for departure to Loonplage. It was a full three hour journey to the west of Dunkirk. From there, Sarge said we'd march to Fort Mardyck, a camp just outside Dunkirk port, to await orders from Major Mackay. Eventually, we would be going to Rousdamme, and Sarge reckoned we'd stop to have routine inspections, baths and a camp drill there before moving on.

"It'll only be another brief stop, before we head-on out again," he said.

He was right. We hardly had any time to get cleaned up, before orders came to load our gear into trucks again. We then spent a further five-and-a half hours travelling shell-pocked roads, tossed around like washing in the wind, before eventually reaching our final destination, Avecapelle, four miles south of Nieuport. We stashed our gear, and immediately relieved the 66th Division, who were building a light railway.

The July day was unbearably hot and, lacking sleep and feeling worse for wear, we stripped down to vest and braces ready for work. Pick axes were wielded over and over again, as mile after mile of railway line was laid. I thought about Albert and could almost hear him laughing at me doing anything as physical as this. I was a railway clerk not a bloody platelayer, I thought to myself just as the pick axe hit a solid piece of ground, sending vibrating waves of pain up my arms as it came to a sudden stop.

"Bloody 'ell," I muttered as I rubbed them, cursing. I looked at my hands. All softness gone, replaced instead with blisters and hard roughened calluses. Labourer's hands.

My neatly manicured nails and velvety skin associated with being a 'white collar' worker at York railway office, were long gone.

"Just look at these hands," I said, showing them to Bill as he lit up a cigarette for both of us.

"It'll be bloody months before Alice will let me touch her with these."

"You should be so lucky," exclaimed Bill, as he handed me the woodbine, and tried to swat bothersome flies away.

"Sorry mate. I didn't mean anything by it," I said, realising I'd put my big foot in it again.

"Oh, it's not you, John-boy; it's these bleeding flies. They're worse than the bloody Jerries," he said, hot and frustrated, as he blew smoke at them.

The flies were big, fat, juicy blue-bottles, and the heat of the July day had brought them out in droves. We were often plagued by them in the trenches, where you could watch them laying eggs in the decaying bodies heaped up ready for collection. Sometimes the bodies would be left to fester for days in no-man's land until it was safe to bring them in. It was then the eggs would hatch out into maggots and emerge to feast on the decaying matter, before turning into these monster flies now circling around us.

I wiped the sweat off my forehead, trying not to think about them as I threw my cigarette butt away and swung the axe back into action. The quicker we got the job done, the sooner we'd be able to have a well-earned rest at Rousdamme, Sarge told us.

By the 17th, we were done, pleased to be rid of railway drudgery, and ended up moving to billets at Oostdunkerke.

"How about those rainbows?" said Bill, nodding his head towards twenty-seven brand new soldiers who'd joined our battalion.

"Poor buggers. They've no idea what they've let themselves in for," I commiserated.

"Don't they look young?" I added.

"Didn't your Mam tell you John-boy that when men start to look young, you're getting old?"

"Just so mate, and I bloody well feel it as well."

"Hey up, Sarge. What's afoot?" asked Bill, as Sarge wandered over.

"Plenty's afoot. We're set for another offensive at Ypres to capture Ostend and Zeebrugger. It's Haig's third attempt to push the Germans out of Belgium," he said, full of scepticism.

"Do you reckon its going to be any different to the other two attempts then?" Bill queried.

"Well, let's put it this way. Nothing's changed so I can't see it will, but we won't know till we try."

As the sun started to set, we prepared for a night's kip. Sarge left us, reminding us about tomorrow's agenda.

"Early start lads. Don't forget there's a kit inspection and box respirator drill as well, so be sure to look sharp all of you."

It was the last thing I wanted to hear, especially as my kit needed some attention.

"Oh, what the hell," I said to Bill.

"I'll do it in the morning and if it's not right, then sod it, I'll take the consequences."

Bill laughed, as the pair of us settled down for the night.

In the blink of an eye, morning came. There were some groanings, as everyone stirred from the confines of their sleeping quarters, and headed for the wash tents.

"Looks like we're in for another lot of gassing if we're back to practising respirator drill," said Bill, as he collected his things together.

"God I hope not," I replied, "I can still remember the last lot we had."

The drill was routine and repetitive.

SIX

"You have to be able to do it in your sleep," said Sarge.

When he was satisfied with our efforts, he gave us half an hour to prepare for kit inspection.

"Oh, by the way, we've just had orders we're to relieve the 16th Lancashire Fusiliers tonight, in the left sub-sector of St Georges. Looks like Haig's push has begun. Pass the word around," he added.

"Where's St Georges, Sarge?" asked Bill.

"On the River Yser, just inland of Nieuport, not far away."

In the early hours of the morning, we were in position. Jerry started a heavy bombardment welcoming us, and it gave little time to acclimatize. My company was actually in support when the front line to the left was badly knocked about. 'C' company were in Nun trench. 'A' company were on the right, in Nice trench, but there was nothing 'nice' about it. 'B' company were in reserve at Nieuport. For a while, all hell was let loose and I could see we'd suffered many casualties. As support battalion, it was our job to bring them in.

In between the spats, Old Picky sent out several patrols to do a recce. The patrol sent to the right, encountered a small group of Boche, which scattered and fled back to their lines. The patrol on the left listened by Rat Post for a considerable length of time, but nothing was seen or heard there, and Sarge thought maybe Jerry had retreated.

"I reckon old Picky's spoken too soon, don't you," I said to Bill, at dawn on the 21st, when the enemy opened up a heavy barrage.

It lasted an hour, and the front and support lines, along with the communications trench, suffered extensive damage, resulting in several more casualties. It could have been much worse if Jerry had followed up with an infantry attack but astonishingly they didn't.

Instead, they waited until the following day to dish out the worst. They shelled Nieuport with at least two thousand gas shells, followed by a heavy barrage on our front, which lasted for well over two hours. Fire broke out in various places along Nice Avenue and Nice Walk. One of our lot managed to bring down an enemy plane, just as Brick Stacks was shelled. Bill and I brought in one-hundred-and-forty-one casualties from 'B' company, who'd all been gassed. We collected up the rest of the bodies, several hours later, their purple torsos with puce swollen tongues and grotesque expressions, told of the horrors they'd endured.

We found bodies for several days, as gas shells rained down, and despite wearing our gas respirators, our eyes watered relentlessly, just as Mam's eyes did when peeling onions. Exhausted and somewhat disorientated from wearing the masks all the time, we received orders to stand down.

"Get yourselves up to the huts at Ribaillet Camp, and get some kip if you can. I'll be up there shortly," ordered Sarge.

By 11pm, all of us were in a deep sleep, when the camp was shelled. One minute I was sound asleep, the next I was wide awake, and on my feet, running. I don't remember scooping up my gear as we blindly headed out of the huts, zigzagging around the explosions raining down on us. We were like rabbits running for cover, fearing to breathe until our gas masks were on, knowing instinctively there was gas, by the colour of the mist.

By the time I'd run out of breath, I was like a rubber man with bendy legs, unable to stand. Pain shot through my chest with every intake of air and I started to twitch and shake all over as if possessed by some evil spirit.

"Bloody 'ell… Christ Almighty… what the bleeding 'ells happening?" I gasped, shaken to the core.

It was some time before we gathered ourselves together. Sarge ordered us to stay put, amid the chaos that ensued, whilst several Company Commanding Officers advanced with a number of units to secure the defences at Nieuport, just in case the enemy should attack again.

When dawn broke, all available hands busied themselves restoring what normality they could, as we waited for further orders. Once certain the camp was safe and located further away, we were sent to get cleaned up.

"Who's holding the front?" I asked Bill.

"The 1/7th West Yorkshires, and Duke of Wellingtons. Apparently they're doing a splendid job in disrupting the enemy by raiding their lines," responded Bill.

As we came out of the wash house, the alarm was raised again. Despite the camp's new location, the enemy dropped further gas shells on us in a tit-for-tat response. The pungent smell of mustard infused the air. Our look outs gave warning when they saw the spine-chilling mist drifting towards us, and it didn't take us long to put our box respirators on before it reached us.

We wore the respirators all day as the 'stand to' order was given, and eventually, just after midnight, we stood down again without having received any further orders to move out. Sick to death of wanting the darkness to end and the security of daylight to arrive again, I drifted in and out of a light sleep, with my box respirator close to me. I was petrified to let myself go completely in case we had a repetition of last night's events. I was conscious of the claustrophobic effect the night had on me, and I fought off the urge to run outside and get away from it all.

At first light we started to pack everything up, in readiness to move out. The incredible sunrise gave a rose coloured hue to the gas clouds now hanging over Nieuport. The beauty of the morning, and the horror of the night, mingled together in an unforgettable spectacle, as the effects of the gas were still being felt by all of us.

"Where are we going this time?" asked Jock wearily.

"With a bit of luck, out of bloody Jerry shell range, to billets at Coxyde to recover. Then most probably to billets at Ghyvelde, east of Dunkirk," said Bill.

"How do you know all that?" he asked.

"Old Picky told me this morning," he replied.

By the time we got to Ghyvelde, our numbers were considerably reduced. In order to give the Generals time to rethink, a decision was made to march us on to Teteghem, south of Dunkirk, to regroup and undergo training on the beaches.

"You alright John-boy?" asked Bill, when he noticed one of my hands trembling.

"Not really… I feel as if my nerves are all shot to pieces and I'm all shaky inside. I've got chronic belly ache and I need the lav."

"Don't worry lad, it's just the after effects of gas. Sarge reckons we'll be staying near Dunkirk until 28th August, so you'll have plenty of time to rest up a bit. Let's make the most of it, eh?" he said reassuringly.

"Sure," I replied, rubbing my eyes, as I headed for the latrines, now looking forward to being out of it for a while.

Later, as we headed for the beach, the sea looked magnificent. Our unit headed into the sand dunes to wait training orders. Bill and I sprawled out and lit up a smoke as the mid-day sun beat down on us, making us feel hot and sweaty. We were tempted to strip off and jump into the rolling white breakers now crashing invitingly on the beach. The hypnotic effect of the waves called out to us. Looking towards the horizon, I breathed in the salty air, and thought of home.

"Do you think anyone would notice if I just got up and swam home?" I asked Bill, who was chewing idly on a blade of grass, looking as if he hadn't a care in the world. He followed my gaze lazily.

"I doubt it."

As I got up seriously considering the task, he saw the look of contemplation in my eyes, and got up to stop me.

"Don't be bloody daft, its bloody miles away and the cold water would see you off before you could swim a bloody mile... and what's to say you'll keep swimming in the right direction, eh?. The sun's sent you barmy, John-boy. Leave it another day, eh lad?"

I decided to give the matter further thought, as I took off my jacket and sat back down again. Closing my eyes, I listened to seagulls squabbling in the distance. The summer breeze now felt fresh on my face, cooling me. For several hours whilst we languished in the dunes on the winds of time, far, far away from war, I drifted in and out of sleep. I dreamt of a better life... of Alice and of our future together, and all the wonderful things I was going to do, until Sarge rudely interrupted this one moment of pleasure.

"Come on lads, time to move out."

By the afternoon, our turn to practise new manoeuvres on the beaches had arrived. When we eventually got back to our billets, we were all shattered. Letters from home had arrived, and the usual air of excitement when news from home was delivered, temporarily put an end to the overwhelming desire to sleep.

I had five letters in all, and as soon as I picked them up, I recognised Matthew's handwriting, and instantly sensed, without opening it, he'd rejoined his unit and was back on active service. With a sense of foreboding, I put his letter aside and glanced at the others, which were from Alice and Mam. I lit up a woodbine, savouring the taste of the tobacco, before deciding to read Matthew's letter first.

Tearing the envelope evenly, I began to read his news. It was just as I suspected. He was back on active service.

SIX

"Bloody 'ell," I exclaimed, reading on.

"What's that," enquired Bill, glancing up from reading a letter from his Mam.

"Our Matt's renounced his rank of Company Sergeant Major and reverted to the rank of Private. He says he doesn't want the responsibility of other men's lives anymore. It's all been too much for him. It looks as if he's been giving things a lot of thought whilst being laid up in hospital."

"He's obviously decided that's best for him. I don't blame him, do you?" responded Bill.

"No, not at all, if that's what he wants. I'm just bloody annoyed he's back on active service."

Reading between the lines, I suspected it had something to do with seeing Fred, teetering on the brink of death. Apparently Matthew had spent several days beside his bedside before leaving England. He'd watched him seemingly waste away, as hospital staff tried to keep his body and soul together. The last of Fred's surgery had been done, but he'd lost a lot of weight and needed building up again.

Matthew described him as skin and bone. His mind had been affected, and it was highly unlikely he would ever return to active service. He told me there was another world which Fred sometimes slipped into. Fred was also a Company Sergeant Major and in the confusion between wakefulness and unconsciousness, he led his men time and time again into battle, where he lost them, and himself. The doctors were hopeful that such mental turmoil would pass, but knew little of these things. Matthew understood the responsibility a Company Sergeant Major all too well, and not long after seeing Fred, made the decision to return to the rank of a Private.

When we eventually heard from George, he too reported these kind of disturbances, and I thought of my own, realising now such things were more commonplace than I had first thought. As I folded Matthew's letter back into the envelope, some of the men had already fallen asleep and were snoring. The camp began to settle as I quickly opened Alice's and Mam's letters. Alice was missing me, and begging me to take care, whereas Mam was praying for me, and begging me to come home. Mam made it sound so easy, as if all I had to do was wave a magic wand and it would happen. I wished life was that simple, but it wasn't. Settling down myself, I fell into a deep, deep sleep, dead to the world. I didn't move all night. It was the calling sounds of seagulls, echoing

SIX

eerily throughout the tranquil camp, as dawn approached, which woke me.

Others were still hanging on to the last remnants of sleep and I contrasted their etched faces with those of the fresh recruits eager and waiting to get their first taste of war. A bitter taste entered my mouth and my right hand resumed its twitching again. I fought to regain control of it by holding my fingers, and noticed Old Picky about to do a wakeup call. Seeing me awake, he came over.

"You alright, Jackson?"

"Yes, sure Sarge, just a bit of cramp in my hand, that's all. It'll pass," I quipped, eager not to show I had a problem.

Chapter TWENTY-EIGHT

...my boyhood friend hath fallen, the pillar of my trust,
the true, the wise, the beautiful, is sleeping in the dust.
(George Stillman Hillard 1808 - 1879)

We trained for nearly a month, and were involved in several brigade practice attacks before moving on to Coudekerque, south of Dunkirk. From there, we began another time on the hoof, marching south through Wylder to Wormhoudt, Ledringhem to Arneke and on to Noordpeene. We stopped at Noordpeene to celebrate the first anniversary of our capture of the Schwaben Redoubt, on the Somme.

"Drinks on me," said Sarge, to a few of us propping up the bar in the local estaminet. He was obviously in a good mood.

"Cheers Sarge."

"Cheers lads," he responded.

"Where are we off to next?" asked a big lad, who'd just joined our lot.

"We'll be moving on to Clairmarais and then to St Marie-Cappel, just south of Cassel."

"Can we go back through Hout Schoubrouck, Plattebeurzs or Staple, Sarge? I left a girl in each of those places and she'll be waiting for me," he said laughing.

"No way!"

Instead, on 3rd October, we passed Rattekot Inn and Steenvoodre Road junction, near St Janster Biexen, just west of Poperinge.

"Hey Sarge, any chance I could go to Hospital Farm to visit Albert's grave?" I asked.

He looked at his watch and thought for a moment, wondering whether to let me go or not.

"I tell you what, Jackson, take this message through to headquarters and you can call in on the way back," he replied, writing down something on a piece of paper.

"Thanks, Sarge. I won't forget this. I'll buy you a beer next time we're out," I said.

"Go on, get on," he said, waving me on my way.

As it happened, I managed to borrow a bicycle from one of the locals and sped down the lane towards headquarters, getting there in no time.

"Shall I wait for a reply, Sir?" I asked the Officer.

"No, private. That will be all for now."

Tickled pink that my job was done, I cycled hell for leather to catch up with Albert. Hospital Farm was as busy as ever, as I made my way to the makeshift cemetery at the back. It took me a while to find Albert's grave, as the cemetery had filled up, and I lost my bearings, with so many now around him.

Eventually, I found him.

"Hello lads," I said, including several others in my greeting.

Distant guns could be heard "booming" in the background almost as if alerting them to my presence. I sat down at the foot of his grave and stared at the grave marker with his name on.

"Your Dad says, "Hello." He gave me your pocket watch. I hope you don't mind. Look... it's working fine, in fact it's been keeping right good time. He misses you... I do too..."

A tear escaped and I quickly brushed it aside, turning my face away, so he wouldn't see.

"He hasn't said much, though I know he misses you," I continued.

"He says he doesn't blame me. You don't blame me for letting you down, do you Albert? I couldn't bear it if you did. I've tried hard to avenge your death."

"I know you have John... I know..." whispered his voice in my head.

For a while I sat looking all around to see how large the cemetery had become. It was good to be back with Albert.

"Alice and everyone from home send their love. I suppose you know about Robert. He's buried at Lijssenthoek. He died four months after you."

My eyes wandered to the far end of the cemetery where the wood was. The sun sparkled magically through the trees, as it travelled downwards, almost as if it was heading below ground to see Albert.

"Does the sun ever shine where you are?" I asked, hoping it did.

"Our Matt's been in hospital in England for a while, but he's back here now, silly bugger. George is about ten miles from here, and Fred's hanging on by a thread in a London hospital. If you get the chance, put in a good word to God. Tell him we'd like to hang onto him for a bit longer."

The wind gently blew across the graves as I continued.

"We're moving out tomorrow to relieve the 2nd Wellingtons at Vlamertinge. They're in German trenches now. They're much better than ours. The bigwigs reckon that by 5pm on 9th October, we'll be assembling in shell holes near Calgary Grange. Fat chance. You remember Calgary Grange, don't you? Its part of Haig's third offensive at Passchendaele. We're battling for Poelcapelle. Third time lucky, eh? I bet you're glad you're out of it, aren't you? I wish I was. I feel sick at the thought of all this war and killing."

A brightly coloured goldfinch twittered back agreeing with me, as I continued to linger away the hours with Albert. All too soon, the sun began to set. I reluctantly got up to leave, whilst there was sufficient daylight left to get me safely back to camp.

"I'll write to your Dad to let him know I've seen you and that you're OK. Maybe he'll come to see you for himself one day... anyway, take care of yourself. I'll try to get here again sometime... that is... unless you see me first!" I said light-heartedly, hoping Albert understood the joke.

As I got up, I gave a final wave to them all.

"Bye..." I whispered softly.

I turned to go back through the Farm feeling calm, as if Albert had somehow put my mind at rest. It was just as if he'd wrapped me in a blanket of peace. Suddenly, a poem popped into my head, which a doctor at the front had jotted down and shown me, only a few days ago.

> *"Take up our quarrel with the foe, to you from failing hands we throw the torch, be yours to hold it high..."*

I quickened my pace to match my new found energy, as I carried Albert's torch, realising how apt the doc's words now seemed to be.

"Hurry up John... It doesn't do to be out in the open as night draws in... Hurry John," I heard Albert saying.

Breathless, I made it back to camp just as the light faded completely and silently sneaked to where my unit was.

"Did you find him?" Bill asked, giving me a fright, as he moved out of the shadows. He was having a quick smoke as he waited for me.

"I was just about to send a search party out for you," he said smiling.

"Yes, I found him... he's got plenty of company. There's a few more moved in with him. Not surprising really. No doubt after the next few days, there'll be even more."

We talked for a while and then decided it was time to turn in before old Picky caught us.

The following day, we relieved the New Zealanders and within two days, were indeed in position at Calgary Grange for the battle of Passchendaele, just as Haig had said we would be. In a way, it was like coming home again. We'd been here before, only this time, there was barely anything left standing I could recognise. There was an odd clump of trees here and there, an odd building or two amidst the rubble, but that was all. Even townsfolk had upped and left in a wave of horses, carts, pots, pans, and baggage.

The landscape they left behind undulated, taking on an appearance of its own. Its swollen surface barely concealed the labyrinth of intricate trench systems, which mimicked ailing blood vessels weaving in and around the hundreds of craters now pitting its surface. The scene was one great big cancerous sore, with men and machines like insects crawling all over it, sucking away the last remnants of its former guise.

Orders came through to attack the lower slopes of Poelcapelle Ridge, and we could see Jerry in the distance firmly dug in, looking down on us. It seemed almost an impossible task. What chance did we have of winning the high ground? Still, what did it matter? If we threw a whole battalion at them, then surely victory would be ours in the end.

I had a coughing fit as old Picky told us the plan of attack, and Bill thumped me several times on the back. Eventually a slug of rum was smuggled across to me from an unknown pocket and I downed it quickly, allowing its warmth to soothe my throat and penetrate deep down.

"Right, then you lot, listen. Here's what we're going to do," bellowed Sarge.

SIX

"Companies 'A' and 'C' will be in the first wave. You lot are to take a line midway between 'Peter Pan' and 'Wolf Copse', on the lower edges of the slope. 'B' and 'D' company will be in the second wave. You're going to leapfrog through and take the next objective, which will be a line roughly one hundred yards north-east of the road, running up from north-west to south-east of the ridge. Is that clear?" he said, pointing to the various positions on a large map of the area.

All of us were nodding.

"Right then, let's move out."

We left the safety of the old Jerry trench just east of Wieltje and set off in pouring rain, to reach assembly positions. The attack was due to start at about 1.20am. The going was heavy, and all of us experienced great difficulty in finding the way through vast areas of mud, which clung relentlessly to us, as if trying to stop this foolish task.

By midnight, all six hundred and forty-two of us, with twenty officers, were in position. With our strength sapped, we lay low, exhausted, waiting. Word was passed down the line to say that zero hour had now been put back to 5.20am and would begin with the usual barrage. The barrage would go forth at the rate of one hundred yards every six minutes, with all of us following behind in the set wave patterns, as planned.

Grateful for the respite, I closed my eyes, listening to the night time sounds as we waited. In my mind I fought the coming battle killing Germans in my way, until I was stopped dead by the thud of a bullet in my chest. The dream was so intense that I jumped when I heard the voice of Sarge.

"Shut it, Jackson."

The thud of the bullet was the thump to my ribs from Sarge's fist, telling me to quieten the noise I was inadvertently making.

"Time to go lads."

For a minute, I was unsure where I was.

"Come on mate, it's time to go. Any minute now…" Bill whispered.

When the whistle blew, we struggled to keep pace with the barrage as we ploughed over the blown up wet land in its wake. By the time we came to crossing the open plain of the Stroombeek, the mud underfoot was more like forging a small flowing stream of sludge, which ran into a marsh about two hundred yards wide.

In crossing this, we slipped and fell about like drunken men, as mud caked itself all over us, holding us down. The men in front tried to free themselves, as the men behind started to bunch up and the battalion lost all its formation. Within five minutes of zero hour, the Jerries opened fire from pill-boxes and shell holes on the Bellevue and Yetta slopes nearby. We were all sitting ducks.

As the bullets zinged all around, there was a frenzied fight to head for cover, and all of us ended up blindly climbing over fellow men as they dropped underfoot. I kept saying "sorry" as I trod on the bodies of men now forming duck-boards in the mud. We were like lice deserting the dying as we dodged the bullets and moved into brushwood a little way ahead.

I threw myself into the undergrowth and re-lived the repulsive squelching sensation I'd felt, when my foot accidentally trod on the face of a fallen man, pushing him further into the mud. I'd seen his eyes staring up at me. On hearing the squelching noise, I'd rushed on, in the footsteps of others who'd done the same. As a mouthful of vomit threatened to spill out, I glanced across at the chaos, and watched 2nd Lieutenant Parker, with a few men, hurry towards the pill-boxes to put them out of action. He got within forty yards of them before he was stopped by wire and brushwood. He quickly dug in to give some counter fire, hoping the rest of my lot would get to a safer spot.

By 6.20am, the first objective had been miraculously achieved, and those of us who could, went forward towards the next objective, leap-frogging through as old Picky had told us to do. Captain Wallace and Lieutenant Birbeck were killed as they attempted to offer further cover for us, just as Jerry continued to hold on doggedly to the slopes. We amazingly broke through, amidst the turmoil and madness that ensued, and captured a small section, but only after further heavy loss of life.

In a fit of madness and anger, we shot at the enemy, forcing them to retreat. A few Jerries surrendered, no doubt thinking they would be taken captive, but we killed them without mercy. This was one time when "D" company would take no prisoners. We were determined to get retribution for the lives of our friends strewn on the slopes of Passchendaele, as we fired each bullet.

For a moment I stood over a badly injured German boy, who was dying. I glimpsed his fear and the pleading look for mercy in his eyes, before I put him out of his misery. The hate within me consumed all instinct to save him. As I looked down at him, I didn't see him as a fellow human being, I saw him as a killer, determined to kill me. I loathed myself for what I had become. The abhorrence I felt, left me with a bitter taste in my mouth, and I turned in anger to God, despising Him for reducing us all to animals.

Amid the chaos of battle, we carried on and on, killing and maiming, just as Jerry killed and maimed us. The senseless 'tit-for-tat' fighting seemed to have no end, and my unit became cut off from the rest. Our runners attempted to get messages through to headquarters for reinforcements, but failed, so we just dug in and did the best we could to stay alive.

Lieutenant Colonel Bousfield realising our dilemma attempted to help, but was wounded before he got anywhere near us. On hearing this, Major Mackay went forward from the old German Reserve line to take command, but within an hour of leaving his position, he was killed, which left only Captain Ablitt to take command, and us still stranded at a point just short of the second objective.

As we struggled to maintain and strengthen our position, "A" and "C" companies managed to secure a support line running from the south edge of Wolf Farm to the eastern edge of Wolf copse, behind us. We were about one hundred and fifty yards out from the southern corner of the copse. It was some time after midnight on the 11th, well over twenty-four hours later, when they managed to reach us. Supplies of food and water quickly followed, but by that time we were seriously dehydrated.

Eventually, we were relieved, and those who had survived, made our way back in dribs and drabs to the old German reserve line. It didn't take us long to re-assemble and slowly march back to Vlamertinge. All of us were in a bad way, caked in mud which cracked and fell from our eyelashes, eyebrows and hair, as we walked wearily to the resting area. The brown earth mingled with sweat and streaks of splattered blood, and unrecognisable bits of human tissue from those who had been blown up. No one spoke. Only the offering of water, and the odd nod of the head to say, "Thanks mate," was witnessed. The silence told its own harrowing story.

The battle for the ridge went on for a further month before it was declared officially over. On the 10th November 1917, having got no further forward, the bigwigs decided it was a waste of time to pursue it any further. Our battalion was warmly complimented on our gallant attempt, but in the end, Haig's third push in the battle of Ypres at Passchendaele failed, just as all of us had known it would. As units dug in to hold positions, paid for with the lives of hundreds of men, the routine of trench warfare reigned once more. We had achieved nothing.

Letters from home confirmed the return to normality. I had a letter from Mam, who told me grandma Jackson had died on the 13th of November. They buried her in the old churchyard at Ebberston where grandad was a sexton. I read Mam's words matter-of-factly, devoid of any emotion. Death was now common place, so much so, it just seemed to be another one to add to the list. It wasn't until much later when my thoughts drifted to Rose Cottage where grandma and grandad had lived all their lives, that I realised the old place wouldn't be the same without her. I wondered how grandad was managing and thought about the lives they'd had together. She was seventy-five and he was six months older than her. I knew he would miss her terribly. The only comforting thought was everyone in the village knew each other and grandad would be well looked after by the hamlet of well meaning folk.

Our family had lived in Ebberston since the dawning of time and was well known. When Dad had moved to York because of work, I'd hated the thought of moving away and leaving the wide open spaces, which the countryside offered. It had only been when I realised I had the best of both worlds, that I had resigned myself to living there. It had enabled me to spend the summers in Ebberston with my grandparents and the rest of the time in the hustle and bustle of the big city and I had soon learned this was an advantage.

I had loved helping grandad in the fields with the cattle and then coming home after a hard day's work to grandma's cooking. I sighed as I remembered the evocative smell of her steak and kidney pie, with rich thick gravy, and home grown carrots sitting neatly next to mashed potatoes, now realising how far away that was from here. For a brief moment, I was happy for grandma. She'd lived a long and contented life, and had lived it well knowing nothing of the horrors of war. Poor grandad. He must be lost without her. He'd been married to her for fifty-five years, and had spent over three-quarters of his life with her. It would seem as if he'd lost a part of himself. Feeling somewhat bereft myself, I couldn't imagine myself without Alice. Instantly I realised how he was feeling and knew if it was me, I wouldn't want to go on.

SIX

Mam continued to say Dad was inwardly upset, and had bottled up his emotion at the funeral. Tears in a man were regarded as a weakness, and I knew he'd be cross with himself if he let them show. It was always the same, a man must maintain a stiff upper lip. I did my best to follow his example but had difficulty in keeping this emotion in check with all that was happening here. Despite Dad's beliefs and resolve, I knew he would be grieving, even if he didn't show it to others, and for once, I was cross with him for hiding his emotion. Afterall, what was so wrong with crying?

The rest of Mam's letter was about getting back to normal. Grandad had refused to go back with them to York, saying he'd be fine where he was, and insisting he could look after himself. Mam had doubted this, though respected his wishes. I smiled realising Mam would think no man could ever manage without a woman to look after him, even though Stephen Seal proved to be the exception. No doubt grandad would too. He had lots to keep him occupied. He'd probably treasure some moments sitting on the Church bench overlooking her grave. His belief in God was strong. There was of course her grave to tend to, which he'd no doubt do lovingly, just as he had tended to her when she was alive. For a brief moment I closed my eyes and imagined sitting on the Church bench with him, feeling the chilled November air cover us, listening to the wind blowing through the belfry, as we absorbed the relative peace...

It was dusk before I reached in my jacket pocket for the bundle of other letters I'd put there. Searching for Alice's amidst them, I wanted to feel her near me, to hear her words echoing in my head. I clutched her letter, desperately wishing she was with me. As I sat there, an intense, almost joyous feeling washed over me, as if she knew, and had answered me. The love we shared seemed to have defied the laws of time, and I felt bathed in its glory, which no-one, not even Jerry, could take away from me. In some strange way, it felt as if the love grandma and grandad had shared for all eternity, now belonged to Alice and me, and I could sense Alice felt that too.

Chapter TWENTY-NINE

As two floating planks meet and part on the sea,
O friend! so I met and then drifted from thee.
(William R. Alger 1823 - 1905)

My lot spent the next few days wiring up the west slope of the ridge at Broodseide, just in case Jerry tried to take it back. Ironically, he continued shelling headquarters further back and attempted to shell where A and C companies were in support, but strangely, left us alone on the slope, almost as if he hadn't seen us. In recognition of Jerry's folly, I felt quite elated and when our relief took over and we moved back down the line to the Brigade Reserve area, where our Nissan hut billets were, I whistled a monosyllabic tune.

There was some confusion regarding how long we would be billeted in this corrugated jungle, and just as we were about to settle down to another night, new orders came through.

"What's the problem, Sarge?" I asked.

"There's no problem, Jackson."

"Why are we being moved out so late then?"

He didn't answer.

"Where are we off to this time, Sarge?" asked Bill.

"Devonshire Camp," he responded tersely, sounding as if he had a bee in his bonnet.

"Where's that then, Sarge?" Bill persisted.

"Look, all of you. This has just been a stop off place, and it's now been decided that we'll relieve the 1/6th Battalion in support at Esplanade Gap in the South West corner of Ypres town. Any more questions?"

"I thought we were going to spend more time here," I said, now disappointed.

"Well you're wrong and when the big-wigs say jump, we jump, OK?"

"What's up with Sarge?" I whispered to Bill, as we collected our gear together.

"I don't know, but something's certainly ruffled his feathers."

SIX

We headed towards tunnels, in the ramparts close to Ypres Railway Station. The town was in ruins, heaving with soldiers on the move. Our new living quarters were underground, which didn't surprise me as there was nothing left standing above that was remotely habitable. I thought I'd seen it all, but as we entered this different kind of setting, the damp claustrophobic atmosphere underground was as if we'd moved in with the grim reaper. His breath flickered our candles and in the stillness of night, he made strange resonant noises as he walked amongst us, surveying his future prey.

Terrified the continual shelling of the city would bring the roof down and bury us alive with him, I stayed close to the entrance, where I slept fitfully for the whole time we were his guests. The entire month of December was spent with him, as we relieved various battalions in the left and right sub-sections of the front line, three days here, three days there, holding our positions, before returning to his parlour.

On Christmas Eve, the 1/6th battalion relieved us and we went into reserve of the left brigade. The day was crisp and bright and I was glad to be outside. Rumour had it we were moving on to Halifax Camp, and when we packed up our gear on 29th December and left, I was elated to be leaving these underground quarters. Life below was certainly not for me and if ever I survived this war, and had a choice, I'd damn well make sure no-one would put me in a coffin and lower me into it.

When the year 1918 dawned, the old familiar 'Auld Lang Syne' was merrily sung.

"Do you reckon we'll go home this year?" I asked Bill.

"I've no idea lad. It doesn't look like there's an end in sight."

"What do you reckon, Sarge?" he asked.

"Doubtful. There's no indication of any let up."

Though the weather was bitterly cold, it was dry. Bill heard there'd been some heavy snow at home, and I tried picturing the family trudging their way to Church on New Year's Day morning. I could almost smell the goose cooking slowly waiting for their return. All the vegetables would be prepared so Mam would only have to put them on when they got back. My stomach started to ache as I thought of it. We were having the usual served up here, with a double ration of rum to keep us warm. There'd be no other festive luxuries, unless someone from home sent a parcel.

The next few days in the front line were spent with gas masks on and off. Jerry decided to release a barrage of gas shells to welcome in 1918 but fortunately our warning party gave plenty of notice, and kept the number of casualties low. By the 11th, we were relieved by the Manchesters and moved back into Ypres to camp near the School. I was silently relieved we hadn't gone back to the tunnels, and said as much to Sarge.

There was very little happening at this time and all of us felt at a loose end. Our mood mirrored the damp weather, so I decided to catch up on letter writing.

"'ere John, this one's for you," said Bill, throwing me a letter which he'd just collected.

It was from Mam. I came to the conclusion she must write a letter almost every day and silently thanked her for caring. As I opened it, I immediately noticed the tone of this one was sombre.

"Oh God, no!" I exclaimed.

"What's up John? Bad news?" asked Bill.

"Fred's back on active service," I said disbelievingly.

"After languishing for months in a bloody London Hospital on the brink of death, he's been posted back to the front lines. It beggars belief. After all he's done for his King and Country, they still demand more," I said shocked.

"The family's distraught. Mam's made an emotional plea to the authorities telling them he's done enough, but Fred said he wouldn't feel right walking the streets of York with his mates fighting on the battlefields. He's lost his bleeding marbles!" I added.

Somewhat distracted with thoughts of Fred, I missed the announcement that our lot had been given a few days' free time to spend in Vlamertinge and Poperinge. Sarge said he hoped we'd regain some zest for life, especially as he knew winter in the front line had eaten away at our very souls, and morale was now at an all time low.

"It'll be good for you lot to get away," Sarge advocated.

"You're ordered to take some time out to soak up any cheer that's about," he added.

Bill heard on the grapevine that some of the back street estaminets were still open and so we decided to take advantage of this, heading for a small bustling café on the Poperinge Road. It was obviously doing a roaring trade from other like minded individuals. On arrival, we fought our way to a little table in the corner. As I downed my third cup of strong coffee, the throng of young men kept coming and going like a tide. I noticed a woman entering, and was startled to realise it was Lisette from Talbot House. I raised my hand but she didn't see me. She was battling her way through to the other side of the room where a young man sat, obviously waiting for her.

"Hang on a minute, Bill. I just want to speak with someone I've seen. I'll be back in a jiff, sit tight," I uttered, heading in her direction.

I squeezed myself around the various tables and writhing bodies and on reaching the now deeply engrossed pair, I took off my cap and interrupted them.

"Excusez-moi… Bonjour mademoiselle…"

She looked directly at me with her dark blue eyes.

"John!" she exclaimed, as it dawned on her who I was.

She immediately stood up and threw her arms around me, obviously pleased to see me.

Turning back to the young man she spoke hurriedly in French, before proudly introducing him.

"My fiancé, Pascal," she respectfully said, in broken English.

We shook hands and I congratulated her as she eagerly continued.

"Z'ere is a message on zee board for you, from your brudder. He was here," she said excitedly, "in Vlamertinge only a few weeks ago. I am certain 'e is still 'ere."

She saw my puzzled look as to which brother it was.

"It was Massthew," she said, shaking my arm as if I should know.

"I will leave a message for 'im if you like?"

"Great," I said, elated.

This was almost as good as actually seeing my brother and I hastily scribbled down a note, telling him where I was, should he get the opportunity to come looking for me. I also told him to keep a look out for George as well. It was a long shot but stranger things did happen, and in any case, one could dream of such an encounter.

After giving her the note, and passing further polite conversation, I began to feel like a gooseberry and so decided to make myself scarce.

"Well, I must be going. Nice meeting you Pascal," I said, shaking hands with him as I turned to Lisette.

She raised her hand to shake mine and instead, I made the over demonstrative gesture of kissing the back of it. Lisette laughed coyly and stood up. She gave me a hug and affectionately brushed my cheek with her lips like a sister.

"Au revoir John. I see you soon, no?"

"Oui mademoiselle Lisette," I said, tipping my cap.

"Good-bye Pascal. Take care of her."

As I left, they both turned towards each other and became eagerly engaged in conversation, and I felt bitterly jealous it wasn't Alice and me.

Bill was twiddling his thumbs, when I returned.

"Who was that then?" he asked, as I sat down.

I briefly explained, and told him about the notice board at Talbot House, and the message Matthew had left. I remembered how the board in the hall was a focal point for all who entered the building. Messages from fathers to sons, brothers to brothers, comrades and friends were written on this board which 'Tubby' kept organised.

Walking back to camp, I studied the faces of the men we passed in the hope one of them might be Matt and almost came to believe Mam's words of, "maybe you could all meet up..." In some strange way, it gave me comfort to think he was not far away.

As January faded into February and then into March, there were no further messages from my brother, nor did I see Lisette again as our battalion moved on to Hussar Camp, then to Garter Camp, and finally to Scottish Wood Camp, to be in reserve again. Relief came at intervals over the next two weeks in April, before 'A', and my 'D' company, were ordered to withdraw completely. We left 'B' and 'C' company manning the posts at Stirling Castle and Glencorse Wood, whilst we moved into Ypres to take the train to Ouderdom. It wasn't until 21st April, they eventually caught up with us on the front line, opposite Wytschaete.

It was there I heard about Fred. He'd been wounded again and had been shipped back to a London Hospital, this time, for good. His fighting days were definitely over. I didn't know the extent of his injuries, but realised they must be pretty bad as Mam and Dad had been summoned to his bedside. This all happened when Matthew was home on two weeks' leave, which was why I hadn't heard from him either. Mam said she got up to find him lounging in the fireside chair in the kitchen and just couldn't believe her eyes when she found him there, as large as life. She always left the latch off the hook in case any of us came home, and this was one occasion when she was grateful she had. As I read her letter, listening to enemy artillery fire in the background, I suddenly became conscious I might never see any of them again, and began to feel lonely and depressed, worried at the uncertainty of everything.

Her letter had been written just before Matthew returned to France on March 30th. They all travelled down to see Fred again, as Matthew had to pass through London on his way back to rejoin his old unit. How I wished I could have been there with them! Mam said she was 'beside herself' with joy, and I smiled at the thought of the surprise it must have been.

Gradually, the pounding of guns in my head became incessant, eventually distracting my thoughts away from her letter. As the noise got louder, I realised they were shelling the roads trying to stop our ration and carrying parties from joining us.

"Four men 'ave just copped it and there's about twenty-three others wounded," said Sarge, as he told us all to get ready.

I quickly put her letter in my pocket and picked up my gear to follow Bill and the others.

By the time darkness fell, it was our turn to be under attack and all thoughts of home were long gone. Jerry was attempting to capture our listening post on the left of 'B' company, but our lot managed to drive them off using rifle and Lewis gun fire. We sent a message through to the artillery section to fire in front of the post, and by 10.15pm, it was all over. We helped carry in the wounded. Three officers were dead and we moved all of them speedily down the line.

24th April was a bright, cold morning, with enemy aircraft more active than usual. Orders came down the line to be ready for action again, as we were told the battle of Lys was about to start in earnest. Listening posts heard mention of a German attack called 'Operation Georgette,' so we knew something was afoot. The battle in the far distance was getting closer by the minute and by mid afternoon on the 25th, Jerry's gas barrage started. They sent over a significant number of smoke shells to confuse us, making the air black and thick like treacle. Our gas respirators stayed on until the all clear was given at 4.50am, when one by one, each of the companies reported everything to be stable.

We anticipated Jerry would follow through with a bombardment, and so waited, knowing it would come soon. The uncanny silence set nerves on edge. We didn't have to wait long. After ten minutes, it started. We moulded ourselves into the walls of the dugouts to become one with the moving earth until it was over. With telephone wires cut and communication with other companies lost, headquarters sent up an S.O.S signal to tell everyone of the imminent assault. It was laughable really. It was bloody evident to all of us the attack had begun.

As we desperately tried to drive the enemy back, further spine-chilling clouds of gas swirled unexpectedly around us. Dying men clawed at our legs in their final moments, as we hastily put our gas masks back on, and clambered out of the trenches, losing all sense of direction. Smoke and gas enveloped us, blinding us as we flailed around, shooting our way ahead, hoping we would kill Jerry before he killed us. We ran for our lives, each man for himself. We had thought the gas attacks had finished, but soon realised such thoughts were a big mistake, and now we were paying the price for such folly.

Our support lot took over, whilst those of us who could, regrouped. Any man able to fight, was sent either to Zero Wood, or to north of the Grande Bois, to fight a rearguard action with the 1/6th West Yorkshires. At 7am, after the gas slowly dispersed, the enemy headed towards Northern Brickstacks, south east of Grande Bois. Their strategic move prevented communication with our front line runners, as they'd come right around the right flank of us and were now working in rear of battalion headquarters. Headquarters relocated to take up a defensive position, whilst we moved into Chinese Trench, under the command of Lieutenant Colonel Oddie. We kept extending our flank in a north westerly direction parallel with the Wytschaete Road in order to prevent the enemy from getting any further round the back of us, but we were unable to establish a hold. A Scottish Rifles company succeeded in momentarily filling the gap before all hell let loose again.

Despite our valiant attempt, the enemy broke through well outside the flanks of the battalion and worked round to the rear of the front line companies. They faced strong resistance from us for about four hours as we doggedly held onto the line, but it came with a price. Eighteen officers and five hundred and forty-eight men were killed, wounded or missing. We stood our ground until relief came, but there wasn't one unwounded man amongst us, including me. I'd been hit in the arm. Bill had copped one in his shoulder, Sarge in his leg. We looked as if we'd been used as target practice. My arm hurt like blazes, but Bill and I carried Sarge between us, until we all collapsed at the makeshift dressing station along with hundreds of others.

Word eventually got back to say that Jerry had been forced to retreat and we'd all done a splendid job. The bullet in my arm had gone straight through and after a few stitches and a pressure bandage I returned with the rest of the patched up men to Ouderdom Camp. Bill returned a day later, along with Sarge, who'd insisted on hobbling around without a problem, but he looked his age and more. His pale etched face and greying hair put a further ten years on him.

"Well, we're all moving further up the queue to Heaven. Soon be at the top!" he joked. We laughed at his cynicism, but in our hearts, we knew he was right.

On 29th April, those of us who could walk, were moved back to the Watou area, west of Poperinge. Others, such as Sarge were transported in trucks. The following day we were inspected by Brigadier General Rennie, the Commanding Officer of 146th Infantry Brigade. After inspection he warmly congratulated us on the stance we'd made yesterday and he read out a letter he'd received from Major General Cameron.

> *"It is with very great pleasure that I forward the enclosed on to you, though I think you have seen it already. The letter reflects great honour on the 1/7th West Yorkshire Regiment. The 1/5th and 1/6th West Yorkshire Regiment battalions had added great lustre to the record earned by your Brigade and by the 49th West Riding Division in the recent fighting. It is a wonderful achievement that these two battalions stood their ground on the Wytschaete Ridge on 25th April without a single unwounded man coming back. My great hope now is that you will find that you have sufficient old hands remaining to carry on the great spirit which has animated the 146th Brigade and infuse it into the new drafts which I hope to see joining you soon, in order that the name of the 146th Brigade shall live for ever. Please let your battalions know that I feel deeply proud of them."*

SIX

Despite this commendation, my heart was heavy. On the very day I'd been wounded, I'd received word to say Matthew had been severely wounded and had been immediately transferred to the 4th Casualty Clearing Station with shrapnel wounds to his legs. A few hours later, a message reached me saying he'd died. By this time, I realised my big brother, who was 32 years old, would have already been buried, no doubt in Pernois Cemetery, close to where he was in France. The telegram said he didn't suffer, and had bravely fought for his country. I reflected on the words 'he didn't suffer', but the bitter phrase of platitude, said to all relatives, belied the truth. I knew the reality of death. I'd seen the suffering of men and knew that death was often a drawn out agony. I visualized him embracing it with open arms like so many others, begging for his deliverance.

I started to count the personal toll of war... Albert, Robert, now Matthew, all dead. George, God knows where, Fred seriously ill in hospital and me, desperately trying to stay alive, with no end in sight... six of us, out of thousands. I imagined Mr Rourke knocking on the door with the telegram and Mam's face wondering which one of us it was. She'd immediately know before opening it, that another one of her sons was dead.

Unrelenting tears washed down my face, as I wished time would go backwards and this madness on earth would end. Sadly, there was nothing in sight. I remembered how everyone had believed the war would be over by Christmas 1914, and yet here we all were, three-and-a-half years on, in the month of May, soon to give way to June.

Our unit spent a few days resting in order to give some time to build up our numbers to full battalion strength again. However, as new men joined us, they were struck down within days, by an illness, so we were no better off. The rest of us soldiered on, seemingly more resistant. We watched these poor souls come and go, too weak to fight this unseen enemy and waited, wondering if, after all what had happened, it would be a bloody flu bug that would see us off. Everyone seemed to be coughing and delirious with high temperatures. Filthy 'white' handkerchiefs were held to streaming noses, as people staggered around battling aching joints and other such symptoms. Only those unable to stand were relieved of duty. The rest soldiered on until they succumbed.

By the beginning of June, those struck down by flu that had survived, were back on active service. Mam wrote a letter enclosing a newspaper article from the Yorkshire Herald. It was dated Tuesday May 14th 1918.

SIX

I was amazed to see photographs of me and my brothers, and read it eagerly, wondering what on earth she'd been saying. I'd been too wrapped up in the events of war and illness, to realise Mam had been blabbing about us, telling the world about how many sons she'd lost, praying there would be no more.

Chapter THIRTY

Now let us sing, long live the king
(William Cowper 1731 - 1800)

Despite worrying, and mourning the loss of another son, Mam carried on. She put all her energy into getting ready for her visit to Windsor Castle.

"I wonder if John got my letter," Mam asked Dad, who was busily polishing his shoes.

"He'll be surprised about our audience with the King at Windsor Castle," she remarked to herself.

"Do you think him and George will be home by then?"

"'Eee lass, don't get your hopes up. By all accounts the war's not over yet," he warned.

"Well, they keep saying that, now the Americans are there, it'll be over soon. Don't you think it will be then?"

She waited for a response, but before Dad could answer she continued talking.

"In any case, this flu bug seems to be killing the Germans in their thousands, and has been since the back end of last year. That'll be the end of them, you mark my words."

"Aye, and it'll be the end of our lads as well, and all of us here in the towns. All it needs is for our John, George and Fred to catch the ruddy thing and the bloody lot of them will be gone," Dad snapped, angrily expressing his emotions.

"I know," Mam said, suddenly bereft. "I don't like to think about such things. I just pray to God they'll come home safe and sound."

She quickly changed the subject.

"You're going to need a new suit and me a new dress when we go to Windsor."

"What's wrong with my wedding suit?" Dad quipped, not wanting to indulge in further expense, as Mam pottered around him.

"Nothings wrong with it, except that it's old and probably won't fit you."

"Rubbish. Dig it out and we'll see if I need a new one," he said stubbornly. "I'm just the same as I ever was. It'll fit, don't you worry," he mumbled, pulling in his stomach.

Mam sighed, but decided that as he was so keen to wear it, it was worth taking it out of mothballs to have a look at it, before committing monies to a new one. However, whatever happened, she was adamant that she would have a new dress. She rarely indulged in such luxuries and decided it was about time she did.

"I might see some nice material and Mrs Naylor could possibly run me up a dress," she thought to herself, as she looked at the invitation again and read it out aloud, as if she couldn't believe it.

> *"By Command of the King... (She sighed)*
> *Admit the Bearer to the State Apartments Windsor Castle, on*
> *Tuesday 23rd July 1918 between the hours of 11am and 1pm.*
> *Signed by - Sandhurst, Lord Chamberlain."*

"Gosh, to think the likes of us will be meeting the King. I wonder what he's really like. I've got it all planned," she said, and when Dad didn't ask what she had in mind, she continued to babble on.

"We'll spend a few days with our Gladys and little Robert in Colchester, and then we'll catch the train to Windsor from there. It couldn't be better."

She stole a look at Dad to see if he approved. To her, his silence meant he did.

"I bet our grandson has grown somewhat. Gladys says he's the image of our Robert. He would be proud, I know," and brushing away a tear, she put the kettle on, satisfied with her plans.

Suddenly, Dad erupted in angry response to all of Mam's planning.

"What do you mean, 'the likes of us'? What's wrong with the likes of us? We're just as good as the rest of them, and it's the likes of us that have sacrificed two of our sons and Stephen's Albert, for the likes of him, so don't you forget it. And, it's not over yet. What's to say the rest of our lads are going to come home safe? I'm going to make damn sure the King bloody well knows this when I see him. Just you wait and see."

"Now then Thomas, you can't go talking to the King like that. Don't you go spoiling everything. I meant it's not everyday 'ordinary' folk like you and me get to see Royalty, and I'm not going to let you make a scene and embarrass me, or I won't go, King or no King," she said stubbornly, and deciding to let matters calm down, she changed the subject, telling him how Mrs Lofthouse was feeling, now the weather had improved.

Over the next few weeks, Mam was careful not to upset Dad. She continued making plans, as the grimness of war was reported in the newspaper. The flu epidemic seemed to be ebbing slightly, for which everyone was silently thankful. She knew no end of people who'd been affected; even some who lived in the same street had died from it. She worried about grandad, but thankfully Ebberston, being a small village, seemed to have escaped the best part of it, and he was managing to stay reasonably well.

Stephen Seal hadn't been quite so lucky. He spent several weeks in bed and was still very weak, even though he was now over the worst of it. Mam did what she could for him, despite him telling her to keep away. The last thing he wanted was for her to come down with it, but she took no notice, insisting she was as strong as an ox. She took him homemade soup every day, and made sandwiches for tea, but he was insistent she left them on the kitchen table and didn't get any closer to him. Dad brought his bed down into the front room so he didn't have so far to walk. It also made it easier to get to the lavatory which was downstairs. He was eternally grateful to both of them and reckoned he wouldn't have survived this awful illness, if it hadn't been for the care they gave him.

By mid June, Mam found some plain crepe material in a pleasing duck-egg blue colour. It had been displayed in a back street shop window, and she impulsively bought it. She called around to see Mrs Naylor, who measured her up, saying she would make it into a simple dress and jacket. After several fittings it was perfect and fitted a treat. She borrowed a wide brimmed, pale straw hat from Mrs Lofthouse, which complemented the outfit. She then dug out her best brown crocodile shoes, with matching handbag which had been great granny's, and was just perfect for such an occasion. The final touches were white lace gloves and some jewellery.

Dad's wedding suit, as predicted, pinched a bit around his waist so Mrs Naylor made a V-shaped piece of fabric to insert at the back of his trousers. It didn't matter it wasn't exactly the same colour. His jacket would cover it, so long as he kept it on, she told him. As the day grew closer, Mam's anticipation mounted.

SIX

Finally, on Friday 19th July, they were ready to go. Stephen Seal called around to see them off and wish them well. Mam was transformed from her usual scullery maid appearance, into a woman from the gentry, and was pleased with the result. As she went upstairs to get herself a handkerchief, she was even more delighted when she overheard Dad and Stephen talking.

"My missus sure does scrub up well, don't you think?"

"'Aye, she sure does," said Stephen, acknowledging that she did.

They set off to catch the 8.30 a.m. train from York station, and after two train changes, arrived at Colchester. There, waiting on the platform, was Gladys, with Robert.

"Nanna, grandad…" a little voice was heard above the hustle and bustle of the station, and looking in the direction of the sound, they saw little Robert running towards them.

He was definitely the image of his father and just for a moment, the clock was turned back thirty years, as Mam remembered the brown haired, little boy who once smothered her in kisses and clung to her skirts, whenever she had to leave him. Instantly, this small version of Robert threw his arms around Mam's legs, and buried his head, hugging her, just like his Dad used to, all those years ago.

By the time Gladys caught up with them and embraced them both, Mam was crying. She swept Robert up into her arms and buried her head in him, squeezing him tightly.

"Oh I could just eat and eat and eat you. You're so lovely."

Robert squirmed to be free, leaning his body towards grandad, waving his arms as he did so.

"Grandad, grandad," he shouted, in his attempt to be rescued.

"I'm here, son. I'm here," said Dad, as he disentangled him from Mam's grip.

Robert gave him a quick kiss and a hug for saving him, allowing himself to be lowered to the ground where he instantly held tightly onto his hand, ensuring he was well out of Mam's reach. Gladys and Mam smiled at Dad's outward display of affection.

Robert was blissfully unaware this was the first time all of them had seen one another since his father's death, and he skipped happily along side them. As they headed out of the station, Gladys helped to carry the bags and hooked her arm through Mam's. Silence now prevailed, leaving only the unspoken thoughts between the grown-ups, poignantly reminding them of memories still raw. The odd tightening hand on an arm, the sympathetic knowing looks, the hastily wiped away tear, spoke volumes, as each of them avoided alerting little Robert to the turmoil of emotion surrounding him. Such expression of emotion was for mulling over when 'little people' had gone to bed. Until then, there was a need to catch up on other news and rein in some semblance of normality once more.

The four days flew by quickly, and before they knew it, Tuesday had arrived. The day was bright and warm and Mam was excited as she paid particular attention to her hair, curling it up into a faultless bun at the back of her head. She left her hat off, telling Gladys she'd put it on in the hansom cab taking them from the station to the Castle. She nervously checked the hat pin threaded through the hat's rim to make sure it was secure. The last thing she wanted was to lose it and her hat to blow off.

"Stop fussing, or we'll be late for the train," Dad quipped.

Mam hated goodbyes and dithered even more, prolonging the event as she hugged Robert, now reluctant to let him go. Gladys, realising the difficulty, quickly exchanged kisses with them, and with promises to write, encouraged them to go as she pulled Robert towards her and waved them on their way.

"He's grown so much. Our Robert would have been so proud of him," remarked Mam, as she sniffled into her handkerchief, and waved them goodbye.

Fighting their way through the hustle and bustle of London, they made good progress and were surprised to reach the Castle a little before 11am. There were a few other people milling around, waiting to go in. Some were officers, some were soldiers, who looked to be recovering from injuries, and there were also other middle-aged couples. Mam wondered if they'd lost sons too. It was a grand sight.

As the small crowd of people gravitated to the main entrance through what was known as Henry VIII gateway, an official guide from the Lord Chamberlain's Office began unlocking the huge mechanism on the wrought iron gates to let them in. He escorted them to the road leading towards the State Apartments. As they passed the Guard Room, they saw soldiers in bright red uniforms, with busbies on their heads which gently rippled in the breeze.

SIX

"Ooo, look at them," Mam said to Dad.

"They're the King's soldiers," he said, enlightening her.

The guide led the procession past the three towers on the town side wall of the Castle, towards St George's Chapel on the left.

"I'm sorry but I am afraid we'll not be able to see the Chapel today as it's not safe to enter. It's going to be restored. I'm told it will take several years," he said.

There was a disappointing "awh," collectively muttered, as they moved on further up the hill.

"Oh Thomas, just look at that," Mam said, pointing to the towering turrets and grand stone escarpment of the Castle.

They continued on, passing the residences of the Military Knights of Windsor, an ancient Order attached to the Castle, and on to the North Entrance. The road opened out onto a square known as 'The Great Quadrangle' and at last, they were looking straight at The State Apartments, the King's private apartments and visitor apartments, which all bordered onto it. The vast space overwhelmed Mam. She teetered backwards, looking up at the large stone escarpment, unable to take it all in.

"That's the Sovereign's Entrance," said the guide, who pointed across the yard.

"But we shall all be entering through this entrance," he continued as he led the way inside.

"Ooo, look Thomas, they've got the red carpet out for us. I bet this is where the saying comes from," she grinned, all knowingly.

The grand staircase was decorated with fine specimens of Arms and Armour from the fifteenth through to the eighteenth century and was absolutely spectacular. Her eyes took in every detail. On the landing was a white marble statue of King George IV wearing a long robe. There were fine specimens of wood carvings which Dad ran his fingers over, feeling the smoothness of the workmanship. That was before noting the large portraits of majestic dignitaries who looked down regally on him, warning him with menacing faces, not to touch.

As they progressed along the lush red carpet, they came across tapestries hung from floor to ceiling, complementing the crimson silk-covered suite of furniture below them. Rooms led off in all directions and the group of people eagerly looked this way and that, taking in the

SIX

richness and opulence of the trappings of Kings and Queens who had walked there before them. Each step, Mam took pleasure in knowing she was treading where royalty had. The guide continued with stories he must have told thousands of visitors before them, but Mam hung on his every word, and eagerly waited for further little gems of information, delightfully recounted. As they approached the State Bedroom, they were greeted with walls covered in green silk damask and furniture upholstered in Chinese style old silk to match. The scene was breathtaking.

Dad, equally impressed, smiled mischievously.

"How about that for a bed?"

Mam quickly elbowed him in the ribs, 'shushing' him, worried he would be overheard, and when no-one seemed to notice, she smiled seductively back at him as if agreeing. As the guide pointed out great masterpieces of enormous value, adorning the walls everywhere, the group slowly moved on, with Mam and Dad grinning like newlyweds on honeymoon.

At last they came to the Grand Reception room where guests were received. This was the personification of the British Empire, and they had arrived at last. Mam looked at her watch, and catching the eye of the guide waved him over.

"Excuse me. What time are we being presented to the King?"

Somewhat surprised, and realising there had been a misunderstanding somewhere along the line, he became uncomfortable.

"Oh madam, I am afraid the King is not in residence today. He is actually visiting the Fleet at Rosyth and will not be back until tomorrow."

Mam looked as if she had been struck by him, and somewhat confused, engaged the guide further.

"But I thought we were being presented to him today?"

She continued to look distressed, as he politely repeated the information again.

"No madam, certainly not today. I'm sorry if you were under that impression. He does sometimes call in to see people as they are wandering about and it's unfortunate he isn't here today. If it's any consolation, he always personally insists that tea and sandwiches are provided, with the instruction we are to make sure you have everything you require, so if you'd like to follow me, it's just through here," and with that, he gently took her arm and led her through to the Throne Room, where tables were set and several butlers, immaculately dressed, were ready to serve them.

"You and your bloody presentation," Dad muttered softly to her, when they sat down and no one was looking.

"I thought it was too good to be true for the likes of us," he continued, noting how upset she was.

"Never mind ole' lass, I've seen him from a distance and he's not much to look at."

"That's not the point, Thomas. I was looking forward to meeting him in person."

She sniffed into her handkerchief and looking up from under her hat, saw a butler approaching them. She gracefully took a cheese and cucumber sandwich from the tray, which he held out to her.

"Thank you. These look delicious," and before he could move on, took several more, obviously determined to make the best of things.

Tea and cakes followed and were served with the utmost care, making her feel like a lady. Thomas, undoing his collar slightly, began to relax and take pleasure in the pampering.

"'Ere, wait till our lot hears about this," he jested.

"Oh stop it, Thomas," she responded, now blushing and wishing the carpet would swallow her up.

"I'll not be able to look that guide in the eye again. What must he have thought," she uttered self-consciously.

After a few more leisurely hours spent eating and drinking, admiring the huge chandeliers and large scenes painted on the walls, they headed for the Grand Vestibule, which completed the tour. The guide courteously said goodbye to everyone, hoping that each of them had enjoyed their visit, and then smiled at Mam, as if to say she wouldn't be the first to make such a mistake. Mam smiled back and giggled slightly to overcome her embarrassment, before thanking him warmly for the tour.

They stood for a moment under the large marble statue of Queen Victoria, which dominated the space outside the State Apartments, and taking several more looks behind them, finally descended down a large staircase leading to the base of King John's Tower.

"This is the oldest and least altered portion of the Castle," Dad told her, having heard someone else mention it.

"Really," said Mam, impressed by his knowledge.

Finally, the visit over, they entered into the sunshine once more, content and full from their feast. They let the sun warm their faces, before admiring the Castle's façade, on the way out.

"Come on, ol' lass. Let's pop into The Old Ship Hotel over there and go to the lav before we move on. Then we'll make our way into town. There'll be a gift shop there, I bet," he said, as he pointed across the way.

"You go on then. I'll wait for you by the gate," she replied.

She'd already visited the lavs at the Castle, when Dad was talking to a soldier, on sick leave from his unit.

As Mam waited for Dad in the sunshine, an elderly couple, also leaving the Castle, stopped to talk to her, telling her they were just on their way to 'Token House.' The guide had told them it was the best gift shop in the area, and a must to visit. Thanking them for the information, Mam said they'd call there as well, especially as it was on their way home. They found the shop on High Street, opposite the outer walls of the Castle, and it was there Mam spotted several pomander balls in the window, in a lovely decorative basket. Tempted to go in, she went up to the counter and asked what they were made up of.

"They're made from a recipe handed down since the reign of Henry VIII," said the shop keeper, handing her one to smell.

"How much are they?"

"2s.6d each, madam."

After humming and hawing, Dad bought one for her. Mam's pleasure was now complete.

"It's been a lovely day," she said, pleased with herself as they headed back to the railway station to catch the late afternoon train to York.

It had certainly been a day neither of them would forget. Meanwhile, they were blissfully unaware of what was happening in Belgium and France.

Chapter THIRTY-ONE

To every thing there is a season,
and a time to every purpose under the heaven...
(Ecclesiastes 3, verses 1, 2 and 4)

Once more I was fighting on the front line, assisting the Americans, at the aptly named, 'Hell Fire Corner.'

Defensive patrols were on the lookout. My nerves were on edge, and my stomach was churning. I waited and waited for the expected, knowing it would come sooner or later, wondering if this would be the time I'd be joining Albert, Robert and Matthew. My thoughts drifted to the inexcusable waste of life. It was exactly three years since Albert had died, followed by Robert a few weeks later and then Matthew, a mere three months ago. Only God knew where George was, and then there was Fred, still languishing in hospital. I wondered if anyone ever realized what it was like in this unimaginable hell, or was it a case of only understanding it, if they experienced it.

And what of Alice, I continued to deliberate. I hadn't heard from her for quite some time now. I missed her softness, the smell of her hair, and the warmth of her body. I tried remembering every detail of her. Oh God Alice, maybe you're gone too, I deliberated as I waited and waited for hell to freeze over.

My thoughts ran away with me, until eventually, the lice made active by the sun on my body, distracted me. The itching drove me crazy until I scratched frantically. Sweat poured from me as I desperately looked for shade, lower down in the trench. We were hoping for water to come down the line, but runners had been cut off from us yet again. We heard they were on their way with their precious booty, but we'd no idea how long it would be. I imagined taking a few sips, then pouring the rest of the delicious cold water over my head, to feel its coolness. It wouldn't be long now, I kept telling myself.

As we waited, I noticed how still it had become.

"'Ere Jackson, keep watch while I have a pee," came a voice down the line. It was Sarge.

The late afternoon heat was now at its height, and mirages played tricks with my eyes, as I kept watch. A wasp buzzed around my head, hovering around the dirt and sweaty grime on my face. It was a persistent little bugger. I tried in vain to swat it, before finally managing to move it on. As I looked down, there were ants playing around my feet, clambering over my boots and up my putties, looking for a way in. I'd given up trying to stop them, as I knew only too well the action would bring me out in more of a sweat and that was the last thing I wanted right now.

When I looked through the periscope across no-man's land, the only things moving were the rats. I could see them in the distance, scavenging bits of human fragments from battles long gone. They were fat on the pickings.

"I wonder what Jerry is thinking," I said to Bill, who'd made his way down the line to join me.

Bill shrugged his shoulders as if to say, "Who knows?" and I turned my attention back to watching anything which moved.

Out of the corner of my eye, I glimpsed a butterfly playing in the wind, fluttering in and out of Jerry's trench. I was struck by its grace and beauty, and wondered where it had come from. For a while I watched it dilly-dallying on thermals generated by the heat from Jerry bodies, telling us where they were, before 'waltzing' across no-mans-land.

"I wouldn't stay there too long," I whispered to it, as it danced a fine line across my field of vision.

It disappeared quickly from sight, almost as if it had heard.

Following in its wake, came birdsong. A sound so rare now, that I began imagining they must be birds from heaven. It was almost as if heaven was orchestrating the view before me, with the butterfly being the conductor, and the birds now following its lead. This orchestrated sound had an iridescent red backdrop to it, as the sun slowly set. It was incredibly beautiful, and as the birdsong grew softer, dusk slowly pulled a blanket over the sun, gently tucking it in. Sarge had been way-laid after his pee, so I continued to watch and listen, waiting for his return. The distant echo of gunfire rumbled like drums, as if proclaiming an end to the synchronized scene, just as the last of the sun's embers were put out.

My fevered hallucinations diminished as the heat of the day steadily cooled. The long awaited water eventually made it down the line, along with someone to take over from me. Sarge was still nowhere to be seen. With my watch now finished, I drank the cool water heartily. I could see the moon, trembling on the surface of the water in the billy can. At last, a curtain of cloud hid it, and darkness became absolute. The performance of heaven was complete. As silence descended with the night, my thoughts also became quiet. With half of me vigilant, the other unprepared, I tried to relax a little, praying to God this war would soon be over, praying he'd heard.

Bill snored loudly, and I gave him a shove in his ribs to shut him up. If Jerry had listeners out, they would certainly hear him. I took a closer look at him in the fleeting moonlight, and saw a wizened old man curled up looking as if he wanted to die. We were all tired. Even old Picky looked different when he returned. He leant across Bill and offered me a fag. Gratefully, I accepted.

"Won't be long now Jackson. Relief is due in the morning," he said, by way of comfort.

"Good," I said, hearing enemy machine gunners in the distance, active on the Menin Road.

The Company stirred restlessly, listening to see if it was coming our way, but it didn't. Time dragged on until dawn broke and another bright hot day began. True to Sarge's words, we were relieved from front line duties and moved down the line to take position at Siege Camp, in reserve.

As I walked up towards headquarters, the adjutant came running after me with a telegram in his hand. I could see it was from York and marked urgent. I instantly felt sick... it could only mean one thing. It must be Fred. I strolled over to sit down on an up-turned cart on the edge of the road. The horse was dead, half buried in the mud, waiting to be burned. I shakily opened the flimsy paper in my hand, as my heart wildly pumped with anxiety and fear.

> "George dead... Stop. Killed 6th June... Stop. Enemy air raid...
> Stop. Penetrating wounds to abdomen... Stop. All of us shocked.
> Stop. Dad."

I stared incredulously at the paper. George. Bloody 'ell, George. Four brothers now dead. Just Fred and me alive. It was unbelievable. How would Harriet manage with three children to bring up alone? Everyone would be devastated at the awful news. Alice would be worried sick.

"What's up, John boy?" asked Bill, who caught up with me.

"It's our George. He's dead."

"Good God! How many's that?"

"Four, and if our Fred doesn't pull through, five. In fact I thought it was a telegram to say it was our Fred. I never thought it would be George. Killed in a bloody air raid."

I just couldn't believe it, and for days after, kept thinking about it.

It was a fortnight later before Mam wrote, telling me what had actually happened. His commanding officer had written to Harriet. It appears George was way back down the line putting new railway lines in place, when an air raid came out of the blue.

"I just can't believe it…"

Bill listened quietly, now speechless. He too was shocked. Throughout the years, he'd got to know my family really well, despite never meeting them.

Over the next few weeks, my mood was sombre. I hated this life. Alice's letters caught up with me, just as we were moving to Pigeon Camp in the Proven area, but even she didn't inspire me as she normally did. She was working in the ammunitions factory and was praying that every bullet she forged, would keep me safe. As predicted, everyone was finding it difficult to cope with the sad news. I kept seeing George's face and remembering the last time we were together. All of us were close and I just couldn't imagine never seeing him again.

As I continued reading Alice's letter, the everyday events she wrote about poignantly reminded me of my brothers, and our lives together. I felt as if my family was being blown away, whilst hers continued as normal.

Connie was still going out with Bert, and Alice reckoned they would be married before us, if I didn't get myself home soon. Ted was his usual mischievous self. Edna had started school and hated every minute of it. Both Connie and she were also helping her mother, ironing in the evenings and parcelling up shirts and other such stuff, ready for collection the following day. She complained the house smelt of wet washing, and she was forever ducking under the many washing lines rigged up in the kitchen, with other people's laundry on it. Great big bloomers and the like, she said, from women down the road, the likes I would never see! I had visions of her tangling herself up in these bloomers, and wished I was there to see it. Her mother sometimes received butter or other rationed food, in payment for their efforts, so they ate slightly better than most, therefore it was worth it, she said.

SIX

Her letter was relatively short, but sweet. As well as the day to day things to tell me, she declared her undying love for me and the longing in her heart for me to be home. I tried imagining both of us lying naked together, doing all the things I ever wanted to do with her, but this time, the image didn't inspire me. I simply felt nothing, and it bothered me.

"Isn't it time you took a cold shower?" Bill said, laughing when he caught me reading her letter.

"Its time they upped the bromide in the tea again! I must becoming immune to it," I responded, trying to sound normal.

I grinned at him, trying to keep up the pretence that sex was constantly on my mind, and was glad he walked on and left me to it.

August and September were horrible months, spent constantly on the move. The heat of summer was overbearing as we marched west to Herzeele, then northeast to Oostcappel, and then by rail to Northkerque, eight miles southeast of Calais. From there we marched to Tournehem, then north to Audricq, and on by train to Brias, twenty miles northwest of Arras, finally arriving at billets in Foufflin-Ricametz village.

We ended up spending a week at Bois de Berthonval on battalion practice attack, before marching on to Wakefield Camp, to relieve the 4th Seaforth Highlanders. By the end of September, we were patrolling the north bank of the Scarpe River in the Plouvain sector of the Divisional front line. It would be several weeks before letters from home would catch up with us, and I worried about Fred, imagining he was also dead, believing it to be just a matter of time before the news caught up with me.

There was no sign of let up by Jerry and it became obvious the 'big wigs' were once again planning a large offensive, which we were being prepared for. We were moved by route march to a new position in 'E' area and waited in bivouacs for orders. They came on 11th October, following several days of heavy rain. The Canadian Infantry Brigade had reached high ground southeast of Iwuy, just northeast of Cambrai. Our orders were to take over the attack, so with a battalion strength of ten officers and five hundred and fifty-four other ranks, we started. It was bang on nine o'clock in the morning, 'bang' being the operative word, and considering the flack we were taking, our casualties were miraculously light.

SIX

We advanced through heavy enemy barrage, and when that didn't stop us, the bastards used a considerable amount of gas. We managed to establish a new front line and dug in at Sunken Road to consolidate our position. We lost eight men, with forty-six others wounded, as we dug ourselves deep into the vast quagmire Flanders had become. Horses, men and mules were sinking into the earth and for once, even Jerry, had a greater enemy to contend with. Its adhesive properties were far superior to any glue on the market. It stuck to everything and dragged us all down. Sunken Road was aptly named.

Ironically, I remembered Albert once likening 'our' determination to overcome such things, to Mark Tapley in Charles Dickens's 'Martin Chuzzlewit', whose fortitude and resolve saw him through time and time again. Why I should have thought of it now, goodness only knew, but I couldn't imagine Mark Tapley surviving any of this as the Earth sucked us down, clawing us into her.

We lay low until the companies in support of us were in place. The battle then started up again. It was mid-morning on the 12th but by 12.45pm, we had reached our objective, the Avesnes-Villers en-Caushies railway. It was relatively easy. Very little of the enemy was actually encountered. Sarge reckoned they had been swallowed up by the mud.

Later that night, we were told to secure a crossing on the River Selle. This was to cover the building of some bridges. Thinking that Jerry would be up to his ears in mud, and would give us no trouble, we got on with the job. How wrong we were! We only just managed to hold onto our position until the following evening, when it became obvious we didn't have enough man power to hold Jerry off. We lost twelve men in the battle that ensued, and as we waited for orders, twenty-nine other poor sods were wounded. We stayed put for the whole of the 13th trying to patch up the wounded as best we could, before eventually receiving orders to withdraw into Divisional Reserve. Sarge told us the 148th Brigade had been ordered to take over from us.

As we withdrew, Jerry started another round of heavy shelling, killing another five men. Fifty-five others were wounded and we precariously dragged them between us for well over six hundred yards, along with several tons of mud, until stretcher bearers reached us and took over. It was too dangerous to go back to retrieve the dead. Sarge said they'd have to wait for collection later.

Just then, a runner came rushing up to greet us.

SIX

"Where's Sergeant Pickles?"

"I'm over here," shouted Sarge, further down the line.

The runner pushed his way through and handed him a wire. We all waited expectantly. It was from Major General Cameron. We gathered around him, waiting for orders, as Sarge read it. He looked up, and with a wry smile on his face, relayed its contents.

> *"Warmly congratulate you and your battalions on the very fine advance you made yesterday. I think that it very materially helped the general situation even though some of the ground won could not be held. Please communicate to all ranks and explain that enemy retreat today largely due to your efforts yesterday."* End of message.

Cheers roared out.

"More likely to have been the bloody mud," I whispered to Bill.

"More than likely, but lets not disillusion the big-wigs. They might give us a couple of weeks' leave."

Sarge echoed our scepticism regarding Jerry's retreat being anything to do with us, but it didn't matter. All of us were past caring.

Bill's idea of two weeks leave turned out to be one day, which we spent cleaning Lewis guns and giving ourselves a well earned foot rub. After that, we were moved into the right sector of the divisional front to take relief of the battalions there. The railway, and the village of Villers, were shelled intermittently with high explosives and gas throughout the whole day. A small patrol was sent out to check the condition of the bridges across the river. They returned in the evening to say they were all down. All our efforts had been pointless.

On the 17th we went into reserve and were route marched to Escaudoevures, where we were ordered to take baths and get a change of clean clothes. Gosh, what it was to be clean! It was like a new injection of energy. I was beginning to feel normal, whatever that was. We spent the next few days tidying up our billets and polishing our equipment, as well as indulging in various training sessions.

A class for stretcher bearer instruction was on, which Bill and I were ordered to attend. The officer giving the talk was new. It was obvious he had never witnessed the conditions under which stretcher bearers brought in the dead and wounded. We tried to enlighten him as to which part of the body was the best anchor to grab hold of to pull them in, and in exchange, received a dressing down regarding the further damage we would be inflicting on the wounded. Bill politely told him his method was straight out of the book and though ideal, risked the stretcher bearer being shot and the likelihood of the wounded man dying anyway. A heated debate ensued, regarding bringing the wounded in quickly and 'any old how,' as against stabilizing them and carrying them carefully on a proper stretcher. He had no concept of shells and machine gun fire zinging all around.

Finally, having been threatened with a court martial, we were silenced and accepted our efforts to enlighten him were pointless, so gave up trying.

"This bloody man's barmy. What does he know about it? We've spent nearly four years picking up pieces of bodies and saving what bits we could, and here he is trying to tell us what we should do. Crickey, we'll all be bloody dead if we did what he said. How many stretcher bearers have you seen walking calmly under fire to bring the lads in, eh? He's no idea," Bill said, heatedly.

I nodded in agreement, thinking about Albert and the higgledy-piggledy way the stretcher bearers had man-handled him away. If he hadn't been already dead, speed would have been his only chance. And then there was the time the stretcher bearers put a rifle under my legs to form a make-shift stretcher to carry me out to safety. God knows what would have happened if they'd gone back for a proper one. I owe them my life. I nodded again to Bill, agreeing.

Bill was still rankled when a few days later we moved on to the Ramillies area. His mood didn't improve either, when we arrived to find there were no billets available and had to move on to Iwuy. Specialist and platoon training sessions were mandatory and the stretcher bearer class was extended. It continued for three days, but Bill and I managed to curtail our attendance, tagging onto a tactic training group instead.

"Any news about what's happening Sarge?" I asked.

"Not really. We'll be moving out tomorrow to Douchy and your lot will be billeted in a house there, before moving up to the railway embankment. No doubt I'll get further orders when we're there," he said.

The railway embankment was just behind the front line. In front of it was the town of Famars, which was in British hands. Old Picky gathered us all together to give out new orders. A gentle breeze blew the map he laid out.

"Grab us a few stones, to pin this bloody thing down," he requested.

"Now then, the sector is split into four. I want 'C' company to the right, east of Famars; 'B' company on the left, north of Famars; 'A' company in close support of 'B', near the Chateau in Famars; and 'D' company, in reserve west of Famars. Is that clear?" he said, pointing his stick to the various areas.

There was a low mumble of acknowledgement heard.

"When's all this taking place Sarge?" asked a voice from behind.

"We're moving out on the 29th."

We crept quietly into place like cats stalking their prey and waited for the signal. Once in position, a message came down the line ordering us to stay where we were. Famars and Maing, were intermittently shelled, but we were told to maintain our position. Our attack was delayed. The 29th came and went and so did the 30th as we waited.

"Bloody 'ell, Sarge, all this nervous energy isn't good for us," said Bill, who was beginning to feel the pressure.

"Won't be long now lads," said old Picky, also feeling the strain.

Later that evening, orders came to say our attack would be at sunrise, and the objective was to knock out Jerry's railway line from Marly, to the Sunken Road. When Sarge checked this on the map, he suddenly realised history was repeating itself.

"Did you realize this is the place where our regiment won the right to have 'Ca Ira' as our regimental quickstep in 1693? And bugger me, here we are again, two-hundred-and-twenty-five years later, back fighting in that same spot. Queer isn't it?" said Sarge amazed.

"Some things never change," added Bill, unaware Sarge was interested in such things.

"Absolutely. Still, it's quite a momentous thing to be back here in the same place. You lot should be proud of your history," he added.

As sunrise lifted the curtain of darkness, our barrage started moving forwards at the rate of one hundred yards every three minutes to a point just east of the Rhonelle River, with us following in its wake. As it slowed to one hundred yards every four minutes, we reached the outskirts of Aulnoy. We knew we had twenty minutes to cross the river, and form into two lines, with two platoons in front and two in support. It all sounded so easy on paper, but in reality it was very different.

Unfortunately, there was a lot of confusion, as one of the seven, twenty foot bridges, was blown up. The first wave of men suffered several hundred casualties between the river and the outskirts of Famars, before the rest made it through to reorganise. Whilst all this was going on, 'C' company managed to round up a small group of German soldiers, who surrendered without much resistance. We made small gains here and there but in the end, it was our relief who eventually secured our objective.

As we entered the village of Aulnoy, the villagers were amazed. At first they thought we were American soldiers, because the Germans had told them all the English had been killed. Most of the civilians were hiding in their cellars and as they came out they greeted us warmly, so much so, that our advance into the village was held up.

On the morning of the 2nd we rested up. The attack had been deemed a success, but we had suffered heavy losses. The weather which had favoured us, now deteriorated and it became cold and miserable. It matched my gloomy mood. The thought of another winter here depressed me. Mulling things over in my mind, I felt I couldn't take any more and decided that enough was enough, and it was time to court death.

The mood was catching.

"I've had it up to here," I said to Bill, lifting my hand up to neck level.

"All of us have, except for the bloody new ones who arrived this morning, and they haven't a bloody clue as to what it's really like. They're still wet behind the ears, playing at being soldiers," he remarked.

He was right; they didn't understand this reality was depressingly different and unyielding. In a sense I felt sorry for them. I had once been like them and look at me now. I hadn't a spark of energy left in me. My life had become automatic, meaningless, accepting and unquestioning. Inside I felt dead. Instantly, the face of the soldier who bumped into me on the dockside all those years before came back into my mind. My own haunting expression now mirroring his was on the faces of all those who'd been to hell and back.

"Just wait till they've been here as long as us, then they'll know what its like," I responded.

"That's if they last that long," Bill snapped, angry at their folly.

Later that day we received orders to proceed to Lieu-St-Amand via a cross country route, skirting Thiant and Noyelles-Sur-Sec. The going was very scary. Somehow, the Brigadier's congratulatory words on the fine work we'd done in the sector seemed hollow. Our situation was just as bad as ever. Constant machine gun fire picked us off one by one, as if we were ripe cherries there for the taking. I didn't care anymore. Bill and I just carried on regardless, with debris flying everywhere, as we tempted death to come and get us.

By the end of the night, we arrived in a zombie like state at Lieu St. Amand, where our billets were. Bill walked slowly by the side of me.

"It's foot inspection tomorrow," he informed me.

"Here, put a bullet through mine then," I begged, as I held it up for him.

"Tempting, I know, John-boy, but don't be bloody daft," was his response.

We knew the consequence of such an action would be a court martial and death, not a fair trial, I thought. Better to go out in a hail of bullets, I reasoned. Bill and I walked on, as I collected my platoon together.

"We're moving out again on the 5th. Sarge has sent orders for us to have baths, and disinfection of blankets and kit in the Foden lorry," I said, addressing them.

"I reckon we're in for some more praise as well," said Bill.

"Oh aye?"

"Yes, I heard the C.O. saying General Godley had sent a wire congratulating us."

"They'll probably tell us at the company parade then. OK, let's all jump to it," I said.

The cleaning up period took longer than predicted, probably because we all took our time, savouring the sensation of hot water on our skin, and on the morning of the 5th, as predicted, we received the praise Bill had seen coming...

From Major General Commanding Officer, N.G. Cameron...

> "I send you herewith a copy of a message from the Corps Commander XXII Corps. My own very hearty congratulations go with it. Apart from the actual fighting, you have all had many serious difficulties, and much hard work to contend with, especially

in connection with the rapid changes in plan brought about by frequent changes in the situation. I admire immensely the spirit of initiative and enthusiasm with which your infantry artillery and engineers alike have met and overcome those difficulties; and I congratulate you all most warmly on the well earned success which has crowned your efforts. You have added an honourable page to the history of the 49th West Riding Division."

And From General Godley, XXII Corps…

"I wish to heartily congratulate you and your division on the successful capture of all your objectives and the heavy losses inflicted on the enemy as the result of your two days hard and gallant fighting. All three infantry brigades, your artillery and engineers, have added another page to the distinguished record of the division."

Old Picky was nowhere to be seen, which wasn't that unusual, but he missed the praise. I wondered where he was. It was odd for him to be gone for so long without telling any of us, and I began to think that maybe he was resting. Just recently, he'd been looking pretty rough. Life was certainly taking its toll on him. As we waited to move out, I turned to Bill, voicing my concerns. Surely someone would know.

"Hey, Bill have you seen Sarge lately?"

He thought for a moment.

"No, come to think of it, I haven't."

He turned, shouting out loud to the group of lads we were with.

"Where's Sarge? Anyone know?"

There were a few muted murmurings, but no-one seemed to know.

"How about asking that batman over there," I said to Bill, pointing to him.

Bill went over, whilst the rest of us packed up our gear.

"Hey up there," Bill called to the batman.

"Where's Sarge gone?"

The batman looked bereft.

"Sarge took a bullet in his chest three days ago. He died instantly. They're bringing in his body later today."

Bill looked aghast, and instantly we all knew. He didn't have to tell us. I suddenly realised Sarge must have been one of those 'cherries'.

"Sergeant Pickles is dead? Old Picky dead after all this time? Bloody hell," I uttered in complete amazement.

Bill and I couldn't understand why we hadn't heard or seen him fall. After all, he'd only been yards away from us that day, and as we tried to piece together images of our last sighting of him, it became obvious others hadn't realised he'd gone down either. We were rendered speechless, and the long wait in the rain for buses to move us out, deepened our sombre mood.

"Takes the wind out of your sails to hear he's gone," said one bloke. "He was just like a father to me," he continued, as he offered me a cigarette.

"And to all of us," shouted another.

"He'd been with us from the start and here we are, now almost four-and-a-half bloody years down the line and he's gone. Bloody 'ell!" uttered another.

Bill and I stood in silence, as the convoy of buses arrived. We listened to various comments about Old Picky and what a jolly good sport he'd been. There was speculation as to who would stand in his shoes, and murmurings as to who they didn't want, but Bill and I continued to stand motionless, immersed in our own thoughts, not really giving a damn. We knew there would always be someone eager to jump into his shoes. Rain now poured relentlessly down, almost as if heaven was crying. It ran down all our faces, hiding the deluge of tears, for a man we all respected.

It was a further forty minutes before we got on the buses and set off into the pitch darkness of the unknown. We were thoroughly wet, and steam condensed on the windows, obscuring any fleeting moonlit view of the area we travelled, as we bounced around over the pock-ridden roads. The journey was fraught with problems and several of the buses became separated from the convoy in the darkness. By the time we reached Douai, we heard that some buses were stuck in mud and had ended up being ditched.

We were lucky: we made it through to Auby, but it was well after midnight before we arrived at our billets in Evin Malmaison. On assembly, company commanders realised there were still three buses missing. Two eventually turned up, leaving the third bus stranded at Douai. That didn't arrived until 3am.

The following day, reveille and breakfast were late, and all companies were at the disposal of company commanders for cleaning up and the improvement of billets. In the afternoon, officers got together to talk about various training sessions and recreation time. A decision was made to have a fund for the Band. Platoons and specialist training sessions were to start up again under specialist company officers. The stretcher bearer course was again on the menu, but under the care of a more experienced Medical Officer this time, who knew what war was all about. The Lewis Gun officers were instructed to run sessions, and other training sessions were organised, in readiness for the next military objective, still to be decided. It was almost as if we were back in limbo land, and the never ending waiting game, waiting in reserve for the big-wigs to make a decision.

The next day, whilst all this went on, the commanding officer, his second in command, the adjutant, and the company commanders, went to divisional headquarters for a conference, as they too waited for orders.

On Sunday morning, 10th November, the whole battalion attended Divine Services. Bill and I went to the Church of England parade service, near the makeshift football ground. Others joined Roman Catholic mass in Evin Church, and the Wesleyan lot crammed into the recreation room. Afterwards, our commanding officer inspected our billets. It was a bloody cold day. The fog rolled over the area like a proper pea-souper. The Front line in our sector was still being held and thankfully stayed quiet. The rest of the day passed like any other day with routine duties and training, and the inevitable stretcher bearer course was still ongoing.

"How many ways can you bring in the dead and wounded without being blown up or shot yourself?" Bill asked, in a loud voice, as we walked past the group queuing up for instruction.

"Only two," I uttered… "Grab 'em and run," and we laughed as we made our way to the hand combat training course we'd been assigned to.

By ten o'clock that night, the Brigade received a wire from Divisional Headquarters, saying that all hostilities were to cease at 11am tomorrow. Captain Mackay received the information and just couldn't believe it. Word spread like 'wild fire' that Germany had surrendered.

SIX

At sunrise on the 11th, the Armistice with Germany was signed, and at 11am, a cease fire alarm echoed piercingly throughout the land. It was finally over… the war was finally over.

Bloody hell it was over. I still couldn't believe it was true. Morning parade was cancelled, but it all seemed surreal. Church bells peeled out enthusiastically. Cheering, clapping, boisterous squeals of delight were heard in a confusion of sounds, as we threw our helmets in the air, and hugged one another. We gathered in small informal groups near our billets, before setting off to wander through the village streets. Bill and I chatted excitedly with villagers, accepting hugs and kisses from unknown women, and we allowed ourselves to be dragged into several kitchens, where we were given chunks of bread and cheese, washed down with glasses of home made wine. For hours the news seemed incredible. We meandered around in a wonderful trancelike state of euphoria, unable to take in reality.

"Pinch me. Go on, pinch me," I said to Bill, as we headed back to billets for a Brigade Parade at 1.30pm.

Lt. Col. Oddie addressed the parade, confirming it was finished. It was then that I dared to believe it was finally over. Germany had indeed signed the Armistice, and he held a short thanksgiving service. It seemed strange, and I couldn't help but ask God in silent prayer, what had taken him so long. I was twenty years old, and I'd seen untold horrors, and witnessed hatred in all its manifestations. If only Old Picky could have held on for another nine days. Bloody hell, just nine more sodding days, and then he would have made it out alive.

"Strange that our last action of the war should have been where our lot attacked the French and won the Regimental March all those years ago," Bill uttered.

"Yes. Strange too that Sarge said he was honoured to be there on the very day he died," I reflected.

"Perhaps he wanted to be a part of that history," Bill conjectured.

"Maybe he knew his number was up and couldn't think of a better place to be," I said, realizing that we'd all certainly remember him.

As guns became silent, the war diaries recorded "Casualties – nil" on every page. Only the sound of spades and the clearing up could now be heard. Peasants worked alongside army men to clear away debris, and make roads passable. Hundreds of letters were written home, and there was a longing to be there. Army existence relaxed somewhat and daily structure lessened. There were still parades where medal ribbons were presented and congratulations bestowed, but we spent most of our time helping hoards of returning locals rebuild their lives. All the while, we were waiting to hear when we'd be going home.

Christmas came and was soon over, along with the cakes and sweets and excesses of drink that were sent in numerous parcels. There were sing-songs and brief flirtations with local girls, but underlying this frivolity, there was a need to make sense of it all.

"Sometimes all I see is darkness and fragments of who I am. Do you think it's possible to forget such horrors?" I asked Bill. He thought for a moment…

"I think it's possible to block 'em out, but not forget. No, we'll never forget."

By the time January arrived, we were getting more and more impatient to be home. All of us kept asking if demobilisation would be soon. In answer to this, our commanding officer fixed up a lecture on the 28th, entitled "Home" by Lt. A. Stevens. We crammed onto the parade ground, eager to hear him describe the logistics of actually going back to England.

The 1st and the 8th West Yorkshires had temporarily left for Germany, with the Army of Occupation. They were now stationed at Cologne. Meanwhile the rest of us were told we'd be demobilised over the next week or so. 'D' company was now under the command of Lt. C. Beall, and Bill and I wondered how long 'a week or so' really meant. Beall wouldn't enlighten us any further.

"Patience lads. It'll happen soon enough," was all he said.

"What will you do Bill?" I asked, as I gave him a smoke.

"I don't rightly know. Probably stay with Mam for a while 'til I get sorted out."

He gazed absentmindedly into space, thinking as he drew smoke into his lungs.

"You can always come home with me. We can make room for you. My Mam won't mind."

"Thanks John-boy, but I'll go home if it's all the same with you. My mother wouldn't want it any other way. I'll get by, you'll see. What about you?"

"Oh I'll probably see if my railway clerk's job is still there. Knowing Mr Prince he's probably forgotten his promise, and Mr Green will no doubt have conveniently forgotten he was keeping my seat warm, but what the hell! I'll do something. And of course, there's Alice."

"What about Alice? Will you marry her?" Bill persisted.

"I've changed. She may not like what she sees anymore," I replied.

We sat in silence, each of us engrossed in our own thoughts. I did want to marry Alice, but I'd become part of a sub-human race. I'd killed my fellow man. I'd broken God's cardinal rule, "thou shalt not kill." Visions of death haunted me and now I wasn't sure if Alice could love the person I'd now become. I loathed myself. There was nothing left inside. I hated what I'd become. It came from courting death, and if Alice knew, she'd hate me too.

Bill tapped me on the shoulder.

"Won't be long now John-boy and we'll be on our way home."

Chapter THIRTY-TWO

It isn't for the moment you are struck that you need courage,
but for the long uphill climb back to sanity and faith and security.
(Anne Morrow Lindbergh 1906-2001)

On 19th February 1919, our papers were signed, and the words "disembodied" stamped across them. It sounded as if someone had taken us apart and left us. It was an apt description. I felt as if nothing held me together any more. The boy I had been before the war, was missing, presumed dead, and in his place was this "disembodied" man held together by the threads of a uniform, just like the broken pieces of skeletons rotting in no-man's land, their skulls now laughing at my predicament.

"Look John-boy... home!" pointed Bill, as the white cliffs of Dover came into view.

I strained to see them through the sea mist. Yes, we were going home I told myself, still unable to believe it. It was all I had ever wanted to do and yet, I was strangely fearful of it. There was no structure to my life anymore and I wasn't sure how I would manage. Bill had written to tell his mother to expect him, but I wanted to head into London to see how Fred was doing first.

I said goodbye to Bill on the dock side, promising to keep in touch, and told him that if ever he needed me, he had only to let me know. We shook hands in the approved manner of 'goodbye' and then feeling stupid about such formality after all we'd been through, we hugged one another. I watched him go as he headed to catch his train. We'd been together through thick and thin, and I knew I was going to miss him. He was quite a bit older than me, but he'd been just like a big brother. I hoped he was going to be ok.

I slowly headed towards the train at platform three going to London, and saw it was already heaving with people, excitedly talking about how we'd won the war. I jostled for a seat listening to the stories of enemy encounters and the thwarted attacks they'd made, but as the train pulled out of the station, the carriage became quiet, almost as if the excitement of going home had somehow become personal.

I eventually located the hospital and found Fred lying on his hospital bed looking straight up at the ceiling. There was an air of melancholy rising on the thermals of disinfection. It was outside visiting hours, but the ward sister had kindly let me in, after I'd told her I'd just come straight from France.

"It'll do him good to see you," she'd said, as if I was a dose of medicine.

"He's over there... the third bed from the end," she'd added, pointing to where he was, not sure whether I'd seen him or not.

Fred didn't bother to look to see who was walking down the ward. He seemed to be wrapped up in a world of his own.

"Hello Fred. How are you doing?"

"John! Good God, when did you get back?" he responded, shocked to see me standing by him.

"Just now."

I laughed at the expression on his face, as I bent over to hug him. His face contorted into a grimace as he fought back tears, and the brotherly bond between us, was renewed.

"It's just the two of us now, you know," he said.

"I know... I know."

"I can't believe they're all gone. It's like a nightmare."

"I know... I know."

"It's been so long. I can't sleep, thinking about them. Any idea what happened?" he asked, brushing away escaping tears.

"Albert got a bullet through the head," I said, automatically touching my head, tracing the bullet's path.

"Robert died of wounds. The bloody French hadn't even gotten around to helping him. George intervened, but by then, it was too late. He was with him when he died. Unfortunately I got there just after."

I stopped for a minute, to let the information sink in before continuing. Fred just stared up at the ceiling, imagining Robert's suffering.

"Matthew got wounds to his legs, and died the next day at a casualty clearing station, and George died in an enemy air raid attack. He was constructing a railway line when a jerry plane came from nowhere. He copped a bullet straight through his abdomen. According to his C.O., it ripped him apart, and he died within minutes. That's about it," I said, matter of factly.

SIX

The words came out so easily, leaving behind the inner turmoil of their true meaning. I looked at Fred, who silently absorbed the impact of what I'd said.

"What about you?" I now asked, breaking the tension between us.

"Oh, I'm pretty much on the mend now. I copped a bullet. They tell me it's been touch and go, but I'm alright now. They reckon I should be able to go home in a few weeks. It's been so depressing here though. Mam and Dad visited me when I first got here, and again when our Matt went back, but it's now been a while since I've seen anyone. It's been difficult, I know. Mam's been trying to get me transferred up to York, but it's only just recently that I've been stable enough to move. Sister says they'll be moving me up there next week to convalesce for a week or two and then I'll be able to go home for good."

We talked on and off for several hours. Our silences spoke volumes. Our chatter united us as kindred spirits. Our nightmares were similar, and our killing of fellow human beings, distressing and haunting. We justified our actions, acknowledging we had had no choice, and in an attempt to appease our souls, we spoke about our brothers and the killing being retribution for their deaths. Both of us had lost sight of 'God' and I told Fred of my 'pact' with Him when I was so scared of dying. Fred understood. He'd been there. He knew fear. He knew the horror and the carnage of war. He'd been face to face with death and won. Yes, he understood, and we shared a common bond that no-one else could, unless they'd been there and seen it for themselves.

I decided to stay in London and told Fred I'd head on home when he was transferred to the convalescent hospital in York. He was grateful of the company each day and I was grateful for some time to adjust and make sense of civvy life again. It was Fred who wrote to tell Mam and Dad I was with him, and that I would be home soon.

I tried explaining to Fred my reluctance to go home, after he'd sensed there was something wrong. I told him I had difficulty in facing everyone. I felt guilty at being alive when my brothers were dead. I also felt different. I couldn't understand what was happening to me. I seemed to be without form. There was no structure to myself anymore. Before, all I had had to do was accept orders, eat when told to, sleep when told to, go when told to, kill when told to, and now, there was nothing. I wanted to go home but was frightened that everything would fall apart. I feared I might disintegrate. I felt that none of it was real.

Fred was a tower of strength. He explained it had been the same for him, but lying in his hospital bed had enabled him to have some time to work through it all, and gain a sense of order.

I told him about the nightmares and the voices in my head, the constant deafening sound of shells exploding, and the visions of black nothingness, from which intolerable fear erupted, and tore my guts apart. And then there was Albert, who stared up at me as I held him, with his blood flowing like a river into the ground as he left me. I would try reaching out to him as he faded away but there was only the darkness again, like a bottomless pit, which left me teetering on the edge of it. Sometimes it would happen during waking hours, when I'd be left shaking uncontrollably, not knowing where I was. It was terrifying.

"It's OK, John. You just need some time to rest and work things through. It's going to take time."

"Maybe it would be better if I didn't go home just yet," I said.

"Rubbish!" said Fred, horrified at the thought.

"The best place for you is home, with familiar things around you and people who love you. Don't worry about it, John. It'll turn out alright, and I'll be there soon. Mam and Dad will understand. They'll help you get through it... no, the best place for you my lad is definitely home," he reiterated.

Not letting on, Fred wrote to tell Mam and Dad I was struggling to come to terms with civvy life, and was in need of a bit of peace and quiet, and daily routine. He told them I'd be with them for definite by next Thursday, when I'd be travelling up with him, to the convalescence hospital.

As it happened, the hospital transferred Fred a day earlier than expected, and before we knew it, we were in an army ambulance, and on our way. Being a Company Sergeant Major definitely had its perks. Within no time, we were at Clifford Street Military Hospital, and Fred was settling in. It was only a stone's throw away from home, so after leaving him in the caring hands of Sister Kenyon, a pretty, dark haired woman, not much older than me, I set off to walk the short distance home.

My leg was playing up again. Maybe it was the damp weather, or maybe my reluctance to face everyone. Either way, I was fearful of breaking down and not maintaining that 'stiff upper lip' required. I hesitated at

SIX

the door before lifting the latch. It was off the hook as usual. Mam and Dad were sitting around the kitchen fire. Dad was smoking his pipe. They looked up as I entered, surprised to see me.

"Oh my word, it's our John," exclaimed Mam, putting her knitting down and throwing her arms around me.

"Oh lad, you're home," she continued.

"Come on, come on in and sit down here. It's nice and warm by the fire, and I'll put the kettle on. Eee bah gum, he's home," she said to Dad, as she manoeuvred me towards the fire.

Dad was by this time standing. He put his arm on my shoulder.

"Good to see you son," he calmly said. His voice was steady and sincere.

His eyes glistened revealing the emotion he felt as he kept himself in check.

"Good to see you, too, Dad," I said softly, as I now hugged him.

"Oh son, it's good to have you home again. Now you just sit there and don't move whilst I get a cuppa," Mam continued, scurrying around to put the kettle on the fire plate, and take the teacups out of the cupboard.

I settled back into the fireside chair as she bustled around, talking to herself about putting a hot pan in my bed, and moving Charlie into Wilf's room, to give me a bit of space until Fred came home, and how I needn't think I was going to go back to work until I was well rested.

"I must tell our Wilf that he's not to let on you're home, like he did last time, until you've had a chance to rest up a bit and get used to being home again," she muttered.

"Where are Charlie and Wilf?" I asked.

"Oh they're both at work son. It'll be another hour or so before you'll see them. It'll give you time to shut your eyes for five minutes or so, if you want to," she declared.

"Nah, I'm alright Mam."

"Did they say when our Fred will be home?" she now asked.

"Probably in a week or two depending on how well he does. He's still a bit weak. He's only just started to eat more solid food again. He's lost a lot of weight but I reckon he's turned the corner."

"I'll bake some scones tomorrow and take him some. There's nothing like home cooking to put the stuffing back in you," she said, talking to herself again.

It was good to be home. Fred was right. The familiar smell of freshly baked bread in the kitchen and the routine of family life was exactly what I needed. Mam and Dad continued as usual, chattering between themselves, with the odd snippet directed at me. Other than the perfunctory "yes" or "no" answer, they didn't expect anything. They didn't ask about the war, and I didn't say anything about it either.

Wilf was first to come through the door, and greeted me, like a long lost brother should be greeted. He didn't ask if I'd killed any Jerries. It was almost as if he knew, and didn't need to ask anymore. Charlie strolled in about ten minutes later, surprised to see me back earlier than expected. A punch to the shoulder, with a "You alright then, bro?" and then a hug, said it all. They both fussed around me, laughing and joking about what they'd been up to and which girls they were seeing, and took the mickey out of me for being so surprised they were courting. I kept reminding myself that Charlie was now eighteen and Wilf nearly sixteen, the age I had been when I left home. It was like looking through a mirror and seeing myself in 1914. The only difference was that I hoped he had more sense.

As the days passed almost in the blink of an eye, Fred came home, and the pair of us shared the back bedroom. I eventually returned to the railway office clerk's job and Fred returned to being a railway fireman. Gradually, a different kind of daily routine emerged. I kept the picture of Alice in her red dress, in my jacket pocket, along with her handkerchief. It was a kind of security, something that rooted me to reality.

It was Alice who held me together over the next few months, and I fell more and more in love with her. She became the stabilising influence I needed, and in essence, nursed my soul back to life. For quite a while I felt as if I was two people. There was this person who carried on as if nothing had happened. He was the one who got up, had breakfast, went to work, had dinner, had tea, came home, saw Alice, went to bed and did the same thing again and again, day in, and day out, with a slight variation on Saturday and Sunday. But then there was this other person, who re-lived untold horrors, slept fitfully and was haunted by images of war. This person tended to appear whenever I was alone. He would highjack my thoughts, making it difficult to function, leaving me fearful and unsure. It was with Alice's help, that I managed to keep this 'other' me at bay.

"Try not to be on your own," she told me. "That way, you'll always be the 'you' you want to be, and eventually, the troubled 'you', will leave you alone."

Her logic was a bit crazy, but bit by bit, the troubled me settled. When I was with her, she showered me in kisses, stirring a longing to want more, and gradually, I dared to feel alive again.

Victory day for the Nation was set for 19th July, and in the weeks running up to it, the 'troubled' me threatened to take over again. I had been dreading it. I wasn't on my own. There were others who remembered the war and the horrors, and the price freedom had cost. When the day finally arrived, both Fred and I were deep in thought, trying to enter into the spirit of jubilation that spilled over into numerous street parties. Everyone gave thanks for the end of the war and lost loved ones were remembered for their sacrifices. Mam cried.

Alice sensed the tension within me and took me into the back yard. She kissed me sensuously, tempting a response. She was so lovely. Her body teasingly rubbed against mine.

"Let's fix a date to get married," she said.

"What date do you want?" I answered, kissing her neck, and exploring her body with my hands.

"How about Christmas Eve, when everyone will have finished work and will be off on Christmas Day?"

"A Christmas wedding?"

"Why not?"

"Why not, indeed," I added, confirming the day.

And so it was, on Victory Day, Alice and I fixed our wedding day. I asked Fred to be my best man and he agreed. Everyone shook hands with us, and the womenfolk talked about 'bottom drawer stuff' and where we would live. In the end, the Victory party turned out to be more of a celebration of things to come, and seemed a fitting tribute to everyone who'd died. It would be a new start, a new beginning together, but first, Alice had to know the truth...

-o-o-o-o-

Back in the park with Alice, the light was fading, and I was beginning to feel cold, unsure of Alice's reaction.

"So now you know what happened," I said, wondering whether she still wanted to marry me.

"I've done some horrible things Alice. I've killed men. I've seen such terrible sights, and so many people have died. It's been awful, and I know that's no excuse, but you've got to believe me when I say, if I could turn the clock back, I would."

Alice immediately put her arms around me.

"Let's put it behind us John," she said reassuringly.

"Do you still want to marry me? Even after all I've told you?" I asked hesitatingly.

"Yes. Even after all you've told me," she repeated, as if trying to set my mind at rest.

As we stood up, my leg ached, reminding me of war, and I held onto her for support, trying to banish all thought of it. The sun was settling and it was definitely becoming cold. I pulled her towards me, holding her close, wanting to kiss every part of her. Her body responded, and for a while we were lost in each other's embrace, with only the old oak tree looking on. We didn't see the few remaining people leave the park area. We didn't care. We had each other, and that was all that mattered.

On Wednesday, 24th December, I waited for Alice in the chilly interior of St. Lawrence's Church, in York. Fred stood next to me. Both of us were nervous. Fred kept checking to see if he still had the ring, and I kept rubbing my hands together to generate some heat. I fiddled with my chrysanthemum buttonhole, making sure it was secure. The Church was decorated in holly, covered in an abundance of red berries. Red flowers decked the alter and candle light gave a romantic warm glow, despite the cold. Charlie and Wilf were ushers, busily showing guests to their seats. The grand organ was playing as we waited for Alice, and I momentarily thought of Tubby's old groan box, in the loft of Talbot House. It seemed almost a lifetime ago.

"Stop fidgeting," said Fred.

"Do you think she's changed her mind?"

"Don't be daft. The bride is always late," he reassured me.

At last, the bridal tune was played, announcing her arrival. I turned around to get a sneak preview of her coming down the aisle. She wore a cream 'V' necked dress with long sleeves. The dress came down below her knees. Her gloves and tan coloured shoes matched the mustard colour of the chrysanthemums she carried. She held her bouquet at waist height and the flowers trailed down the front of her almost to her knees. A lace bonnet decorated with little flowers hid the long curls of her hair, and the attached veil cascaded down her back. She looked like a scared rabbit.

As we sang the first hymn, she smiled shyly up at me. The minister did the reading, speaking of God's gift of love, and the joining of man to woman, and prepared us both to take our vows.

"Wilt thou, John Edgar Jackson, take thee, Alice Emma Johnson…"
"Who the 'ell's Alice Emma?!" said a voice at the back of us.

It was our Charlie… forever the comedian. As we turned around to look at him, he was grinning from ear to ear. We were just in time to see Mam give him the usual clip around the ear-hole, amidst great amusement from the congregation.

In the prayers and silence that followed, I made my peace with God. I didn't know why I had survived the war when so many others hadn't, but I breathed a sigh of relief it was finally over, and a new life lay ahead.

I made a silent promise to God that Albert, Robert, Matthew, and George, would never be forgotten, nor the thousands of others who'd perished in a war that was meant to end all wars.

And the Son of God said, 'Greater love hath no man than this, that he lay down his life for his friend'
(John 15:13-15).

Alice and I would cherish their wedding gift.

Smiling, I turned to look at Alice and, kissing her gently, dared to dream that God was in his heaven and all was now right with the World…

SIX

POSTSCRIPT

John Edgar Jackson kept his promise with God, and became a 'lay preacher' in 1920. He continued to work on the Railways and became the Station Master for Brafferton and later Kippax Station in Yorkshire. He died on the 13th June 1985 at the age of eighty-seven. He never did forget his best friend Albert, or his brothers Robert, Matthew and George, who died like so many others in a War that sadly did not end all wars.

I don't know what happened to Robert's wife Gladys, and his son Robert, after those war years, nor what happened to George's wife Harriet, and their three children. They are part of the never ending research that makes genealogy great fun to do. No doubt in the fullness of time I will find a link to someone who knows.

As you know, Fred survived the war years. He married Renee, and they had three children, before he eventually died in 1964 at the age of sixty-nine. Charlie married Miriam, and they had one child before he died a few years after Fred, in 1970, also aged sixty-nine. Wilfred, the 'baby' of them all, married a woman also called Gladys, and they had two children. He lived to the age of ninety-two, eventually dying in 1995.

John, Fred, Charlie and Wilf, all bore witness to a Second World War. They carried scars in one way or another from World War One. Mary, their mother, died on the 25th April 1944 aged eighty-one, twenty-six years to the day on which Matthew had died, and their father, John Thomas, died nine years later at the age of eighty-eight in 1953.

Even though I was only three years old at the time of John Thomas's death, I have fond memories of our daily walk down 'Ha'peny Lane where he would use his walking stick as a pointer, to reveal the hidden wildlife we would look for. My final memory of him was being 'laid out' in the front parlour of grandma's house, with a stream of sunlight shining through the window onto him in his coffin. He looked so beautiful and peaceful. My mother lifted me up so that I could give him a big kiss goodbye. It was only after they took him away in what I thought was a black taxi, that I discovered what it was like to miss someone.

As you know, John married his Alice on 24th December 1919, and they had sixty-five wonderful years together before she eventually died in March 1984, aged eighty-two. They only had one child, a daughter, who was my mother. She in turn became a 'lay preacher' and married John Amos Webster. They had Michael, David and me. My name is Elizabeth. David was born on the 23rd July, 1945 – thirty years to the day on which Albert had died. My grandfather loved us all, but he had a special place in his heart for our David, often commenting on how much he was like Albert. He once talked of re-incarnation and I think, liked to believe his best friend was still near him.

The traumas of the First World War stayed with my grandfather all his life, and when the Second World War was declared, he joined the 'home guard'. During an air raid warning, he fell off the platform at Kippax station and broke his leg. His leg healed quickly, but as the war began to take a hold, he mysteriously became paralysed from the waist down. The hospital carried out extensive tests, but could find no reason for this. Eventually, they came to the conclusion his paralysis was psychological and similar to the neurasthenia which had been seen during the post war years.

The horrors of WW1, which he'd shut away deep in the recesses of his mind, had become real again in the face of another war. The specialists concluded that his unconscious brain could not cope with such a prospect and had manifested his abhorrence in the form of a paralysis. There were no treatments in those days for such illnesses and the paralysis lasted for almost the duration of the Second World War. Gradually, with patience and support and help from my father, he learnt to walk again, but it took him many years to achieve full mobility and to become 'well' again.

As I grew up, I became fascinated with war. This was partly due to listening to WW2 sing-along-songs, which Dad played on the piano in the 1950's when this was the fashion, and also partly due to listening to him recount his navy days. As a family, we watched numerous war films on the television in those years and the early sixties. They were victorious manifestations of war, with heroes and heroines, and I loved them, not really understanding at that time what war was all about.

However, it was when I was twelve years old, in 1962 that my real fascination for war took 'hold'. It was when I proudly showed grandad a photograph of my German pen pal. My school had been twinned with a German school and all of us were given a pen pal to write to. I think it had something to do with 'building bridges' after both World Wars. My pen-pal was called Regine Beckenbauer.

On this particular day, I showed grandad a photograph of Regine, who was the same age as me. I can still see that photograph in my mind. It was a head and shoulder view of a girl with short blond cropped hair, and a round robust looking face. She was smiling, and the top part of her neat dress was a rich multicoloured gingham pattern of black, red, blue and white. She was immaculately groomed, clean and fresh looking and I imagined her to be from a very wealthy family. So great was grandad's abhorrence of the German race at that time, that he took one look at the picture and without further ado, threw it on the floor.

"All seeds which have sprung forth from the loins of Germans are evil," he said, almost without thinking.

I was so upset, and not understanding his hatred at that time, I quickly told him Regine was not evil and that she was my friend. I had never seen my grandfather so openly repulsed by anything before, and in order to justify his vigorous detestation, he told me the first of his war stories in graphic detail. It was the death of his beloved Albert. He ended with a declaration that he would never speak to a German again, if he could possibly help it. His voice was full of emotion and his eyes full of tears, as he recalled Albert's last moments of life.

Because I was at such an impressionable age, it became something I never forgot. It was this memory that created an urge within me to learn more about such things. It was a 'side' of my grandfather I didn't know. For many years after that incident, grandad never spoke about the war. Gradually as I got older and interested in family history, he would speak about his brothers and bit by bit, I managed to piece together some of his experiences of the First World War from the odd glimpses he would occasionally share with me. As time went on, I started to record these stories and as they came to light, slowly began to understand his extreme dislike of German people, and of war. Eventually, he was to recall many more accounts that made my hair stand on end.

This book has been based on those true stories which he recounted to me, mainly in the latter years of his life. With family memorabilia such as the war postcards he sent home, which his mother had kept, the use of the West Yorkshire War diaries, and a newspaper article about him and his brothers, written in 1918 under the headline...

"YORK SOLDIER BROTHERS FALL IN ACTION,"

I have tried to re-create what his life was like in those years. For a while, my eyes have tried to see what he saw, and my feet have attempted to walk in his shoes. Now, I have a greater understanding of his reaction to the photograph of my pen-pal. Though he became a 'lay preacher' and found God again, the commandment of:

"Love one another as I have loved you,"

…didn't quite seem to include 'his enemy,' though in his later years, I know he struggled to do that.

I now look back and still find it hard to believe that my kind, unassuming grandfather, like so many men, killed other men, in a war that was supposed to end all wars, but then sadly, that's what happens. As I read Ecclesiastes Chapter 3, verses 1-8, maybe a better understanding is gained.

> *~ For everything there is a season,*
> *And a time for every matter under heaven:*
> *A time to be born, and a time to die;*
> *A time to plant, and a time to pluck up that which is planted;*
> *A time to kill, and a time to heal;*
> *A time to break down, and a time to build up;*
> *A time to weep, and a time to laugh;*
> *A time to mourn, and a time to dance…*
> *A time to keep silence, and a time to speak;*
> *A time to love, and a time to hate,*
> *A time of war, and a time of peace.*

This book is meant to be a testament to the lives of all those men who died in those terrible years, as well as all those who survived and had to pick up the pieces and live on. I hope the book has demonstrated their bravery and their abhorrence of war, and how it changed them. It's a story of survival, and is dedicated to my grandfather, John Edgar Jackson, who believe it or not, was a quiet, gentle, loving man, whom I loved with all my heart.

Liz Moran

13th June 2005

John Edgar Jackson
Born 28th February 1898
(Photograph taken in 1919)

Alice Emma Johnson (later nicknamed 'Betty')
Born 9th August 1901
(Photograph taken in 1919 – the dress was red!)

John Thomas Jackson & Mary (Polly)
(The photograph was taken in the war years in the back yard of
15 Brunswick St, York)

Jackson Family Tree

John Thomas JACKSON (21 Feb 1865-9 Nov 1953)
+ **Mary (Polly) CROSS** (25 Aug 1862-25 Apr 1944)

1. **George Ernest JACKSON** (13 Jul 1884-6 Jun 1918)
   + Harriet Ethel FOWLER (1888-)

2. **Matthew William JACKSON** (21 Mar 1886-25 Apr 1918)

3. **Robert Henry JACKSON** (15 Oct 1888-10 Nov 1915)
   + Gladys Violet ENGLISH (-)

4. **Thomas Alfred JACKSON** (17 Mar 1892-17 Jul 1912)

5. **Fred Oswald JACKSON** (4 Apr 1895-1964)
   + Sarah Irene (Renee) KJELGAARD (1897-)

6. **John Edgar JACKSON** (28 Feb 1898-13 Jun 1985)
   + Alice Emma (Betty) JOHNSON (9 Aug 1901-18 Mar 1984)

7. **Charlie Cross JACKSON** (31 Jul 1901-1970)
   + (1st wife) Frances UNKNOWN (-)
   + (2nd wife) Mirium GODDARD (-)

8. **Wilfred JACKSON** (14 Dec 1903-16 Dec 1995)
   + (1st wife) Gladys MARTIN (7 Aug 1905-11 Oct 1972)
   + (2nd wife) Beattie UNKNOWN (8 Apr 1907-27 Nov 1994)

- **Albert SEAL** (28 Jun 1898-23 Jul 1915) - best friend and
  'Indian blood brother' to John Jackson.

YORK SOLDIER BROTHERS FALL IN ACTION.

TWO WOUNDED AND ONE ON ACTIVE SERVICE.

Pte. M. Jackson
(died of wounds).

Sergt.-Major R. Jackson
(killed in action).

C.-S.-M. F. Jackson
(wounded).

Lce.-Corpl. J. E. Jackson.

Pte. G. Jackson.

Of the five soldier sons of Mr. and Mrs. J. Jackson, 15, Brunswick-street, York, two have given their lives in the service of their country, a third was recently wounded, and two others are on active service. The family formerly resided at Ebberston, near Pickering, but removed to York some years ago, and Mr. Jackson is in the employment of Mr. R. F. Dunnell, St. Paul's Lodge.

Private Matthew Jackson, the second son, emigrated to Australia seven years ago, where he was engaged in farming up to the time of joining the Australian Forces in December, 1914. He was drafted to Egypt in 1915, took part in the landing in Gallipoli, and fought all through that campaign. In 1916 he was moved to France and took part in the Battle of the Somme. Wounded in March, 1917, he returned to active service again in the following June, and on April 24th last was badly wounded and died the following day in a casualty clearing hospital overseas. The deceased was 32 years of age, and before going to Australia was engaged in farm service at Ebberston.

Sergeant-Major Robert Jackson, aged 27, served in the Durham Light Infantry for six years. He went to the front on January 4th,

1915, and was killed in action on November 10th the same year, leaving a widow and one child, who reside in Colchester.

Company Sergeant-Major Fred Jackson, aged 25, joined the Durham Light Infantry in September, 1914, and proceeded on active service in April of the following year. He was wounded on April 9th, 1917, and, returning to duty again, was moved to Italy. Early this year his unit was brought back to France. He was severely wounded on March 24th, and is now in a London hospital. He has been awarded the Military Medal, and has also a certificate for distinguished service bearing date February, 1916. Before enlisting he was a fireman on the North Eastern Railway.

Lance-Corporal John Edgar Jackson, aged 20, West Yorkshire Regiment, joined the Forces in August, 1914, being at that time under military age. He went on active service in April, 1915, and has been twice wounded—once in June, 1915, and again in September, 1916—and once gassed. He was formerly a clerk in the solicitor's office of the North Eastern Railway Company.

Private George Jackson, aged 34, the eldest son, is in the West Yorkshire Regiment, which he joined in November, 1915, and has been abroad since January, 1916. He was previously an agent of the Refuge Insurance Company, and his wife and three children reside in York.

Newspaper Article, Tuesday, 14th May 1918. The report was before George had been killed.

SEAL, ALBERT.
Private, 1/5th West Yorks. Regt. Aged
17 years. Born at York. Last resided
at 8, Beresford Terrace, York. Killed
in action 23rd July, 1915, at Ypres.

John's best friend and 'Indian blood brother'

YORK BURNING FATALITY
YORKSHIRE HERALD NEWSPAPER

8TH DECEMBER 1911

TRANSCRIPT OF
CHILD IN FLAMES IN MOTHER'S BEDROOM

THE INQUEST AND VERDICT

An inquest was held at the York County Hospital last evening by the City Coroner (Mr J. R. Wool), on the body of Hilda Louisa Johnson, aged 4 years, daughter of Mr. And Mrs. G. W. Johnson, of 4, Bexley Square, Cemetery Road, York, who on Wednesday received injuries by burning to which she succumbed the same night.

ELIZABETH JOHNSON, wife of George Wm. Johnson, residing at 4, Bexley Square, Cemetery Road, said that her husband was a carter employed by the Corporation. Witness left home on Wednesday soon after 3 o'clock to help her aunt, who kept a shop, to do some paper hanging. Her daughter Alice, aged 10 years, was left in the house, as well as the deceased, there was a fire lit in the kitchen and a fire in the bedroom upstairs. Two pillows and a piece of cloth from the child's cot were being dried in front of the fire in the bedroom. There was a fender in front of both fires, but no fireguard. Witness had left the children in the house alone before, but she frequently went back to see that everything was safe. She had only been in her aunt's shop a minute or two when her daughter Alice ran into the shop and said, "Hilda is ablaze." Witness ran back to her house and upstairs as fast as she could. The child's clothing was on fire, and she was standing near the bed. The bedclothes were also on fire. Witness picked the child up and ran downstairs with her, and Mr. McTernan took the child. Witness stood looking at the child a minute or two and then, remembering that the bedclothes were on fire, she went back and put them into the fireplace. Mr. McTernan looked after the child, who was afterwards taken to the Hospital.

THE CORONER: Was the child very much burned? – Yes, sir.

What clothes had she on? – She had on her skirts, a frock made of a kind of flannelette, and a Holland pinafore.

THE CORONER: I suppose there was no other person in the house? – Yes sir. There was a little girl from next door.

ALICE EMMA JOHNSON, aged 10 years, said that the deceased was her sister. Her mother baked the bread yesterday and then went to her aunt's. As soon as her mother went out her sister went upstairs. Witness went upstairs to fetch her down, and she came a short way down the stairs. Then witness went into the front bedroom to see if the baby was asleep. And her sister followed her. Deceased refused to go downstairs. Witness got her to the top step, but she sat down, so witness left her. Witness went downstairs, and was about to put some water into a bucket to wash the floor for her mother when she heard three screams. She ran upstairs and found her sister on fire. Witness told her to stand still, and then witness tried to get her pinafore off, but could not. Witness ran for her mother. On the way she did not tell anyone what had happened.

THE CORONER: Was she near the fire when you went into the room? – No, sir; she was running about the room, and when I told her to stop she was near my mother's bed.

ADA HURWORTH, a neighbour, said that yesterday afternoon Mrs. Johnson called at her home and told her that she was going to wash some paint at her aunt's house. She had not been gone more than five minutes when witness heard her neighbour scream Witness rushed to Mrs. Johnson's house, and Mrs. Johnson was just coming downstairs with the child in her arms. The child's clothing was on fire.

JAMES McTERNAN a cattle drover, residing at 15 Bexley Square, said that yesterday afternoon he heard a scream from Mrs. Johnson's house, and on proceeding there he saw Mrs. Johnson bringing the child down the stairs. The child's clothes were on fire. Witness picked up a rug or something and wrapped it round the deceased, and then sent for a cab and conveyed the child to the hospital.

DR. S. F. A. CHARLES, house surgeon at the York County Hospital, said that the child was admitted to the institution yesterday afternoon and died at 6.45. She was most extensively burned all over the body, with the exception of her feet and the lower part of her legs. The case was quite hopeless from the first.

In summing up, **the CORONER** said it appeared to him that it was another case which showed the folly of people leaving their children in the house with fires which were not protected by fire guards. This case had occurred early in the winter, and he hoped that it would be a warning to others not to leave their children alone with unprotected fires. He thought that the girl who had given evidence was a very capable child, and had done everything she could for her sister.

A JURYMAN asked Mrs. Johnson if she possessed a fireguard, and he replied she did not, as she could not afford to buy one.

The CORONER: If we give you one will you use it? – I will, sir.

The CORONER: Then we will make you a present of one.

The jury returned a verdict in accordance with the medical evidence, and found that the deceased had died from burns arising through her clothes having caught fire whilst left in the house with her sister.

-o-o-o-o-

My grandmother never forgot the incident. It haunted her all her life, and once when she was looking after me, she caught me standing with my back to the fire with my dress hitched up, exposing my bottom and legs to the flames to get warm, as one did in those days. Her face went pale with horror. She rushed into the room and pushed me away from the fireplace with such force that it knocked me off my feet. She had never laid a finger on me before, so it came as a bit of a shock to find myself knocked over. She then explained her reaction, and warned me that if I did it again, I would end up dead like 'Molly'.

It took quite some detective work in later years to find the newspaper article, as grandma didn't know the year this had happened, only how old her sister had been at the time. I didn't know Molly's year of birth then, until grandma remembered she herself had been about the age of ten. I searched for the death certificate first in the St. Catherine's index, but initially couldn't find it. It eventually came to light when I discovered that 'Molly' was actually a nickname, and her proper name was Hilda Louise Johnson. In the end, a York Registrar found the death entry for me, and from the certificate I was able to locate the inquest in the local newspaper.

-o-o-o-o-

The Jackson Brother Survivors…
John, Fred, Charlie and Wilf in the 1950's

Order of events in the lives of the Jackson family in the years 1914 – 1918.

1914 August	John Edgar Jackson & Albert Seal, join the West Yorkshire Regiment.
1914 September	Fred Jackson joins the Durham Light Infantry.
1914 December 29th	Matthew Jackson joins the Australian Imperial Force, 14th Inf. / 2nd Bn.
1915 February 5th	Matthew on active service abroad.
1915	Robert Jackson joins the Durham Light Infantry, 2nd Bn.
1915 April	John & Albert on active service abroad.
1915 April	Fred on active service abroad.
1915 May 7th	Matthew on Gallipoli Peninsular.
1915 June	John wounded.
1915 July 10th	Matthew admitted to the 2nd Field Hosp (Gallipoli).
1915 July 23rd	Albert Seal killed in action, aged 17yrs.
1915 November 10th	Robert dies of wounds aged 27yrs.
1915 November	George Jackson joins the West Yorkshire Regiment.
1915 December 28th	Matthew in Alexandria, Egypt.
1916 January	George on active service abroad.
1916 February 28th	Matthew in Tel-el-Kebir with 54th Div.
1916 June 18th	Matthew in Alexandria again.
1916 June 27th	Matthew in Marseilles, France.
1916 July 1st	Battle of the Somme.
1916 September	John wounded.
1916 December 20th	Matthew a driver with the 54th Division.
1917 February 26th	Matthew admitted to the 15th Australian. Field Hosp, France.
1917 March 1st	Matthew admitted - 3rd Canadian Field Amb. Hosp, Boulogne.
1917 March 2nd	Matthew admitted to Edmonton Military Hosp, Eng. until 17.7.17.
1917 April 9th	Fred wounded.
1917 August 31st	Matthew rejoins his unit.
1917 September 16th	Matthew 14th brigade - Reverts from CSM to Private (own request).
1917 November 13th	Mary Jackson (nee Vasey), grandmother, dies at Ebberston, aged 75yrs.

SIX

1918 February 24th	Matthew on leave in England until 13.3.1918.
1918 March 24th	Fred wounded.
1918 March 30th	Matthew rejoins 14th Brigade in France.
1918 April 24th	Matthew wounded, shrapnel wounds to legs.
1918 April 25th	Matthew dies of wounds aged 32yrs, Pernois, France.
1918 June 6th	George dies in enemy air raid aged 34yrs, France.
1918 July 23rd	John and Mary Jackson (parents) are 'presented' to King George V at Windsor.
1918 November 11th	War ends.
1919 February 19th	John Jackson 'disembodied'.
1919 July 19th	Victory Day.
1919 December 24th	John marries his beloved Alice.

Footsteps of Grandad ~ 1914~1919

FRANCE ~ **Apr 1915** ~ Boulogne ~ Merville ~ Le Sart ~ **May 1915** ~ truck to Estaires ~ marched to Bac St. Maur ~ Fauquissart ~ Rue Petillon trenches ~ **Jun 1915** ~ Rue de Quesnes ~ Rue Petillon ~ **BELGIUM** ~ **Jul 1915** ~ Proven ~ Ousthock ~ Turco Farm ~ Chateau les trios tours ~ Poperinghe area ~ Hospital Farm ~ **Aug/Sept 1915** ~ Turco Farm ~ the canal bank ~ Estaminet ~ Algerian Cottage ~ **Oct/Nov 1915** ~ Coppernolle ~ Brielen ~ La BelleAlliance ~ Elverdinghe Chateau ~ Hale Farm ~ **Dec 1915** ~ Houtkerque ~ Wormhoudt ~ **FRANCE** ~ **Jan 1916** ~ Route march to Calais ~ **Feb 1916** – Longeau Station ~ train to Amiens ~ marched to Ailly Sur Somme ~ Ailly town ~ marched to Rubernpre ~ marched to Bouzincourt ~ marched to Martinsart ~ **Mar 1916** ~ Harponville ~ **Apr/May/Jun 1916** ~ Naours ~ Albert ~ **Jul 1916** ~ Aveluy Wood Passerelle de Magenta ~ Thiepval wood **Aug 1916** ~ Schwaben Redoubt ~ Fort Schwaben ~ Aveluy Wood ~ Martinsart ~ Hedauville ~ Leipsig Salient ~ **Sept 1916** ~ Thiepval ~ Gordon Castle ~ Malincourt wood ~ Speyside ~ Martinsart wood ~ Forcewith ~ bus to Arqueves ~ marched to Halloy ~ **Oct/Nov 1916** ~ marched to Humbercamps ~ Hannescamps ~ St Amand ~ Bienvillers ~ **Dec 1916** ~ Souastre ~ Henu ~ Pas ~ Mondicourt ~ Lucheux ~ Bouque Maison region ~ **Jan 1917** ~ Baillemont (near Arras) ~ **Feb 1917** ~ Gastineau and Lincoln Lane ~ Berles ~ Pommier ~ Humbercamps ~ Bavincourt ~ Pommier ~ Berles ~ Lesouich ~ Lacauchie ~ Coiturelle ~ Humbercourt ~ Lucheux ~ Le Souich ~ Bouque Maison ~ Monleblond ~ Bonnieres ~ Frevent ~ St Pol ~ Gauchin ~ Wavrans ~ Hestrus ~ Tangry ~ Sains Les Pernes ~ Fiefs ~ Heuchin Rd ~ Nedon ~ Lilliers ~ St Venant ~ Gauarbecque Rd ~ Beaupre ~ Lestrem ~ Bout Delville ~ **Mar/Apr 1917** ~ Laventie ~ Rue Bacquerot ~ Fauquissart ~ **May/Jun 1917** ~ Fauquissart ~ Picantin Rd ~ Rue Tilleley ~ Bertha Trench ~ Irma Trench ~ La Gorgue ~ Fauquissant ~ **Jul 1917** ~ marched to Estaires ~ Lestrem Station ~ train to Mardyck ~ Loonplage (west of Dunkirk port) ~ marched to Fort Mardyck ~ by road to Rousdamme ~ Avecapelle (4mls south of Nieuport) ~ **BELGIUM** ~ Oostdunkerke ~ St Georges (River Yser, inland from Nieuport) ~ Num trench, Nice trench, Pat post, Brickstacks, Rosy trench ~ Ribaillet Camp ~ Nieuport ~ **Aug 1917** ~ Oost Dunkerque ~ Coxyde ~ Ghyvelde ~ Uxem ~ Teteghem ~ **Sept 1917** ~ Ghyvelde ~ Coudekerque ~ **Oct 1917** ~ Wylder ~ Wormhoudt ~ Ledringhem ~ Arneke ~ Noordpeene ~ Clairmarais ~ Hout Schoubrouck ~ Plattebeurzs ~ Staple to St Marie Cappel (south of Cassel) ~ Rattekot

Inn & Steenvoodre Rd junction ~ St Janster Biexen (west of Pop) ~ Poperinghe ~ Vlamertinge ~ Spree Farm ~ Calgary Grange ~ Poelcapelle ~ Passchendaele ~ Peter Pan, Wolf copse ~ Wieltje ~ marched to Vlamertinge ~ marched to Looge Hoek ~ Poelcapelle ridge ~ Steenvoodre ~ **Nov/Dec 1917** ~ Bus to Zonnebecke ~ Halfway House ~ Ridge at Broodseide ~ Esplanade Gap (south-west corner of Ypres) ~ Ramparts at Ypres Railway Station ~ **Jan 1918** ~ Bus to Bavinchove just west of Cassel ~ marched to Zuytpeene ~ **Feb 1918** ~ marched to Ebblinghem Station ~ train to Watten ~ marched to Moulle ~ marched to St Martin au Laert ~ St Omer ~ Arques ~ Zuytpeene ~ Bavinchove ~ Oxelaere ~ Caestre ~ train to Brandhoek, Devonshire Camp ~ train to Gordon House ~ marched to Broodseine ~ Hussar Camp ~ **Mar 1918** ~ Molenaarelsthoek and Moulin Farm ~ Zonnebecke sector ~ **Apr/May/Jun 1918** ~ Garter Camp ~ Scottish Wood Camp ~ Train to Ouderdom ~ Wytschaete ~ Scherpenberg Ridge ~ Kemmel ~ Grand Bois, Zero wood ~ marched to Watou ~ Hoograaf ~ **Jul 1918** ~ Brake Camp ~ Ypres, Hell fire corner, Menin Rd, Rifle Farm, Goldfish Chateau ~ **Aug/Sept 1918** ~ Proven, Pigeon Camp ~ Herzeele ~ Oostcappel ~ Train to Northkerque ~ Tournehem ~ Audricq ~ Train to Brias ~ Foufflin Ricametz ~ Bois de Berthonval ~ Plouvain sector, Scarpe River ~ **FRANCE** ~ **Oct 1918** ~ Iwuy ~ Avesnes ~ Villers en Caushies railway ~ Villers ~ Escaudoevures ~ Ramillies ~ **Nov/Dec 1918** ~ Iwuy ~ marched to Douchy ~ Marly to Sunken Rd ~ East of Rhonelle River ~ Aulnoy ~ Famars ~ Maing ~ Aulnoy ~ Lieu St Armand ~ Thiant ~ Noyelles Sur Sec ~ Douai ~ Auby ~ **11ᵗʰ Nov 1918** ~ Evin Malmaison ~ Evin ~ map reference Valencienne 1.100000 ~ **Jan 1919** – Moncheaux ~ Evin ~ **19ᵗʰ Feb 1919** - Boulogne ~ Home.

SIX

The Graves

Private Albert Seal – died Friday 23rd July, 1915 aged 17yrs. Buried Hospital Farm Cemetery, Belgium, Row B, grave 16; 1st/5th West Yorkshire Regiment (Prince of Wales's Own) Regimental number - 1838. Bullet through the head.

CSM Robert Henry Jackson – died Wednesday 10th Nov, 1915 aged 27yrs. Buried Lijssenthoek Military Cemetery, Belgium, plot 4, row B, grave 8; 2nd Battalion, Durham Light Infantry, Regimental number 9549. Died of wounds at a Casualty clearing station.

Private Matthew William Jackson - died Thursday 25th April, 1918 aged 32yrs. Buried Pernois British Cemetery, Halloy-Les-Pernois, France, Plot 1, row A, grave 13; Initially taken to 4th Casualty Clearing Station, Regiment 14th Australian Brigade – Regimental Number - 1575. Died of wounds to legs.

Pioneer Sapper George Ernest Jackson – died 6th June, 1918 aged 33. Buried Croix-Rouge Military Cemetery, Quaedypre, France, Plot 1, Grave A2. Royal Engineers, 118th Railway Construction Coy., Regimental number 249843. Died from penetrating wounds to the abdomen from enemy aircraft fire.

May they all rest in peace...

SIX

Structure of an Army

There were Five Armies on the Western Front, commanded by a Commander-in-Chief (Sir John French until Dec 1915 and Sir Douglas Haig for rest of war).

Each Army was commanded by a full General and was made up of several Corps.

A Corps was commanded by a Lieutenant General. Each Corps was made up of two or three Divisions.

A Division was commanded by a Major General. There were approximately 15,000 men in each division, which was made up of three Brigades.

A Brigade was commanded by a Brigadier General. Each Brigade was made up of four Infantry Battalions.

An Infantry Battalion was commanded by a Lieutenant Colonel and had 800 officers and ranks. Each Battalion was made up of four Companies, within which was a Regimental Sergeant Major RSM who was its senior NCO.

A Company was commanded by a Major or a Captain. Each Company was made up of several Platoons, within which was a senior NCO Company Sergeant Major (CSM).

A Platoon was commanded by a Lieutenant or a 2nd Lieutenant. Each Platoon was made up of four sections.

A Section was commanded by a Sergeant or a Corporal. Each section was made up of small squads of men.

A Squad of men was commanded by a Lance Corporal.

A Regiment is the title under which a number of Battalions are formed and maintained. It is not an actual body of men. **Abbreviations:** Regimental Sergeant Major (RSM); Regimental Quartermaster Sergeant (RQMS); Company Sergeant Major (CSM); Company Quartermaster Sergeant (CQMS) are all ranks known as Warrant Officers, as they were appointed by Warrant rather than by Commission.

SIX

References

Poor Bloody Infantry by Bernard Martin

The Long Trail by John Brophy & Eric Partridge

Poems by Longfellow

John McCrae poem – In Flanders Fields

Rossetti's Poem – Remember Me

Browning's Poem - Fear Death

Trench Fever by Christopher Moore

The West Yorkshire War Diaries

The Durham Light Infantry War Diaries

The Commonwealth War Graves Commission

The West Yorkshire Regiment, Vols 1 & 2, by Everard Wyrall

The Australian War Records Department

The Yorkshire Herald Newspaper

'The Bible'